T0157092

"Piper—hell, woman, don't make me chase you."

She didn't stop to argue. The stars and sliver of a moon provided just enough light for Clate to make her out as she lurched away from him.

Then she tripped, going down face first, cursing vociferously.

She was still cursing, up on her hands and knees, when Clate caught up with her. She seemed to have on a long black dress or nightgown that had tripped her up. Without thinking, he grabbed her around the middle and hauled her to her feet.

It was as big a mistake as he'd ever made.

She blew a strand of hair out of her mouth and fastened her eyes, luminous in the near-darkness, on him, and he sucked in a breath at what he was thinking, feeling. Every muscle went rigid, as if that could force common sense back into him. He wanted to kiss her, he wanted to scoop her up into his arms and carry her upstairs to his bed.

Her eyes narrowed, and she whispered, "Oh, dear," and he knew they were lost. . . .

Books by Carla Neggers

White Hot
Night Scents
Just Before Sunrise
A Rare Chance
Finding You

Published by POCKET BOOKS

CARLA NEGGERS

NIGHT SCENTS

POCKET BOOKS
New York   London   Toronto   Sydney

This book is a work of fiction. Names, characters, places and incidents are products of the author's imagination or are used fictitiously. Any resemblance to actual events or locales or persons, living or dead, is entirely coincidental.

An *Original* Publication of POCKET BOOKS

POCKET BOOKS, a division of Simon & Schuster, Inc.
1230 Avenue of the Americas, New York, NY 10020

Copyright © 1997 by Carla Neggers

ISBN 13: 978-1-4767-2546-8

First Pocket Books printing August 1997

10

POCKET and colophon are registered trademarks of Simon & Schuster, Inc.

For information regarding special discounts for bulk purchases, please contact Simon & Schuster Special Sales at 1-800-456-6798 or business@simonandschuster.com

Front cover illustration by Melody Cassen

Printed in the U.S.A.

For Pop,
well loved, never forgotten

NIGHT SCENTS

Chapter

1

The moment Piper Macintosh heard the screen door bang open and shut, she knew she was caught, and probably by Clate Jackson himself. He'd made it plain he wouldn't tolerate trespassers. He'd instructed the realtor who'd sold him Hannah Frye's two-hundred-fifty-year-old Cape Cod house—who'd told everyone else in Frye's Cove—to have his property posted in accordance with Massachusetts law. Hannah and Piper had always shared responsibility for the hedgerow that divided their property. Not Clate Jackson. It was his. He'd had a No Trespassing sign posted smack in the middle of it, marking out his territory like a grouchy old wolf.

So here she was, Piper thought miserably, out in his back yard at four o'clock in the morning, clearly trespassing.

Footsteps sounded on the stone terrace up one level from the overgrown herb garden where she crouched. Not tentative, I'm-not-sure-what's-out-here footsteps, but confident, I've-got-me-a-trespasser footsteps.

A fat earthworm oozed out over the cool, moist dirt.

The wet leaves of tall yarrow and foxglove dripped on Piper's army-green poncho. The rain had stopped. Too bad. It might have kept her neighbor inside.

A cool breeze floated up from the bay, bringing with it the scents of salt, wild grasses, and scrub pine that mixed with those of the extensive Frye gardens. It was June on Cape Cod, and Piper could smell roses and honeysuckle and a touch of mint in the clean night air, even as her heart pounded.

The gate to the wrought-iron fence that enclosed Hannah's garden of medicinal herbs—her witch's garden, she called it—creaked open.

Piper knew she was doomed.

"All right. Up on your feet. Slowly."

Slowly? What, did he think she had a couple of grenades tucked under her poncho? That arrogant tone decided it. She wasn't going home empty handed. Giving a final tug, she broke off the hunk of valerian root she'd been digging. She ignored the horrendous smell. Worse than dirty feet. *Only for you, Hannah.*

As instructed, Piper rose slowly. She didn't know if her new neighbor came complete with shotgun. He was from the South. He was rich, a prominent Tennessee businessman. He owned one of Nashville's most exclusive hotels. He'd paid Hannah Frye every nickel of her exorbitant asking price for her house and thirty waterfront acres.

Hannah also claimed that Clate Jackson was destined to be the love of her grandniece's life, but Piper had dismissed that crazy notion as just another case of Hannah being Hannah.

She turned—slowly—and prepared herself to smile and talk her way out of getting hauled down to Ernie at the police station. Ernie had been saying for years, long before he'd been named police chief, that one of these days Piper was going to let Hannah land her in serious trouble.

"You must dig up the valerian root before the sun has fully risen."

2

Now that she was caught, Piper wondered if her aunt had known that Clate Jackson would be arriving tonight, late. She'd checked his house at eleven, before getting a few hours' sleep, and there was no sign of him.

She pulled her poncho hood down off her hair and smiled, then nearly choked as she focused on the dark figure over by the gate. He wasn't what she'd expected, had *hoped* for. No one in town had actually seen the grumpy, mysterious Tennessean, and so she had nothing to go on, was completely unprepared. He was young. Mid-thirties. Thickly built, an inch or two under six feet, with dark, tousled hair and the dangerous look of a man who'd just rolled out of bed to roust a trespasser off his land. He wore ragged jeans and an unbuttoned denim shirt, and he was barefoot. Even in the milky predawn light, even from over by the yarrow, Piper could see that his eyes were a searing, penetrating blue, and at the moment were entirely focused on her.

No, definitely not what she'd hoped for. Her reaction would thrill Hannah. *"He's the man for you, Piper. I know it in my soul."*

Her smile frozen, Piper said, "Well. Good morning. You must be my new neighbor. I'm Piper Macintosh. I live just beyond the privet." She pushed through tall, wet, weedy-looking herbs toward the gate, aware of his unrelenting gaze. "I was just digging a little valerian root."

"Is that what I smell?"

"I expect so." She held up the fibrous root with its hairy offshoots and distinct, unpleasant odor. "Sort of smells like a dirty locker room, doesn't it? My aunt, Hannah Frye, wants it for some new medicinal tea she's got in the works. She couldn't think of another immediate source for it but here."

Clate Jackson seemed unimpressed by the desires of an eighty-seven-year-old woman. "Any particular reason you had to collect this root at four o'clock in the morning?"

"Yes, supposedly there is, only Hannah didn't give me

the specifics." And Piper hadn't asked, having learned from hard experience that her aunt's reasoning often made sense only to her, which didn't make her any less tenacious. "I wouldn't have agreed to dig it for her, except I didn't think you were here."

"I see." A faint note of amusement had crept into his deep, rasping drawl. "Smarter to trespass when no one's around."

She checked her annoyance. "Really, I don't think of myself as trespassing."

"No?"

"No." Her tone was firm. He would not get to her. "It's sort of like the case of the tree falling in the woods. If there's no one to hear it, did it really make a noise? I figured, if you weren't here, I wasn't really trespassing."

"I am here, and you are trespassing."

"Then I should get out of your way and let you get back to bed." The problem was, he was blocking the gate. The fence was waist high and had spikes, tough to leap over. "If you'll excuse me."

He didn't move, just rocked back on his heels and studied her through half-closed eyes. She'd dragged herself out of bed after barely four hours' sleep and had brushed her teeth, splashed cold water on her face, and pulled on black leggings, her oversized Red Sox sweatshirt, sneakers, and her poncho. Not the sort of attire she'd have chosen to meet her new neighbor. Her hair—dark chestnut, long, and straight—hung in tangles.

"I can't imagine valerian root makes a very palatable tea," he said.

In other words, he didn't believe her story. "All of Hannah's teas taste lousy. One of the local selectmen swears she tried to poison him. But valerian is known to ease insomnia, headaches, nervousness—basically it's a mild sedative."

Jackson glanced away from his trespasser for the first time and took in the small, wild-looking garden. None of the look of the trim, well-planned Frye terrace gardens

4

here. This one was pure Hannah Macintosh Frye. Each plant was carefully identified by its common and Latin names, the poisonous ones marked with a prominent skull and crossbones. Piper had helped Hannah paint each one.

Her neighbor turned back to her. "What is this, some kind of witch's garden?"

"My aunt has considerable knowledge of the medicinal qualities of many different plants." There. That was diplomatic. "Used properly, all of these plants have beneficial qualities, although some are quite poisonous if misused. Monkshood, for example. Even brushing up against it can cause topical numbness."

"Charming."

"My aunt couldn't very well have taken these plants with her to her new condo. She hasn't found a new source for valerian root, and probably a few other plants as well."

Clate Jackson's eyes fell on her. "Mrs. Frye doesn't own this property anymore."

Piper stifled a wave of irritation. This was no time to lecture him on the finer points of life in small-town Cape Cod. "Right."

A strained smile took a bit of the edge off his words. "I'm not being very diplomatic, am I? I didn't get in until after midnight, and I can't say I expected to be awakened by a woman stealing plant roots from my back yard."

Stealing? *Stealing?* Piper's spine straightened. "I wasn't stealing."

"You are removing something from my property. I consider that stealing."

His tone wasn't so much cold as firm, as if he wasn't accustomed to having his view of things countered. Piper had a good mind to shove the smelly, dirty, wet valerian root at him and let him stick it back in the ground or wherever he saw fit. He could have it for breakfast for all she cared. "I can't believe anyone would

5

deny an eighty-seven-year-old woman access to a bit of valerian root. Mr. Jackson, around here it's considered the neighborly thing to do to—to—"

"To sneak onto someone's property before first light and dig up their crops?"

Amusement had crept back into his tone. It was even worse, Piper decided, than suspicion and irritation. Clutching the foul-smelling valerian root in one hand, her trowel in the other, she marched another few steps closer to him. He'd moved back from the gate. He would let her go home with fair warning. He wasn't going to turn his only neighbor in to the police on his first night in town.

As she shot him a sideways glance, she saw, against the slowly brightening sky, that he had a small scar on the outer corner of his left eye, another longer, deeper scar on his collarbone. She decided she might be wise not to make too many assumptions about Clate Jackson.

Nonetheless, she held her ground. "You're determined to put as negative a face on this as you possibly can, aren't you? My aunt planted every one of these plants—"

"And sold them to me. Look, I don't want to—"

Piper paid no attention to his conciliatory tone. "She lived in this house for twenty-five years, not counting the year she lived here after she was orphaned at age seven. She needs some time to adjust to her new life. Around here people understand that."

"I'm not from around here."

His words—matter-of-fact, spoken in an easy Tennessee drawl—brought Piper up short. No, he wasn't from around here and didn't want to be. There'd be no getting involved with the locals, no establishing ties with the community beyond finding someone to mow his lawn, sell him food and supplies, and clean his house.

"Miss Macintosh—"

"Piper." But she spat it out through half-clenched teeth, just daring him to treat her like a small-time nuisance. "We're neighbors, remember?"

"Piper, then." His tone was cool and deliberate and he stayed on the *i* longer than any northerner ever would, the result giving her name an unexpected lazy, sexy quality that rippled up her spine. "I'll let this one go. Take your aunt her valerian root. Next time we meet, I hope it will be under better circumstances."

He thought he was being magnanimous, Piper realized in disbelief. Magnanimous would have been to offer her all the valerian root she wanted, to have Piper tell her aunt that she was welcome to any of the herbs and other medicinal plants she'd left behind, just to call ahead next time. Instead, Clate Jackson thought he was being magnanimous simply because he wasn't having her arrested for trespassing and stealing.

"You know," she said coolly, "one of these days a hurricane's going to churn up the east coast and try to rearrange your little Cape Cod refuge here. You're going to want good relations with your neighbors, and if you haven't noticed, I'm it."

His eyes darkened, but she thought she noticed—or imagined—a slight glimmer of humor. "Miss Macintosh, I'd cut my losses while I could and get on home. You wouldn't want me to change my mind."

"Gladly," she said, just like her ten-year-old nephew, and marched through the gate.

Never mind Hannah's pronouncements on the subject, Piper did not consider Clate Jackson a likely prospect for the love of her life.

She decided a quick retreat was a more judicious course of action than arguing about the true meaning of magnanimity. The sky had turned a dusty lilac, daylight coming fast. She was normally a feet-flat-on-the-floor type, but Hannah's talk had thrown her off. Salt in the fire, muttered spells, casting out into the universe for a man whose attraction to her niece was so powerful, so irrevocable, that it would draw him to a place and a community he didn't know or understand.

It was weird stuff, and the physical reality of Clate Jackson—the muscles, the stubble of dark beard, the piercing eyes, the scars—wasn't helping, never mind that he showed no sign of looking upon her as anything beyond a pesky neighbor, a trespasser, and a thief. He had bought the Frye House not for its history or the prospect of a new community, but for its private, coveted location on a spit of Cape Cod occupied only by it and its neighbor, a tiny half-Cape that Piper was in the process of restoring. Surrounded by thirty acres of his own and a sprawling wildlife refuge of marsh, dunes, woodland, and an undisturbed coastal pond, the Frye House was an ideal and rare spot on the fragile, often overcrowded arm of land that jutted out into the Atlantic Ocean.

Gad, she thought. I have to get out of here.

"Well," she said, glancing back at him, "I guess I should thank you for your understanding." Such as it was, she added silently. She beamed him a fake smile. "And I'm sorry for having gotten you out of bed."

A narrowing of his deep blue eyes stopped Piper short, making her regret her ill-chosen words. He smiled sexily, deliberately. "No problem."

Love of her life, right. He was just another rake. It was an old-fashioned word that suited most of the men she'd encountered. Their idea of romance was sex and a hot meal. She liked sex, and she enjoyed good food, but she wanted more. Hannah's talk of the love of a lifetime had fired Piper's imagination. It involved a linking of souls that was seductive—and utterly hopeless.

Nearly slipping on the wet grass, she scooted down the well-kept, sloping lawn that gradually bled into marsh and water. She didn't linger over the sunrise. She had Hannah's valerian root, and she'd met Clate Jackson, and that was enough for anyone before sunup.

Sleep eluded Clate after he went back inside. He put on a pot of coffee and sat at his rickety antique kitchen table while it brewed. The kitchen was located in a one-story ell, a later addition to the main body of the old house. A double, small-paned window looked out on the terraced gardens bursting with late spring flowers, the early morning sun glinting on everything from creamy yellow day lilies to clumps of black-purple irises.

The smell of the strong, dark coffee eased his tension. He hadn't met Hannah Frye in person. He knew she was elderly and presumed she was eccentric, given that she'd sold him a house that had been in her husband's family for more than two centuries. Everyone in town, apparently, had assumed she would live there until her death, then the house would go to her husband's granddaughter by his first marriage. But she'd had other ideas, and the granddaughter apparently hadn't minded. Since he didn't plan to involve himself in the affairs of the people of Frye's Cove, Clate didn't care.

Nor did he care about living in an historic eighteenth-century house. He knew nothing about the Fryes and little about Cape Cod. He couldn't say why he'd even picked New England, except that it was far removed from the pressures of his life in Nashville.

He poured himself a mug of coffee and returned to the drop-leaf table, staring again down across the terraced gardens toward the water. He'd opened windows when he came in late the night before, and now he could hear the gentle wash of the incoming tide, smell the salt on the breeze, hear the water and shorebirds calling. Privacy, isolation, solitude. After a long, intense winter, their promise had finally lured him to this quiet, beautiful spot.

All he had to do now was to keep his nosy neighbor at bay.

With a heavy sigh, he leaned back in his antique chair and sipped his coffee, shifting his attention to his new kitchen. New to him, at any rate. Except for minor repairs, he guessed the house in general hadn't been touched in twenty years, at least. The kitchen appliances were in reasonable working order, and the cupboards were a rich, dark cherry, built around windows and doorways that had sagged and settled with time. He doubted if there was a level square foot in the entire house. Whatever minimal work they'd done over the centuries, the Fryes had preserved the architectural integrity of their historic house: the wide pineboard floors, the stone fireplace, the post-and-beam construction, the moldings and wainscoting, the suffocatingly low ceilings. No expert in old houses, Clate knew enough about construction to realize that much more could be done to update the place without sacrificing its authentic characteristics. But he didn't expect he'd bother, not for a while, perhaps not at all.

He set down his mug. It wasn't old-lady fussy, but of sturdy, dark brown pottery. Leave it to a Yankee, he thought, suddenly amused.

And he thought of his trespasser.

Piper Macintosh. A hell of a name. Yankee to the core, no doubt about it. Green eyed and porcelain skinned, she had a fetching spray of freckles across her nose and dark, straight hair with a hint of red. She hadn't expected him and didn't like him. She'd clearly planned her herb-stealing escapade for when he wasn't around. Made sense. But he'd decided to leave Nashville suddenly, on impulse, as if running off to Cape Cod could postpone the inevitable.

But it couldn't. He'd learned that lesson early in life. Running left you with the same problems, just different scenery.

He shot to his feet, refilled his mug. Gulls swooped and swarmed down in the marsh. He'd have to get used to the lay of the land up here, the smells, the sounds, the colors. A walk on the beach and a trip to town for provisions would occupy him for the day. If necessary, he'd again remind his one and only neighbor that her aunt no longer owned the property next door. Things changed.

Eventually, he supposed, he'd have to decide what to do with Hannah Frye's weird little garden, the poisonous plants, the skull-and-crossbones markers.

But not today. Today he would feel his way into life on Cape Cod and wait for the call from home.

He hadn't lived in the tiny, hardscrabble village in the Cumberland hills where he'd grown up since he'd left at sixteen. But like it or not, it was home, and when the call came, he knew he wouldn't be ready.

Chapter

2

∞

A hearty breakfast of homemade oat bread smeared with chunky peanut butter and honey helped clarify Piper's thinking about her new neighbor. She reluctantly decided that Clate Jackson hadn't responded that unreasonably to finding a woman digging up his garden at the crack of dawn. Perhaps she'd overreacted just a tad. She *had* willfully and deliberately trespassed on his property. He'd had no idea who was in his back yard at four in the morning. All in all, she supposed she was lucky he hadn't hit her over the head with a garden hoe and asked questions later.

Her defensiveness had sprung from an uneasy mix of embarrassment, irritation, and worry. Embarrassment because she'd been caught doing something truly stupid. Irritation because Clate Jackson had different ideas about property and neighborliness from hers.

And worry because of Hannah.

"Valerian root," Piper muttered, shaking her head as she started up the steep stairs in the small vestibule to her tiny, traditional half-Cape with its side entrance and massive brick chimney. Unlike many antique houses throughout New England, hers hadn't been expanded over the centuries. The first floor consisted of a small front parlor, a fair-sized keeping room across the back, off of which were a tiny borning room and buttery. The keeping room, with its large, open-hearth fireplace, served as her kitchen and main living area. She'd converted the borning room, where in past centuries women gave birth, into her office and had kept the buttery as a pantry; it had its own trapdoor down to the dirt cellar. A cozy bedroom and bathroom under low, slanted ceilings comprised the upstairs. The chimney served fireplaces in the parlor and bedroom as well as the keeping room, a plus on frigid, damp winter days.

Putting thoughts of her elderly aunt out of her mind for the moment, Piper pulled on shorts and an old polo shirt one of her brothers had thrown out two years ago. It wasn't one of her dress-for-success sort of days. She peered at her reflection in an oval mirror above a battered pine bureau that had come with the house. Dark circles under her eyes, freckles standing out in her pale face, worry etched in her brow. Hannah would see the worry and be annoyed. She hated having anyone fretting about her, although it seemed as if everyone in Frye's Cove did.

Piper quickly brushed and braided her hair. Given its weight and straightness, the braid wouldn't last past noon.

Two minutes later, she was on her mountain bike with the valerian root tucked in her knapsack and the breeze in her face. It was a warm, beautiful morning with low humidity and not a puff of fog in sight. Only a few fair-weather clouds dotted the sky. Every oak leaf, every pine needle, every blade of marsh grass was in sharp focus, and the air smelled clean and fresh, scrubbed by yesterday's rain. The only sounds were of birds, the wind, the tide, and a few distant boats.

Slowly, Piper relaxed as she pedaled along her narrow, winding, isolated road, a rarity on Cape Cod. It dead-ended behind her, just past the Frye House, at the back of a wildlife refuge that was accessible only at its opposite side, which was actually within the boundaries of the next town over; visitors were discouraged from making it that far out. Tourists would sometimes drive out her road, missing or ignoring the dead-end signs, then have to turn around and head back through the protected marshes and meadows to the village of Frye's Cove.

Frye's Cove wasn't a tourist town by Cape Cod standards. It didn't have spectacular beaches or cute, upscale shops and restaurants or even that many places to stay. There were beaches, if not miles of them, and there was breathtaking scenery, and there was potential, a lot of it, for Frye's Cove to become a favored tourist destination. It had its share of summer people who preferred a quieter retreat and didn't mind its shortcomings, but the year-round residents of what was just, in their view, another historic village on Cape Cod Bay had simply never given much thought to tourism. Frye's Cove was where they lived, worked, and usually died. That was it. They had exploited and battled both land and sea for centuries, but now, for the most part, had made their peace.

Piper paused at the sliver of a town green to catch her breath. There were a post office, a pharmacy, a hardware store, a bank, an iffy antiques shop, and—the big news in town—the almost-restored Macintosh Inn. A Macintosh had built the place as a tavern back in the 1840s, only to lose it, in true Macintosh fashion, to mounting debts and another failed moneymaking scheme. In their three hundred years on Cape Cod, the Macintosh family had made and lost fortunes in shipping, salt making, cranberries, whaling, and who knew what else. Theirs was a history filled with tragedy, bad decisions, shortsightedness, and relentless optimism buoyed by an occasional bit of glory. Having a notorious whaling captain in the family tree would have been plenty for Piper, but every manner of hero, victim, and scoundrel seemed to lurk in the Macintosh past.

Eighteen months ago, Paul and Sally Shepherd had stunned Frye's Cove when they purchased the crumbling colonial, which had become a village eyesore. Sally was the only grandchild of Hannah's late husband, Jason Frye. He and Hannah had married late in life. Jason, who'd lived in the Frye House his entire life, had a grown daughter by his first marriage. She'd stayed in Boston after college, married, and raised Sally in an upscale suburb. No one, apparently least of all Sally, ever expected she'd come to live on Cape Cod year round. But she and her new husband, Paul, a Boston attorney, couldn't resist the charm and potential of the Macintosh Inn.

Ironically, the Shepherds had called upon the expertise of the descendants of the original owners of their Cape Cod inn to help in its renovation and restoration. Macintosh & Sons, experts in old houses, did the carpentry and construction work; Piper, an expert in early American crafts, consulted on the decor. She was emphatically not in business with them. Life in the same town with them was claustrophobic enough without having to work side by side with her father and two older brothers.

Macintosh Inn had opened for limited business Memorial Day weekend while work continued. Piper recognized the Macintosh trucks out front, signaling another day on the job. They liked the work, they liked the Shepherds, and any hard feelings a Macintosh had had about losing the inn had been dealt with a hundred and fifty years before.

She decided not to pop in to say hello. Andrew and Benjamin, and maybe even her father, would sniff out the foul-smelling valerian root or ask about her obvious lack of sleep or otherwise guess that Hannah had put her up to another wacky scheme. She could never explain her encounter with Clate Jackson. They simply wouldn't understand.

Or maybe they would, she thought dryly, remembering Jackson's expression as he'd stared at her in the milky darkness. Nope. Her overprotective father and brothers didn't need to know about that particular predawn escapade.

She climbed back onto her bike and pedaled along the green and out to the main road, following it to the edge of town where a full-care, upscale housing complex for elderly people had gone in two years before. Few locals lived there or knew anyone who did. Nestled amidst lilacs and rhododendrons, with trim shrubs and decorative maples and oaks, the complex was determinedly Cape Cod with its clusters of cedar-shingled, white-shuttered townhouses and its small, tasteful nursing home. Strict rules about plantings, exterior decorations, and curtains were enforced by a committee of residents. To Piper's surprise, her independent-minded aunt, who ordinarily balked at anyone telling her what to do, didn't object. She'd even cheerfully removed a pot of peppermint from her doorstep when it didn't meet the committee's standards. As far as Piper was concerned, this was just another sign that Hannah Frye's mental state needed watching. Her aunt just wasn't herself these days.

Piper stood her bicycle in the short, smoothly blacktopped driveway and took the stone walk to Hannah's brass-trimmed front door. She hated the creeping doubts about her aunt. If she reached eighty-seven, she wouldn't want people thinking she'd gone daffy just because of a few odd incidents.

But there had been more than a few, chief among them selling the Frye House to a cranky, reclusive Tennessean. Grimacing, Piper pressed the doorbell, which was just a courtesy. Hannah had presented her with a key when she'd moved into her new home, insisting she was long past getting into compromising positions and never had cared if anyone caught her in her skivvies.

Without waiting, Piper unlocked the door and pushed it open. "Hannah? You up and at it?"

There was no answer. Hannah's hearing wasn't the

best. Piper slipped inside and shut the door hard behind her, her usual way of alerting her aunt that she had company.

The pungent odor of some concoction drifted in from the kitchen. The townhouse was a one-floor design: two small bedrooms down the hall to the left; combination living-dining room to the right; den and kitchen in back, where sliding glass doors led out to a shaded deck. The interior was traditional Cape Cod with its muted, gray colors, tab curtains, and mix of Queen Anne and Shaker furnishings, every stick of it fresh off a furniture showroom floor. Hannah hadn't kept so much as a silver teaspoon as a memento of her twenty-five years in the Frye House, eighteen of them after her husband's death. All the Frye family antiques, such as they were, now belonged to Tennessean Clate Jackson.

As Piper approached the kitchen, the smell of whatever Hannah was brewing got stronger and nastier.

"I have your valerian root," she said from the doorway. The kitchen was done in white and gray-green, pleasant, sunny, fresh, everything sparkling and new, a radical departure from the old Frye kitchen with its views of the bay.

Hannah glanced up from the steaming, shiny pot she was stirring with a long-handled spoon. "Excellent. You didn't wash it, did you?"

"It's fresh out of the ground."

"Good. I have special springwater I want to use."

"Hannah, I could have rinsed it off at home. I have a well."

"I'm using the water from a surface spring in the wildlife refuge. Your father fetched me several gallons last evening."

Robert Macintosh indulged his only aunt. Everyone in Frye's Cove did—and had, apparently, ever since Hannah had been orphaned at age seven. The deaths of her parents, Caleb and Phoebe Macintosh, eighty years ago remained one of Cape Cod's most celebrated mysteries. Phoebe had left her young daughter with the Fryes—

Jason was seventeen at the time—while she went to meet her husband upon his return from fighting in the Great War. During his long absence from Cape Cod, Caleb had often expressed his deep longing to get out on the water again, and so Phoebe arranged for them to travel home from New York by boat.

What was to have been a romantic voyage turned into a nightmare. A fog bank rolled in, throwing them off course. Experienced sailors both, they might have survived, if someone hadn't decided to take advantage of their predicament, waving a lantern they assumed was meant to lead them to safety. Instead, it lured them onto a dangerous sandbar, where they were robbed and left to fend for themselves. They'd died of exposure before anyone could reach them.

Little Hannah was forced to wait nearly a year with her future husband's family until her older brother—Piper's grandfather—returned from war to raise her. Ever since, people in Frye's Cove had indulged Hannah Macintosh Frye more than most, and perhaps more than was wise.

Piper was no exception. Only her reasons were different. Having lost her own mother at two, she identified with her great-aunt in a way few others could. Hannah was mother, aunt, friend—someone who understood Piper and accepted her unconditionally. The bond they shared was unlike any Piper had with anyone else, including her father and brothers. Much as she loved them, they weren't Hannah.

Which explained why Piper had ventured out at four in the morning for valerian root.

She set her backpack on Hannah's gleaming new kitchen table and fished out the foul-smelling stuff.

Her old aunt beamed. "Wonderful! Just set it on the counter."

Piper obliged, aware of Hannah's watchful eye. She was a tiny woman, slim and snowy haired. Over the years, her fair skin had taken on the quality of crumpled crepe paper. Her eyes were as green as those of any

Macintosh, infamous or celebrated, her approach to life as optimistic and impractical. She hadn't married until sixty-two. Her many years as a single woman had only further solidified the general tolerance for her eccentricities. She'd kept books for the town for forty years. Everyone in Frye's Cove knew her; she knew everyone.

Her most noticeable eccentricity was her style of dress. After her husband died, Hannah, then not quite seventy, had taken up wearing long dresses distinctly nineteenth century in design, which she sewed herself, almost entirely with needle and thread, while sitting by the fire during Cape Cod's long, cold winters. Sometimes Piper would join her and help, feeling as if she were stuck in a chapter of *Little Women* as the fire crackled and the winter winds howled.

Today's dress was a high-collared cornflower calico that made her look as if she'd just stepped off the stagecoach. It made no sense to Piper that a woman so attuned to the past would give up her antique house for life in a posh housing complex for the elderly.

Unless she was willing to believe Hannah's mutterings about spells and the love of a lifetime and one rich, unsociable Tennessean.

"Which I'm not," she said under her breath.

Hannah frowned. "What?"

"Nothing."

"You look tired," her aunt pronounced. "Would you care for some tea?"

Tea in Hannah's kitchen usually involved experimental concoctions and potions and odd bits of dried things floating on top. Seldom did it involve the Twinings family. Piper politely shook her head. "No, thanks. I'll just have a glass of water."

She filled a new, inexpensive glass with water from the tap—she didn't necessarily trust Hannah's spring-water—and leaned against the kitchen counter as she drank. Her aunt examined the valerian root, but Piper wasn't fooled. "Hannah, I know what you're thinking."

"You met him, didn't you?"

"Yes, unfortunately, I did. He caught me red-handed. He wasn't very happy about it."

"He wouldn't be," Hannah said knowledgeably.

"You've never even met the man! How would you know how he'd—" She caught herself and held up a hand before her aunt could get started. "No, never mind. I don't want to know. Hannah, you know I love you, and you know I'd do anything in the world for you, but this notion of yours about Clate Jackson and me is just—" She struggled for the right words. "It's just plain loony."

Unoffended, Hannah settled into an oak chair at her kitchen table. "Tell me about him."

"There's nothing to tell. He heard me digging in *his* garden, came out to investigate, caught me, maintained I was trespassing and stealing, warned me not to do it again, and let me go."

"Let you go? He had you in his clutches?"

Piper contained an unexpected smile. "No, he just threatened to call the police."

Hannah seemed disappointed. "Why on earth would he have called the police?"

"I was trespassing, Hannah."

"Phooey."

"You sold your house to him. You can't come and go as you please anymore, and neither can I. This is the last valerian root you'll have picked before dawn unless you manage to plant some off your deck."

"The committee would consider it a weed."

The committee might have a point. "Look, Hannah, I know this isn't easy for you—"

But her aunt wasn't listening. "Was he pleasant?"

"He wasn't totally insufferable, but he was not in any sense of the word pleasant." She quickly dismissed an image of his searing eyes, his tousled dark hair, and stubble of beard. "He made it quite clear he expects to be left alone and didn't come to Cape Cod to mingle with the locals."

"You're his only neighbor—"

"He's rich enough that he doesn't need neighbors."

"Nobody's that rich," Hannah said with a sniff.

"Well, he obviously chose your house because of its isolation. I wouldn't count on him indulging the eccentricities of its former owner."

Her aunt blinked in surprise. "I've never been an eccentric."

There wasn't a person in Frye's Cove and probably not on Cape Cod who didn't think Hannah Frye was an eccentric, one of the few things saving her from having her mental fitness openly challenged. As it was, there were stirrings. Worrisome stirrings. Piper pushed them aside. "I'm sorry you were wrong about Clate Jackson."

"Wrong? Oh, I'm not wrong. He's the man for you, Piper. What does he look like?"

Piper hesitated, a mistake.

Her aunt pounced, smiling. "Ah."

"It was still dark, I wasn't really paying attention, I couldn't—"

"Nonsense."

But Piper didn't want to admit that she'd paid very close attention to Clate Jackson in his tattered jeans and unbuttoned denim shirt. "He's not particularly good looking, I can tell you that much."

"He wouldn't be. According to my vision—"

"Hannah." Piper gritted her teeth. "You know I don't believe in that stuff."

Hannah calmly tucked wisps of white hair into a hand-crocheted bun cover. "It doesn't matter what you believe. Your destiny is your destiny. And so is his."

"I don't believe you put a spell on him."

She snorted. "This isn't 'Bewitched,' Piper. I don't put spells on people. I merely appeal to the life force and—well, I won't get started."

"Thank you."

Hannah had been muttering about romance, destiny, vision, and the stars for weeks. In Piper's estimation, it was all an attempt to justify selling her house to the first buyer willing to meet her price and set her up with a microwave, new dishes, new furniture, good wiring, town water, and a bathroom with a whirlpool tub.

"Fate and destiny don't have anything to do with Clate Jackson buying the Frye House," Piper said. "You just got tired of dealing with extension cords."

"I have at least one outlet on every wall. Do you want to see?"

Piper laughed in spite of her frustrations and concerns. Okay, so her aunt was not only incorrigible and maybe dotty, but she was also very happy in her new life. That had to count for something. "I'll pass, thank you."

Hannah grinned. "Come, Piper, sit down. I have a nice peppermint tea that will soothe your nerves. You need to calm down after your first encounter with your Mr. Jackson."

"He's not my Mr. Jackson. He just wants to be left alone."

"No." She spoke with certainty, her faith in her vision, or whatever it was, unshakable. "On the contrary. That's the last thing he wants."

"You haven't even met him!"

"Not in this life, no."

That did it. Piper headed for the doorway. "I've got a full day ahead. Enjoy your valerian root, Hannah. Don't do any mischief with it."

"Mischief? Me? What do you mean, Piper?"

She glanced back and saw, amazingly, that her aunt was truly mystified. "I mean Stan Carlucci."

Hannah waved a bony hand. "That fool. I served him a perfectly ordinary medicinal tea that was meant to benefit him and everyone else in town. We'd all have an easier time of it if Stan Carlucci had improved digestion."

Carlucci was a recently elected member of the board of selectmen whose ideas about the future of Frye's Cove differed from Hannah's. She generally considered people who disagreed with her narrow-minded and dead wrong, but at least she would grudgingly acknowledge their right to hold an opinion different from hers. Stan Carlucci, however, tested her ability to agree to disagree, particularly when he sneered at the way Frye's Cove used to do things, namely when Hannah was keeping the town's books. She'd taken his comments as a personal affront. Possibly they had been meant as such. A relative newcomer to town, Stan Carlucci didn't have the benevolent view of Hannah-as-orphan that so many did.

"He said he had cramps for three days," Piper pointed out.

"If he had a more settled temperament, he would have been fine. He was even crankier than I had anticipated. The tea helped bring his system into balance."

"Maybe so, Hannah, but he's telling anyone who'll listen that you tried to poison him."

She snorted. "If I'd tried to poison him, I'd have succeeded, make no mistake about it."

"Hannah—"

"Oh, Piper, stop fretting. I am in full possession of my faculties. I despise Stan Carlucci's know-it-allness and his disdain for others and his politics. But I gave him that particular tea because I believed it would help him and for no other reason."

Even if she was telling the truth as she saw it, everyone in town still believed that she'd intended to give Stan Carlucci cramps and diarrhea. He was ruthless, divisive, and insulting, and many rued the day they'd voted him into office and couldn't wait to vote him out again. But that didn't mean anyone would touch anything Hannah Frye offered in the way of food and drink. Right now, most were willing to give her the benefit of the doubt because it was Stan Carlucci calling her a menace. A few more similar incidents, however, and people would start seriously wondering about the state of Hannah Frye's mental health.

That scared Piper. Conjuring up a Tennessean for her niece and compelling her to dig valerian root at the crack of dawn were just the sort of incidents that Stan Carlucci needed to lend weight to his assessment that her aunt was a dangerous nut. But it wasn't his accusations that worried Piper, it was the possibility that her aunt could be on her way to becoming a menace to herself and her community. In which case something would have to be done to keep her from hurting herself or anyone else.

"Piper, Piper." Hannah sighed, shaking her head, as if reading her niece's thoughts. "I'm not out where the trains don't run just yet. Now, I know you must have a million things to do today, but I do want to talk to you about something."

Piper groaned to herself. Now what? She manufactured a smile. "Sure, Hannah. What's up?"

"Last night was a test."

"A test? What do you mean?"

"I wanted to see if you could sneak onto my—onto Mr. Jackson's property at night and do a bit of digging. I needed the valerian root, so it was a good choice."

"It didn't have to be dug before full light?"

"Oh, it did, just not for medicinal or spiritual reasons." She smiled, pleased with herself. "For practical reasons. I wanted to see if this could be done."

Piper was getting a bad feeling about where her aunt was going with this one. "Well, it couldn't. I was caught."

"But you'll know what to do next time."

"Uh-uh. There's not going to be any next time."

Hannah shook her head, confident. "Oh, but there will be. You see, Piper, I need you to dig up my parents' buried treasure."

"Hannah?"

She got jauntily to her feet. "I'll make tea, dear. We'll talk."

Clate pulled his car into a narrow space in front of the pharmacy in the village of Frye's Cove. Earlier, on his way to the grocery up near one of Cape Cod's main thoroughfares, he could have sworn he had spotted his next-door neighbor streaking along on a mountain bike. It was a weekday. Friday. She'd been up at four stealing herbs, then off on her bicycle by midmorning. Didn't the woman have a job?

He pushed aside the thought. He didn't want to get involved with the locals. He knew next to nothing about his neighbor and would have preferred to know less than he did. He was here on a much-needed break. He meant only to get acquainted with his new property and try to understand the strange impulse that had led him to buy an eighteenth-century house on Cape Cod.

He'd learned to rely on his instincts. They, coupled with hard work and a bit of luck, had served him well over the years. But usually he understood, if sometimes only in retrospect, the source of his impulses, the logic and rationality behind buying a run-down block in Nashville that he'd rehabilitated into prime office space, the vacant, trashy lot near Opryland where he'd built his exclusive hotel. He could trace those decisions back to concrete information, rumors he'd heard, studies he'd glanced at, musings while driving—a maze of facts and suppositions that ultimately made sense.

Buying a sagging antique house on Cape Cod made no sense. Not even in retrospect.

"You're Clate Jackson, aren't you?"

A tall, dusty man with dark reddish hair approached him on the steps of the pharmacy. He had a familiar look about him. Clate said, "Yes, I'm Jackson."

"Heard you were in town. Thought I recognized you from a description someone gave me. I'm Andrew Macintosh."

Another Macintosh. Was everyone in town related? Clate decided not to ask who had provided the description of him. Frye's Cove, he was coming to discover, was the sort of town where talk of newcomers spread fast. He shook hands with Andrew Macintosh, who appeared to be a few years older than he was; his hands were thick and callused, as Clate's had been when he'd worked construction. "Pleased to meet you. Is Piper Macintosh—"

"My sister. She has another brother and a father in town, too." Deep green eyes assessed Clate with remarkable frankness; Andrew Macintosh didn't smile. "We look after her."

So, he was serving notice that his little sister wasn't just out on her isolated road all by herself; she had meaty men folk checking up on her. Clate didn't blame the man. In Andrew Macintosh's place, he'd do the same. "Tight family?"

"Very."

"That's nice. I doubt if I'll be seeing much of your sister. I'll be in and out of town. I have no intention of becoming a permanent resident."

That seemed to sit well with Andrew. "You've met Piper?"

"Briefly." Prudence kept him from going into detail about where, when, and how, although he suspected Andrew Macintosh was less likely than his little sister to skin the newcomer in town alive.

Andrew grunted something about welcoming Clate to town and departed. Message delivered, message received. He didn't like it that his sister no longer had an eighty-seven-year-old woman as her only neighbor, but Clate was to have no illusions that Piper was on her own, unwatched and unprotected.

As he pushed on into the old-fashioned pharmacy, he wondered what Piper herself might make of her big brother's warning. This, after all, was a woman who'd gone toe-to-toe with a stranger before sunup over some damned stinky hunk of root.

Leave it alone, Clate warned himself as he soaked in the atmosphere of the turn-of-the-century pharmacy and found his way to a bottle of simple, no-nonsense aspirin. His gaze traveled to the prophylactic section, then darted back to the aspirin. Hell. If Andrew Macintosh saw that, he'd jump to all the wrong conclusions and there'd be fur flying in Frye's Cove. Clate had no designs on anyone's little sister.

None.

Not even when he thought of her trim body marching off with her smelly root.

He swore to himself, viciously, and grabbed the bottle of aspirin before he drove himself mad. Quiet, isolation, solitude, rest. They were what he needed, what he wanted, and why, ultimately, his instincts had drawn him to Cape Cod.

Chapter

3

Piper stared out across a narrow strip of sandy beach, her bicycle parked next to her on the side of the road. She tried to concentrate on the scenery. A few people were out surf fishing, a half dozen children were racing across the wet sand. The tide was out, the water in the bay as blue as the sky, sparkling in the early afternoon sun. There was almost no wind. It was still early in the season. After the Fourth of July, even Frye's Cove would be crowded with tourists, sightseers, summer residents.

She heard a car on the road behind her, but didn't bother turning around. She wasn't in the mood to talk to anyone. Then the car stopped next to her bicycle, and finally she turned.

Clate Jackson had his window rolled down, his eyes on her. He drove a BMW, probably rented or leased if he'd flown up from Tennessee. "Must be your day off."

"I'm self-employed. I can make my own hours."

"What do you do?"

"A bunch of stuff." She took a breath, calming herself. He couldn't read minds. He wouldn't know what she and

Hannah had discussed that morning. Her bike ride and her aunt's bizarre talk about buried treasure had her hot and jittery; she could feel sweat trickling between her breasts. "I'm sort of an expert on traditional early-American crafts. I teach, consult, write. I sell some of my own stuff, mostly just breads and open-kettle jams."

"You work out of your house?" His question was matter-of-fact, but his eyes were a dark, deep blue, unreadable, as if he were still gauging just how big a pest his only neighbor would prove to be.

"I converted a shed on my property into a small studio and I have an office in my house."

He didn't seem too pleased by that idea. She could see him calculating her opportunities to get in his way if she didn't go off to work.

"I stay very busy," she added, then grinned. Or tried to. She felt stiff and self-conscious. She was rattled and tired, and a day of bike riding and Hannah had taken its toll. She wished she'd worn one of her own shirts, at least, instead of her brother's. "Just not today. I'm teaching a class tonight in yarn dyeing. Actually, valerian makes a decent yellow dye." She was deliberately goading him and had no idea why. "But I'm using chamomile flowers tonight."

"From your own garden, I trust."

"And one of my student's." Her tone cooled. "Chamomile's a relatively common herb."

"Harmless?"

His drawl rolled up her spine. "Quite."

He shifted, and the light caught a two-inch white scar along his jaw. She'd missed that one last night. She didn't know how. With the nick of a scar at the corner of his left eye, he looked tough, masculine, not a man she would want even to attempt to deceive.

Which was precisely what Hannah had asked her to do.

Piper groaned to herself. It would have been ever so much easier if Clate Jackson had been a slick, shallow executive, unappealing on any level. Even Hannah would have had to admit the universe had coughed up the wrong man.

"By the way," he said, "I met your brother Andrew in town earlier."

Perfect. Just what she needed on top of Hannah's buried treasure. One look at Clate Jackson and Andrew would be on high alert. She'd taken a detour around the center of town, just to make sure she didn't run into her father and brothers after her unnerving talk with Hannah. They always had a way of seeing through her. They'd know something was up. But she couldn't explain. If she did, the Macintosh men would haul Hannah straight off to the loony bin.

Clate had those searing eyes narrowed on her. Piper tried to look less distracted, less guilty. "And how's big brother?"

"Seemed fine. Told him you and I had met."

"Did you say how?"

"No." A flash of unexpected humor softened his eyes. "Figured I'd leave that up to you."

"Good of you. Andrew—both my brothers are protective of me. And my father, although he's not quite as bad."

The humor drifted from his eyes to his mouth. "So I gathered."

"But I guess I'm protective of them, too, in my own way. If Andrew stops by to see Hannah, she'll tell him about the valerian root herself. She doesn't understand why I shouldn't be traipsing off to your place in the middle of the night."

Clate's eyebrows raised, and too late, Piper realized she could have chosen her words more carefully. She took a step back from his car, feeling hotter and even more self-conscious, as if every part of her were somehow exposed to him.

"Anyway," she added briskly, "I told Hannah that you wanted to preserve your privacy. She just needs a little time to adjust to not having all her herbs right on her doorstep."

"She's happy with her valerian root?"

"Seems to be."

"I hope she'll find another source for it in the future. Well, I'll leave you to your bike ride." But he didn't pull away from the road, eyeing Piper instead; his eyes seemed an even deeper blue in daylight. "Are you all right?"

"Yes, fine. I think I might have strained a calf muscle, that's all." Nothing was wrong with her calf muscles, but she'd needed a simple explanation; the truth was out of the question. But her lie sounded false even to her own ears. "I sometimes overdo it bike riding when the weather's this gorgeous."

"I understand."

Something in his tone—it wasn't obvious—suggested he knew she had fibbed. She forced a smile. "Thanks for stopping."

"If you need a ride—"

"No, that's okay. I'll just ice my calves when I get home."

"I hope they feel better soon." Sarcasm dried out his drawl, the humor and suspicion lingering in his gaze. No doubt about it, he knew he had a liar living next door. "See you around, Piper Macintosh."

She had to fight herself not to dig herself a deeper hole by telling him she did, too, have sore calves and he could damned well come back to her house and watch her ice them if he didn't believe her. The truth was, although her calves were fine, she wasn't. And for once, common sense kicked in before she could compound her problems.

His car disappeared down the narrow road and around the bend out to their spit of marsh, sand, and scrub trees. If Clate Jackson was a light sleeper, he'd see her around sooner than either of them wanted.

Provided, of course, she did Hannah's bidding.

"Buried treasure."

Piper's shoulder sagged. It was nuts.

"Try under the wisteria first," Hannah had advised. "That's my best guess."

Naturally, the wisteria in question was in Clate Jackson's back yard. There would be no asking his permission. Not only did Hannah forbid it, but Piper would have refused. This latest mission made her elderly aunt look goofier than ever, something her aunt couldn't afford these days. Being known as a harmless eccentric was one thing, a dangerous nut was something else.

No matter how hard she tried, Piper just couldn't dismiss Hannah's haunting tale of her parents' deaths. She couldn't pretend she'd forgotten their conversation that morning or simply dig in her heels and refuse to act. After eighty years, Hannah believed she had the long-denied answers to the deaths of her parents within her grasp, and she needed Piper to help her reach them.

Piper climbed onto her bike and pedaled slowly toward home. As she'd listened to her aunt talk, the pain of her terrible loss seemed so fresh. Piper could imagine a seven-year-old child waiting up late into the night, eager to see her father again after his long months at war.

"Father wrote to me every week while he was away." Her face was old and worn now, decades later, her voice quiet and steady as she spoke, but Piper could see in her eyes the hint of the little girl Hannah had been, vivid and curious, determined to see life as it was, not just as she wanted it to be. "He told me an elaborate tale of how he'd saved a Russian princess from certain death at the hands of a roving gang of miscreants. She had already escaped the Russian Revolution, and here she was about to die on a lonely French road, when my father appeared on the scene and rescued her, bringing her to safe quarters. She was so impressed by his courage that she insisted upon rewarding him. She had no money, only gemstones and a Fabergé egg."

Piper had been skeptical. "Hannah, that sounds like the sort of fanciful story a father would tell a precocious seven-year-old daughter to keep her from worrying about him getting killed in battle."

"I know. For years that's what I thought. But now"—she'd exhaled deeply, fixing her gaze on her only niece—"now, I'm not so sure."

And so she'd explained.

In the weeks since she'd moved out of the Frye House, new details of her memory of that night eighty years ago had emerged from deep within her subconscious. "It's as if they've lain dormant all these years, and only now, free of that house, could I bring myself to remember. And now that I do, Piper, I remember so clearly!"

In her excitement at the prospect of seeing her father, she'd been unable to sleep. She reread his letters to her, which she'd kept in an iron box, and played in bed, until the scent of roses and the sea in the cold night air drew her to her window.

"The wind had shifted, as it often does. I thought nothing of it at the time. But now—I don't know if I can explain. It's as if my parents were sending those scents to me as they died, enticing me to the window so that I would see what I saw, knowing that I was too young to understand, that it would be many decades before I would seek the answers I'm now seeking." She'd paused, her jaw setting. "It all comes back to destiny."

Afraid Hannah would drift back to the subject of Clate Jackson, Piper had steered her aunt back on course. "What did you see?"

"A shadowy figure. It was dark and cold, the wind was gusting. I heard digging. Then the clouds shifted, and in a quick ray of moonlight, I saw a small trunk sitting on the ground."

"A trunk," Piper repeated.

"Correct."

"Did you mention this trunk to anyone at the time?"

"I told you, I've only remembered seeing in the past few weeks."

"So after eighty years, you suddenly, out of the blue, recall a scene you witnessed on the most traumatic night of your life." Piper didn't bother hiding her skepticism. "Hannah, repressed memory is a tricky thing."

"Of course it is. That's why I'm dispatching you instead of calling the police. My parents were murdered, and I think it's because of the gems and Fabergé egg— the treasure—the Russian princess gave to Father. Piper, someone else must have read my letters and known about the treasure, and then deliberately set out to rob him and Mother that night."

There were a million holes in Hannah's story. Caleb and Phoebe were off course. How could the perpetrator have known where to find them? Even if they hadn't been that far off course, how could he have known it was their boat in the fog? Premeditation made little sense— not, Piper thought, that happenstance made any sense, either.

And treasure buried for eighty years in the Frye back yard made no sense whatsoever. Why risk being seen by a Frye, never mind a seven-year-old?

Even if Piper indulged Hannah and chose to believe in her conveniently recovered memory, any treasure would have to be long gone by now. Whoever had buried it surely would have dug it up some time during the past century.

But Hannah was visibly tired and shaken after telling her story, and Piper didn't have the heart to blow holes in her theory. "Well, I just wish you'd thought of digging up this treasure of yours during the umpteen years you lived in the Frye house."

She sniffed. "I didn't think of it then."

Piper had sighed, exasperated, worried, haunted by the palpable horror of that night almost a century ago.

"I know nobody's going to believe me," she said calmly. "That's why you have to find the treasure first, Piper. Discreetly. Then I'll know for sure. You do see, don't you? I have to know what happened to my parents. Before I die, I have to know."

Getting morbid had always been one of Hannah's last-ditch ploys to persuade Piper to do her bidding. This time, it had the ring of authenticity. She'd convinced herself the notorious mystery of her parents' deaths was within her power to solve—with Piper's help, of course.

"It's as if I couldn't let myself remember while I was living in that house."

"But you didn't live there until you and Jason were married. You were sixty-two! You had a lot of years you could have remembered—"

"Ah, but I was in love with Jason from the time I was seven. His hold on me was staggering."

Piper had lurched forward in her chair. "You don't think a Frye killed your parents, do you?"

"I only know what I know."

Drama—or evasiveness. Hannah wasn't above holding back pertinent information as a ploy to get her way. "Are you sure you didn't recognize this shadowy figure?"

"I never saw his face."

"But it was a man?"

Suddenly her bony shoulders sagged, and she seemed little more than a pile of bones in cornflower calico. "I don't know. I've told you everything. After a lifetime, I finally remember that night, the scent of roses and the sea, the sound of digging—" She'd swallowed, tears in her eyes. "The shock of losing my parents must have blocked my memory all these years. But now—now, Piper, I remember."

And so it was that Piper had agreed to check into the possibility of treasure buried in her neighbor's back yard.

She breathed in the cool June air as she pedaled toward home, noticed the scent of roses and the sea even as she tried not to think of a seven-year-old girl staring out into the night while her parents died together on the other side of the windswept peninsula.

Unless the whole story was a tactical move on Hannah's part to throw her grandniece and the Tennessean together. But as devious as Hannah Frye could be, Piper didn't believe she'd stoop that low. Hannah really believed she'd seen someone in the Fryes' back yard that night.

Still, with any luck, her aunt would move on to something else before Piper got to the point of digging under Clate Jackson's wisteria.

Clate squinted out at the tall hedges dividing his property from that of his closest and only neighbor. He couldn't see her house from the stone terrace where he stood. On his way home, he'd slowed in front of her little Cape and had taken note of the rambling pink roses on the white picket fence, the terra-cotta pots of wispy flowers, the spikes of pink and yellow and white and orange in gardens all around the old house, and the trim, pretty shed that served as her studio. To live and work out here by herself had to require a certain courage and independence, something he wondered if her brother Andrew recognized in his little sister.

Well, it wasn't his problem.

He could smell the sweet scents of his own flower gardens. He distinguished honeysuckle and wisteria among them, and for a moment he might have been home, not in Nashville, but in the Cumberland hills where Irma Bryar's honeysuckle and wisteria grew in unmanageable tangles. Spring came late to New England and lasted only a short time, unlike the long, slow, fragrant spring of Tennessee. Cape Cod was foreign territory for him. The locals had little interest in celebrity, none at all in his particular brand. He grimaced at the thought of his unsmiling face on a recent cover of a slick Nashville magazine touting him as one of the chosen new architects of the growing, changing city. *He's rich, he's successful, he's respected . . . So why isn't Clate Jackson smiling?*

A dumb-ass headline if he'd ever read one.

He tore his gaze from the hedges. To have his place on Cape Cod be what he wanted it to be—what he needed it to be—he would have to keep the locals at arm's length, Piper Macintosh most especially.

She'd looked preoccupied standing by her bicycle, looking out at the water. Troubled.

The rattle of a truck engine interrupted his unwelcome thoughts. Company? More Macintosh men to warn him off? He headed around to the gravel driveway and garage at the side of the house.

A big, muscle-bound man stepped out of a rusted pickup. He looked about thirty, give or take a year, and had tawny, curly hair, a tawny beard, and a meaty, friendly face. "You Clate Jackson? Hi. I'm Tuck O'Rourke. Figured I'd stop by, see if you could use someone to take care of your place here. I can do pretty much whatever you need doing. Cut grass, prune, trim, odd jobs. Don't matter."

After less than twenty-four hours up north, Clate was having his doubts about tales of standoffish Yankees. "You have references?"

"Yeah, sure. You got a minute? I can look around the place, see what needs to be done, and maybe we can work something out. Probably should have called, but I didn't know if you had a phone yet."

He did. The number wasn't listed. But hiring a caretaker was on his to-do list, and he supposed he should look upon Tuck O'Rourke's visit as a convenience rather than an intrusion. He motioned for the big man to go on ahead of him, and they walked around to the back yard together, Tuck explaining that Jason Frye had employed his father as a caretaker. "When Jason died, Mrs. Frye let Pop go. She never liked the idea of someone else doing work on the property."

"She did it herself?"

"Or didn't do it at all."

Added insight into the Macintosh personality. Clate let Tuck take him around the lush, old yard as he pointed out its many problems. Rotted trellises, bees' nests in inappropriate places, brick that needed replacing, cracked stone, washed-out spots along the foundation, a robust crop of poison ivy vying with grape vines off along the far edge of the yard. When they finished, they returned to the stone terrace, which was in danger, apparently, of eroding and washing down into the marsh.

O'Rourke shrugged his massive shoulders. "Sorry for all the bad news. I guess Mrs. Frye didn't keep up the place that well."

"Did she decide to sell because upkeep was getting out of hand?"

"I don't know. I just heard it had to do with one of her spells."

"One of her what?"

"Spells. She's a witch." He spoke in that blunt, Yankee manner, then grinned at Clate's mystified look and rubbed his short beard. "You didn't know, huh?"

"No, I didn't." Although the skull and crossbones in the enclosed herb garden should have been a tip-off, he supposed. "Well, that's her business. It has nothing to do with me."

Tuck shifted, suddenly looking uncomfortable.

Clate felt a twist of foreboding. "There's something I should know, isn't there?"

"It's just idle talk."

"I'll take it in that light, then. I've had experience with gossip and rumors."

Avoiding Clate's eye, O'Rourke mashed the toe of a work boot into a crack in the terrace. "I've heard Mrs. Frye put a spell on you."

Clate nearly choked. "On *me?*"

Tuck nodded.

"Why in hell would she do that?"

"Don't know. Some say because she thinks one of your ancestors is haunting the house."

"My family came to this country via Baltimore and headed south from there."

Tuck squirmed, and Clate could see that he was a taciturn man by nature. "I just hear things, you understand. Doesn't mean I believe them."

"Acknowledged. What else do people say about this supposed spell?"

"I guess some folks are saying the devil himself made Mrs. Frye put a spell on you to get you to come north, buy this place, and develop it."

Clate couldn't stop a grin. "The devil, eh?"

"Yeah." Tuck wasn't grinning back. His idea of witches seemed rooted in horror movies and popular stereotype, not contemporary understanding of witchcraft as one of the world's oldest religions. "I mean, I don't believe any of that."

"That's it, then? I'm here either because of ghosts or devils?"

"Or Piper," O'Rourke added almost inaudibly.

Clate didn't know why he wasn't surprised. "Mind elaborating?"

"There's talk—I know it's crazy—" He flushed, his cheeks red above his tawny beard. "There's talk Mrs. Frye's been working her magic to try and get a man up here for Piper, seeing how she hasn't had any luck with the guys around town."

"I beg your pardon?"

"It's just crazy talk. Small town, you know?"

Witches, ghosts, devils, romance. Small-town talk indeed. Clate took a breath. No wonder Andrew Macintosh had made a point of introducing himself. If even a scrap of this crazy talk was accurate, his aunt was a lunatic. And his sister wasn't far behind if she was indulging the old woman.

"I suppose." He tried to sound good natured about the whole thing, but he hadn't considered the possibility of an eighty-seven-year-old woman casting spells on him when he'd tried to understand his impulse to buy property up north. "Thanks for stopping by. Let me know what you can and can't do around here and how much you'll charge, and we'll talk."

O'Rourke still was looking awkward and embarrassed. "I wouldn't worry about Mrs. Frye, really. I've been talking out of turn. I've known her all my life. She's harmless." He started off the terrace, apparently wishing he'd kept his mouth shut. "I'll get you that bid by tomorrow."

"Thanks."

Clate waited until he heard Tuck O'Rourke's truck rattle off down the road before he headed back inside. If he were smart, he'd pay no attention to local gossip. An eighty-seven-year-old widow and her green-eyed, chestnut-haired niece living alone out on this road were bound to stir up imaginative talk, especially in a small town. Add him to the mix, and the talk could get interesting. It wasn't every day that a rich Tennessean bought a two-hundred-fifty-year-old house and thirty acres in Frye's Cove.

He checked his voice mail, his mind still on his bizarre conversation with Tuck O'Rourke. Most of his messages were routine.

But there was the one he'd expected, dreaded. His assistant, the young, smart Mabel Porter, delivered it in her polished eastern Tennessee accent.

"She's gone, Mr. Jackson. I'm sorry."

Chapter

4

Piper sat at her picnic table with a cup of coffee, her portable telephone, and her binoculars. She thought she'd spotted a piping plover in the marsh from her bedroom window. It was an endangered species, distinguished by its unique, twisting flight, and it was rigorously protected on Cape Cod. Enough reason to breakfast outside. The glorious morning only added to her satisfaction. There wasn't a cloud in the sky, sunlight sparkled on the quiet bay, shorebirds plundered the marsh for food, bees buzzed in the flowering herbs around her. She'd planted ordinary, innocuous culinary herbs: several kinds of thyme, mint, basil, tarragon, oregano, sage. Nothing remotely poisonous. Sage supposedly was good for female complaints, but she just used it for stuffing.

She sipped her coffee, wishing she hadn't thought of Hannah. Not yet, not before her second cup of coffee at least. She'd had a good night's sleep. No predawn forays into her neighbor's yard for medicinal herbs or buried treasure. Even Hannah couldn't have expected her to dig for treasure last night. If Clate Jackson had caught Piper two nights in a row, there was no doubt in her mind he'd have her explaining herself to Ernie down at the police station.

After her yarn-dyeing class had let out last night and she'd cleaned up her studio, she'd pondered a delicate course of action that would manage to satisfy Hannah without further fueling people's concerns about her mental health. Without her aunt breathing down her neck, her sense of urgency almost palpable, Piper could think.

What she'd thought, quite simply, was that it wouldn't be smart to head next door with shovel in hand and start digging willy-nilly for buried treasure that might not even exist.

She snatched up her binoculars and scanned the marsh. She had a busy afternoon and evening ahead, but her morning was hers. She could head into town and sneak into a quiet corner of the library, away from prying eyes, and look up newspaper accounts of the shipwreck that had killed her great-grandparents. Maybe there'd be some long-lost hint that Caleb Macintosh really had rescued a Russian princess and Hannah's memory wasn't a fairy tale, a ploy, or a trick of her mind.

Her telephone rang, startling her. She picked it up, the binoculars still in place. "Hello."

"Stay off Clate Jackson's property if you know what's good for you."

She dropped her binoculars. "What? Who is this?"

"Do it."

The voice was muffled, gravelly. Piper felt a stab of fear and started to say something, but stopped when she heard a click and a dial tone.

She switched off her phone and stared at it. What the hell was that all about? Her hands shaking, she pressed the on button, hit the memory button for Hannah's number, and snatched up her binoculars while the phone rang. Her heart raced. Who would want to make such a call?

Hannah answered after four rings.

"That wasn't you, was it?"

"Who wasn't me? Piper? What's wrong?"

She ran a trembling hand through her hair. "I just got a weird phone call. I'm okay."

"Tell me about it."

Piper wanted to. A few months ago she would have, without thought or hesitation. Now, she reconsidered. "It was probably nothing. I should have listened to Andrew and Benjamin and never put my name in the Yellow Pages. I'll talk to you later."

"Piper—"

"Gotta run. Bye, Hannah. Love you."

She gathered up phone, coffee mug, and binoculars and charged inside, adrenaline still pumping. All right, so Hannah wasn't above sending her out for valerian root at the crack of dawn to force an encounter with Clate Jackson. She would never do anything deliberately to terrify Piper, just to encourage romance between her and the man of her destiny.

Unless Stan Carlucci was right and Hannah really was unbalanced.

Piper stopped in the middle of her keeping room, wide boards under foot, dried herbs and flowers hanging from exposed beams. What if it had been Clate Jackson on the other end of the phone?

No. That was absurd. He'd told her right to her face to stay off his property. Why be sneaky about it?

An associate?

"Geez," Piper breathed, "I'm losing it."

She grabbed one of the handmade baskets hanging amidst the bunches of herbs and flowers. The first of the strawberries were ripe. She'd planned to pick them this morning and make a batch of open-kettle jam, and that was just what she would do.

"Stay off Clate Jackson's property."

With a shudder, she slipped back outside and took several deep, cleansing breaths before heading to her strawberry patch. She needed to clear her mind and consider her options instead of doing something precipitous, like marching next door or, worse, calling her father and brothers or Ernie at the police station. Berry picking, she hoped, would do the trick.

A narrow, well-traveled footpath took Clate through a break in the hedge that divided his and Piper Macintosh's property, then up through tall, wild grasses, the marsh creeping further up the gentle slope toward her house. None of the Frye House's terraced gardens and lush grass here. The marsh gave way to a yard that was more meadow than suburban lawn. He noticed wild-looking gardens of vegetables, herbs, flowers, trellises of pink roses, a grape arbor, bird feeders, a rooster weathervane, a neatly stacked woodpile. A brightly colored windsock danced in the breeze from a low-hanging branch of an oak.

Clate spotted her in her vegetable garden, a floppy straw hat protecting her face from the strong midmorning sun. He didn't think she'd seen him. She seemed absorbed in her work. As he came closer, he saw that she was picking strawberries, her small hands moving rapidly, surely, among the low vines.

"Nice garden," he said.

Her head shot up, and her hat fell back off her head as her eyes, their green blending in with their environment, focused on him. Her hat had a long, loose, ropy tie that kept it from falling into the strawberries. The sunlight struck her chestnut hair, and she stood up and brushed her hands on her berry-stained shirt, sending an arrow of lust straight to its mark. Clate felt his throat tighten. Shapely breasts, flat stomach, taut legs. A pity the eighty-seven-year-old aunt wasn't his neighbor instead of the niece. He hadn't come north for this kind of distraction.

"Thank you." But her smile didn't quite reach her eyes, and he remembered her troubled look yesterday when he'd stopped alongside the road. "It's just enough garden for me to manage on my own."

He pushed back questions about her troubled state; it was none of his business. "It's organic?"

She nodded, some of her obvious distress easing. "A lot of it's just knowing what to plant where to discourage pests and promote growth. Synergy. That and a few of Hannah's natural remedies work fine for me. But I can always run down to the grocery if the deer and the bugs get everything."

"Your strawberries look as if they've done well. I didn't mean to interrupt."

"No problem. My back was starting to give out anyway. What can I do for you?"

Picking strawberries in the June sun, Cape Cod Bay sprawled at her feet. Clate inhaled. Life could be worse. He remembered Irma ladeling sweet, juicy strawberries onto warm biscuits, lecturing him about family and community and duty, ever the idealist, ever the believer in what he could do and who he could be, and he felt himself withdraw into a grief that had caught him by surprise. Irma Bryar's death at eighty-nine was not unexpected, and yet she had been a presence in his life for so long, she'd cared about him in a way his own parents were incapable of caring, that he simply couldn't imagine what his life was going to be like without her. Never mind that he seldom saw her, that he'd gone way beyond even what she'd imagined he could do with his life. Irma had always been there. And now she wasn't.

He saw Piper's eyes narrowing on him, knew he must look haggard and on edge.

"I came to ask your opinion, if you don't mind." He straightened, reined in his grief, his purely physical reaction to her. That had been a distraction, nothing more. "I need to leave town today."

"Business?"

"No. Personal."

"Oh." She wanted to ask more; he could see it in her expression. But his tone had cut off further questioning. "Well, I can look after your place while you're gone."

"That's not necessary. I just wanted your take on a man who stopped by yesterday and offered his services as caretaker. Tuck O'Rourke. Do you know him?"

"Sure, I know Tuck." She scooped up her basket of strawberries, snatched up a fat one and twisted off its green top, popping it into her mouth. He watched her swallow. "He's a good guy. Solid, hardworking, not a whole lot of imagination."

"Honest?"

"So far as I know. You want him just to mow and stuff like that or really do some work on the place?"

"I'm considering having some landscaping and other work done."

She frowned. "Landscaping? Like what?"

Her matter-of-fact curiosity took on a proprietary tone. Clate cursed himself for asking her opinion. He'd operated on gut instinct from the time he could walk. He could have decided about Tuck O'Rourke on his own. "I'm not sure yet. The place needs a lot of work."

She flipped the strawberry cap into the dirt. "Well, if you're going to start digging stuff up, I hope you'll let me know before you throw anything out. Some of the Fryes' flower varieties are really old. I'd hate to see them land in a compost heap."

Not that she wouldn't help herself if he neglected to include her in his plans. Clate didn't wonder that the locals were speculating about her aunt resorting to magic to lure a man to Frye's Cove for her niece. Even if the rumor were wholly untrue, he could see that the local male population wouldn't have an easy time of it romancing Piper Macintosh. She was direct, determined, insistent upon seeing people as they were, not simply as they wished her to see them. A man would have to have a good opinion of himself to stand up to her scrutiny—not to mention that of her father and two brothers.

A rough lot, the Macintoshes.

But Clate was unintimidated. He considered asking Piper about O'Rourke's tales of witches, ghosts, devils, and romance. He'd like to see her squirm her way out of that one, whether fact or mere gossip. He decided against it, only because he didn't want to get Tuck O'Rourke in hot water with a woman who knew her way around poison herbs. The poor bastard could never hold his own with Piper Macintosh.

"About Tuck O'Rourke," he said curtly, putting aside speculation about his neighbor's love life. "Any hesitations?"

"No, he'll do a good job. When are you leaving?"

He thought of Irma in her rocking chair on her front porch, needlework and a book always at hand. "Immediately."

He could see the spark of curiosity in Piper's eyes, watched her force it back. "I'll keep an eye on Tuck and make sure he does right by your lawn and gardens."

"I wouldn't ask you—"

"Of course you wouldn't." She grinned, the distress he'd seen when he first arrived completely gone now. "Afraid I'm going to become a pest, Mr. Jackson? Not to worry. I've plenty to do without interfering in your affairs."

He sighed. The woman saw too much, and yet not nearly enough. He'd wager she had no idea he found her attractive. "I just don't want to put you out."

"You're not." She scooped up a handful of berries, let them fall one by one through her splayed fingers, a gesture Clate found impossibly erotic. "Have a good trip."

"Thank you."

"Oh, and if your place starts smoking or something or you remember you left the coffeepot on, I still have the key my aunt gave me. Unless you've changed your locks."

"I haven't," he said, "but perhaps I should."

She gave him a mystified look, as if she couldn't imagine what he'd find wrong in her having a key to his house. "Do you practice getting on people's nerves or is it just a gift?"

"I say what's on my mind."

"Well, that's something we have in common. If it makes you feel any better, there's probably a key to my house tucked away in your kitchen somewhere. Frye's Cove is a small town. Neighbors rely on each other, and it's just you and me out here."

He gave her a slow smile, just deliberately sexy enough to knock her off her high horse. "So it is."

She popped a strawberry into her mouth, stem and all. "How long will you be gone?"

He was unaccustomed to answering such questions. "Four or five days."

"That's all? It's not as if your place'll go to hell in just four days."

"Thanks for your help, Piper. I'll call Tuck O'Rourke before I leave."

She tilted her head back, studying him. A bit of color went out of her cheeks, and she seemed to have tightened her grip on her basket of strawberries. "You didn't happen to call here a little while ago, did you?" she asked suddenly.

Clate shook his head, saw the fresh signs of strain in her expression. He went still, sensing something was wrong. "No, I didn't. Why?"

"It's nothing, never mind." She took a deep breath, her hat hanging down her back as the breeze caught the ends of her dark, straight hair. "Tuck'll be fine, and I'm sure you won't leave the coffeepot on. Have a good trip."

Dismissing him, she negotiated her way through neat rows of strawberries, peas, new onions, tiny stalks of corn, and feathery carrot tops. Clate didn't move. She was barefoot, he saw. And shaken. Something about this mysterious phone call.

Why hadn't she known who it was?

"Are you sure you're all right?" he called.

She glanced back at him, smiled a phony smile. "Nope. I'm crazy. I picked too many strawberries and now I have to do something with them. Maybe I'll save you a jar of jam for when you get back."

"That would be nice."

But his words were distracted. She wasn't telling him the whole story, not even half of it. He had a mind to call her brother, put Andrew Macintosh on the case—a notion he immediately rejected. If Piper was in trouble, she would know where to find her family, and she had an entire town of friends who would help her, even if they believed she needed a witch's spell to improve her love life.

First she'd have to ask for their help. Piper Macintosh didn't strike him as a woman who would want to admit there was anything she couldn't handle on her own. She lived alone at the end of an isolated road, after all, and had her own woodpile, her own vegetables, her own quiet, independent life.

Clate sucked in a breath and started back down the sloping field, onto the worn path between their houses. Whatever her troubles, Piper just wasn't his problem.

Instead of taking her bicycle, Piper decided to drive to her three o'clock appointment with Sally Shepherd. She'd changed into nice pants and a silk blouse and was much calmer after her morning encounter with Clate Jackson. He'd already left for Tennessee. She'd driven past his house just to make sure. To accustom herself to his ideas about property, she'd even forced herself to turn around in the road, not his driveway.

She parked behind three trucks belonging to the men of Macintosh & Sons. She hadn't seen her father and brothers in days. Luckily she'd brought along extra jars of strawberry jam, still warm from the kettle—not that they'd be pacified. They would know why she was avoiding them: Clate Jackson and Hannah Frye. Both had her confused, disturbed, frustrated. She'd practically accused her new neighbor of making a threatening anonymous call. Of course he hadn't done such a thing! She had no reason whatever to suspect him, and now she'd succeeded in alerting him to just how jittery she was.

But something wasn't right with him, either. She

suspected he'd left Cape Cod over something more serious than a business deal gone sour. Which was none of her business, of course, as he'd be the first to tell her.

She headed up onto the inn's front porch, with its rockers and potted plants, and into the entry, where the scent of old wood, lemon polish, and potpourri immediately soothed her spirits. After completing massive structural repairs on the historic old house, Macintosh & Sons had gone to work on its individual rooms, starting with the first floor. It was a century newer than her tiny Cape, with twin chimneys on either end and a beautiful center staircase. Additions and modifications had made it less a classic colonial, more a wonderful mishmash of a century and a half of American architecture. The ceilings were higher, the rooms bigger than a Cape Cod, the feel was richer, less claustrophobic, and purely functional.

Piper joined Sally and Paul Shepherd in the front parlor, where they sat together on a Queen Anne sofa, poring over stacks of fabric swatches, wallpaper books, and paint chips. They made all decisions about the inn together. Although they were committed to preserving the sprawling house's historic flavor, they weren't afraid to mix in contemporary touches, refusing to be stuffy or overly proper. Sally, known for her exquisite taste, had called on Piper to help her decide how to use and place various reproduction and original crafts she'd collected.

"Right on time," Paul said with a pleasant smile.

Piper laughed. "What, did my brothers bet you I'd show up late?"

He grinned, a dark, good-looking, charming man. "Early."

"They're such teases," Sally said. "You're lucky to have each other."

"Sometimes," Piper acknowledged. "Not that I'd know what life was like without them. They're working upstairs still? I'll have to stop up and see them after our meeting." She tried to keep any dread out of her tone. She did want to see her family, provided they didn't force her to talk about things that didn't concern them, like Hannah and Clate Jackson. "I made strawberry jam this morning. Here, I brought you a jar."

It was a deft change of subject. Sally beamed, taking the jar. "Oh, Paul, it's still warm! We'll have it with scones later on with tea. Have you heard we've hired a new chef, Piper?"

"No, I haven't."

"She's excellent. She worked at an inn up in Provincetown. She suggests we serve afternoon tea on a regular basis. You'll have to bring Hannah by."

Paul cleared his throat pointedly, a glint in his dark eyes. "Not that we serve her kind of tea."

Sally flushed. She was a plain, fair-skinned woman with hair that was dyed too dark for her coloring and a wardrobe of sturdy, preppy clothes. She had married for the first time three years ago at age thirty-five. Both her and her husband's stock had gone up considerably in Frye's Cove when they hadn't made a peep about Hannah's inexplicable decision to sell her historic house and acreage. Sally was Jason Frye's only living direct descendant. Many in town considered her to have more claim to her grandfather's property—morally if not legally—than his wife of seven years. But Sally had long said she had no interest in the Frye House and was content with her and Paul's pretty house in the village and their up-and-coming inn.

"Oh, Paul, you're awful," she said affectionately. "Don't worry, Piper. We don't believe any of those silly rumors about Hannah trying to poison Stan Carlucci. She'd never deliberately hurt anyone."

"A pity," Paul put in, grinning. "I have a long list of people I wouldn't mind her treating to a pot of tea."

Sally giggled, her husband's irreverence having a positive effect on her. She was more spontaneous and flexible than Piper remembered, less bound by her natural reserve and sense of propriety—simply put, less of a prude.

Piper tried to share their good-natured response to Hannah's latest eyebrow raiser. "I'm surprised Carlucci hasn't had her bound up and tossed into the bay as a witch by now."

Paul waved a hand. "She's an old woman, for heaven's sake. People tend to tolerate the eccentricities of old people. Stan got what he deserved, and he knows it—not that there's any proof Hannah's tea was responsible for his difficulties." He grinned, as most everyone did at the mention of Carlucci's cramps and diarrhea. "Last I heard, he's still not a hundred percent."

"I worry about her," Piper blurted.

"We all do," Sally cooed, immediately reaching over to pat Piper's hand. "But I've no doubt Hannah can handle Stan Carlucci or anyone else who'd dare to think she'd stoop to poisoning people. Now. Shall we get started?"

Paul bent down and kissed his wife on the cheek. "I'll leave you two to it. Piper, good to see you. Remember, tea and scones, okay?"

An hour later, her meeting with Sally successfully completed, Piper felt calm enough to venture up to the second floor, where Macintosh & Sons were working on a suite well to the back of the old inn. Of course, it wouldn't have mattered if she'd been keyed up and out of sorts. If she didn't pop in to say hello, her father and brothers for sure would know she was hiding something from them, which she was.

When he saw his daughter, Robert Macintosh grinned, dusted off his big, callused hands, and declared, "Time for a coffee break."

He looked every inch the carpenter with his overalls, tool belt, and muscular build. Flecks of white paint and a layer of plaster dust clung to his thinning gray hair and dotted his nose and bushy eyebrows. He was precise in his work, not his appearance. Despite an occasional relationship, he had never remarried after his wife's death in a car accident when Andrew and Benjamin were ten and twelve and Piper, who'd been in the car with her mother, barely two.

Andrew glanced up from a section of tile he was

repairing on the fireplace. Piper immediately recognized his critical look. He knew about her valerian-root escapade. Hannah must have blabbed.

Before he could say anything, Benjamin spotted the jars of jam his sister was carrying. "All for me?"

Piper laughed. "No, you have to share."

"You're no fun."

"You do get an extra jar for Liddy and the boys."

Liddy was his wife, a fifth-grade teacher; they had two sons, eight and ten. Andrew had been married once, briefly, in his twenties and, at thirty-eight, seemed to have no intention of repeating the experience. Benjamin was taller and leaner than either Andrew or their father, his dark hair without a hint of red, his eyes more blue than green. He grabbed a squat jar from his sister and held it up to the light streaming in from the windows. "Color's perfect, kid."

Her father handed her a mug of coffee he'd poured from his ever-present Thermos. "Glad to see you making jam, Piper."

Andrew grunted, getting up from his work. "Better than letting Hannah lead you around by the nose."

Piper sipped the coffee; it was strong, rancid, lukewarm. "What's that supposed to mean?"

"Means we heard you got caught trespassing the other night."

"Hannah told you?"

"She let a few clues drop," Andrew said. "I had to pry the rest out of her. Don't worry, I didn't get out the thumbscrews. Once she got started, she was happy to talk, damned proud of herself if you ask me. Jesus, Piper. What were you thinking?"

"I was thinking of her."

He snorted in disgust. "If you were thinking of her, you'd tell her you can't trespass and you can't steal on her behalf."

"Hannah can be damned persuasive," their father said mildly.

Benjamin sighed. "I have to agree with Andrew on this

one, Piper. You're as crazy as Hannah is if you start listening to her."

"Hannah's not crazy. She's just eccentric."

"Tell that to Stan Carlucci," Andrew muttered.

Piper nearly spilled her coffee. "There's a big difference between a medicinal tea and poison."

"And there's a big difference between a doctor and an eighty-seven-year-old lunatic." Andrew was incensed. "Piper, I love Hannah as much as you do, but she's got to watch herself. I'm not even going to go into what all I've been hearing around town. She's going to land herself in a padded cell and you in jail if you're not careful."

"Hannah's been taking care of herself longer than you and me put together. She's just trying to stay interested in life. And I'd hardly call helping myself to a bit of valerian root a major crime."

Andrew inhaled, ready to go off again, but Benjamin got in the next shot. "Never mind Carlucci. I'm worried about you and this Clate Jackson character, Piper. He put up those No Trespassing signs for a reason, you know. He guards his privacy. They say his place in Nashville's like a damned fortress."

Piper had heard enough. "Then I'll watch for land mines next time I sneak onto his property."

Benjamin hissed through clenched teeth, and Andrew glared at her. Piper took their irritation in stride. At least Hannah hadn't blabbed about her buried treasure. Her brothers would have been even more insufferable. They'd never sympathize with the poignant emotions, the tantalizing mystery of what had happened to their great-grandparents eighty years ago.

Their father held up a hand. "All right, all right. The boys have a point, Piper. I'm not sure I like the idea of you out on that road with just this guy for a neighbor. It probably makes sense for you not to go digging up herbs for Hannah in the middle of the night."

What about digging under his wisteria for treasure? But Piper had been dealing with her father and brothers' protectiveness since she was a tot. She smiled. "That's just what I told her."

Benjamin wiped his hands with a dirty rag. "Hannah could have stayed put if she'd wanted to keep her herb garden."

Piper resisted comment. She didn't know for sure if anyone in town had dared relay to her brothers the rumors about Hannah's efforts to lure a man to Cape Cod for her niece. She was betting not. Andrew and Benjamin would have mentioned it by now, even if they wouldn't want to do anything to encourage their sister to think about Clate Jackson in romantic terms.

"I don't trust Jackson," Andrew said. "Guys like that don't sit around on their back porches watching the tide roll in. They thrive on the next deal."

"Well, I only met the man for two seconds." Not counting yesterday on her bicycle and that morning while picking berries, and never mind her reaction to him.

"Point is, you should watch yourself with this guy."

As far as her brothers were concerned, there wasn't a man alive she shouldn't watch herself with. She'd heard that advice from high school on. When she returned to Frye's Cove after college, she'd taken great pains to fashion an independent life for herself. To a large degree, she'd succeeded. Still, her social life largely consisted of dates that didn't go anywhere.

Tuck O'Rourke was one example. Two movies with her, and the prospect of dealing with her brothers if he tried anything they didn't like inhibited him to the point that he simply didn't call again. Andrew and Benjamin Macintosh cast long shadows. They knew too much about the men in town.

Of course, so did Piper. Sometimes it was convenient to use her brothers and even her father as an excuse, thus enhancing their reputations for being overprotective. Her last real relationship was with an oceanographer in Falmouth, with whom she shared a love of Cape Cod but little else. She couldn't have said what was missing and sometimes wondered if what she wanted in a relationship, in a man, was unrealistic, unattainable, ridiculous.

Hannah said she just hadn't met the right man.

Piper groaned to herself and changed the subject, allowing her father and brothers to show her their work on the Macintosh Inn. Whatever project they were involved in captured their full attention, no detail too small for their notice. When she said good-bye, their talk was of floorboards and plaster, not stolen valerian root and cranky Tennesseans.

Once home, Piper checked the answering machine in her borning room office. There was just one message. "Piper, it's Hannah. I understand Clate's out of town. It's a perfect night to dig under the wisteria. Call if you need my help."

Piper sank into a chair at her worktable. A small window looked out onto a sunny garden of pink and blue bachelor buttons, old-fashioned white nicotiana, a half-dozen kinds of poppies. She'd scattered the seeds herself in early spring.

So, Hannah didn't mind her digging when Clate wasn't around. Did that mean her tales of buried treasure weren't meant to force another encounter between him and her niece? Or were Hannah's tactics more labyrinthine than usual?

Piper just couldn't see how she could trust a suddenly resurrected memory of a night eighty years ago.

"Stay off Clate Jackson's property if you know what's good for you."

Who had made that call?

Why?

She stared out at the riot of June colors. She was afraid if she didn't cooperate, Hannah would find someone else to do her bidding, and that could be disastrous. So long as Piper could get her aunt to filter her increasingly odd behavior through her, she figured she could keep Hannah happily making her decoctions and infusions in her new townhouse.

But if she started digging for treasure without more to go on than Hannah's slippery memory, the men in white coats would probably carry them both off . . . unless whoever was on the other end of the phone that morning decided to stop her first.

Or unless Clate Jackson lost all patience and simply called the police. At that point, who cared about the men in white coats?

With a loud groan of pure frustration, Piper flung herself to her feet and into her keeping room, where she dragged out crocks of flour and sugar and a tub of frozen homemade butter, a bit of wheat germ, some yeast, a little salt, and started to throw some bread dough together.

Chapter

5

The proliferation of gas stations, motels, and fast-food places along interstate exchanges hadn't reached the winding roads deep in the hills of east Tennessee, where Clate had spent his first sixteen years. Nothing much had changed in his tiny, poor hometown since he was a scraggly eleven-year-old with a tattered fishing pole and a bad attitude.

He eased off the gas pedal as he came to the crossroads that passed for the center of town. A little white church stood on one corner. He could see cars and pickups crowded in the gravel parking lot. He cut off his air-conditioning and rolled down his window, feeling the drop in humidity from the Nashville basin, smelling the fresh-cut grass, the cedar trees, all the rich, fragrant smells of a southern summer.

His grip tight on the wheel, he pulled into the church parking lot. Two or three dozen people were gathered out back. Young, old, black, white. He could see picnic tables laid out with coleslaw, biscuits, ham, tomatoes, fried corn, fried pies, watermelon. He used to crash funerals, just because the food was usually good.

The service itself would be over. Irma's friends and neighbors, many of them former students, would be laughing, crying, remembering how she'd badgered, cajoled, done whatever she had to do to persuade even the most troubled and stubborn of her sixth-graders that poverty and isolation didn't mean they couldn't learn, couldn't make a contribution, whether they stayed in their little town or left, whether they got rich or stayed poor. She'd already retired by the time she'd got hold of Clate. But that hadn't stopped her or even slowed her down. She introduced him to books, manners, the peace and power of sitting quietly on her front porch and watching the sun set, odd ways, perhaps, to save a boy's life, but without them, he knew, he would have crashed and burned long before now. He doubted he'd have lived to twenty-one. From the time he turned eleven, he knew he was destined for jail or an early grave.

Irma Bryar had helped him see his destiny in a new way, as something that was entirely within his control.

A warm breeze carried the smoke from the barbecued chicken and ribs. Clate climbed out of his car and stood there in the hot sun, breathing in the smells, absorbing the sounds. His chest was tight, his throat raw. There was no blaming the southern air, the long trip from Cape Cod, the phone calls and meetings and catching up he'd done at his offices in his Nashville hotel before heading into the Cumberland hills. He was home for the first time in years and he was tense as hell.

He smiled, almost hearing Irma's reproach for swearing. She had saved him from himself, set him free, and had never asked him one thing in return.

He crossed the crabgrass-infested yard in front of the church. In spite of the crushing heat, he wore a dark suit. Irma would have expected that much courtesy from him. He could hear a booming laugh from the crowd behind the church, but forced himself not to speculate whose it might be. He'd given jobs over the years to people from his hometown, people who still had family there, friends. Irma usually sent them. She never asked him to provide a job, simply had them stop by with a bit of country ham from home, a peach cobbler, a batch of fried apricot pies. Mabel Porter, his new assistant, was one. She was smart, crafty, and maybe as ambitious and jaded as he'd been when he'd first arrived in Nashville.

A rickety wooden gate opened into a small graveyard where Clate would sometimes hide from his father when he was in a violent, drunken rage. Irma had taken him out once to show him where she would be laid to rest, in a shaded plot between her husband, who'd died in World War II before they'd had any children, and her parents. The visit had been one of her ways of impressing upon her recalcitrant, angry student that life was short and death certain, and he'd best make good use of his time and talents. Irma Bryar had always operated more on gut instinct and example than whatever educational theory was currently in vogue during her long life and career. She did whatever she thought was right, and whatever she thought might work.

Her grave was covered with fresh dirt, flowers all around, wilting in the strong afternoon sun. Clate could feel the sweat dripping down his temples, matting his shirt to his back. He keenly remembered Irma's disappointment in him when he'd left town before graduating, a disappointment coupled, not incongruously in her own mind, with an uncompromising faith in him. His mother had just died. His father had been too drunk to come to her funeral. There was nothing to keep Clate home. He had no money. Eventually he'd earned his G.E.D. and gone on to college. He seldom returned home. Irma put him on the mailing list for her church newsletter and issued an open invitation for him to stop by her house and have iced tea with her on her porch.

He hadn't often enough, and now it was too late.

Wild daisies swayed in the hot breeze over in the

small, oak-shaded field that would, in time, provide ground for more graves. Clate walked into the tall grass and picked a handful, their long stems turning his palms green. Bugs that he'd barely have noticed as a kid found him, buzzing in his ears, lighting on his neck, his hair. Ignoring them, he ducked under the low branch of a huge old oak and made his way without thinking, without feeling, to his mother's grave.

He used to pick wildflowers for her as a small boy, and he could remember, even now, the sense of urgency he'd felt as he scooped up handfuls of daisies, black-eyed Susans, dandelions. He'd wanted to make her happy. It wasn't until years later, long after he'd buried her, after he'd become a wunderkind of Nashville business, that he understood his mother had spent her short life trying to fill an abyss that couldn't be filled, that his flowers were just one more thing that had gone into the void. She couldn't be happy; she wouldn't. There was nothing he or anyone could do.

"Peace to you, Mama," he whispered, still feeling a stab of that desperate five-year-old who'd wanted, needed, the reassurance that Lucinda Jackson was happy. She'd been just thirty-two when she'd died. Younger than he was now.

He left her the daisies, went back to Irma Bryar's grave for a final good-bye, then headed out through the gate, across the churchyard, and back into his car.

He didn't breathe again until he was out of the church parking lot and onto the main road.

But he couldn't stop himself from glancing in his rearview mirror.

A man in his early fifties stood at the edge of the graveyard, watching the expensive car head out of town. Clate didn't stop, didn't even slow down, although he knew the man was his father.

Clate Jackson didn't stay in Nashville for four days as he'd estimated. He stayed for three. This Piper knew because she and Hannah were standing out on his terrace when he returned, discussing the night her parents had been lured to their deaths.

Alone, Piper could have scooted back to her property before he was any the wiser, but with her elderly aunt at her side, there'd be no escaping. They had heard an engine out front, assumed it was Tuck, then heard a curse from the kitchen. Now there were sounds of locks being unlocked, the back door banging open. Piper deliberately kept her back to the commotion because to have looked around would have indicated she was aware she was doing something wrong.

"Just let me do the talking," she said in a low voice to her aunt, still absorbed in memories of mooncussers who would deliberately lure boats onto sandbars and treasure and paying no attention to the man who'd bought her house. She had insisted his No Trespassing signs didn't apply to her. "Do *not* mention buried treasure."

A shadow fell over them. "I see you've yet to learn the difference between mine and thine."

Piper knew he was addressing her, not Hannah. She could tell by his tone, a husky mix of drawl and fatigue that somehow made her feel warm, despite the persistent drizzle and the cool breeze off the water. Hannah glanced back at the man she believed she'd summoned north, then raised her eyebrows at Piper and smiled with satisfaction. Obviously Clate had passed muster, not that Hannah had had any doubts he wouldn't.

"Oh, hello." Piper gave her hair a flip, a transparent attempt to look unchagrined. "I didn't realize you were back."

"I take it you only trespass when you think no one's around."

"Be dumb to try it when I knew you were home."

Even so, she'd tried to persuade Hannah of the folly of venturing onto posted land. What if Clate had asked the police to swing by his place from time to time while he was gone? After the Stan Carlucci incident, it wouldn't be in her best interests to get caught trespassing. But after two days of Piper dragging her heels, her aunt's patience was worn thin. She wanted her treasure. She was convinced of the accuracy of her restored memory.

Piper kept her tone light, as if she didn't believe she'd done a thing wrong. "You haven't met my aunt yet, have you? Hannah, this is Clate Jackson. Clate, my aunt, Hannah Frye."

Hannah put out a bony hand. "It's a pleasure to meet you at last, Mr. Jackson."

The way she said "at last" made it sound as if she'd anticipated their meeting for years, not just the few months since he'd taken an interest in her house. Clate didn't seem to notice. Piper suspected he was distracted by her aunt's odd appearance: her homespun dress reminiscent of times gone by, her antique cameo brooch, the calico kerchief holding back her wisps of snow-white hair, and her new, top-of-the-line Reeboks.

"Likewise," he murmured, the Southern gentleman.

"Are you enjoying my home?"

A trace of irritation crept into his eyes, but he seemed to direct it more at Piper than at Hannah, either because it wasn't in him to be rude to old women or because, like most everyone else in Frye's Cove, he was holding Piper responsible for her aunt's behavior. "I've only spent a couple of nights here, but so far it's been . . . interesting. Is there something I can help you two with?"

Hannah opened her mouth to reply, probably to suggest he grab a shovel and start digging under the wisteria, but Piper shot forward. "My aunt and I just came to see about the hummingbirds."

He tilted his head back slightly. "Hummingbirds."

"Yes, she's always put out feeders, and she was worried they wouldn't adapt to having to fend for themselves. We planted bee balm last year—hummingbirds love it—but I don't know if it's well enough established to make up for the loss of the feeders."

Hannah picked up on Piper's half truth right away.

They *had* discussed hummingbirds along with buried treasure. "Have you seen any hummingbirds since you've been here, Mr. Jackson?"

"No." His jaw seemed stiff. He glanced at Piper with those searing eyes. No way did he believe she and Hannah were there about hummingbirds and bee balm. "I haven't."

Hannah was oblivious to the tension between them. "Piper can show you where the feeders are, should you want to set them out."

"That won't be necessary. I'm a great believer in animals' survival instincts. The hummingbirds will figure out soon enough they're on their own."

Piper rested back on her heels and gave her conniving aunt an I-rest-my-case look. Maybe she'd reassess her opinion that Clate was meant to be the love of her niece's life. But Hannah pressed ahead. "Well, perhaps you'd let Piper set up the feeders in her yard."

"She's welcome to them. Now, I've had a long day. If you two ladies don't mind—"

Piper seized her aunt's hand in an attempt to coax her out of there before she could say anything else, but Hannah didn't budge. Her brow was furrowed as she stared at Clate. Finally, she said, "Someone close to you has died."

His head jerked up. His eyes darkened. Suspicion, fatigue, grief, irritation—Piper sensed a dangerous swirl of emotions as any trace of patience and humor ebbed out of him.

"I'll be back for the feeders another time," she said quickly.

He said nothing. Piper half led, half dragged her aunt down the terrace steps. Hannah seemed in no hurry to go. Probably still trying to read Clate's mind. "Geez, Hannah," Piper said when they were out of Clate's earshot. "Whatever possessed you to suggest that someone close to him died?"

"Because someone did."

"How do you know?"

She shrugged. "It was in his eyes."

Piper groaned as she slipped through the break in the privet, then waited for her aunt to join her. "Well, you see what he's like. You went and conjured up the wrong man. Clate Jackson is impossible."

"Of course he is," Hannah said placidly.

"He hates people, he's mean to birds—"

"He's suffered and survived. He thinks it builds character. You've never been booted from the nest. You can't judge."

"You don't know anything about the man!"

"Oh, but I do."

"Hannah, I swear, you are the most exasperating person I've ever known. You're lucky I love you so much."

She smiled, the corners of her eyes crinkling. "Yes, I am lucky. You'll see to my hummingbirds?"

Piper sighed. Hannah wasn't worried about her hummingbirds until Piper had done some fast thinking to placate Clate. "Of course."

"And my treasure? No more dragging your heels?"

"I haven't been—"

"You have been dragging your heels, Piper. Please don't insult my intelligence by trying to deny it. You missed your chance to act while Mr. Jackson was away. Now you'll have to risk his catching you again."

"Hannah, you've seen what he's like. He'll call the police next time he catches me trespassing."

She waved a hand in dismissal. "Ernie would never arrest you for trespassing on Frye land."

"It's *not* Frye land anymore."

"Phooey," her aunt muttered as she walked around to Piper's driveway and her brand-new, neon-bright raspberry car, complete with its own compact disc player and cellular phone. Hannah Frye was undaunted by modern technology. She'd had the soundtrack to *South Pacific* playing when she'd arrived two hours ago. She opened up the driver's door and looked around at her niece. "I've waited eighty years, Piper. I want to know what really happened to my parents before I die."

"Hannah—"

"If I could, I'd do the digging myself, but I'm afraid I'm just too old."

Piper felt the drizzle damp on her hair. "You're trying to manipulate me with all this talk of getting old and dying."

"I *am* old, and I *will* die."

"Neither of which has anything to do with me going up against Clate Jackson."

Hannah sniffed as she slid behind her leather-covered wheel. "Honestly, Piper, I'm tempted to put a spell on you to make you cooperate. You're lucky I don't do that sort of thing."

With that, she flicked on her CD player, pulled her door shut, and eased off toward town and her luxury townhouse with "There Is Nothin' Like a Dame" at top volume.

A crazy aunt and a cranky neighbor. "Just what my life needs," Piper grumbled, and headed off to her studio.

Clate turned up at her door an hour later. She had left it open while she prepared for her evening class. He had changed from his travel clothes into frayed, stained khakis and a denim shirt, making him look untycoon-like, more real, more a man she could understand. She shook off her reaction. What was she thinking? He wasn't a man she could remotely understand!

"I brought your hummingbird feeders," he said in that rasping, sexy drawl.

"Oh. That wasn't necessary. I could have fetched them myself."

"I'm sure."

His wry tone kept his response from being totally insulting. He set the feeders just inside the door as he gave her small studio a quick scan. It wasn't expensive, high tech, or elegant. Having scavenged what she could from her father and brothers, Piper had built floor-to-ceiling shelves, now crammed with supplies, books, equipment, and a big sawhorse worktable made out of two-by-fours and a slab of birch plywood that she'd sanded and stained herself, with much unsolicited advice from Macintosh & Sons.

She noticed Clate taking in the array of flowers, leaves, spices, bits of root, citrus peel that she'd spread out on the table for her evening class. "Relax, I didn't swipe anything off your property."

"You're working?"

"I have a potpourri-making class tonight."

"Your classes meet in here?"

"Most of them. I teach my cooking classes in the keeping room in my house."

"You enjoy crafts," he said.

"I don't really view what I do as crafts, but skills once needed to survive or maybe to make life more pleasant. If I were transported back a century or two, I could probably make a go of it." She grinned suddenly, adding, "Except I'd miss the Red Sox, of course. Or maybe not, the way they play half the time. Point is, I like knowing how to make dyes, pottery, how to weave, make dress patterns, grow vegetables, cook on an open hearth."

"Your aunt taught you?"

"Hannah? No way. She says only someone who grew up with permanent-press sheets would want to learn how to tat. I don't romanticize the past. I just think some of these lost skills help connect us with previous generations, make us more confident, less mystified by a hand-woven place mat."

He smiled. "I don't know if I've ever been mystified by a place mat."

"Well, you know what I mean. There's something—I can't explain it, but I love getting a beautiful red dye from plants that grow in the marsh outside my door, knowing how to do it. Besides, it's fun."

"Right."

She laughed, even as that long, southern *i* rolled up her

spine. "You don't get it, do you? Well, neither do my brothers. They think I should have gone to law school."

Her laughter faded, and when he said nothing, she became aware of the stillness of her surroundings. No radio, no television, no cars, not even much in the way of birds and sea. The gray, drizzly weather contributed to a heightened sense of intimacy, as if the fog and rain had enveloped them in their own world, separate from the rest of Frye's Cove.

Piper shook off the feeling. She'd been spending too much time with Hannah. "Thanks for the feeders. Hannah will be relieved to know her hummingbirds are being taken care of."

"You two are quick on your feet, I'll give you that much."

"Are you suggesting—"

He held up a hand. "I'm not here to argue. If you and your aunt want to pretend you were on my property to look after hummingbirds, you go right ahead."

"We're not pretending anything."

"Ah-huh."

They weren't. They simply hadn't explained everything. She and Hannah both cared about the fate of the hummingbirds that had come to rely on feeders at the Frye house. That just had nothing to do with why they'd been there.

Which Clate obviously knew.

Instead of further dancing around the truth, Piper kept her mouth shut. Clate made no effort to pretend he wasn't studying her and her studio. She fingered a dried rosebud, trying to look as if she didn't care if he scrutinized her all night. And, damn it, she didn't, because not in a million years of scrutinizing her would he guess that she was thinking about how she was going to dig under his wisteria and satisfy Hannah there was no treasure buried there.

"You're aware, I assume, of what people are saying about your aunt."

Heat radiated up from her neck to the roots of her

hair. She dropped the rosebud and shot him a look. His intensity was disconcerting, unnerving, utterly mesmerizing. "What people?"

"People in town. I've hardly spent any time at all here, and already I've heard things."

"Hannah's an old woman, and she's lived in Frye's Cove all her life. People talk. I wouldn't pay any attention—"

"Then she doesn't fancy herself a witch?"

Piper took a breath. Who had he been talking to? But he'd never tell. Clate Jackson was the kind of man who listened to and remembered everything, but said nothing unless it was to his advantage. "Hannah's beliefs are her business and no one else's. I will say this: the witches I know are kind, knowledgeable, self-reliant, attuned to nature—and they make a vow to do harm to no one."

His intensity didn't let up, his eyes, even with the gray light, that searing, unsettling blue. "Not intentionally, presumably."

"You mean Stan Carlucci." Piper could hear the weariness in her own voice. "He's never going to let that one little mistake go. Well, you can forget whatever you've heard. Hannah doesn't go around deliberately poisoning people, not even Stan, who's as big an ass as they come."

Clate was staring at her in such a manner that she decided, belatedly, that perhaps he hadn't heard about Stan Carlucci's misfortune. She swore softly to herself. The best defense was sometimes a good offense, but other times it was knowing when to keep your mouth shut.

"And Stan Carlucci is who?" he asked mildly.

"A local selectman. I—you—" She winced, calming herself, then cocked her head at him. "Um, what exactly have you heard about Hannah?"

A smile tugged at the corners of his mouth, only increasing Piper's dread about just what he'd heard. He fingered a cinnamon stick. She noticed a tiny scar on his thumb, the dark hairs on his tanned wrist. "I gather there are competing theories as to why she sold her property and how I ended up as the purchaser."

Piper swallowed. When she was ten years old, she had vowed never to let anything her great-aunt did embarrass her. Hannah's actions were a reflection on her, and she was accountable for what she did, and Piper loved her unconditionally, totally.

But her aunt had never before claimed to have conjured up a rich, sexy Tennessean for her one and only niece.

Clate rested those mesmerizing eyes on her. "You've heard these theories, too, I take it?"

She cleared her throat. "Probably not all of them."

"You want me to run them by you?"

"Please."

He smiled. He knew she didn't want to hear the first thing about any competing theories. This was revenge, pure and simple, for having caught her trespassing again and then lying about it. Piper raised her chin, determined to hear him out without squirming.

"Let's see if I can remember." He narrowed his eyes a moment, as if thinking. She didn't for a second believe he didn't have this entire scene rehearsed. "First is the ghost theory. Supposedly Mrs. Frye believes one of my ancestors is haunting her former house—"

"Not true."

"No, I didn't think so. Then there's the devil theory."

The devil theory? Piper hadn't heard that one. "Go on."

"The devil made her cast a spell on me to lure me north so I could buy her house and land and build a resort that would forever change the destiny of quiet, picturesque Frye's Cove."

"That's crazy. Hannah's no tool of the devil. She's a sweet, caring woman."

"What about me?"

Piper shrugged. "I can't vouch for you. I hardly know you. Did you buy her land for a resort?"

He gave her a small, mysterious smile that didn't quite

reach his eyes. "That's irrelevant. In this particular theory, we're both tools of the devil, not just me."

"Just because Hannah has unorthodox interests doesn't mean she's evil. That's just people's ignorance of what real witchcraft is, not that Hannah's even a witch. So you can cross that theory right off your list if it means Hannah's involved with the devil."

"All right." He boldly settled onto a high stool at her worktable. The smell of spices, orange, lemon, lavender, and roses mingled with the cool, salty scents of the fog and the rain. "Well, then we come to the romance theory."

Piper was silent.

"The romance theory," Clate went on in that smooth, all-too-sexy drawl, "has it that your aunt sold her house as part of a spell to summon a man to Cape Cod who would fall in love with her niece."

"The man being you," Piper said neutrally, "and the niece being me."

"Presumably."

She cleared her throat. "Well, all these theories are very interesting, but Frye's Cove is a small town, and people will talk. Right now I have work to do."

"You haven't dismissed this particular theory."

"I haven't? Oh. Well, consider it dismissed. My love life isn't anyone else's business, and I'm sure yours isn't either."

"It's not, but that doesn't stop people from trying to make it their business."

No, it certainly didn't. Hannah Frye for one. Suddenly restless, Piper grabbed a bolt of blue calico cloth from the shelf behind her. She would cut swatches for simple potpourri sachets. "I'm not so desperate for a man that Hannah would need to conjure one up for me." Not, of course, that Hannah had acted out of a sense of Piper's desperation. She maintained it was all because of a dream, the universe urging her to provide Piper and the love of her life the little push they needed to get together.

Clate held his ground. "This isn't about you or me. It's

about your aunt and whether she thinks she got me up here through some kind of spell."

"Not a spell," Piper blurted. She set the bolt on her worktable with a loud thump. Clate didn't move. She caught her breath, raked a hand through her hair even as she knew she'd already said too much. "It was more like . . . I don't know, a prayer. A wish. A dream of what life could be like for me but never was for her. She threw salt in the fire every night over the winter and asked the universe to send me—well, a man, I guess."

"How does she know I'm that man?"

"She doesn't, and you're not. It's all just some bizarre notion of hers." Piper groaned, exasperated. How could she explain Hannah, their relationship, to a man as concrete in his thinking, as obviously jaded, as Clate Jackson? "Just because Hannah says she summoned you up here doesn't mean she did summon you up here. It's all in her head."

"She didn't even meet me until today. For all she knew, I could have been old, married, decrepit."

"I was hoping you would be."

Amusement flared in his eyes, and Piper immediately realized the impolitic nature of her words. She'd as much as admitted that she was attracted to him, a complication none of them needed right now.

"I only meant," she added quickly, "that Hannah doesn't need any encouragement. Just because you're not a geezer or unavailable or—or whatever doesn't mean I have any designs on you. I mean, I don't think you're the love of my life."

Clate slid off the stool and came around the worktable toward her. She was shaking, she realized. Not with trepidation or nervousness, just sheer mortification and anticipation. She *was* attracted to him. She did think he was good-looking, sexy, earthy, appealing on a basic, elemental, biological level. His eyes, his scars, his stubble of beard, his flat stomach, the way his frayed khakis hung low on his hips.

But she wasn't the type to let her attraction to a man ease out into the open. She was accustomed to playing her feelings close to her chest. It wasn't just her brothers, her shaky romantic past, it was her personality, the emotional reserve that was natural to her. Long ago, she had accepted that her life could well end up being more like Hannah's than like either of her brothers' or, certainly, her parents'—her mother who'd died too young, her father who'd learned to go on without the love of his life.

Of course, the physical sensations coursing through her as Clate came closer didn't necessarily have anything to do with romance.

For the first time in her life, one of Hannah's schemes had succeeded in throwing Piper for a loop.

"Don't be embarrassed," Clate said, and that soft, rasping drawl only made her knees go liquid under her.

"I'm not embarrassed."

"Of course you are. Anyone would be. Who would want their eighty-seven-year-old aunt conjuring up romantic prospects for them?"

"Hannah never meant for me to feel . . . inadequate. If you and I could have met some other way, then—" Piper stopped herself, grimacing. "Not that there's anything between us or ever will be. I'm not saying that."

"It's complicated," he said, deadpan.

"Yes! She really believes she had to sell her house to you in order for me to fulfill my destiny. Or something like that. Look, Clate, I love my aunt. I want her to be happy. She doesn't mean any harm to either of us. She's convinced she's right about us. I know it's crazy, and it puts you in an awkward position."

He shook his head. "Not me. If people want to think your aunt put some spell on me, it makes no difference to me." He leaned against the worktable, studying her with half-closed eyes. "But it does to you."

Piper found his certainty both irritating and intriguing. She grabbed a pair of scissors from a cracked, misshapen urn, one of her early works of crockery. "If it does, it's because I care about the people who're doing the talking. They're my friends, people I've known all my life."

"My point exactly. Provided it doesn't interfere with my privacy, your aunt and the rest of Frye's Cove can think I'm the devil incarnate or the man for you." He grinned, the gray light catching the scar under his left eye. "Or both."

"In other words, so long as she and everyone else in town leaves you alone, you don't care what they think."

"That's a bit harsh."

"But it's true."

He sighed. "Basically, yes, it's true. I came here to get away from the complications in my life, not add more."

"What complications?"

Some of the earlier edginess and fatigue crept back, but he covered with a half smile. "Nothing like witches, ghosts, devils, and romance. I just climbed the ladder fast and hard. I decided I needed to catch my breath."

"I understand," Piper said quietly, stifling her sudden curiosity about his life in Tennessee. Maybe it didn't include witches, ghosts, and devils, but she'd bet he'd had his share of romances. But that was none of her concern, and she'd put her foot in her mouth enough for one day. "Well, I have no intention of complicating your life, I can assure you."

He laughed unexpectedly. "Oh?"

"If you hadn't come home when you did, you'd never know I'd trespassed. And Hannah—" Piper set down her scissors. She could hear her aunt pressing for immediate action on her buried treasure. She hated to be so duplicitous, but how on earth could she explain without having Hannah sound like a lunatic? She sighed deeply. "My aunt complicates everybody's life."

"You know, I'm not so sure she's not a witch." His laughter had faded, and the shadows suddenly seemed to draw out the small scars on his face, to make his eyes seem more remote. "Someone close to me did die. A woman I've known all my life. She was eighty-nine." He breathed. "Anyway, that's why I had to head back to Tennessee."

"I'm sorry."

"How your aunt knew—"

"I don't know. She never said anything to me."

"She calculates her moves, doesn't she?"

"Always." Which was part of the reason no one in Frye's Cove believed she hadn't deliberately thrown off Stan Carlucci's digestion.

Clate nodded. "I should leave you to your work. Have a good class, and I hope the hummingbirds find their feeders."

"Thanks," she said, her voice thick as he retreated through the screen door. She couldn't figure him out. Her nerves and emotions were a jumble. She sensed kindness and deep feeling one moment, remoteness the next, and all the while she'd noticed muscles in his arms, the shape of his fingers, the occasional strand of gray in his dark hair. Could she trust him? Should she just tell him about Hannah's buried treasure?

Suddenly she plunged through the door out into the wet, cold, foggy early evening. The drizzle had turned into a light, steady rain. He was just a few yards off, her windsock flapping above him.

"My aunt means a lot to me. I hope you understand that." She pushed back her hair with both hands, her heart pounding at her own impulsiveness. She was open by nature. Secrecy and deceptiveness weren't her style. But her urge to protect Hannah was stronger than anything she'd ever known, her desire to come clean with Clate Jackson notwithstanding. She took a breath, calming herself. "I just want her to live out her life on her own terms."

Clate glanced around at her, his eyes taking on the gray of the fog. He said nothing.

Piper exhaled at the sky, felt the drizzle on her face as she fought for the right words, for some semblance of control over her emotions. Finally, she leveled her gaze on him. "Not everyone around here thinks Hannah's as harmless and innocent as I do."

His mouth was an unreadable slit. "Go on."

Piper chose her words carefully, reining in the impulse that had pushed her outside. "Some people are afraid she's going to end up hurting someone, or even herself."

"That doesn't seem an entirely unreasonable fear." There was no trace of humor in his tone or expression. "Do you share it?"

"No, of course not." But the words tumbled out fast, as if she'd been saying them to herself too many times, almost like a prayer she wasn't quite sure she believed. "I'm just worried about her. I'd hate to see her forced into a situation where she has to be . . . watched more carefully."

"You mean put in a home."

Piper hated even the thought. "She's so happy with her microwave and her remote control. She just figured out how to do faxes off her computer and plans to pepper the local papers with her opinions. I don't want to see her lose what she's worked so hard to get." Rain pelted onto her hair, further distracting her. Clate seemed oblivious. "I hated to see her sell the Frye house for selfish reasons. But I can understand. You must realize its problems. Selling it and all its furnishings has given her an infusion of cash she's never had. She's enjoying herself."

"But there's all this talk of poison, witches, ghosts, devils, romantic spells."

Her shoulders slumped. "Yes."

"Piper." His voice was liquid, melting into the fog. He moved toward her. "No one will hear any talk from me."

"Really?"

He smiled. "Really."

"Thanks. I guess that's what I wanted to hear."

She expected him to continue on his way. The rain had picked up, glistening on his dark hair, soaking into his shirt. A wayward image flashed, and Piper could see herself rubbing her palms across his rain-soaked chest.

Nuts, she thought. Her attraction to him wasn't going to help her decide what to do about Hannah and the eighty-year-old mystery of the deaths of Caleb and Phoebe Macintosh.

"Piper, what's wrong?"

His question startled her. "What?"

"The other day when I stopped alongside the road, then before I left for Tennessee, you seemed rattled about something. I had the feeling something was wrong. I just had it again."

Something *was* wrong, she *was* rattled. But she couldn't admit it without admitting everything, and she'd promised Hannah. That was all there was to it. "It's nothing, really. I just worry about Hannah. Moving was a big change for her."

He didn't back off. "Piper, you're hiding something."

She shut her eyes, took a breath. It would be so easy to tell him. All she had to do was start.

She could hear his soft sigh. "But you'll tell me when you're ready." He curled a lock of her damp hair around his finger, tugged on it gently to draw her forward. She had her eyes open now, pinned on him. "And I will be ready," he said, very close to her mouth. "Anytime."

She couldn't speak, could almost not breathe.

He kissed her lightly on the side of her mouth, gave her a wink, and retreated into the fog.

Chapter

6

"Bitch. I warned you."

Piper bolted upright in bed. She'd fumbled for the phone on her nightstand and was still half asleep when the venomous voice assaulted her. Muffled, yet each word distinct. "What? Who are you? Never mind. I'm calling the police."

"You're making a mistake if you do."

She slammed down the phone. She didn't want to hear more. She jumped out of bed and forced herself not to throw up. *Think. You have to think.*

Yesterday's rain had pushed out to sea, and the sky vibrated with streaks of pink, lavender, orange. She checked her clock. Not much after five. She was wide awake now, heart pounding, knees shaking, stomach lurching. She knotted her hands together and stifled a sob. Her father. Andrew, Benjamin. They'd come if she called.

And do what?

Make her pack her bags and go stay with one of them. And that was just for starters. Then they'd comb the streets of Frye's Cove for whoever was harassing her, drag everything about spells and treasure out of her, interrogate Hannah, put the thumbscrews to Clate Jackson. They would be thorough and relentless.

They'd never trust her again to live out on her isolated spit of land alone.

Right now, she didn't care. She was afraid, and she wanted the bastard caught. Who would know she'd been out to Clate Jackson's yesterday? It wasn't as if she'd done any digging for treasure. Hannah had dragged Piper out there in an effort to spur her to action, to see if being back at the Frye house would jog her own memory of that night eighty years ago when her parents hadn't come home.

Piper choked back a sob of frustration and fear. Who would care what she and Hannah were up to?

She picked up the phone, dialed the police.

Hung up.

Hannah cared. Hannah cared desperately. She wanted the answers to the infamous crime that had led to her parents' death, and she was out of patience, had waited eighty years already. She believed those answers lay under Clate Jackson's wisteria.

Piper sank onto the edge of her spindle-post bed. Tears clouded her eyes. It wasn't that she herself had enough doubt of her aunt's sanity that she could imagine, if never believe, that Hannah Frye was capable of making such a disgusting phone call to get her way.

It was that she didn't know what anyone else would believe.

She brushed angrily at her tears, leaped up off her bed, and stumbled down the steep stairs. Should she call Clate? What if it had been him on the other end of the line?

But that was ridiculous. He had no reason to threaten her. He didn't even know about the treasure.

The voice on the other end of the phone hadn't mentioned treasure, she reminded herself.

She flipped on the radio and made coffee, her hands

shaking as she fumbled for a filter, dumped in the fragrant grounds, filled the carafe with water. Obviously she wasn't going to call the police or she already would have by now. There was nothing they could do. They would have no more idea of who had threatened her than she did. They could view the calls as simple harassment, or even random acts, rather than a specific threat toward her.

There hadn't been a specific threat, she reminded herself. Just a general air of menace.

"I warned you."

She shuddered, getting a pottery mug down from a shelf. Hands still shaking. Heart still skidding. Not good signs. She poured her coffee and went outside in her nightgown. The sun had burned off the pale colors of dawn and a gentle breeze soothed her troubled spirit. She walked through her herb garden and out to her sloping back yard, down through her meadow—basically unmowed lawn—toward the marsh. The grass was damp and cool on her bare feet. Hot coffee splashed out over her hand as she came to the narrow path.

A few weeks ago she could have slipped through the privet and had her coffee with Hannah.

Instead, she headed into the marsh, through cordgrass, sea lavender, beach peas with their pretty pink flowers. They slapped her legs, drenching her nightgown from the knees down. Sand clung to her feet. She crossed a long two-by-four she'd laid over a wet section of marsh, then came out onto the narrow strip of beach.

The breeze was cooler on the water, not as gentle. Boat engines purred in the distance. It was just past high tide, the surf up. She drank more coffee, sniffled. She'd be all right. She'd make sense of it all. Who on earth would want to hurt her over pestering her new neighbor? Harass her, maybe. Scare her, obviously. But not actually hurt her.

It wasn't Hannah. Piper knew that, even if her aunt would be everyone else's first suspect because of her odd behavior lately. Hannah's rendition of reverse psychology, a ploy to force her niece and Clate Jackson together. Nobody was looking for Hannah's logic to make sense anymore. Piper preferred to have a stranger on the other end of the line to *anyone* she knew. Let it be someone she could have arrested, sic her brothers on, punch out herself. Not someone she knew—and certainly not someone she loved, worried about, wanted so desperately to live out her remaining years in happiness and comfort.

"I'm old, Piper. My husband's dead, most of my friends, my brother. I've had my happiness. Now I want to ensure yours."

"A hell of a way of doing it, Auntie," Piper muttered, as if hearing her own voice out loud would help calm her nerves.

"Well, good morning."

Her coffee went flying. She screamed and swung around, stopping herself just short of clobbering Clate with her mug. "Good God, you scared the living daylights out of me!"

"So I gather. Sorry. I thought you heard me. I was out on the beach taking a walk and saw you, figured I'd be neighborly and at least say good morning."

That wry tone again, half teasing himself, half teasing her. But as she brushed coffee off the front of her cotton nightgown, emblazoned with an enormous moose, she felt his scrutiny, the wryness going out of his expression. A fine mess she must be. Coffee down her front, wet from the knees down, hair unbrushed, face pale.

"All right," he said in that deceptively mild drawl. "You're telling me everything."

"What do you mean?"

"Everything, Piper, or I call your father and brothers."

"Call them about what?"

He just glared at her.

She glared back. What made him think he could squeal to her father and brothers? She set her jaw. "There's nothing to tell."

"Bullshit." Still that mild drawl. He picked up her

hand and pried her stiff fingers from her coffee mug. He held the mug, and she began to shake. She couldn't stop herself. He hissed through clenched teeth. "I rest my case. Now. What the hell's going on?"

"A phone call." She sucked in a breath, grateful for the fresh sea air, the wind in her hair. "I just got a nasty phone call. It's the second time. The first was on Saturday, before you left for Tennessee."

"I remember you were disturbed about something. Any idea who it was?"

She shook her head.

"Male, female?"

"I don't know."

"Did they use your name, threaten you in any way?"

"Depends on your point of view. The first phone call suggested I stay off your property if I knew what was good for me. The second—just now—called me a bitch and said I'd been warned. Whoever it was must have known Hannah and I were out at your place yesterday."

Clate frowned, remaining silent. Piper could feel his intensity. He was barefoot, his feet covered with the white sand of the beach and marsh, and he wore canvas shorts and a black-and-gold Vanderbilt T-shirt. She noticed the thick, corded muscles in his arms and legs, a two-inch scar on his knee. His presence left her feeling raw and exposed, had her pulse jumping in a different way from the anonymous call, her nerves a jittery mess.

The breeze picked up, whipping her nightgown against her, outlining her figure in excruciating detail. She shivered when she noticed his eyes on her breasts. "You don't have any ideas, do you? The calls couldn't have something to do with you instead of me, could they?"

He shifted his gaze to her face. "Not that I know of. I won't pretend I don't have enemies."

"Personal or business?"

"I don't make those kinds of distinctions. My personal life and business life are more or less one and the same. You can't do what I do without someone ending up wanting your hide."

"Who's running the show while you're up here?"

She could tell she'd struck a nerve. "I have people I trust working for me. I'm in constant touch with my office, but—" A self-deprecating twitch of a smile. "I'm not known for taking much time off."

"Control freak?"

The smile broadened. "I've heard you Yankees are a blunt lot."

Piper laughed, which felt good mixed in with all her tension. "Sorry. It's just that local gossip has it that you're—I don't know if ruthless is the right word, but a tough businessman. I guess it takes focus and commitment and a lot of hard work to do what you do."

"It does."

"So, who knows that you bought the Frye house?"

"A few people. Not many." He gave her a long look, a half smile. "And no one knows I've been dealing with a trespassing neighbor."

Piper grinned. "You mean you didn't call home and gripe about me stealing valerian root out of your back yard?"

"I did not."

She stared out at a seagull wheeling over the marsh, and suddenly she could hear the voice on the other end of the phone, hear its fury and determination. Her throat tightened, her light mood gone. She turned back to Clate. "You know, if you were planning to build a resort out here, you'd want to get hold of my land. It'd be to your advantage. The nature preserve limits what you can do to the north. The only way you could expand would be to gobble up my land."

"Honey, if I wanted your land, I'd get it some other way besides making mindless phone calls."

He'd get her land. Not he'd try to get it. If the rumor mill in Frye's Cove was to be believed, Clate Jackson was a successful, driven businessman who didn't regard land, family, or community in the same way she did.

Her gaze drifted to a No Trespassing sign posted on a

pitch pine. It said everything. "I suppose you would, at that."

"What about you, Piper?" he asked. If he'd noticed her irritation, he wasn't calling her on it. "Any enemies?"

"Me? No. Not anyone who'd deliberately try to scare me. I'm not naïve. I know not everyone likes me, but I can't think of anyone—*anyone*—who'd do this to me, not out of plain hatred. There'd have to be a more concrete motive."

"Such as?"

Piper exhaled, turning her gaze back to the water. The wind was cold now, and she wished she'd thrown on a sweatshirt before heading down to the beach. Motives for harassment, for someone not wanting her messing around on Clate Jackson's land. Hannah was trying to get her to dig for supposed buried treasure and uncover the answers to one of Cape Cod's most notorious incidents. Who on earth would care? Who even knew?

Piper's immediate impulse was to lie outright and deny anything and everything. She couldn't stand to have Clate suspect her aunt or apply that hardheaded thinking of his to her claims about what she saw as a girl of seven.

But she didn't want to lie to him, either. "I can't think of any motives that make sense." That was true, as far as it went. "If I do, I'll let you know."

Clate settled back on his heels, studying her through suspicious half-closed eyes. Piper tried not to squirm. This wasn't a man who'd take well to lies, dissembling, or foolishness, a quality that no doubt served him well in business. She didn't know how her latest mission on Hannah's behalf would fit into his scheme of things, but she wouldn't expect patience or understanding.

She was accustomed to sparing the men in her life details they didn't need to know, especially when they involved her great-aunt. The Macintosh men were less indulgent of Hannah's whims. For years they'd warned Piper that her propensity for doing her aunt's bidding would get her into trouble one of these days. If she told them about the calls, they'd jump way ahead of the facts and there'd be no peace. She had no reason to believe Clate would be any different, and she didn't need a man breathing down her neck while she was still trying to sort out her options.

But to her surprise, once again he didn't pressure her to talk. "All right. If you decide you want to tell me what you know, I'll be around most of the day."

If similarly provoked, her brothers would have had a totally different reaction. Probably it would have involved dunking her into the cold tide until she talked. Piper nodded. "Thanks." She lifted the damp hem of her nightgown. "I'm a mess. I should go back up and get dressed. I didn't expect you to be out this early."

"Nice sunrise."

She managed a smile. "Yes. Are you technically on vacation?"

"No. I've got a hand in things back in Nashville. I just came up here to get a feel for the place. I'm hoping to come back for a couple of weeks later in the summer."

"Then you don't plan to stay long?"

He grinned at her. "Do I see a gleam of hope in your eye?"

Piper suppressed all thought of Russian princesses and buried treasure. "No, certainly not. I—"

He laughed. "Well, if your aunt wants more valerian root, she need only ask."

"That's a softer stance than you had when you caught me."

"I'm not at my best at four in the morning, and I did say she should ask."

Piper nodded thoughtfully, wondering how he would respond to a request from his house's former owner to dig under his wisteria.

No. She wouldn't tell him. She needed to keep things simple. In her experience, the fewer people who knew about Hannah's missions, the better.

"Well," Piper said breezily, "have a good day."

He hung back, suspicion flaring again in his eyes. "You, too."

He was not a man to go plunging in whenever suspicion beckoned. He would bide his time, observe, remember. If she intended to continue to play loose with the truth, she thought, she'd have to be careful to keep her story straight. One misstep, and Clate Jackson would swoop in for the kill.

He remained on the beach as she walked back up the path through the marsh. She could feel his eyes on her. A hot shower, clean clothes, breakfast. They'd put her back on track, and then she'd figure out what to do about the phone calls, Hannah, and buried treasure.

She was halfway through her breakfast of homemade granola, fresh strawberries, and yogurt when her telephone rang. Her heart skidded. She decided to screen the call. If it was the same jerk as earlier, she wanted his voice on tape.

But it was Hannah. Piper snatched up her cordless phone at the sound of her aunt's voice. "I'm here," she said.

"Why didn't you answer?"

"Because I'm screening my calls. Remember that weirdo who called the other day? He's bugging me again. Or she. I really couldn't make out the voice." She tried to keep her tone light, not to let her earlier panic and fear show in her voice. "Hannah, you're sure you haven't mentioned your treasure to anyone else?"

"Absolutely."

Which didn't mean, at eighty-seven, she hadn't.

"Why?" her aunt asked. "Did the caller mention it?"

"No—no, not at all. I just wondered at the coincidence." The caller must have known she'd been out on Clate's property last night. She considered telling Hannah, then decided better of it. There was nothing Hannah could do but worry, and Piper preferred her aunt to enjoy boiling up her herbal concoctions and playing with her new microwave and computer. "Well, it's probably nothing. What can I do for you?"

Hannah took an audible breath. "You can stop humoring me and either get going on the treasure or let me find someone else who will. I can't stand any more of your delaying tactics, Piper." Even miffed, Hannah was too gentle a soul to manage more than mild reproof. "Once we find the treasure, all your doubts will be proven to have been for naught."

We. As if Hannah were going to venture out to Clate Jackson's property in the middle of the night. Piper sighed. "I'm doing the best I can."

"Your best. Ha."

"Hannah, what's that noise I hear? It sounds like a siren."

"I think it is. I hope I'm not being stopped for speeding."

"You mean you're on your cell phone? Hannah, geez. You shouldn't be driving and talking on the phone at the same time. It's dangerous, especially—well, you just shouldn't do it."

"Especially at my age, you were going to say. Phooey. You sound like Andrew. I only take calculated risks." The sound of the siren faded, and Piper could hear her aunt's smug little snort. "There, he's gone. Now, I wanted to tell you that I have a black dress that would be perfect for midnight digging."

"For who, me?"

"Yes, you. I think it will fit you. You can come for it later today." Her voice lowered to a near whisper. "Piper, I had another dream last night. I don't have much more time to solve this mystery."

Piper felt a jolt of fear. "What do you mean? You got a clean bill of health at your last checkup."

"I don't know what I mean. I just know."

"Right." She poked at her granola with her spoon. "Look, you should get off the phone and concentrate on driving. I'll come by later, okay?"

"Good," Hannah said, not bothering to disguise the note of victory. She knew how to motivate Piper. She always had.

Giving up on breakfast, Piper grabbed her knapsack and headed out front, where the wind had died down and the sun was boiling down from a cloudless sky, stirring the scent of the roses that grew in tangles over her picket fence.

"Bitch. I warned you."

She shook off the disturbing words, hoisted her back-pack onto her back, and climbed on her bicycle. First stop the library, then Hannah's. By this time tomorrow, she decided, she wanted to have this buried treasure business finished.

Before she'd even cleared the driveway, Andrew's battered brown truck rolled to a stop on her narrow blacktopped road, and her brother poked his head out his window. "Christ, Piper, you look like hell."

"And a good morning to you, Andy."

No one called him Andy. "What did you do, spend the night digging up Jackson's back yard?"

She gave him a sarcastic smile. "No, I'm saving that for tonight."

"You're such a pain in the ass," he said good-naturedly. "Here. Benjamin dropped this by last night. Thought you'd find it interesting reading."

He shoved a magazine out the window at her. She immediately recognized Clate's picture on the cover. He was wearing a charcoal suit and red tie, his arms crossed on his chest, everything about him dark and devastating.

Her brother observed her closely. "Jesus, Piper, are you drooling?"

She scoffed. "Don't be ridiculous."

"Hell of a guy for Hannah to conjure up, huh?"

"So, you heard."

"Oh, I heard." He didn't sound at all happy about what he'd heard.

"Well, she didn't conjure him up. She just thinks she did."

"What do you think?"

She rolled up the magazine and shoved it into her

knapsack, aware of Andrew's probing gaze, accustomed to it. Together, he, Benjamin, and their father knew the bad habits of every man in town and half on Cape Cod. "Be serious. I don't believe in all her spells and potions."

"Just don't let her get you in over your head. You know how you are with her."

"Andrew—"

"Relax. I'm not criticizing. We all know you and Hannah have a special bond. We understand. She was your anchor after Mother's death in a way none of us ever could be. So, don't get your back up."

Piper sniffed at him. "You aren't any more objective about her than I am."

"Maybe not, but I never would have dug valerian root for her at the crack of dawn, never mind if it didn't involve trespassing. Which it did."

"That was an innocuous favor."

"Yeah. Sure. Read the article on your neighbor, Piper. Then we'll talk about what's innocuous and what's crazy."

He rolled off, and Piper made a face just as if she were four years old and her big brother had pulled her out of a tree she'd been climbing. At least neither he nor Benjamin pulled any punches with her. They were straightforward in their opinion that she needed them in her life to keep her from walking off the plank and landing in shark-infested waters, figuratively speaking. They'd defend her without question, and for that she was grateful. It was just their insistence on prevention—on defending her before anything had happened—that annoyed her.

She gave Andrew time to get well ahead of her, then started down the road, welcoming the warm sun, the rain-scrubbed air, the smell of pitch pine and ocean, and wondering what he'd have thought if he knew Clate Jackson had kissed his baby sister last night.

Clate stared at the shadows on the low, slanted ceiling of the upstairs bedroom he had chosen as his own. It was a cool, quiet, still night. His room had a view out across the marsh to the bay, which was all he cared about. The antique furnishings and the quaint decor didn't interest him. Half awake in the shifting darkness, he was eerily aware that virtually nothing in this house was his. Everything *belonged* to him, but that was something different. He felt like a guest, as if he were sleeping in someone else's bedroom.

An owl hooted in the distance. He could hear the wash of the tide. Hell, what was he doing this far north, this far from his office, his routines, his dogs? He'd left his two big mutts at home with the caretaker while he checked out Cape Cod.

Maybe that damned scrawny old woman *had* put a spell on him.

After watching a troubled Piper Macintosh head up through the marsh, he'd checked with his office, made some calls, and tried to imagine what it would be like to spend a summer up here, the routine, day-to-day operating of his business in the hands of trusted associates.

But there weren't too many people he trusted.

Tuck O'Rourke had come over around noon, and they'd discussed his plans to repair the damage, erosion, and wear and tear he'd spotted outside. Some projects would be simple and quick, others costly and time consuming. Clate was still debating what he wanted Tuck to do. He didn't know why he was hesitating, he knew what needed to be done. But he couldn't dispel an image of himself with shirt off, sweat pouring down his back, as he did the work himself. When he'd first rolled down out of the hills to Nashville, he'd had nothing going for him but his strong back and willingness to work. He had the scars to prove how hard he'd worked. Until now, he hadn't missed physical labor. He couldn't say why he did. Or, really, *if* he did.

He pushed the thought aside. He hated obsessing on things in the middle of the night. Yet he was wide awake, sleep eluding him.

He and Tuck had also discussed the Macintosh family.

Despite O'Rourke's taciturn nature, he talked readily about the people he'd known all his life. From their conversation, Clate gained a better understanding of Piper's attachment to her elderly great-aunt. She had lost her mother at two and had latched onto Hannah as her central female role model, and a bizarre one at that, especially in the years since Jason Frye's death. Her nineteenth-century dresses and witchy ideas were legendary in Frye's Cove, and she had a penchant for leading Piper down the so-called primrose path. There'd been various incidents with experimental teas and possible spells.

Then there were her brothers, who had apparently combated their own grief over their mother's death by becoming very protective of their much younger sister. From what Clate could gather, her romantic life had suffered as a result—at least in townspeople's minds.

"I took her out a couple times myself," O'Rourke had admitted. "Andrew and Benjamin made it pretty damned clear they were keeping an eye on me."

Maybe, Clate thought, they'd had good reason. O'Rourke didn't strike him as a man who'd want much more from a woman than what she could provide in bed and in the kitchen. If Clate saw that after only a couple of encounters, Piper's brothers must have seen it after knowing him all their lives.

Still, if the Macintosh men underestimated her capabilities and her self-reliance, this would annoy her, and could explain why she was hesitant about telling too much too soon about her disturbing phone calls.

Clate could understand their impulse to protect her. The spray of freckles, the straight, chestnut hair, the faith in people, the single-minded determination to stand by her crazy aunt, even the kind of work Piper Macintosh did made her seem more vulnerable than perhaps she was.

He flipped over onto his stomach, irritated with himself. It was the middle of the damned night. He should be sleeping, not brooding about his neighbor and her troubles. He was accustomed to being alone. Solitude suited him. As a kid, an only child, the kind of boy other parents didn't necessarily want their own kids playing with, he'd fished, walked in the hills, just sat for hours watching the creek. Only when Irma Bryar had taken him by the ear after he'd been rude to a clerk in the corner store had he begun to make his peace with who he was. He got along all right with people. He just needed his time alone. For a while his place along the river outside Nashville, with his dogs, was enough. But it was harder and harder to keep friends and colleagues away without being rude, and so he'd ended up buying a place on Cape Cod. It was his personal retreat. He wasn't looking to develop it, and he sure as hell hadn't bought it because of some old woman's damned spell on him.

The plain muslin curtains billowed in a sudden breeze. He'd have to pull up a blanket in a minute. He was sleeping nude, as was his custom, even when alone, which had been the case more often than not in the past year. He wondered if old Hannah Frye knew that one.

"Ouch! *Damn it!*"

He went very still. The voice—a loud whisper more furious than pained—had come from outside, somewhere beneath his window.

He'd bet a nickel it was Piper Macintosh.

In case he was wrong and it was her anonymous caller, he rolled out of bed and stayed low as he crept to his dormered window.

Silhouetted against the starlit background of sky and sea was the distinct figure of a woman. Clate set his jaw. She must have tripped in the dark. She wasn't moving, probably waiting to see if he'd throw on a light and yell out his window. It was tempting.

Instead, he felt his way to the blanket chest at the foot of his bed, found a pair of shorts he'd tossed there, and pulled them on. He groped for a sweatshirt, pulled it on. Late at night, the mosquitoes could be fierce. He even took time to locate his sneakers, in case Piper tried to run off and he had to lay chase.

He hissed in annoyance. "What the hell's she doing this time?"

Not procuring smelly roots for her lunatic aunt, he'd wager. He remembered her scared, wild look that morning on the beach. She'd fought herself over how much to tell him. There was more. Whatever it was would explain why she was out there now.

He slipped through his bedroom door out to the hall, down the steep stairs, not moving with his usual assurance. It was pitch dark, the ground unfamiliar. He half expected to bump into sharp-cornered secretaries, some damned fussy antique table. In Nashville, he had space, light, tall ceilings, tall windows, spare furnishings. Here, everything was cozy, cramped, intimate.

Maybe old Hannah Frye *had* put a spell on him.

He was through the kitchen, moving fast now. He didn't care if Piper heard him. She wouldn't have time to make her escape.

He tore open the back door, banged open the screen door, and was out in the cool, fragrant night air.

"Oh, damn!"

Her voice, not pleased. There was a clattering sound, then her silhouette streaked down the slope toward the marsh.

Clate jumped after her. "Piper! Hell, woman, don't make me chase you."

She didn't stop to argue. The stars and sliver of a moon provided just enough light for him to make her out as she lurched away from him.

Then she tripped, going down face first, cursing vociferously.

She was still cursing, up on her hands and knees, when Clate caught up with her. She seemed to have on a long, black dress or nightgown that had tripped her up. Without thinking, he grabbed her around the middle and hauled her to her feet.

It was as big a mistake as he'd ever made.

She blew a strand of hair out of her mouth and fastened her eyes, luminous in the near darkness, on him, and he sucked in a breath at what he was thinking, feeling. Every muscle went rigid, as if that could force common sense back into him. He wanted to kiss her, he wanted to scoop her up into his arms and carry her upstairs to his bed.

Her eyes narrowed, and she whispered, "Oh, dear," and he knew they were lost. Her fingers dug into his upper arms. Whether she found his mouth or he found hers, in the next moment he was consumed by the taste of her, the heat of her, the feel of her small, lithe body against his. She responded eagerly, moaning softly. It wasn't instantaneous. It couldn't have been. She must have been thinking, imagining, what could happen if he caught her this time.

With a sharp jolt, Clate realized he wanted nothing more, now, than to sweep her down onto the dew-soaked grass and make love to her until dawn. But Piper had boldly lied to him, snuck onto his property every time he turned his back, and had troubles and distractions that could make her regret what she'd done come morning, no matter how much she wanted him now.

He'd have no regrets, Clate thought with another sharper, deeper jolt, even as he eased back from their kiss. He slid his hands down along her hips, finally noticing her outfit: a high-collared, simple black dress right out of a mourning scene in a John Wayne movie. "What the hell do you have on?"

"One of Hannah's dresses." Her voice wasn't shaky, even if her eyes were shining, fiery with desire. "Actually, she's never worn it. It was one of her first efforts, and she got the size wrong. It fits me okay—"

"Why one of Hannah's dresses?"

"I don't own anything all black."

Matter-of-fact. As if that explained everything. Clate noted, his hands still light on her hips, that she wasn't nervous or intimidated by him, just boldly buying herself time. "This is right up there with bee balm and hummingbirds as far as tall tales go, Piper."

"Hannah also believed the dress would bring me good

luck. I figured, why not? But obviously she was wrong."
She screwed up her face, frowning at him. "Don't you
ever sleep?"

"Uh-uh. You're not blaming me. You're the one in the
wrong here. I heard you yell."

"I hit a tree root and banged my shovel against my
ankle. And that was a stifled yell, not a full-blown yell.
You must have already been awake."

"Why did you run?"

She blinked at him as if she were dealing with a
moron.

Clate grinned. "Knew what would happen, did you?"

"You know, for a man who doesn't want any more
complications in his life—"

"This wasn't complicated, Piper." He let his hands
drop to his sides. "This was damned simple."

"For you maybe," she said under her breath.

"All right. Two questions. One, why would you need to
wear black? Two, why would you need luck?"

"Same answer to both." She squared her shoulders
and tilted up her chin, and he wondered if she had any
idea how beautiful and sexy and ridiculous she looked in
her nineteenth-century, ill-fitting black dress. "I didn't
want you to catch me. You seem to have this thing about
trespassers."

"That's why I had the signs posted."

"I know that, but Hannah—" She gave her head a
toss, her hair, straight and thick, had been whipped into
tangles by the breeze and her race across his yard.
"Hannah insists you posted the signs to draw me over
here."

"I'd never even met you when I decided to post my
land."

"That wouldn't matter to her."

No, he thought with a resigned sigh, it wouldn't. The
woman was an eccentric, her grandniece one in the
making. "It's all part of our destiny?"

"I think so."

"Why the shovel?"

She hesitated. "I needed it."

He wasn't letting her off the hook, not this time. "For what?"

Her eyes leveled on him, steady, gleaming in the soft starlight. But she didn't answer him.

"You managed to dig your valerian root the other night with a trowel. What were you planning to dig up tonight, a whole damned tree?"

"Actually, no." Her voice was cool, just a hint of annoyance. "If you really must know, I was digging for buried treasure."

He thought she was being sarcastic and bit off a hiss, but then he saw that she was perfectly serious. Buried treasure. He inhaled sharply. "Hell." It came out as a low growl of exasperation, irritation, resignation.

"Well, I'll just get my shovel and head on home."

"Uh-uh. No way." He pointed toward the Frye house. "Inside."

She looked mystified. "For what?"

He could think of a thousand answers to that one, not one related to buried treasure and the whims of an eighty-seven-year-old. His thoughts must have revealed themselves in his expression, because Piper took a step back, wariness flashing in her eyes, a little thrill. He saw a wink of what must have been a white petticoat, and his gut twisted at the image of dispensing with nineteenth-century undergarments as well as a nineteenth-century dress before getting to her trim body.

But he reined himself in and said, "I'll make coffee, and you can tell me about your buried treasure."

"It's not my buried treasure, it's Hannah's."

"All the more reason you're going to tell me about it."

She tilted her head back, staring up at the stars scattered across the night sky, contemplating her response. She had a choice, and she knew it. As determined as he was, Clate couldn't drag answers from her that she had no intention of giving him. Finally, she leveled her gaze at him once more. "You have decaf?"

"What?"

"You might never sleep," she said, turning her back to him as she started up the sloping lawn, "but I need my eight hours or I don't function well. I'm teaching open-hearth cooking in the morning. I don't want to burn myself on a cast-iron kettle because of lack of sleep." She paused, glanced back at him, her chestnut hair trailing down her back. Right then, she could have passed for an old-fashioned, horror-picture-show witch herself. Beautiful, tempting, dangerous. "Coming?"

"Right behind you, sweetheart," he muttered through clenched teeth, and followed her up the rise.

Chapter

7

As she poured extra milk into the steaming mug of coffee Clate had handed her, Piper decided Hannah must have put something in her tea yesterday. It was the only explanation for why she'd agreed to wear a nineteenth-century getup and dig for treasure when Clate Jackson was home—why she'd kissed him.

She felt drowsy yet edgy, watching him move about in a kitchen as familiar to her as her own. His dark sweatshirt made his shoulders seem even broader and more muscular. He looked rugged, physical, his presence in Hannah's old, quaint house incongruous. But he owned it now. She was on his turf.

The stove clock read two-forty-five. Her class in open-hearth cooking was at eleven. Time enough to tell Clate what she would tell him—she wasn't yet sure exactly what that would be—and get a few hours' sleep.

He dropped onto the chair opposite her and settled back, the muscles in his jaw tensing as he looked at her. Finally, he sighed. "Trust me, Piper. I'm not in to burning bamboo shoots under the fingernails. I'd like to know what's going on, and that's all. You want to tell me about this buried treasure?"

She sipped her coffee, inhaling its strong aroma, painfully aware of what kind of loony figure she must cut in her nineteenth-century black dress and white petticoat.

"You do have a choice," Clate said in that quiet, deceptively reasonable drawl. He had his emotions under tight control. Whatever had propelled him to kiss her with such hunger, such ferocity, was well banked down. "Either your forays onto my property stop or you explain them."

She shot him a look. "Meaning you'd have me arrested for trespassing."

"Meaning exactly that."

"Even after what happened out there?"

His grim expression lightened, and a sexy half-grin reminded her that she wasn't the only one who'd enjoyed the experience. "Piper, it was only a kiss."

She pursed her lips. "You're a cad, Clate Jackson. My brother dropped off a magazine article about you, and it as much as said so. You're rich, successful, driven, but a cad."

"It didn't say 'cad.'"

"That's my interpretation." She sounded high and mighty and a bit nineteenth century even to her own ears, but she didn't care. "It indicated you wouldn't hesitate to take advantage of a woman who found herself in an unfortunate position."

He was unmoved. "You didn't find yourself in an unfortunate position, Piper. You put yourself there."

She peered at him over the rim of her steaming coffee. "Only because I tripped."

"Uh-uh." That rasping drawl wasn't so easy and reasonable now. "Because you deliberately dressed yourself in black from head to toe and snuck onto my property in the middle of the night. You made your choice."

She sniffed. "It wasn't my choice to kiss you."

He had the audacity to laugh.

"I'm not saying I objected or have any regrets, but . . ." She trailed off, suddenly realizing she wasn't getting anywhere. He held the cards. Every damned one.

"But what?" he asked.

She squirmed on her rickety old chair. He wasn't about to let her mount a graceful retreat. "I don't think I need to spell it out. You pounced, Clate. Let's just leave it at that."

He stretched out his muscled legs, at ease. "Honey, that wasn't pouncing."

"It was in my judgment, and right now, my judgment is the only one that counts."

"Piper." He leaned forward, the light shifting on his face, his eyes, making what he was thinking even more difficult to read. "Can you honestly sit there and tell me you know which one of us started that kiss?"

She clamped her mouth shut and refused to answer. She didn't care if she seemed like a prude. She should have refused to discuss this topic altogether, but it was too late—too late to stop the memory of the taste of his mouth, the heat of his tongue, the feel of his arms around her.

Her throat went dry. She managed to shake her head. "But it doesn't matter. Nothing would have happened if you'd just stayed in bed and let me do what I came to do."

"Piper, we did what we did because it felt like the right thing to do at the time. Period, end of story."

She had to admit that kissing him *had* felt right, that it still did.

"And if you ever don't want me to"—he smiled slightly, sexily— "pounce, all you have to do is say no."

She acknowledged his words with a curt nod and drank some of her coffee. Three o'clock in the morning and she was sitting in Clate Jackson's kitchen. The Nashville magazine had profiled him as hard edged, sexy, driven, a man who fiercely protected his privacy. He had started in construction at age sixteen, doing grunt work. At twenty-six, he had his own company. With relentless commitment, long hours, an eye for calculated risk, and an ability to pick and motivate good people, he had defied his doubters and become one of his city's most successful businessmen. Now, he owned an exclusive hotel, exclusive office buildings acclaimed for their character and beauty as well as their functionality. He had built a house in a private location on the Cumberland River. Always, profit was at the center of what he did. His integrity was unquestioned, but no one pretended Clate Jackson wasn't capable of playing hardball if he felt the situation called for it.

There was no mention of his family, parents, siblings, cousins, what he'd been before age sixteen, beyond a cryptic line that said he didn't discuss his past.

He pushed his chair back, its legs scratching on the pineboard floor and lurching Piper back into the present. Three o'clock in the morning, Clate Jackson's kitchen, she in one of Hannah's *Little House on the Prairie* dresses. They'd have had a heck of a time with all the buttons and hooks and eyes if they'd decided to make love out in the moonlight. Of course, maybe they wouldn't have bothered disrobing.

Warmth spread through her. It was wild thinking. Insane.

"Tell me about your aunt's buried treasure," Clate said, giving no sign he had a clue of what she was imagining.

Piper cleared her throat, glad for the distraction. For years her father and brothers had drilled into her the necessity and the advantage in keeping her emotions in check and her mouth shut. She was accustomed to doing what she had to do without a lot of introspection and angst, without expecting anyone else to understand.

But she found herself wanting Clate to understand why she'd put on a black dress and snuck onto his property in the middle of the night, why she was indulging her aunt in spite of threatening phone calls, him, her brothers, her father, and common sense.

"All right. I'll tell you."

He listened without interruption. He gave her that much courtesy. His expression remained neutral, even when she got to the part about the Russian princess and Fabergé egg. But she had no illusions. This was a man who was concrete in the extreme, not one given to flights of imagination. He wouldn't easily accept that some things were not subject to logical explanation. Hannah's recovered memory and her firm belief in what she saw that night eighty years ago required a leap of imagination that even stretched Piper's capabilities.

"I've been dragging my heels," she said finally, "and Hannah knows it. She called me on it yesterday. I came out here tonight because I was more interested in pacifying her than finding buried treasure. I just had to act— results didn't matter."

"How far did you get?"

"I didn't even break ground."

"You were going for under the wisteria."

She nodded, suddenly feeling foolish. "If I was eighty-seven and believed the key to my parents' death lay under a wisteria, I'd want someone to dig for me and prove it one way or the other."

"What about the phone calls?"

"I can't explain them. I can't imagine why anyone would care if I were messing around on your property. Hannah says she didn't mention the treasure to anyone." Piper jumped up and returned her mug to the sink. A good thing she'd requested decaf. She'd have trouble sleeping as it was. She turned around and glared at Clate. "She has no reason to lie."

"I didn't say she did."

His tone was mild, not defensive. Piper reeled in her frustration. "I'm just so damned confused. I tried to do some research at the local library, but too many people I know were around. I managed to read one of the major accounts of how my great-grandparents died. People up and down the Cape were outraged and horrified that someone—probably one of their own—would lure two people to their deaths."

"Any proof that that was what happened?"

"A lantern was found on the beach, and an old fisherman said he'd seen a light waving in the fog. There were never any suspects, though."

Clate had his eyes narrowed, and Piper knew he was listening intently, that she had his full attention. "Is there any chance the ship wasn't purposely lured onto the sandbar? Could whoever had the lantern have been trying to help a lost ship and things just went awry?"

"I suppose it's possible, but it's unlikely. Presumably if it was an accident, this good Samaritan would have gone for help. Instead, it was hours before anyone realized a ship was stuck."

"All right. Suppose the guy with the lantern initially wanted to help. The ship hits the sandbar, he goes out to do what he can, but by the time he gets there, there's nothing he can do to help your aunt's parents. He's too late. He decides he might as well have a look at their belongings—"

"Finds the treasure and helps himself."

"Exactly."

"So he'd be a vulture stealing from dead people, not a murderer. I don't know. For the past eighty years, everyone around here has believed that Caleb and Phoebe Macintosh were lured to their deaths by a mooncusser."

He frowned. "A mooncusser?"

"They're sort of a Cape Cod legend. They'd use a lantern to deliberately strand ships, then rob them and leave them to fend for themselves. I'm not sure how many actual incidents of mooncussing occurred, but the legend persists."

"Your basic land pirate."

"I guess you could say that."

"No mention of Russian treasure in the account you read?"

Piper didn't like his disbelieving tone. "No, but I'm not finished with my research." She heard the defiance in her own voice and leaned against the counter, feeling her fatigue now, the aching in her mind and body. "Missing jewels and Fabergé eggs. I know it sounds far-fetched. But Hannah—" She sighed. How could she possibly explain her elderly aunt to a man who had as low a tolerance for whim and fancy as Clate?

"Repressed memory is fairly unreliable from what I understand," he said, skeptical but not unkind. "This could be some fantasy your aunt's created to get closure on a traumatic event in her childhood. Her motives may be above reproach, but it doesn't mean she saw a thing that night."

"I think she knows that. I think she's just trying to sort out what's real and what's not."

"But it's been eighty years."

Piper thrust out her chin. "That's why she can't wait any longer."

"Okay." Some of his skepticism eased, but Piper had no illusions that he was relenting. He'd come to Cape Cod for privacy and quiet, not unraveling an old mystery. "Suppose I allow that she's really trying to sort out a haunting memory—even one she's only recently, and rather conveniently, recalled—it's still a big leap to think there's treasure buried under my wisteria. Even if she saw what she thinks she saw, the chances of that chest or whatever it was still being out there are next to none."

"I know," Piper said, fatigue overwhelming her. "I could have just told her I'd dug out there and didn't find anything, but—"

"But she deserves more than that from you," Clate finished.

His answer surprised her. "Yes, I guess that's it. She's always been there for me."

"And you for her."

Piper sucked in a breath. She was tired. That was why she was feeling so emotional. She knew Hannah wouldn't live forever. She only wanted her to live out whatever was left of her life happily, finally with the answers to what she'd seen, or what she thought she'd seen, that night at age seven. Piper knew she couldn't be objective where her aunt was concerned. But was her devotion to Hannah so obvious that even a man new to Frye's Cove, who wanted nothing to do with the people there, saw it?

He broke the silence. "Irma Bryar, the woman whose funeral I went home for, was that kind of presence in my life. I understand your loyalty, Piper."

"Was she your aunt?"

He shook his head. "Just an old woman in town, a retired teacher, who took an interest in a bad-mannered kid on all the wrong roads to all the wrong places."

"You miss her," Piper said with conviction, suddenly seeing past the hardness of the man, straight into his heart. An old friend had died, and he mourned her passing.

"We weren't as close as you and your aunt are. We had a different kind of connection." He got to his feet, moved toward her. "But if she'd asked, I'd have gotten my shovel and gone onto my neighbor's property to dig under a wisteria." A flash of humor. "I'm not sure I'd have worn a getup like yours, though."

As he came closer, Piper noticed the scars, the signs that life hadn't always been easy for him, Irma Bryar notwithstanding. She smiled. "I don't know. I can see you in a ruffled shirt—"

"You're exhausted, Piper." He touched her hair, trailed the back of his hand down her cheek. "Come on, I'll walk you home."

"I can manage on my own."

He laughed. "Don't get your back up, sweetheart. I'm not trying to snatch your independence from you. I'm not one of your brothers, I assure you."

"No kidding. They'd string up you and me both if they could see us now."

"Never mind the kiss?"

Her grin broadened. "They'd string us up and shoot us if they knew about the kiss."

"They look after you."

"They have their good points, meddling in my life not being one of them. Anyway, we can blame the kiss on adrenaline, circumstances, the night air. Whatever."

"Why blame it on anything?"

She licked her lips, remembering the taste of his. "Because it's the smart thing to do. Better yet, I'm just going to pretend it never happened."

Clate smiled knowingly. "Sure. You do that."

The Russian princess stuff almost had Clate on the phone with his realtor the next morning. He'd get rid of his place on Cape Cod and buy in Wyoming or Montana, find a quiet, peaceful Caribbean island. Hell, he'd do without a retreat. It was too damned complicated with his work and his dogs anyway. He belonged in Tennessee, not up here with all the sand and sea and crazy Yankees.

"Actually," Piper had said, "I doubt if she was a real Russian princess. She might have been just a baroness."

Gritting his teeth, he ducked under the rotting wisteria arbor in what purportedly was his back yard. It felt more like Hannah Frye's. He imagined her standing out on the terrace in one of her costumes, perhaps remembering yet not remembering the night her parents died.

A hell of a lot more convenient if she'd done her treasure digging before he'd moved in.

He wasn't convinced this sudden recovered memory wasn't just a ploy on the old woman's part to throw him and her niece together.

Still, here he was, under the wisteria.

The blossoms hung in thick, violet clusters, their sweet scent almost overpowering. Maybe Piper was humoring Hannah to keep her from finding someone else to dig for her buried treasure, meanwhile trying to establish some reason to believe in her recovered memory.

It wasn't treasure Hannah Frye wanted. It was clarity,

answers, to what she saw that dark, terrible night eighty years ago. Clate could understand that compulsion. He remembered coming home from a solitary fishing trip when he was twelve and hearing his parents fighting, yelling, cursing, hitting, throwing things, both still just in their twenties. Alcohol, youth, ignorance, poverty, irresponsibility. They'd all taken their toll on them, on him. Yet he'd often wondered, less and less now, how it had all come to be. He'd tried to make sense where there was none to be made. In her own way, Hannah Macintosh Frye could be doing the same thing.

He breathed in the sweet smells of the wisteria, remembered the rambling wisteria Irma had on sagging trellises. He'd talked over these same issues with her on her front porch, after she'd insisted he wash up and dispose of any gum, cigarettes, and chewing tobacco. Instead of discussing his parents, she'd discussed books. Instead of answering his questions, she'd asked more. Clarity, she would say, was something one discovered, not something one had imposed upon one.

He shook off his sudden nostalgia, the nagging grief he felt for a woman he'd seen only sporadically in the past eighteen years. What if he'd seen her every day, as Piper Macintosh and Hannah Frye saw each other?

"Hell," he grunted, tearing himself back to the present. The salty breeze, the cloying wisteria, the prospect of a treasure chest buried under his feet. He saw that Piper had left her shovel behind after all. He thought of her anonymous caller. Hannah might not be interested in gems, gold, Fabergé eggs, but that didn't mean someone else wasn't.

He grabbed the shovel and stabbed it into the soft ground, not sure what the devil he thought he was doing. The day was warm, a bit cooler under the wisteria. Piper's shovel was well worn, and he imagined her tilling her garden with it, imagined the tightening of the muscles in her legs, the perspiration beading on her brow.

He turned over a spadeful of dirt, then another. The soil was sandy and porous, not hard digging. He pulled off his shirt. If he'd shipwrecked, robbed, and left two people to die, he wouldn't have buried his bootie in someone's damned back yard. He'd have gone out into the woods, far away from the prying eyes of a lonely seven-year-old. And if he had been dumb enough to leave treasure buried under a wisteria, he wouldn't have left it there for eighty years.

Before long, he had a three-foot hole dug. Sweat poured down his back, bugs buzzed around him. He was breathing hard. He'd worked fast, furiously, as if physical exertion alone could keep him from applying the slightest bit of logic to what he was doing.

He threw down Piper's shovel and slipped out from under the wisteria, where the air seemed clearer, less cloying. He sat in the grass and let the sounds of sea and wind and birds soothe his raw nerves. Cape Cod was a pretty place. He'd give it that.

He checked his watch. Past noon. He had a conference call in an hour. Work beckoned. It always did. He hadn't learned the fine art of delegating. He suspected there were those in his company eagerly anticipating the day he did. He had good people, a handful he'd trust as chief executive.

He breathed a long sigh, staring at the hole he'd dug. There was no treasure buried under his wisteria.

Piper must have guessed as much, or she'd have been out here at her aunt's first mention of what she'd seen that night. She wasn't one to wait. First chance he got, here he was digging a hole big enough for a dead elephant. A wonder he hadn't gone out before dawn. That Piper had been more deliberate and cautious than he had didn't sit well with him at all.

Pride compelled him to fill his hole. No need to have his neighbor slip through the hedges and discover he'd gotten caught up in her aunt's dotty ideas, too.

"Russian princesses," he muttered, stabbing at the mound of dirt. "Hell."

He'd get cleaned up, he'd do some business, and then

1 0 8

maybe he'd wander into town and pay old Hannah Frye a visit.

Piper taught her open-hearth cooking class, picked a quart of strawberries, and was off to town on her mountain bike by four o'clock. Her life wasn't ordered, but it was endlessly stimulating.

She was not encouraged when she arrived at the Macintosh Inn and found four trucks outside belonging to her father, her brothers, and Tuck O'Rourke, and one BMW belonging to Clate Jackson.

In her experience, nothing good came of that many men conferring in one place, particularly when three were Macintoshes and one she'd kissed within the past twenty-four hours.

She ran into Sally Shepherd in the front lobby. "I suppose you're looking for your father and brothers. They're all in the tavern."

Even worse. With foreboding, Piper headed back to the tavern, a dark, wood-paneled room that called up images of revolutionaries plotting mischief against the British and sea captains telling tales of far-off lands. There was one notorious whaling captain in the Macintosh family tree. Piper sent in a donation to the New England Aquarium every year in his name.

The only customers, gathered at a round table, were the Macintosh men, Tuck, and Clate. They looked as if they'd been devising ways to purge a local witch and her cohort from their midst.

"Piper!" Her father rose, sounding delighted, as always, to see her. "Come, sit and have a drink with us."

Their work finished for the day, he and his two sons were sharing a pitcher of beer. Tuck had his own beer, Clate a tall glass of iced tea. As she leaned over and kissed her father on the cheek, Piper was aware of Clate's eyes on her, and Andrew's and Benjamin's eyes on *him*. She'd changed from her teaching outfit into bike shorts and her Red Sox shirt for her bike ride into town and had pulled her hair back in a hasty ponytail that was already coming undone.

"I'm on a bike ride," she said before any comments were forthcoming about her ragged appearance. "I saw all the trucks parked outside and figured I'd better stop in, make sure you boys weren't up to no good."

Andrew leaned back, his hands folded on his middle. He had on a dusty work shirt and jeans, his standard outfit for as long as Piper could remember. "Such as?"

Such as persuading Clate to repeat every word she'd told him last night and rat out her and Hannah. Such as making sure he had no designs on his new neighbor. Such as generally meddling in her life. But she manufactured a bright smile, just in case her foreboding was misplaced this once. "I never know with you guys. Hey, Tuck, how're you doing?"

"Not bad. You?"

She wondered if he or her father and brothers noticed the dark circles under her eyes that had made her scream at her own reflection when she'd rolled out of bed at nine. She'd slept fitfully, dreaming dreams her brothers would not want to hear about and Clate Jackson just might delight in. She was sure *he'd* noticed the dark circles.

"I'm fine," she said breezily, not too phonily. "Busy. I have a few summer students who are looking for a property manager. Can I give them your name or are you too tight right now?"

He gripped his beer bottle with a huge, stained hand. "Sure, go ahead."

He was beefier than the other men at the table, dressed in work clothes that were close enough to presentable; Clate's attire was canvas and denim and unquestionably presentable. He did nothing to call attention to his wealth or away from it. She wondered if he knew she'd dated Tuck way back when. Her brothers claimed they'd never said a word to him, which—if true—in no way exonerated them. A look, a gesture, just their mere presence in the same town were enough to scare off someone like Tuck. It never bothered her, but the men in her life just didn't like the prospect of going up against her brothers.

"Clate, nice to see you." She acknowledged him with a polite nod, knowing she had to get it over with. She felt all eyes on her, and it wasn't just her imagination.

He smiled and said in that slow, liquid drawl, "Nice to see you, too."

Andrew sat forward a fraction, just enough to alert Piper that he'd noticed the electricity between her and Clate. According to the article in the Nashville magazine and every rumor anyone in Frye's Cove had ever repeated or heard about him, Clate Jackson was exactly the sort of man her brothers had warned her about for years.

"Haven't seen you around much, Piper," Benjamin said.

"Summer's my busy season."

She was avoiding Clate's eye, probably being so obviously nonchalant that her brothers would know for sure something was up. Ordinarily she wouldn't have given a damn—or not much of one. But this time she really did have something to hide, not only her tumble of feelings about her Tennessean neighbor but also Hannah's treasure, the disturbing phone calls, more trespassing. Her life was out of control enough without her father and brothers diving into her problems and lecturing her on how she could have avoided them in the first place.

"We made bread this morning in my open-hearth cooking class," she said. "I have a couple of extra loaves. I can bring them out later."

Benjamin smiled. "I'll save you the trip to town and stop by. I haven't been out to your place in a while. Liddy and the boys love your bread."

Piper wasn't fooled. He was coming out to her place to spy on her, just as Andrew had yesterday when he'd delivered the Nashville magazine. "Well, I should be back in a couple hours. Bring the boys by if you want, Liddy, too." There, that'd prove she had nothing to hide. "I should get going. See you guys around."

"You won't stay and have a drink with us?" her father asked.

Not a chance. They'd notice the signs of fatigue and trouble, the way her pulse jumped when she was around Clate. It wasn't that she didn't trust her family or generally lied to them. She simply knew they'd demand explanations where she couldn't give any and offer help where she didn't want to be tempted to take any. This time, she preferred to do without her father or her brothers' advice, interference, opinions on Hannah's mental health or her own, or even their loving support. If they found out about the threatening phone calls, she was doomed. There'd be no peace, no room to maneuver. For Hannah's sake if not her own, she needed that room.

She retreated before she could arouse their suspicions further. Her head was spinning, her pulse racing, her mind a jumble of crazy thoughts and conflicting emotions. A good, long bike ride would help her get a fresh perspective.

She was all the way out to the front porch before she realized someone was behind her. She spun around, almost landing against Clate's rock-hard chest. "Geez, you're light on your feet," she said.

"Not really. You're just preoccupied."

"I admit I'm jumpy."

He frowned, blue eyes narrowed, suspicious. The man definitely had a different view of the world from hers. "You didn't get another phone call, did you?"

She shushed him and whispered, "I don't want my father and brothers to know about the calls. No, I didn't get another one."

"Your father and brothers strike me as solid allies, men I'd want on my side."

"They are on my side. They don't need to know details to be on my side."

He thought that one over with a frown. "I guess there's a certain logic at work there. Not that you asked for my opinion, but I think they have your best interests at heart."

"Of course they do. That's half the problem. Look, I just need to do this thing my way. They don't understand Hannah the way I do."

"They're not attached to her in the same way."

His tone was mild, observational, not critical, but Piper felt herself go on the defensive. "When they're eighty-seven, I hope they have someone who'll put up with their whims instead of a couple of cranks who'll doubt their sanity at every turn." She tightened her hands into fists, became aware of the rocking chairs that Paul and Sally had put out, the flower boxes, the cheerful atmosphere of their inn. Tourist traffic was picking up, the summer season closing in. She glanced at Clate, calmer. "You know, you're not helping matters by following me out."

"Bit protective of you, are the Macintosh men?"

"I'm glad you find my life so entertaining."

"Piper." He leaned toward her, a gleam of amusement in his very blue eyes. "I'm not afraid of them. Or you. Or Hannah and her witchy ways, for that matter. I had a drink with Tuck and your father and brothers. Nothing more."

"You didn't pump them for information?"

"No."

"Did they pump you?"

He grinned. "Of course. And I cooperated, to a degree." At her look of panic, he added, "About my background, not about what you and I did last night."

"Benjamin will probably check for footprints between my house and yours when he stops by, you know. Don't think an afternoon drink has won them over. They're as curious about what brings you to Frye's Cove as anyone. Probably more so."

A cool distance came into his eyes. "I gather few believe my stated reason."

"Correct. A man with your money and reputation—" She shook her head and trotted down the front steps to where she'd left her bicycle, unlocked. Come July and August, she'd be more cautious. "Not a chance. People still insist on thinking you'll tear down the Frye house and put in a ritzy resort just as soon as you can sneak it by the review boards."

He'd followed her down the steps into the shade of a huge old maple, a rarity on Cape Cod since many of the early settlers had denuded the forests. "What about you? What do you believe?"

"I tend to believe what people tell me until I have reason to do otherwise." She pulled on her helmet, hooked it under her chin. "But my brothers think I'm too trusting."

"I operate the same way," he said softly, moving from the shade, "and nobody's ever said I'm too trusting."

She grinned. "That's because you have more scars than I do."

"The life of a construction worker with a bad temper." But he didn't smile, a seriousness coming over him. "I wanted to tell you, I went to see your aunt this afternoon."

"Alone? Why?"

"To talk to her. She offered me tea, which I declined, and we had a nice chat on her back deck." He drew a finger along the handlebar of her bike. "Piper, I don't think she's told you everything she knows. I think she's holding back something."

"What? Why would she hold back? I'm doing her a favor."

"I don't know why, I just believe she is. It wasn't anything concrete, but I came away with the distinct impression that if she's not exactly playing us for fools, she's at least slipped a few cards up her sleeve."

"You told her I'd confided in you?"

He dropped his hand to his side. "She already knew."

"Did she know as in you think I told her, or did she know as in . . . well, as in she just knew."

He bit off a sigh. "The latter."

"That's silly."

"Then you told her?"

"No, but she probably just took one look at your face and leaped to the conclusion that I'd told you about the treasure. You're not that hard to read, you know, especially when you're on a tear." At his amused look, she climbed onto her bicycle. "Not that I know you that well, of course. But you don't know my aunt."

"She's not telling you everything, Piper."

She waved a hand in dismissal. "So, what else is new? Look, you caught me at a vulnerable moment last night. I don't think well on that little sleep." Or after kissing a man in the starlight. "I should have been more circumspect. Please don't go tearing uptown and pestering people on my account. I don't need this thing to get any more out of hand than it already is. Right now, I can handle Hannah's treasure and the calls—which for all I know have ended, I might add—on my own."

He settled back on his heels, unperturbed. "And what are you doing to handle everything besides baking bread and teaching open-hearth cooking?"

She eyed him. "Making strawberry-rhubarb jam."

Before she could let his growl of impatience get to her, she eased off on her bicycle, pedaling hard, trying not to wonder if he was standing there on the sidewalk appraising her behind.

Chapter
8
∽

Tempted to head straight to Hannah's townhouse to find out what else she and Clate might have discussed outside her presence, Piper instead wound her way to her favorite road along the water, where it was cool and beautiful and where Frye's Cove's few summer people were out enjoying the scenery. She passed other cyclists, in-line skaters, walkers, cars with out-of-state plates. Tourists tended to cluster near the town's limited beaches, bypassing the village to stay in more popular nearby towns that better catered to their needs.

When the Macintosh Inn was fully opened, that would change to a degree, but it was too small to make much of an impact. A Clate Jackson resort on his waterfront property could dramatically change the character of the town, and certainly of her quiet road, but Piper wanted to believe his declaration that he had no interest in building on Cape Cod.

By the time she coasted back along her road, she was sweaty and aching, but her spirits were revived. Seeing how Clate had already been out to see Hannah, Piper could put off her own visit to explain her abortive foray under the wisteria. Instead, she'd cut rhubarb, cap her strawberries, and round off a perfect afternoon with jam making.

Once she got rid of Paul Shepherd and Stan Carlucci, she thought with a groan as she spotted them standing in her gravel driveway. They'd come in Paul's car. They'd passed her on the dead-end road, but she'd hoped they were just checking on something in the wildlife refuge. Traffic wasn't unheard of on her road, and she seldom paid attention to cars belonging to locals.

Their grave expressions gave her a start. She pushed down her kickstand and climbed off her bicycle. Stan was a big, balding man in his late fifties. Although she disagreed with him on almost everything, and on a personal level considered him pompous and arrogant, she had to admit he cared about their town and was willing to do the difficult work of sitting on the board of selectmen. Hannah, as much as she grumped about not getting her way, had steadfastly refused to run for office.

"We need to talk to you, Piper," he said. "It's about Hannah."

Her stomach lurched. "Is she all right?"

"She's fine," Paul said. He was dressed casually and expensively, the typical Cape Cod inn owner. He gave Piper a weak smile. "It's Stan we should be worried about. He stopped by the inn with an alarming story. Uh—can we talk?"

Slightly calmer, but with a sense of dread, Piper led them inside, through her in-progress front parlor back to her keeping room. It still smelled of bread from her morning class. She offered the two men something to drink, but they declined. She poured herself a glass of water, noticing that Stan was tense and awkward as he scanned her cozy, unusual kitchen. One of her first tasks had been to uncover the plastered-over fireplace, where she'd discovered beehive ovens and even an old iron kettle. She'd since added more kettles and pans, storing them in and around the fireplace.

No one sat down. Piper leaned against the sink and drank her water, wondering what Hannah had done now.

Paul did the talking. He was tall enough that her dried herbs skimmed the top of his head. "Stan came to me because of Sally's and my close relationship to Hannah. Sally's gone to Hyannis for the evening or she would certainly have come with us. However, I don't think we're the ones who can help with this situation. You've always been the closest to her, Piper. If anyone can get her under control, it's you."

Piper could feel her leg muscles seizing up. She'd planned on a long session of stretching, an invigorating shower, then her jam making. "Has she done something?"

Carlucci took a breath. "She's tried again to terrorize me with her witchcraft."

He sounded like a Puritan prosecutor at a seventeenth-century witch trial. Piper gulped more water, trying not to let Stan's gravity and hyperbole affect her. "Hannah would never deliberately harm you or anyone else."

"Show her," Paul said to Carlucci, his tone resigned, even a bit depressed.

Stan withdrew a black velvet pouch from the pocket of his seersucker sport coat and tossed it on the counter. Piper eyed it, then him. Perspiration dotted his brow. "I hope there's nothing dead inside," she said, trying to inject a little levity into the conversation.

Neither he nor Paul responded. "Open it up," Stan said.

Piper's first impulse was to argue, but she thought better of it. Best to get this over with. Apprehensively, she loosened the string on the pouch and felt inside. No dead bat or anything, just a little bottle, about two inches tall. She lifted it out. It was made of brown glass, typical of what Hannah used for her various tinctures and essential oils. A simple label stuck to the outside identified the contents as tincture of bistort and agrimony.

Piper choked back a laugh.

"I'm glad you're amused," Stan Carlucci grumbled.

"I'm sorry. Really." But she had to cover her mouth to keep from sputtering from her laughter, prompted as much by relief as amusement.

"I take it you recognize the contents," Paul said seriously.

"Mmm. Bistort and agrimony are two common astringent herbs used in the treatment of diarrhea." The previous tea that Hannah had prepared for Stan Carlucci was to relieve constipation. Piper chewed on a piece of ice, trying to contain her inappropriate fit of giggles. "Maybe it's Hannah's way of making peace between you."

Stan was unpersuaded. "There's no note, nothing."

"Maybe she expected you to be home, and when you weren't, just left the tincture, assuming you'd figure out what it was for."

"Oh, I figured it out all right."

"Under the circumstances," Paul said, "perhaps Hannah should have at least called."

"She probably didn't think of it. She's eighty-seven. Allowances—"

Stan snorted. "She's had all the allowances I'm going to give her. The woman's a menace."

"Oh, come on, Stan." Piper set her glass down on the sink, ignoring a slight tremble in her fingers. "It's not as if she left a bag of henbane under your pillow. Now that would worry me. Henbane's highly poisonous, but tincture of bistort and agrimony . . ." She shrugged. "Sorry, but that just doesn't move my needle."

"It's harassment," Carlucci said, refusing to back down.

"How do you know? Have you talked to her? You know, if you're so worried about my aunt, why don't you ask her what she intended by leaving a tincture on your doorstep?"

Paul intervened before Piper could work up a really good head of steam in her aunt's defense. "We understand how devoted you are to Hannah, Piper. That's why we've come to you. Neither Stan nor I was ever worried the tincture was poisonous. But Hannah can't—she just shouldn't be doing this sort of thing. You can see that, can't you? People are going to get the wrong idea about her, or one day she *will* hurt someone, however unintentionally."

"She has to stop," Stan said, more reasonably. "For her own good and the good of the community."

Piper inhaled, every muscle in her body aching, her earlier sense of energy dissipating fast. "Leaving a common medicinal tincture on someone's doorstep isn't a crime. Anyway, who's to say it was Hannah? It's not exactly a secret she's into herbal remedies and tried one out on Stan. Maybe someone else who doesn't like his politics took up the cause." She threw up her hands, thinking on her feet. "Maybe it was a joke."

"It was no joke," Carlucci said.

"Well, if you want my advice, I say go ask her."

He looked as if he'd rather have tea with Medusa. Paul Shepherd didn't look much more enthusiastic. That was why, Piper realized, they'd come to her. She sighed, moving off from the sink. "All right, I'll talk to her. But if she says she didn't leave the tincture or simply meant it as a peace offering, I'm going to believe her. I'm not going to be a party to turning this into a witch hunt."

"Fair enough," Paul said. "We'll keep this among ourselves, then, for the time being."

Piper couldn't resist a wry smile. "Yes, I suppose it wouldn't be good for Stan's political career if people knew an eighty-seven-year-old woman in town offered him a little bistort and agrimony to help with his digestive problems."

"Which she caused," Stan pointed out, red faced. "My system has been off ever since I drank that woman's tea. I should have known better. She deliberately gave me . . . problems."

"She just believed your poor digestion was making you cranky and causing you to make unwise political decisions."

"My digestion is none of her damned business!"

Paul stepped between them, holding up one hand in a mollifying gesture. "Look, that incident's water over the dam. We're all just trying to do the right thing here. Stan, let's see what Piper can do. She has a good rapport with Hannah. Maybe this will all turn out to be an unfortunate misunderstanding."

With that, the two men departed. Piper followed them back through her parlor and out the front door. They complimented her on her roses and all the work she'd done on her little antique house.

"You've a talent for this sort of thing," Stan said. "Of course, things will change here if and when Clate Jackson decides to develop his property."

Piper tried to seem unconcerned, only mildly interested in her new neighbor. "He hasn't approached any of the selectmen yet, has he?"

Carlucci shook his head. "But I've made it known that I'm receptive to hearing his ideas. I'm not going to dismiss them out of hand before I've even heard them. It would ease the burden on Frye's Cove property owners to have more business in town. I believe in good growth, the wise use of our resources and natural beauty. From what I understand, Mr. Jackson could bring the kind of tasteful, upscale development this town would welcome."

He was off and running, still rhapsodizing about the virtues of a man he hadn't, as far as Piper knew, even met. Paul gave her a sympathetic smile as he climbed into his car, Carlucci still going on about development being good for democracy, allowing more people to see a part of Cape Cod most didn't even know existed. "Thank you, Piper," Paul mouthed, and they headed out.

Her lack of sleep and her worries about her aunt suddenly overwhelming her, Piper went back inside, stretched, took a shower, and headed out to cut rhubarb, never having felt so damned alone and isolated. What if Clate were right and Hannah was holding back something? What if Paul and Stan were right and she was a menace to herself and the community?

She brushed back tears, remembered a long-ago foggy Cape Cod morning when Hannah had taken her by the hand and walked with her along the beach, showing her horseshoe crabs, bits of kelp, oyster and clam shells, and sea urchins, understanding what it was like to grow up without a mother. They did share a special bond. Because of that bond, Piper was not prepared to lose her aunt to the eroding effects of time, mental illness, disease, or her own nutty ideas. Bad enough that Hannah had sold her house and moved across town.

"Bistort and agrimony," Piper muttered, hacking at a long, tender stalk of rhubarb. "Geez, Hannah."

Best, she decided, to let this one run itself out before sharing Stan Carlucci and Paul Shepherd's suspicions with anyone else, especially the man who had bought Hannah Frye's pretty Cape Cod house—he said—as a refuge.

Clate sat up late into the night watching "The Three Stooges" on the ancient black-and-white television that came with his house. It was in the library, a small, fireplaced room of musty glass-fronted bookcases, stuffed raptors, and threadbare couches and chairs. Give him a pipe and a smoking jacket, he thought, and he could pass for a turn-of-the-century gentleman, except, of course, for his choice of entertainment.

Hannah Frye had a new, nineteen-inch color television with remote control, stereo sound, and a VCR. She'd had an afternoon talk show on when he'd arrived at her townhouse. He was struck by the contrast between her elegant, modern surroundings and her hand-stitched, anachronistic attire, the wisps of white hair straying from a crocheted snood. Comfort, she explained, was the motivation for the way she dressed, not coyness, eccentricity, religious belief, or a need for attention.

In their hour together, Clate came to see Hannah Frye

as a woman who would stop at virtually nothing to see her grandniece happy. "We're not the same, Piper and I," she said. "Only sometimes I think Piper believes she needs to be like me."

As content as she was with her own life, as satisfied with the choices she'd made, she didn't believe that Piper's destiny was to live alone, marry late in life, have no children.

No. She believed *he* was her niece's destiny.

She'd smiled at his reaction. "That makes you uncomfortable, does it?"

"You're welcome to your beliefs, Mrs. Frye."

"It's not what I believe, Mr. Jackson. It's what I know."

And how far would she go to make sure she wasn't proved wrong?

Clate shook off the uncomfortable thought. Hannah Frye would never deliberately terrify her niece, even as a means to an end. She would find other ways, like the predawn foray for valerian root, to throw him and Piper together.

Did Piper suspect her aunt, even a little?

It was possible. More likely, she would worry that someone else in town would, especially given Hannah Frye's well-known eccentricities. That would explain why she hadn't told her father and brothers by now. The Macintosh men seemed friendly enough, just wary of him, an outsider, the sole neighbor of their daughter and sister.

Clate had no doubt that between them, Piper and her aunt had given the men of the family plenty of reason to keep an eye out.

With a growl of impatience, he switched off the old television. Sitting around watching "The Three Stooges" wasn't going to get him any answers. He headed up to bed, noticing the darkness of the old house, the eerie shadows, the creaks and groans of its centuries-old beams and floorboards. He could imagine a little girl wandering these halls eighty years ago, out on this lonely strip of land, waiting for parents who would never come home.

If her elaborate tale of buried treasure and a rescued princess was a way for Hannah Frye to cope with the horror of her parents' deaths, Clate could understand. He could even understand if she truly believed it. But if it was a way to ensure her niece's so-called destiny, then she'd gone from being harmless to being manipulative and potentially dangerous.

He'd tried to impress upon Hannah Frye that he wasn't the right man for her niece. Piper had faith in family and community. She would turn to them, no matter how much her father and brothers bugged her, in times of stress, pain, suffering.

He didn't share that faith. He'd learned at a very young age that his family caused most of his pain and suffering, and his community, poor and isolated as it was, could do damned little to help him. It wasn't a question of self-pity but of taking a hard, cold look at reality and seeing it for what it was. Pure, dumb luck had thrown him in with Irma Bryar, but she couldn't change what was. She could only help him accept it and move on.

If Hannah wanted her niece to be happy, she should think up a new spell to send him back to Tennessee.

He glanced out his window, half expecting to see Piper's silhouette out under the wisteria. Instead he saw only the starlit sky, heard only the wash of the waves on the sand.

Isolation. Solitude. A retreat from the pressures of his life in Nashville, the cover articles in slick magazines, the constant speculation about his social life, his next goal, his next hill to conquer. That was what he'd expected from Cape Cod. Yet here he was, staring out his window for a woman digging treasure.

He cursed himself and climbed into bed, listening to the wind howl until sleep finally claimed him.

He cursed himself again, even more soundly, when morning came and he took his first mug of coffee out to the terrace with him. There, just inside Hannah Frye's peculiar little witch's garden, he found unmistakable signs of digging. Loose dirt, an overturned clod of weeds, a spot that looked as if it had been refilled and flattened by the back of a shovel.

"Piper."

Coffee in hand, he marched down the slope, through the break in the hedge, and along the path up to her house.

He stood on the spotty grass next to her vegetable garden with its flourishing tomato plants, its mounds of summer squash and zucchini, its rows of peas, their ripe, heavy pods hanging thickly, as if eager to be picked. Wind rustled in the tall marsh grasses, and he could hear the trill of a strange bird as he soaked in a world so very different from his own. He thought of his sprawling office high in the luxury hotel he had built, the bustle of staff, the high-tech equipment. Piper had made bread in a beehive fireplace oven yesterday morning.

"My mama don't cook much, Mrs. Bryar."

"I know she doesn't, Clayton. You just eat all you want. You picked that corn yourself. You should be proud. Enjoy your meal and be thankful for these little things in life."

His eyes stung, his pain so fierce, so unexpected, that all the fury went out of him. Irma Bryar had taught him the power of the individual, the strength that could come out of adversity. She had understood that he couldn't rely on his family, couldn't even rely on her. She was too old already when she'd taken him under her wing, too uncertain about her own future to do more than help him learn to rely on himself, to trust that courage and a sense of honor would see him through almost anything.

He walked around front and saw that Piper's bicycle was gone. She wasn't home. He finished his coffee breathing in the scent of her roses on her white picket fence. What did Piper Macintosh want from life?

"Drop it," he muttered under his breath.

He headed back through the hedges and examined the area of digging under tall, weedy-looking plants. If this was Piper's work, he thought he'd have sensed her presence during the night or that she would have seen to it he did. She'd have tripped, struck a stone with her shovel, accidentally whistled, somehow goaded him into coming out and catching her one more time.

She was like that, daring, willing to play with fire, never mind that she didn't know that the fire she was playing with this time was too damned hot for her own good.

For his, either.

He supposed the damage could be the work of dogs or raccoons or some other Cape Cod animal. That was how Piper would dismiss it. In her world, the idea that it could be the work of someone who didn't wish her well, who didn't have her best interests at heart, just didn't fit.

In Clate's world, it fit quite well. Whoever had made those calls warning her to stay off his property could easily have snuck into his yard last night and tried his hand at digging for buried treasure.

Piper eyed the something-or-other tea Hannah had served her on the deck of her townhouse. It wasn't tea colored. It was more the color of swamp water. Hannah had claimed it was ordinary herb tea, which could mean anything.

"Oh, stop glowering at it and drink it," she said, plopping down on a cushioned chair. She sat in the sun. She was old, she maintained, and got chilled easily, and she figured if she didn't have skin cancer by now, if she got it, she wouldn't live long enough to die of it. Not that she'd left much uncovered for ultraviolet light to do its damage. She had on a blue gingham dress and floppy hat that made her look a bit like Old Mother Hubbard. "It's a perfectly neutral tea."

"Why's it this color?"

Hannah leaned forward, peering at Piper's cup. "Hm. I'm not sure."

"That's encouraging."

"I wonder . . ." She frowned. "I might not have

poured from the right pot. I'm trying a new tea for my digestion, and perhaps—I hope I haven't mixed them up."

"You and me both. Why are you so preoccupied with your digestion?"

"Ask that question when you're my age. Neither tea will hurt you. You know that. It's just an inconvenience if I've mixed them up. So just drink and enjoy."

Piper thought of Stan Carlucci. "There's nothing wrong with my digestion. Anyway, I'm not thirsty."

Hannah sat back in her chair, clearly disgruntled. "You always used to sample my teas. Even when you knew you wouldn't like one, you'd at least try it. Do you think I'd give you something that would harm you?"

"No, of course not." But she made herself add, "Not intentionally."

"Oh, I see. I'm just so dotty I can't be trusted."

"That's not what I said."

"It's what you meant."

Piper set her teacup on the small table between them. "Hannah, even you have to admit you're more into this herbal remedy stuff than you used to be. Before, it was a choice between Twinings and Celestial Seasonings. You know, Earl Grey or Red Zinger. Now . . ." She stared at her cup of swamp-colored liquid and teaspoon of honey. "I just worry that in your enthusiasm to apply this new knowledge, you get a little carried away sometimes."

Hannah snorted. "Nonsense. If anything, I'm overly cautious."

Piper didn't remind her about her doubts about which tea was in which cup. "Well, you know I love your spiced tea with a cinnamon stick for a stirrer. It's my favorite, and I don't care if it's good for me or neutral."

But Hannah wasn't mollified. "You know I hate being humored, Piper. If you don't want to drink my tea, don't."

"I'm sorry. I certainly didn't come here to harass you. I wanted to ask you something. Have you made any tincture of bistort and agrimony recently?"

"No, but it's a staple. I have plenty. Why, are you having problems?"

Only Hannah, Piper thought. She shook her head, and with as little emotion as possible, related the basic facts of her visit from Paul Shepherd and Stan Carlucci.

Hannah reacted with neither annoyance nor consternation. She simply gave a flip of her bony hand and dismissed the whole thing as absurd. "First of all, I no longer concern myself with Stan Carlucci's health. He can consume Pepto Bismol for the rest of his life for all I care. Secondly, if I did want to help him, I wouldn't leave a vial of bistort and agrimony with no instructions."

"Hannah, he doesn't think you want to help him. He thinks you want to poison him."

"With tincture of bistort and agrimony? Phooey." She sniffed. "I assure you, if I were trying to poison Stan Carlucci, I wouldn't use anything that benign. And leaving it on his doorstep . . . I might be old, Piper, but I'm capable of devising a less self-incriminating plan than that."

Piper hoped she wouldn't feel called to the test. "Then who did it?"

She shrugged. "Someone who doesn't like him any more than I do, which is a growing number of people, I might add."

"Or someone who doesn't like you."

She seemed shocked at the idea. "Me?"

"Someone who knew Stan would hold you responsible for the tincture and wanted it that way. Even if it's harmless, it's harassment, scaring Carlucci, setting him up as the butt of jokes, making people think he's preoccupied with his digestion."

"He *is* preoccupied with his digestion. Why do you think I gave him that tea in the first place?"

"Nonetheless," Piper said, careful not to revisit Hannah's defense of her original run-in with Stan Carlucci. "I don't like this, Hannah. Maybe I should talk to the police. Between this and the phone calls—"

"Have you had another?"

"No, but that doesn't mean I've forgotten the two I did get."

Hannah shot to her feet as nimbly as a woman half her age. "There's no need to involve the police. Someone just got the idea for the tincture after my incident with Stan and seized the moment without thinking. I wouldn't make too much of it."

"You wouldn't, and maybe I wouldn't, but Stan and Paul—"

"I'll speak to Sally. She'll understand, and she'll calm Paul down, and he can calm Stan down." She took a breath, calmer herself. "There. Now. Come inside. I want you to test a new insect repellent I've mixed. It's a blend of pine oil in a carrier of sweet almond oil."

"Hannah—"

"We're finished discussing tincture of bistort and agrimony, Piper."

"Hannah, not everyone understands you."

She glanced back, a tiny scarecrow of a woman in a high-collared, Ma Ingalls dress. "No one understands me."

"I do."

"You love me. There's a difference. I hope you'll understand that one day soon."

Chapter

9

Piper was shelling peas at her picnic table when Clate walked up from the marsh. "Funny," she said, "how this trespassing thing only works one way."

"You can post your land, same as me."

"Would it stop you?"

He slid onto the bench across from her. "I'm not trespassing, I'm coming over for a visit."

"Good. Be neighborly and help me shell these peas."

Her basket was overflowing, picking peas her second act after arriving home from town. Her first had been to listen to her messages. A mistake.

Clate studied her from across the table she and her brothers had made when she'd first moved in. He had on jeans and a black polo shirt, and something about the light—or maybe just her mood—seemed to bring out the scars on his face and arms. He'd come up in the world the hard way. That much was obvious.

"Something's happened," he said, studying her.

She grabbed up another handful of pea pods, laid

them on the table, lifted up one, split it, shelled it into her colander.

"Piper."

"There's a message on my machine. You can go in and listen to it if you want."

He didn't answer, didn't immediately head into her house and invade her message machine. She continued to shell her peas. Her hands were trembling. Her stomach ached. She was glad for his company, yet disconcerted by his presence. Hannah, the treasure, the phone calls—they were her problem, not his.

Finally, he said, "I'd rather have you tell me about this message."

She scooped up empty pods and flung them into her herb garden, where they could rot. She had a proper compost pile. Another of her many undertakings. Maybe she'd just sell the place and buy a condo. She could understand Hannah's sense of freedom. No more leaky roofs, no more mice in the bathroom, no more fretting whether the furnace would last another winter.

"It's a line from a recording," she said. "A rap song, and not one of the good ones. But I got the message. Whoever's calling me wants me scared enough to stay home and—and shell peas, I guess."

"Any mention of staying off my property?"

"Not specifically. The general idea is for me to pay attention to previous warnings and keep quiet and mind my own business."

"Your aunt—"

Tears welled; Piper sniffled angrily. "There's a reference to crazy old bitches. I don't know if it means me or Hannah."

"Anything about treasure?"

She shook her head. "I can't even imagine this bastard's motive. Is he just guessing or does he know I've been over digging on your property? How would he know? Is he—" She gulped for air. "Is he *watching* me?"

Clate's expression hardened; he didn't move. It was as if he'd withdrawn into a cold, dark place where self-control meant the difference between life and death. "Do you want to call the police?" he asked quietly.

"Of course I do! I want to find this bastard and knock his damned head in!" She snatched up more peas, dropped them on the table, isolated one, split it, crushing half the tiny peas inside. She flung it, peas and all, into the garden. No self-control for her. She didn't care. She looked around at him and sighed, trying to penetrate the fog of emotion—fear, anger, the humiliation of having her space violated by the vile message on her machine—to the calm island of common sense. "But the police can't do anything, and neither can I. All I have is a nasty message on my machine. It could be from a kid and I'm reading into it what's just not there."

"The police might have similar incidents that they could link with this one."

"It's unlikely. I'd have heard."

"Maybe they're not confined to Frye's Cove."

She stared at him. "Clate, do you really believe these calls are a coincidence? That they have nothing to do with you, me, Hannah, or eighty-year-old Russian treasure?"

His expression didn't change. "No."

Her energy was flagging. "Somehow, I figure the police'll just end up pinning everything on Hannah."

Clate watched her with narrowed eyes, his gaze unyielding. "Are you afraid they'll be right?"

"No, I'm afraid of what everyone in Frye's Cove, from Ernie at the police station to my father and brothers, will say when they find out Hannah's talked me into digging for buried treasure. They'll think I'm crazy and she's crazier."

"But the calls are real, Piper."

"I know they are."

"If Hannah didn't place them—"

"She didn't."

"Then she has nothing to worry about. And neither do you."

"You don't know Ernie," she said lightly, as if being

flip could help her make sense of what, ultimately, made no sense. She should call the police. Something in her tale of threatening calls might lead them to the culprit. But it was too slim a hope for her to risk having Hannah's deepest, most private yearnings splashed across the front page of the local newspaper.

Clate reached into her basket. Some of the hardness had gone from his expression. He seemed less stiff, less tightly controlled. His hands were bigger, more tanned, more scarred than hers. But as he pulled out a palmful of peas and started snapping off their ends, opening them up, releasing their contents into the colander, Piper noticed that his movements were sure, experienced. He worked automatically, without thinking, without awkwardness. It wasn't that it was a tough job. It wasn't that she didn't expect him, or any man, not to know how to shell peas. It was that he did it as if he'd been doing it since he was a kid, as she had. Maybe they weren't as different as she thought.

"Someone was out digging on my property last night," he said without preamble. "It wasn't you, was it?"

She watched his thumb run across the bumpy shell of an overripe pea, felt a flutter of awareness. "No," she managed. "It wasn't."

"I checked with Tuck in case I'd missed something he'd done. It wasn't him. It could have been animals, but I don't think so." He heaped his empty pods into a neat pile. "I can't imagine it was your aunt."

"Neither can I. I mean, she gets around well for her age, and she certainly knows your property—"

"And she's getting impatient with you."

"True."

"Could she have found someone else to do her digging for her?"

He was like a hound on a trail. Focused, relentless. Suddenly Piper imagined going to bed with such a man, having all that drive and concentrated energy centered on making love.

She wriggled on her bench, shook off the image. What

was the matter with her? They were discussing threatening phone calls, mysterious signs of digging, and here she was, thinking about sex. It was a defense mechanism, she rationalized. Perfectly normal.

"Piper?"

"No—no, not a chance. I saw her today. She'd have told me if she'd given up on me, I can assure you. Instead, she strengthened her case." She swung her legs up over the bench and got to her feet. "Come on, I'll show you."

She led him through her keeping room back to her front parlor, where, under the watchful eye of her brothers, she was in the midst of sanding layers of paint from the original wainscoting.

Clate remained standing while she sat on a sheet-covered loveseat. She gestured to an ancient shoebox she'd laid atop a stack of magazines on her battered butler's table. It was so old the cardboard had softened and yellowed and the sides were splitting apart, held together only by a series of brown, brittle rubber bands. "Hannah gave me that today."

"What's inside?"

"Letters from her father and brother during World War One." She brushed a hand ineffectually through her hair. "At least that's what she told me."

"You haven't looked?"

"No, not yet." She smiled weakly. "I picked peas instead."

He seemed unsurprised. "You're afraid of what you might find."

She shook her head. "Not that. I'm just—I don't know if I can explain. I feel as if I'm a voyeur of sorts, peering into a private, personal part of Hannah's life. The lives of my grandfather and great-grandfather." She paused, her pulse quickening as she took in his muscular frame, that tousled dark hair, that constant alertness. "It's a strange feeling. These people are family. It's not like reading a letter from Woodrow Wilson."

"That's the whole point, isn't it? A letter from Woodrow Wilson wouldn't help you figure out what really happened eighty years ago."

She rubbed the tips of her fingers over the brittle ripples of old rubber bands. They'd dissolve or break apart on their own before long. "I suppose. Hannah said I should open the box, read what's inside, study, imagine. She thinks this will make that night when she was seven real to me. But it feels real enough right now. I don't know if I want what she must have suffered to feel any more real. She was just a little kid."

"And her memory of events could be skewed by her age. Seven then, eighty-seven now. The letters might help clear up whether her story of her father rescuing a Russian princess was something he told her because it was true, something he told her as a sort of fairy tale, or something she just made up to help her survive the trauma of losing her parents."

Piper nodded. "I know. I'll read them."

He relaxed his stance. "If you need an objective perspective on anything, you know where to find me."

She watched him head back to her kitchen under the low ceiling of her tiny, antique house. She didn't move from her position on the loveseat. He would go. She would read the contents of Hannah's shoebox. Alone. Maybe before she cooked up her peas, maybe after.

"Wait."

He glanced back at her from the doorway, his eyes lost in the shadows.

"I'm steaming the peas, and I've a little grilled chicken in the fridge and some of my dill-oat bread. Would you care to stay for dinner?" She jumped to her feet. "There is one more thing I should tell you."

"I'd love to stay for dinner, even if you don't have one more thing to tell me."

"It's a doozie."

A twitch of a smile. "Of course it is."

Clate watched Piper slather on bug repellent— another Hannah Frye special, apparently—just outside the back door off her kitchen. They were headed outside for a walk on the beach. He observed her with a strangled feeling, aware of every move of her fingers and palms against her bare flesh as she rubbed on her goo. It smelled spicy and sweet, an ungodly cross between perfume and aftershave. He had declined her offer to try some. He'd take his chances with the mosquitoes.

"Poisons can enter through the skin, you know," he told her.

She shrugged, matter-of-fact. "Only the right poisons, none of which are in this particular preparation since it's meant to be applied to the skin."

"You're sure?"

She lifted her mane of hair with one hand and, with the other, dabbed the goo on the back of her neck, oblivious to the effect she was having on him. "Hannah's very good at bug repellents."

Clate made no reply. He was reserving judgment on Hannah Frye's skills as an herbalist. After Piper's tale of Stan Carlucci and the tincture of bistort and agrimony— her doozie—he wasn't even convinced that her intentions were all as sweet and innocent as her niece wanted to believe. Misapplied, her knowledge of plants could be dangerous, even lethal.

Over dinner, he'd learned that a tincture was a mixture of herbs and alcohol—brandy or vodka, not rubbing alcohol—that sat for two weeks or so, with a daily shaking, and then was strained and stored in a dark bottle, just like the one Stan Carlucci had found on his doorstep.

It was straightforward herbal medicine, Piper claimed, and didn't mean Hannah was a menace or thought she was Matilda the Witch.

Clate wasn't so sure.

He'd also learned that Piper Macintosh had eclectic tastes in music and books, had done much of the work on her house herself, was a die-hard Red Sox and Bruins fan, didn't like basketball, and had a keen appreciation for the fragility of the environment in which she lived.

She also worked hard, teaching, consulting, crafting. Her idea of a vacation was a long weekend skiing in Vermont. During the summer, she found no reason to leave Cape Cod, except for the occasional trip to Fenway Park.

She had never ventured south of the Mason-Dixon Line. She failed to convince him that her three trips to Florida, one to Disney with her nephews, counted.

He found himself wondering about her dreams. He sensed in her a desire for adventure and excitement, for challenge. Maybe it was projection. He would find her day-to-day routines stifling after a while. When he tried to push her on her future goals, on what she wanted from her work, her life, she frowned at him and declared, "I have no desire to be Martha Stewart. I'm happy with my life the way it is."

She left her bottle of goo just inside the back door, and they headed across her yard. The air was still and warm, and shorebirds swooped and wheeled, hunting food at dusk. They took the path through the marsh, walking in silence, until Piper grabbed his wrist, stopping him short. She leaned toward him as she pointed out over a stand of dwarf red oak, whispering, "There—a roseate tern."

He would have to learn his Cape Cod birds. He noted a streaking bird and assumed he'd seen his first roseate tern.

"They're endangered," she said.

They continued down to the strip of narrow, isolated beach, unsuitable for beachgoers because of the encroaching marsh, the tufts of beach grass, the wildlife that didn't distinguish the boundaries of their nearby refuge. Ducks, gulls, terns, songbirds, deer, fox, all used the area. Piper moved with the casual assurance of a woman who'd lived her entire life amidst dunes, marshes, tide pools, and the pounding surf. She'd tossed a deep red cotton twill shirt on over her T-shirt and shorts, trim legs moving gracefully, feet digging into the shifting sand.

She walked out onto the hard, damp, packed sand

where the tide hadn't come back in and kicked off her sandals, scooping them up and hooking them on one finger as she let the water seep over the tops of her feet. She yelped, laughing. "It's so cold!"

Clate eased in behind her. "Then get out."

"Oh, I'll get used to it." She plunged in up to her knees, shuddered at the cold, and ran back out again. She gave him an evil grin. "It feels good. Really. You should try it."

"I might in a bit."

A huge swell caught her by surprise, nearly knocking her off her feet. Water swirled up to the hem of her shorts. She gave a soft moan and a shiver that derived more from pleasure than pain. A sharp, hot jolt of awareness nearly had him tumbling into the water with her. He shifted his stance, but it did no good. His throat ached, his breathing was ragged, and an arrow of fire shot straight through his loins.

Piper took no notice. "Take your shoes off and get yourself anointed as a real Cape Codder."

"Now why would I want to do that?"

"Chicken?"

She had the devil in her eye, did Piper Macintosh. She'd lived a life surrounded by people who'd loved and protected her, hadn't had to face the kind of deprivation and hardship he had as a child. Physical and emotional neglect, the helplessness and unspeakable pain of watching two young, vibrant people he loved slowly destroy themselves. An old woman had saved him, had helped him learn from his parents' mistakes or not, shown him that he had choices. But in the process, he'd come to believe that warm, nurturing families were a myth. He expected a dark side to Piper's relationship to her family and community. She wouldn't even think to look for one.

Her teeth were chattering, her lips purple, but she splashed out to catch the next wave. She hooted and hollered and whooped, as if there were no ancient box of letters waiting to be read, as if townspeople weren't worried her beloved aunt was a nut, as if she'd never received a single nasty phone call. She'd played him the message left on her machine. There was no mistaking its intent to unsettle, unnerve, make her feel exposed and vulnerable in her own home.

This was her answer, he thought.

She was out deep enough that the next powerful swell soaked her up to the waist, and the thought of the cold salt water coursing over her hips and thighs, swirling between her legs, was almost more than Clate could stand.

"You're missing a real treat," she called, teasing him, no idea how he was twisting her words to suit his tortured state. Her twill shirt had slipped off her shoulders and was halfway down her upper arms, its hem skimming the water. The cold had her nipples pebbled against the fabric of her T-shirt. "There's nothing like a nice, cold dip in the bay after a long day."

He didn't move. He knew if he did, there'd be no telling what he'd do.

She splashed water ineffectually in his direction, missing him by yards. It was just to make her point. "Of course, if you're chicken . . ."

And there was a gleam in her eyes—he finally saw it—that told him she knew damned well what would happen if she succeeded in goading him into the water.

"Piper—"

"It's not that cold, even for a Southerner."

That did it. He raced in after her, the water shockingly cold against his overheated skin. He caught her around the middle, and at her howl of laughter, acquainted the rest of her with Cape Cod Bay.

Only she had experience with this sort of thing. She had older brothers, nephews, friends who'd grown up on the water, and she knew where, and how, to place a strategic kick that would buckle him at the knees. He went down and under, and when he popped up, spitting salt water, freezing vital parts solid, she was practically doubled over with laughter.

"Proud of yourself, are you?"

She tossed her head, virtually every strand of chestnut hair still dry. "Next time don't underestimate me."

"Damned straight I won't."

Being of an arrogant Yankee nature, she proceeded under the assumption that next time wouldn't be within the next ten seconds. Which was to underestimate him.

As much as he wanted to get out of the icy water, he swooped in on her, caught her low, and dragged her into the bay with him.

"Uh-uh, no, you don't," she yelled and hooked her legs around him, determined that he should go wherever he meant her to go.

He could have pried her loose and dunked her good and proper in a dozen different ways, but instead he went down with her, into the next swell, knowing they'd end up a tangle of arms and legs on the sand.

"Oh, hell," he murmured, breathless, as he stared down into the dark green of her mercurial eyes.

His mouth covered hers. He tasted salt, the cold of her lips contrasting with the heat of her tongue as she greedily plundered, flicked, explored. They were both soaked to the bone, chilled, shivering, and the breeze off the water only made them colder, but as their kiss deepened and their pulses raced, he knew the cold wouldn't stop them.

He felt her body—soft breasts, firm stomach and thighs—beneath him, felt the smooth silk of her legs. She smelled of sand and sea, her crazy aunt's bug repellent washed off in the bay.

"You know I want you," he said in a ragged drawl, "don't you?"

She smiled, trailed fingers up his thigh. "I'd say that's evident."

"Here, now."

"Yes."

His mouth found hers again, his body pressing hard into hers, as if there were no clothes between them. He kissed her throat, tasted salt as he descended lower. She arched under him, and he could sense her urgency even as his own threatened to explode beyond his control. His hands skimmed her breasts. With her wet clothes, she might have been naked.

But he gritted his teeth, sucked in a breath, and rolled off her, sand clinging to his feet, his legs, his rear end. He raked a hand through his wet hair. "Hell."

She sat up, reaching back to lift her twill shirt and give it a shake. "Common sense intrudes, does it?"

He glanced at her, saw her weak smile, her breathlessness. "Making love out here on the sand, in daylight."

She screwed up her face. "Blame those long June days. Yeah, there are too many people out on the water I might know. It'd get around town fast—Piper Macintosh and that rogue Tennessean out here on the beach." She glanced at her watch. "And besides, my brothers will be here any minute."

"Nice timing."

"Nothing new there. But they can't see us from the house."

"Good. Then they won't shoot."

She climbed to her feet, dusting off sand as best she could. "I don't keep a gun in the house."

The cold wind froze his clothes to him. "I didn't want this to happen."

"Oh, really? That's a hell of a compliment." There was little outrage in her tone; she was amused, disbelieving. "Maybe I will sic my brothers on you."

"You know what I meant. I didn't come up north with the intention of having a mad affair with my next-door neighbor."

She grinned at him and scooped up her sandals. "I figured that from the No Trespassing signs."

He got stiffly to his feet, nowhere near as matter-of-fact about freezing his ass off as Piper seemed to be. Damned Cape Codders. She'd already started up the path through the marsh. "I'll go on back to my house and get dry clothes on," he called to her. "Tell your brothers about Hannah's treasure, the tincture, the shoebox, the calls. Everything, Piper."

She stopped in her tracks, glanced back at him. "Or you will?"

"No. I'm just giving you unsolicited advice." Using his toes, he peeled off one shoe, then the other. He hadn't taken them off before chasing into the water after Piper. Now they were stiff and squishy with salt water and sand. "But I'd tell them."

"I don't know enough—"

"You know plenty." He snatched up his shoes and walked toward her in his bare feet, the sand a bit warmer away from the water. "You could be in danger, Piper. You don't know who's placing those calls, who dug in my yard last night."

"In danger? *Me?*" She scoffed, but he could see the spark of fear. "The only danger I'm in is of being annoyed and harassed to distraction. I've lived in this town most of my life, Clate. I know these people."

"So?"

She stared back at him. "I'm not as hard and cynical as you are."

"Maybe that's a good thing, maybe not. You don't have the perspective I do. You can't be objective."

"I'm not that naïve. Look, I know Hannah makes people mad. *I* make people mad. But that doesn't mean either of us is in any real danger."

Clate didn't relent. "Tell your brothers, Piper."

Ignoring him, she about-faced and continued up through the marsh. Clipped pace. A bit of a stomp to it. Hated getting advice, Piper Macintosh did.

But he wasn't finished. "One more thing."

She didn't turn around.

"There's no treasure under my wisteria." He emphasized the *my* just enough to get her back up.

It worked. She flew around, nearly sailing her sandals into the marsh. "Because you don't want there to be any treasure under *your* wisteria or because you know that for a fact?"

"Because I dug a damned three-foot hole and didn't find anything."

She grinned suddenly, devilishly, the orange glow of the sunset bringing out the red highlights in her hair. "Not so hard and cynical as you think, are you, Mr. Jackson?"

Sarcastic, enjoying herself. Clate resisted the temptation to dish her out some of her own medicine. "I'm going to get to the bottom of this thing, Piper. Whatever's at the bottom, I'm going to get to it." He went ahead and made himself sound hard and cynical. He meant what he was saying. "Be ready."

Andrew stood at Piper's back door. "Was that Clate Jackson?"

He and Benjamin, who'd started across the yard to meet her, were both frowning, adding to her self-consciousness. She had sand between her toes, in her hair, all over her wet clothes. "Yes, it was." She kept her tone matter-of-fact as she dropped her sandals on the stone terrace and dragged out the hose. "He saw me down on the beach and came over to say hello. I'm still not used to having a mobile neighbor. Hannah seldom made it that far."

Andrew muttered a *bullshit* under his breath, but Benjamin, being the slightly more diplomatic of the two, touched his younger brother's arm. It wasn't above either of them, Piper knew, to have already examined her sink strainer for signs she hadn't dined alone. Clate Jackson had them on high alert. Well, her, too.

"We're not sure we trust that guy," Benjamin said.

"No kidding." Just enough sarcasm to assert her ability to handle the situation. She turned on the water spigot and hosed down her sandals, glancing behind her at her brothers. Neither was moving. "Something up? Why the family powwow?"

"You know why," Andrew said with a snarl. If he'd arrived with any patience, it had exhausted itself by now. Clate was the sort of out-of-towner that rubbed Andrew the wrong way. Rich, secretive, using Frye's Cove as his personal refuge. Andrew welcomed newcomers provided they made an attempt to be a part of the community, didn't treat it as a fantasy but a real place populated by real people.

But suddenly Piper sensed he and Benjamin hadn't come about her neighbor. She turned off the hose, switched off the spigot, and tried to ignore a sense of dread. "You're here about Hannah."

"She's got to stop," Andrew said darkly.

Benjamin's expression softened. "We don't want her to hurt herself or anyone else. She's a sweet woman. We know that."

"But she can't go around thinking she's conjuring up men for you," Andrew said, "and she's got to leave Stan Carlucci alone. Jesus, Piper. Agrimony and—what the hell was it?"

"Bistort," she said. "It's a common tincture."

Andrew fisted his big hands. "It's *harassment!*"

"There's no proof."

"This isn't a goddamned court of law, Piper. We don't care about proof. We care about stopping Hannah before she lands her little old fanny in jail or somebody else in the hospital."

Benjamin picked up Piper's abandoned hose and wound it into a neat pile, never one to stand a mess. "We're worried about her, kid."

She nodded. "So am I. Who told you about the tincture?"

"We dragged it out of Paul Shepherd," Benjamin said.

If possible, Andrew's frown deepened. "Guess we can't rely on our own sister to tell us what the hell's going on."

"Hannah's our aunt, too, Piper." Benjamin moved from the hose back next to his brother. "We care about

144

what happens to her. No need for you to handle this thing alone."

"Paul and Stan spoke to me in confidence."

Andrew snorted in disgust. "And you can't talk to us in confidence?"

"Well, I—" She sighed. "I just wasn't sure what to do. I did talk to her, and she denies she left the tincture for Carlucci."

"You believe her?" Benjamin asked.

"Yes, I do. That's not because I'm taking her side, either. She's just so open about her herbal remedies, so committed to their safe use, it doesn't make sense that she'd be so sneaky. If she thought tincture of bistort and agrimony would help Stan, she'd hand him a bottle and give him a lengthy lecture on how to use it and why he needs it." Piper threw up her hands in frustration, letting them drop to her wet, sandy sides. "Come on, guys. You know that's what she'd do."

"Unless she's slipping," Andrew said, and for an instant, Piper could see that the prospect of their great-aunt, a steady presence in all their lives, losing it bothered him.

"Stan could have made up the incident just to save face by making Hannah look worse. Or someone else in town decided to capitalize on the tea story and get his goat."

"A copycat poisoning? I doubt it, Piper."

"It wasn't a poisoning in either case. Hannah's tea didn't agree with Stan."

"I'm not going to argue with you," Andrew snarled.

Benjamin gestured at his sister, taking in her disheveled state. "You should go in and change before you freeze to death."

"Why'd you go swimming in your clothes?" Andrew demanded, his tone suggesting it was just the sort of thing his moronic little sister would do. Then his eyebrows drew together. "Jesus. You and Jackson jump into the bay together?"

"No, we did not jump into the bay together, not that it's any of your damned business." She launched herself to her back door. *Tell your brothers, Piper.* Yeah, right. "I'm going in. You two done?"

Benjamin glanced uncomfortably at Andrew. "You want me to tell her?"

"Go ahead."

Benjamin breathed out, shifting back to his sister. "Clate Jackson or someone from his company has been making discreet inquiries into land development on this part of the Cape."

The flush of embarrassment she'd felt a moment ago cooled to ice. "What? How do you know?"

"We hear things," Andrew said before Benjamin could give her a better answer. Payback time for Piper holding out on them. But his expression softened. "Look, it's on good authority, but I don't know if any of it's true. It just seems to me this guy's got a different agenda from yours, that's all. We just wanted to give you a heads-up."

Too late, she thought, remembering the feel of Clate's hard body on hers in the wet sand, the aching need to touch, taste, explore every inch of him, remembering his interest in her, who she was, how she lived, what she wanted out of life, over dinner. No wonder her brothers were warning her. She was out of her mind.

She gave them a faltering smile. "Thanks. I guess I'd do the same for you."

Andrew smiled. "Damned straight you would."

"You go on and get cleaned up," Benjamin said. "Andrew and I will drop in on Hannah tomorrow, see what she says, and draw our own conclusions." At Piper's start, he added, "Don't worry, we'll be subtle. Liddy's going to stop by tomorrow with the boys, too. Maybe we haven't been paying enough attention to her lately."

Piper gave him a noncommittal smile. "Hannah always enjoys seeing Liddy and the boys—and you and Andrew, of course. Pop going with you?"

"We haven't told him all this yet," Andrew said. He

was still leaning back on his heels, studying her suspiciously. "Piper, does Hannah have you on some other mission since the valerian root?"

She hated lying, but she couldn't tell them the truth. She'd promised Hannah her discretion, and if they doubted their aunt on the tincture of bistort and agrimony, her brothers would never believe her on buried Russian treasure. "I'm taking the Fifth."

Andrew swore under his breath.

"She doesn't need to get into any more trouble, Piper," Benjamin said, "and neither do you. Remember that, okay? Now, go get cleaned up. We'll talk tomorrow."

If she played the tape from her message machine for them, they'd talk right now. They'd never leave. They'd call their father, have a Macintosh-male powwow, decide her next moves from then on, until they had everything sewn up and resolved. Clate might not know how her brothers worked, but she did.

"Sure. Tomorrow." She pasted a phony smile on her face. "Thanks for stopping by. I really think we need to be careful of making mountains of molehills."

"Or vice versa," Andrew muttered.

"You need us," Benjamin said, "we'll be there."

That much, Piper knew, and always had known. Which didn't make life with her two big brothers any easier.

Chapter

10

Thunderstorms were moving in over Cape Cod. The air was muggy by northern standards, and Piper Macintosh was pedaling toward town like the proverbial bat out of hell. Clate slowed down alongside her. She gave him a scathing look from under her helmet and kept pedaling.

Embarrassed about last night on the beach?

No. Pissed about something. He expected it had to do with her brothers and what they tended to believe about him, what *she* should believe, maybe even wanted to believe. Falling for him had to give her pause. If she could just dismiss him, maybe next time the opportunity arose, she would resist tumbling around in the bay with him.

Clate understood how she must feel. He'd stared at his dark ceiling for much of the night, warning himself not to get involved with a woman whose life and ambitions were as different from his as Piper Macintosh's were.

She must have realized he'd ride alongside her all the way to town if he had to, because she stopped, rolled off her seat, and shot him a fierce look. Definitely pissed.

Nothing embarrassed about her. She had on an over-sized polo shirt that was probably about ten years old and those strategically cushioned bike shorts that always looked hot and uncomfortable to him.

His passenger window whined down. He peered over at her, resisted a grin. "You look like the Wicked Witch of the West on that bicycle."

"That was Miss Gulch."

He shrugged. "Same difference."

She straddled her bike, and he could see the sweat trickling down her temples, the humidity tough even on the water. She flipped her braid up and let it fall, as if to give her neck some air. Her breasts looked smooshed together under an exercise bra. Even so, a quick arrow of awareness found its mark.

"You want to develop Hannah's land," she told him.

He made sure he displayed no visible reaction. Whatever he did she would misinterpret. She was in that kind of mood. "What makes you think that?"

"I have my sources." She gave an airy toss of her head, which, between the helmet, the braid, and the sweat, she didn't quite pull off. She looked more troubled and irritated than disdainful. "All this stuff about privacy and just wanting to be left alone is just garbage, isn't it? It's a tactic to keep people from poking around in your business. You don't want to get to know anyone in Frye's Cove before you betray them."

She kept her tone cold and distant, but he could see that she was close to crying. She'd told him everything last night. She'd kissed him. She'd nearly made love to him in the sand. Now she was worried her brothers were right and she really was a fool when it came to men, that there wasn't one of them to be trusted.

Of course, her brothers were right.

"Your brothers," Clate said. "They heard a rumor."

"Does it matter who heard what?"

"Piper—"

Her eyes leveled on him. "Obviously I can't trust you."

"I never said you could."

She jumped back onto her bicycle, found the pedals, and launched herself back down the road.

He followed. She ignored him. He cursed under his breath, but loud enough for her to hear through the open passenger window. She ignored that, too.

Finally, he screeched ahead of her, stopped his car, and climbed out. He walked around to the trunk and leaned against it, one heel up on the bumper. She pedaled pell-mell toward him. She had several choices, none of them good. She could turn around and head home, in which case he would follow her back and they could continue their argument in her front yard. She could go around his car and continue on her way, in which case he would follow her all the way to town and they could continue their argument in front of the Macintosh Inn or somewhere equally public.

Or she could run him right up onto the roof of his car, in which case he could have her butt arrested.

She was still cooking along at top speed three yards in front of him. Daring her, he crossed his arms on his chest and didn't move.

For two cents she'd have rammed a nice tire mark up one of his legs. He could see it in her eyes.

But she stopped six inches from his toes.

"See?" He grinned at her. "I trust you."

"That had nothing to do with trust. That was pure arrogance. You made up your mind I wouldn't run you over, and you weren't going to give me the satisfaction of second-guessing yourself."

"Actually, I figured you would run me over, but if I moved, you'd plow into the back end of my car and hurt yourself."

She glared at him in disbelief. "So you were protecting me from myself?"

"We should all be lucky enough to have someone to protect us from our own worst instincts."

That only incensed her more. She leaped off her bicycle and probably would have thrown it at him if she didn't half believe he'd catch it with one hand and hurl it back. They were having that kind of fight, he thought. It was hellishly exhilarating.

"Damn it, I should have run you over!"

"No doubt."

"You arrogant S.O.B. You lying, conniving—"

"Don't forget untrustworthy."

"I haven't forgotten anything."

He dropped his foot to the road and moved toward her, and he skimmed a finger along her throat. "Nothing, eh?"

She licked her lips. "You're trying to distract me from my anger."

He grinned. "Damned right."

"If you were in my position, you'd be angry, too."

"Pissed as hell, probably. If what you heard were true."

"Isn't it?"

He shook his head.

"Why should I believe you?"

Using both hands, he straightened her helmet. "You shouldn't."

Without another word of explanation, he walked back to the front of his car, climbed in behind the wheel, and drove off, leaving her cursing in his dust. Next time, she could damned well ask him if a rumor she'd heard was true, before she jumped to conclusions and made accusations.

Except it was a hell of a lot easier to believe he was—what had she called him? A rogue, a cad, an arrogant S.O.B. Yeah. If he was a rotten bastard, it took her off the hook. It put her back on familiar ground. Piper Macintosh had crummy taste in men. Piper Macintosh couldn't trust herself to fall in love with someone who wouldn't lie to her. Piper Macintosh would end up like her eighty-seven-year-old aunt who'd married, briefly, late in life and had never had children.

Suddenly her face was in his window. He almost had a wreck. He pounded on his brake, and she came within inches of sideswiping him with her bike. He smashed the button to his automatic window, his heart pounding. "What the hell are you doing?"

"Catching up with you. I must have done a world-record sprint." Indeed, she was panting, sweating. "I wanted to tell you I'm off to Hannah's. Then later this afternoon I have an appointment in Chatham. Thought you'd want to know." She gulped in a breath. "In case you worried."

Because of the calls. Because somehow, deep down, she knew he'd passed an uneasy night, alert to every sound, every shadow. If a car had ventured down their dead-end road, he'd have pounced.

"Is this your way of apologizing?"

The muscles in her forearms tensed as she gripped the handlebars. "For what?"

"For believing rumors instead of checking with me first."

But in just a slight shift in her steady gaze, he saw that that wasn't it. The rumors about him wanting to develop his land on Cape Cod were just a convenient outlet for her volatile mood. Something else was wrong. "I've got to go," she said, sliding up onto her bicycle seat.

He kept his foot on the brake. "You went through Hannah's shoebox, didn't you?" His voice was quiet. He knew he'd landed on the real source of her dangerous mood, could imagine her sitting up late last night, poring over those decades-old letters.

She blinked back sudden tears, eased off the seat. "There was nothing—no smoking gun, no proof of treasure, no disproof. I don't even know for sure if my great-grandfather ever rescued a Russian princess. He talks about it in his letters." She swallowed, her eyes pinned straight ahead. "But it could just be a story he told her. He was so lonely, and he loved her so much. And my grandfather—his letters—" She swallowed. "He was so young when he found himself at war, then as sole guardian of his little sister."

"Maybe you can trace something through the dates of the letters."

"Maybe." She squeezed her eyes half-shut in an obvious effort to concentrate, to think beyond the emotions she'd felt as she'd gone through her aunt's ancient shoebox. "They don't say so outright, but you can tell neither my grandfather nor my great-grandfather expected to make it home alive. They were horrified by war. Fear, longing, a sense of duty, a love of home and family." She brushed back tears with her fingertips. "They permeate every line of every letter."

"If Hannah was just seven," Clate said, gently steering Piper back on course, "someone must have read their letters to her. Maybe her father's tale of rescuing this Russian princess wasn't so secret. Someone else could have known about it eighty years ago."

"And planned to rob him when he came home?"

"It's possible."

"They were off course. Nobody could have predicted that."

"Maybe they were drawn off course. Maybe this guy just took advantage of the moment, of coincidence, and lured your great-grandparents onto a sandbar, robbed them, and left them to their fate."

She swung around at him. "And then what? Passed down the information to the next generation? Anyone old enough to have lured my great-grandparents onto that sandbar would be a hundred by now, at the youngest. I can't imagine some hundred-year-old guy making those calls to me. Besides, I know all the hundred-year-old people on Cape Cod, and none's even remotely a possibility."

"All right. Fair enough."

But she was on a roll. "If someone else knows about the treasure, it's because Hannah let something slip. If it was some secret that's been lurking around Frye's Cove for eighty years, I assure you, we'd have known about it."

"You meaning you Macintoshes."

"Yes. And I've been thinking—"

She hesitated. A hot land breeze gusted. She'd never make it to Hannah's and back before thunder and lightning struck, something Clate decided he shouldn't point out lest she think he was trying to run her life or assuming she was incapable of getting out of the rain. But Piper Macintosh had a lot on her mind. That much was clear.

Finally, her eyes as deep and dark a green as the pitch pine around her, she turned to him and said, calmly, "The threatening phone calls could have to do with you, not me. They never mentioned the treasure. My latest mission for Hannah could just be a coincidence. Other people could have heard the same rumors I did about you and land development. Maybe someone's trying to discredit you, get me to blame you for the threatening calls."

"Set me up, you mean?"

She nodded, plainly not liking the thought of it either way: he was the guilty party or he was someone who'd been set up by a local.

She was getting attached to him. Clate could see that much. He could also see she wasn't sure she liked the thought of that, either. He could understand. He presented complications, rubbed rough against all that was comfortable and certain in her life. Easier not to get attached.

"I think it's far-fetched, Piper. I've got enemies, but—"

"I know. I'm probably grasping at straws." She squinted at him in the glare of clouds and hazy sunshine. "I just don't want any of this to touch Hannah."

"Understood."

"She's waiting for me. She was making scones this morning. One of the old ladies in the complex brought her a jar of homemade strawberry-mint jam, and she wants me to try it."

"You two," Clate said, grinning suddenly. Scones. Strawberry-mint jam. No, his life wasn't at all like Piper's. "Have a good time. I'll catch up with you later."

She seemed happier as she rode off. He, however, was feeling a tumultuous mix of emotions, all of which he rounded up, stuffed in a sack, and shut up tight. He needed to keep his wits about him, and letting his emotions run wild would undermine that effort. Lust, dread, anger, exhilaration, confusion, and an undeniable rush of unexpected grief for a life he'd never led, for an old woman he missed, in his own way, perhaps as much as Piper would miss her great-aunt Hannah when she was gone.

And she wasn't ready, any more than he had been. The prospect of that loss—the certainty of it—was what scared Piper Macintosh most.

Hannah guessed what was up the moment Piper walked through the door. "Clate Jackson has insinuated himself into your consciousness, hasn't he?"

Piper scowled. "Not in the way you think."

Her aunt smiled knowingly. "*Exactly* in the way I think."

As tempted as she was to argue her case about a man who would sit on a car bumper and just dare her to bounce him into the next county, Piper resisted. She'd only egg Hannah on. She was sitting at her computer, her color printer feeding out a bright page. One of her family recipes. She was doing them up for Piper to pass down to subsequent generations.

"Have Andrew and Benjamin been out to see you today?" Piper asked, changing the subject.

"The posse." Hannah clucked, climbing to her feet. "They stopped by this morning before work. We had tea."

"They drank your tea?"

"They insisted on inspecting the bags first."

"You have tea bags? How come you never serve me regular tea?"

"You have a more adventurous spirit. I was tempted to add a drop of a new decoction into their cups, but I decided that would be improper, although it certainly would have improved Andrew's mood. He's getting ornery."

Piper laughed. "He's always been ornery. It's just that he's directing it at you for a change."

"Well, he can undirect it. They both kept looking at me to see if I really had gone daffy. I finally got out my broom and pretended I thought I was flying around the room. I even cackled. Andrew was all for calling in the white coats, but Benjamin knew I was just trying to get their goat."

"Oh, Hannah." Piper bit back a laugh, imagining her brothers' outrage when their aunt didn't take their concerns seriously. "Did they believe you didn't leave Stan Carlucci that tincture?"

She waved a hand. "I have no idea and I don't care. Stan can have me arrested as a menace if he has the evidence."

"He doesn't."

"Of course he doesn't. I didn't leave him that tincture."

The doorbell rang, and Piper got it automatically, leaving Hannah to close out her desktop publishing program.

Sally Shepherd smiled from the threshold. "Piper, good morning. I thought that was your bike out front. May I see Hannah a moment? If I'm not interrupting—"

"You're not interrupting. Come on in."

Sally mumbled a thank-you. She struck Piper as even more reserved and formal than usual, her tendency when under stress. Although they weren't really friends, they'd known each other forever; Sally was a part of Frye's Cove because of her grandfather, Jason Frye, and her frequent visits to the Frye house. When feeling squeezed, Sally always fell back on good manners, something Piper couldn't say for herself—her behavior with Clate that morning a case in point.

She did have enough manners to offer to absent herself while Sally and Hannah talked, but Sally shook her head. "No, stay, Piper. I have nothing to say that you can't hear." Her smile faltered, and she twisted her unmanicured hands together. "Hannah, I've heard about the tincture Stan Carlucci found, and I wanted to let you know that I spoke up in your favor. Paul, of course, is keeping an open mind, but I know you'd never deliberately poison or harass anyone."

"Thank you, Sally. I appreciate your confidence in me."

"It's not that Paul lacks confidence—"

"You don't have to explain. I understand. He's trying to remain neutral."

"Yes." She looked relieved. "That's it."

Hannah smiled wryly. "Perhaps someone else in town is concerned with Mr. Carlucci's digestion."

"Or he made up the whole thing because he doesn't like you," Piper muttered.

"I don't think Stan's that devious or clever," Sally said, then blushed at her own impolitic words. "Not that I'm judging him. He's been so supportive of the inn and our move to Frye's Cove."

"I do give him credit for that," Hannah said.

Sally smiled, visibly relaxing. She'd always had a cordial, but not a close, relationship with her grandfather's second wife; she didn't understand Hannah the way Piper did. "I just wanted you to know, Hannah, that I—that Paul and I wish you nothing but the best."

"You're both very sweet," Hannah said. "Thank you for taking the time to stop by. How's the inn?"

They chatted for a few minutes, Sally becoming almost animated as she related the latest news on the Macintosh Inn. She and Paul were working on getting a piece on the inn and its colorful history—especially the Macintoshes—into one of the country living magazines. After his initial uncertainty about their move to Cape Cod, Paul was now fully committed. "He loves Frye's Cove," Sally said. "Not in the same way I do, of course. I feel as if . . . I don't know, as if I've finally come home."

After she left, Piper followed Hannah into the kitchen. "How come I don't get to be sweet?"

Hannah scoffed. "Because you're not. You're a heel dragger."

"Not anymore. Clate dug under the wisteria. He says there's no treasure."

"Do you believe him?"

To her surprise, Piper didn't hesitate. "Yes, I do. He's rich enough on his own not to care about your treasure, but that's not why I believe him."

"Some people can never have enough. But you're right. Money isn't what drives him. He wants to find a home, a place where he belongs, but he's looking in all the wrong places." A flash of mischief in her old eyes. "Until now, of course."

"He's not looking for anything but relaxation in Cape Cod. That's why I believe him. The sooner he finds the treasure or proves it doesn't exist, the sooner he can get back behind his No Trespassing signs and stay there."

Hannah shook her head. "That's what you want to believe because it's less scary for you. No," she went on, checking a pot on her stove, "the reason you believe him is because your soul, the very essence of who you are, knows he's telling you the truth."

"Hannah, are you going to start talking about my destiny again?"

"No. There's no need. Your destiny was determined the moment Clate Jackson bought the Frye house." She inhaled her pot of a whitish, creamy substance. "This is an infusion of chamomile flowers and milk. Lovely, isn't it? It's wonderful for the skin and so relaxing. It needs to sit for a little while longer, but I'll give you a jar when it's ready."

"That'd be nice." She peered over Hannah's shoulder into her double boiler. "I'd like to learn enough about herbal creams and lotions to teach a class next summer."

Hannah beamed. "I'd be delighted to teach you." Without glancing around or giving any indication she was changing the subject, she said, "Stan Carlucci's suspicions about me and these phone calls you've been receiving have upset you. I'm sorry I called you a heel dragger. I wonder if it might not be wise to hold off on the treasure search for now."

"What?" Piper was instantly suspicious. "Why the sudden change of heart?"

Hannah stirred her chamomile-and-milk concoction, then retreated to her little kitchen table, suddenly looking even older than eighty-seven, no mean feat. "I can't let my urgency about the past hurt you now, in the present. That would be wrong."

"Are *you* worried about these calls?"

"Yes. Yes, Piper, I am."

Piper was silent.

Her aunt appraised her, eyes clear, determined to see what they had to see, kerchief in place over her snow-white hair. "Why, Piper Macintosh. Shame on you. You thought I might have placed those calls."

"No!"

"Then explain."

Hannah had always had a disturbing ability to read her only niece. Piper paced in the small, attractive kitchen. "I just worried someone else might think you'd placed them."

"Since when would I care what anyone thinks?"

That was part of the problem. Hannah *didn't* care. "Hannah, I just worry about you. That's all. You know everyone in town's talking about how you think you've lured Clate Jackson north for me. It wouldn't be a big leap for people to start wondering if you're so committed to the two of us falling for each other that you might stoop to—"

"To terrorizing you as a way of forcing you and Clate together?"

Piper nodded, wincing.

Hannah sputtered and huffed, outraged. "Well, I never."

"I've never doubted you, Hannah. It's just that everyone knows how you hate to be wrong."

"I'm not wrong."

Piper smiled. "I rest my case."

But her aunt sprang to her feet, her energy renewed, and dragged Piper back to the living room, where she proceeded to call up onto her monitor a map she'd completed of the grounds around Frye House. "It's rough, I know, but I think it provides a good framework for our plan, when we decide it's safe to dig again."

"Perhaps I should wait until the calls die down. Unless . . ." Piper tried to resist the crazy thought that popped into her head. Hannah's influence. But she continued, "Unless someone else really does know about the treasure and is trying to dissuade me from looking for it. In which case I should try to beat him to it."

Hannah looked up at her. "I don't want you putting yourself in harm's way."

Clate's way, yes. Piper patted her aunt's bony shoulder. "I won't. I really don't think this guy's going to get violent or anything. I think he's just trying to intimidate me."

"You're sure it's a man?"

"I suppose it could be a woman. It doesn't matter. I won't be intimidated."

For the next twenty minutes, they examined, discussed, plotted, suggested, and rejected ideas, never mentioning Clate's No Trespassing signs. When they finished, they had a game plan that neither knew exactly when or if they'd implement.

Before Piper could leave, she had to wait for Hannah to retrieve a little glass pot of her chamomile cleansing milk. "Refrigerate it," she said, returning from the kitchen. "I don't use preservatives."

"Thank you. I love chamomile." Piper cupped the still-warm pot in one hand. "Hannah, thank you for letting me read your letters. It was a privilege."

Her expression softened, her eyes warming, a touch of the seven-year-old she'd once been. "Your grandfather and great-grandfather were good men, Piper. Not perfect, but good. I'd intended you to have those letters after my death. I don't know why I felt the need to wait." In a rare demonstrative gesture, she reached out and squeezed her niece's hand. "My father and brother both would have been proud of you."

Thunder rumbled, too close for Piper's comfort considering she was on her bicycle. Hannah noticed, and smiled. "Relax, you can have Clate drive you home."

"Hannah, I'm not calling him—"

"You don't have to. He will be here momentarily."

"He's coming here? Why?"

"I don't know."

Her words were hardly out, when the doorbell rang.

"You saw him through the window," Piper accused.

Hannah simply shrugged.

"Well, put the maps of his yard away before I let him in."

Piper answered the door, and indeed it was Clate, standing with one rock-hard arm on the door frame and his eyes on her. Their hot words on the road hadn't changed a thing. If he had had her out on the beach right now, she'd do just what she had last night. More. Destiny be damned, the man was all wrong for her! She had to get a grip on her common sense and pull back before she did something she regretted, like really fall for him.

He smiled as if he could read her thoughts. "Fancy meeting you here."

"You have an appointment with Hannah?"

"No, ma'am. Just thought I'd stop by unannounced and talk to her about you."

"Don't say that too loud." Piper glanced back at her aunt, who'd shoved the printed out diagrams of his property in a desk drawer. "She'll take credit for summoning you."

His eyes sparkled with amusement. "Maybe she did."

Hannah joined them in the entry and decided to kick them both out. "I'm tired. I need my nap." Piper had never known her aunt to nap. "Can you come back later, Clate?"

He turned on his Southern charm. "Yes, ma'am."

"Piper here was just about to leave. I'm worried she'll get caught in a thunderstorm—"

"Hannah, if it gets bad out, I'll find cover. I've been riding my bike around town my whole life."

"She's very independent," Hannah told Clate, ignoring Piper completely. "She's had to be to keep from having her two brothers swallow her whole."

"Hannah."

"So, naturally, it pains her to accept help, and she's unusually sensitive to any hint that she might not be capable of managing something on her own."

Piper tightened her hands into fists. "Hannah, you're lucky I love you. You're lucky you're eighty-seven. I swear—"

She waved a hand in dismissal. "I only speak the truth."

Piper groaned, exasperated.

Clate laughed. "Mrs. Frye, if you're asking me to drive Piper home, I'd be happy to."

"My bike won't fit in your car."

"We can leave the trunk open." His voice was liquid sand; he was enjoying himself. "It's not that far to your house."

She opened her mouth to argue about taking her chances, but Hannah gave her a shove, putting all of her insubstantial weight into it. "Piper, for heaven's sake. Get in the man's car and go home."

"Or get struck by lightning," Clate muttered.

Piper made a face. "I've been plotted against."

"You've just come up against common sense," Hannah said, pushing her out the door. "Now run along. I'm falling asleep on my feet."

She wasn't. She was having a grand time. She waited on her doorstep until Piper's bike was safely crammed into Clate's trunk and she was sitting next to him in his front seat. "She doesn't look tired to me," Piper grumbled.

Clate started the engine, his casual attire in contrast with the plush interior of the car. "So far as I can see, you two deserve each other."

She waved stiffly to her aunt as he backed out. "She's going to go right back in there and work on her computer or watch 'Bewitched' reruns or stew up some herbs. She doesn't take naps."

"She's having fun."

"At my expense."

"Well, you've no business riding a bike in the middle of a thunderstorm."

Piper gave him a sideways look, noticed the way the muscles in his forearms worked as he drove. "The thunderstorm was just a convenient way to get me in this car with you."

He tossed her a sexy grin. "Worked."

"I'm still mad at you."

"No kidding. Well, I called my office. No one's admitting to asking anybody anything up here, but if anyone was considering it, they'll think again."

"Then you're saying you didn't put someone up to it?"

He sighed. "I've been saying that."

"And you didn't do it yourself?"

"You'd have heard if I had," he said dryly.

True, she would have. This was her town, not his, which, she reminded herself, was exactly the way he wanted it. "Then Andrew and Benjamin were wrong on this one. Or someone's pulling a fast one on you down in Nashville."

He gave a nearly imperceptible shake of the head. "That wouldn't happen."

"Oh, I see. I'm supposed to entertain every manner of far-fetched explanation for a handful of nasty phone calls, but you can't entertain the idea that someone who works for you has stepped over the line."

"Point well taken."

"But you still think you're right?"

"Yes."

Piper settled back in her seat, strangely comfortable. She appreciated his certainty. It meant he believed he hired good people, that he trusted them. In her view, trust was a positive sign of character. But she decided to change the subject. "I told Hannah you didn't find anything under the wisteria."

"She has new ideas about where to dig?"

Prioritized from one to forty-seven. Piper smiled. "She's a Macintosh. She always has a plan."

"According to what I've learned of your family's history," Clate said, "this isn't necessarily a good thing. Macintosh plans have a way of going awry."

"That's why we've learned to keep them to ourselves."

He glanced at her, the corners of his mouth twitching. "You must have been hell as a little sister. Luckily," he added, "I don't think of you that way."

Chapter

11

∽

Rain slashed the windshield, lightning flashed, and thunder rumbled, but so far as Clate could see, Piper still wished she'd ridden her bike home. "I'll get my bike. No need for you to get wet."

She slid out of the car into the pounding rain. Clate waited two seconds, then decided to hell with it and climbed out, basically ignoring the rain as he joined her at the trunk. She was wrestling with her bike, which had twisted around on itself and didn't exactly fit anyway. A determined woman. He eyed her clamped jaw, the tensed muscles in her arms, her soaked hair and shirt, and wondered why in hell he didn't just scoop her up and carry her inside.

Without asking, he grabbed hold of the handlebars and helped her pull the bike out of the trunk. "I can do it," she said.

"Just smile and say thank you."

She scowled at him, and he laughed. That defiant pride and independent streak were something they had in common, although they'd developed the qualities for different reasons. He because he was alone in the world, she because she wasn't.

"You're getting wet," she said.

"I'm from the South. Thunderstorms don't bother me."

"I'd like to see the South."

Lightning and thunder came together in a crash, the storm moving over their heads. The hard, steady rain dripped off her nose and her hair and made her skin seem paler. They were both drenched. "You'll have to come to Nashville. It's a good city. There's more to it than country-and-western music."

"Are you a fan?"

They were standing in the pounding rain, discussing Nashville. "Absolutely. I'm also a fan of the long, beautiful Nashville springs."

"Summers are hot."

"Hot and humid."

An unexpected flash of memory, Irma serving him fried apricot pies on a hot, still summer night when he'd refused to go home ever again. Thirteen years old and he'd had enough. He'd ended up walking home in a thunderstorm, bringing his mother one of Irma's pies, because Irma had taught him—had almost made him believe—that kindness was its own reward. His mother had cried, sobbing over her own inadequacies and dashed dreams.

"I have a place on the Cumberland, a couple of dogs." With one finger, he flicked rainwater off the end of Piper's nose, then skimmed along her cheek to her dripping hair. He kissed her lightly, softly, tasting the cool rain on her, on himself. "You'd better get inside before you get struck by lightning."

"Too late," she said under her breath, and kissed him hard, fiercely, before darting off into her house.

Reeling, Clate climbed back into his car. He could pour water out of his shoes. The air-conditioning gave him a much-needed chill. When he arrived home, the storm had abated, the rain already dying down to sprinkles, bringing out the smell of roses, honeysuckle, mint, wisteria, grass, pine pitch, seawater. The mix of scents swirled around him as he walked out back and stared out at the bay, choking back the sudden sense of isolation, of strangeness. He didn't belong here any more than he belonged anywhere else. With sheer will power and brute force, maybe he could carve out a place for himself, as he had in Nashville, when he'd arrived with nothing but a tent and a determination that nothing, *nothing,* would stop him.

No, Cape Cod wasn't home. He couldn't squash the urge to head out to the airport, climb in his plane, and get the hell off this elbow of shifting sand and knotted scrub trees and green-eyed, chestnut-haired women who made his blood boil. Put up a For Sale sign on his house and land. Let Hannah Frye conjure up some other poor bastard for her niece to love. Someone who did belong here. Someone who could love her in the way she deserved to be loved, who believed in family and community the way she believed in them.

"Mr. Jackson?"

He started, whipping around at Tuck O'Rourke. "Tuck. I didn't hear you."

"Sorry."

"No, it's okay. I was lost in thought." He got control of himself; he wasn't going anywhere, not today. "And call me Clate, will you?"

"Sure." Tuck scratched the back of his neck. He smelled like dirt and sweat, no problem for Clate, whose first jobs had been working with his hands. He had the scars to prove it—and to prove he'd learned the hard way to control his temper. Tuck cleared his throat. "I worked out here this morning, before the rain. You weren't around. Figured I should stop back and show you what I found."

He led Clate over to Hannah Frye's charming little garden of poisonous and medicinal plants and pointed to an area that looked like every other area. Clate saw no difference.

"That wasn't there last time I was here," Tuck said. "You do it?"

Upon closer inspection, Clate saw that about a dozen of the bushy plants had been cut back, almost to their roots. He glanced at their markers. Monkshood, foxglove, soapwort. The extravagant skull and crossbones on their markers indicated that misused, they could be deadly.

"No," Clate said. "I have no use for any of these plants, but I didn't bother cutting them down."

O'Rourke screwed up his face. "Wasn't animals. Piper?"

"It's possible."

"You know . . ." He breathed in, then out again, before continuing. "I'm not accusing anybody of anything, but I hope to hell Mrs. Frye didn't cut these plants or put Piper up to doing it."

"What are you saying?"

"I'm not saying anything. I'd just hate to see somebody end up poisoned."

Clate eased back, distanced himself from images of Hannah and her niece; he needed objectivity. "Be careful of what you're saying, Tuck. Giving a town selectman diarrhea's one thing—"

"I know, I know." Tuck flushed, rubbed his beard awkwardly. "I've got no business saying any of this without proof, and I'm not making any accusations. I hope I'm way off base. But Mrs. Frye's been acting weird lately, you know?"

"No, frankly, I don't. I've only recently met the woman. What is she normally like?"

He shrugged his big, beefy shoulders. "She's always been one to speak her mind, that's for sure. My father worked for Mr. Frye before he and Hannah got married, maybe a few months after. I'd come out with him sometimes, and she'd be out here fussing with the flower gardens. She wasn't in to herbs in those days. She really settled in here. Didn't take long for her to feel at home."

"She'd lived here for a time as a child, didn't she?"

"Oh, yeah. I forgot about that. The Fryes were taking care of her when her parents died in that shipwreck. Hell, that must have been awful. Maybe that's why she's getting goofy now, who knows? I mean, all that tragedy so young."

"I understand the shipwreck is one of the Cape's most celebrated mysteries, that her parents' ship was intentionally led onto a sandbar."

"That's what everyone says. It was—what, eighty years ago? Hannah's about the only one around here who'd even remember."

And Clate wasn't sure her memory was entirely accurate.

"Look," Tuck went on, "Mrs. Frye and I haven't always seen eye to eye on everything, but, hell, she's an old woman. I don't wish her any harm. But if she's planning to sprinkle a little monkshood on somebody's pizza . . ." His voice trailed off, and he appealed to Clate with a sheepish gesture; gossip embarrassed him. "You know what I'm saying?"

"I do indeed. Thanks for coming to me with this, Tuck. If you find anything else, let me know, okay? Meanwhile, I'll see what I can find out."

After Tuck left, Clate headed inside, changed into dry clothes, and poured himself a glass of iced tea. If there were ghosts in the Frye house, he could feel their presence, and he could imagine it if there weren't. Had Jason and Hannah Frye loved each other? Or had Jason Frye taken pity on her, remembering the little girl who'd waited in vain for her parents to come home? The man had been dead almost twenty years, Caleb and Phoebe Macintosh eighty. Whatever had happened, the past was past and there was no undoing it, only accepting it.

But Hannah Macintosh Frye wasn't after buried treasure because she couldn't accept her parents' deaths. She wanted to find out who'd lured them onto that sandbar, and why, and if her father really had been bringing home treasure to his family. She wanted answers to questions that had haunted her since the age of seven.

Again, Clate had the nagging feeling that she was holding back something, maybe nothing crucial by his standards, but something she didn't want, or couldn't bring herself, to speak about aloud.

Piper didn't have the objectivity to see that however well intentioned her elderly aunt might be, however she might justify her actions, Hannah Frye was manipulating her.

The telephone jerked him from his dark thoughts. It was his assistant in Nashville. "I've done some checking," Mabel Porter said. She still had the sounds of the Cumberland hills in her voice. "No one's saying they called up there and talked to anyone in Frye's Cove. It's become common knowledge, though, that you have a place in one of the last undeveloped areas of Cape Cod."

"So?"

"So, why did you buy it if not to develop it?"

A good question. He could have bought dozens of other properties on Cape Cod more suited to his personality and lifestyle. He didn't have to buy a crumbling eighteenth-century house on a tidal marsh. "It seemed like a good idea at the time." And that was the truth, he realized. He'd had no other rational, logical reason. No wonder people were confused. "Anything else?"

She hesitated.

"What is it, Mabel?"

"Your daddy called."

Only someone from the same, hardscrabble town would have said those words as matter-of-factly. Clate shut his eyes, fought the image of the man in the churchyard. "Any message?"

"He just said to tell you he'd called. He didn't leave a number."

He wouldn't. He wouldn't risk having Clate call back and tell him never to bother him again. "Thank you, Mabel."

Mabel started to say something, but stopped herself. She knew all about Clayton Jackson, Sr. His supposed recovery from alcoholism. His second marriage. His second family. A boy and a girl, half-siblings Clate had never met. Even Irma Bryar had stepped carefully around that one.

His father wanted his firstborn to forgive him, but Clate didn't know if he could, or whether it mattered if he did. Neither of them could relive the past. There was no undoing what was done.

After he hung up, Clate listened to the thunder rumble, even as the sun broke through the clouds. He could see his mother's grave. If she'd lived, would she have transformed her life? Would his father have been able, with Lucinda Jackson alive, to transform his?

For no reason that Clate could fathom, he thought of Hannah Frye. He wondered how he'd feel about his parents after eighty years. Would the rawness and regret and hatred—the love—have eased by then? His father would be long dead. There'd be no more calls, no more chances.

Clate drank more iced tea and pushed on into his musty library, listening to the thunder until it faded into the distance.

Piper reread the magazine article on Clate Jackson before heading off to her appointment in Chatham, a picturesque village on the east side of the Cape. A retired New Jersey optometrist had hired her to help him create an authentic early Cape Cod menu and decor for his new restaurant, beyond, as he put it, clam chowder and watercolors of lighthouses.

On the drive over, she speculated on the past Clate didn't talk about. He'd come to Nashville at sixteen. Sixteen! It had taken that second reading for it to sink in that he'd come without his parents, apparently without any family. As far as she was concerned, the reporter had dropped the ball on this one and should have dug up more on his childhood. But, then, maybe no one else cared.

Quoting from civic speeches, the article praised him for his vision and ability to balance Nashville's need for growth and livability, with an appreciation of its past and an eye toward its future. Clate Jackson was, by every measure, a concrete and logical thinker, a natural businessman who understood, on a gut level, the bottom line and the importance of focusing his energies.

Unlike Piper herself. She wasn't a natural businesswoman. She didn't do five-year plans. She didn't scope out the competition. She didn't do market research. She didn't even have a decent computer for her office, a secretary, a fax machine, or one of those multisectional, compact, specially designed appointment books. She wrote down all her appointments in a datebook featuring Audubon bird prints on the left-hand page, the days of the week on the right. She had a little drugstore spiral notebook for expenses.

Her life just wasn't that complicated. She did work she loved, she tackled new ideas as they came to her, she put in hours that seemed reasonable and didn't interfere with things like watching for piping plovers, walking on the beach at sunrise, taking in the occasional Red Sox game, and watching "Magnum" reruns.

As for money, when she had it, she spent some of it and saved some of it. When she didn't, she resisted dipping into her savings and ate dinner a little more often with her father and brothers.

It wasn't that she lacked drive or ambition, simply that they manifested themselves in different ways in her than they did in Clate Jackson.

She wondered if, deep down, he knew that all those millions didn't take the place of a dinner with friends, a heated argument with a brother, a game of Frisbee with a crowd of nine-year-olds. His money didn't fill whatever hole his childhood had left in him, and there was one, she was sure of that much.

Not that there was anything wrong with money, she thought as she negotiated Chatham's busy, pretty Main Street, hunting for a parking space. From the Fourth of July on through the summer, she'd be lucky to find one. Now, she had only moderate trouble.

She climbed out of her car, didn't bother locking up, and started up Main Street, debating how much to charge the optometrist to distinguish between what was authentic, what was historically accurate, and what was popular and fun, but not necessarily authentic or accurate.

An hour later, she was back on the road, back to speculating on Clate Jackson. The magazine article had provided pictures of his hotel, his sprawling office, the award-winning courtyard in one of his tall buildings, but none of his Nashville home. He had a place on the Cumberland River, not in a fashionable district. Apparently it had a high fence and he owned big dogs.

The man led a life completely different from her own, and it was best if she stopped kissing him in the rain.

She gave a start when her car telephone—a birthday gift from her brothers, who hated worrying she was in a ditch when they couldn't reach her—rang. She grabbed it up, welcoming the distraction.

"You won't leave it alone, will you, Piper?"

She slammed on her brake and pulled over, forcing the car behind her to swerve; the driver gave her the finger as he sped past her.

"Who are you?" she demanded.

"Someone who's lost patience."

"That makes two of us. Look, I don't know what you want me to do. I—*Wait, damn you!*"

But he—or she or it—had hung up. She screeched back out onto the road, pain gathering at the backs of her eyes, her head spinning. She drove through the center of Frye's Cove in a daze, and when she came to her road, to the pretty section closest to the water, she pulled over and jumped out of her car and hurled her cell phone into the bay.

Missed.

She walked out across the sand, her car door open, sand flying up under her heels, and picked up the phone and hurled it again.

It sank beneath a wave.

And a small voice inside her said, "pollution," and without thinking, she kicked off her shoes and waded out into the water. She scooped with her hands and felt with her feet until she'd located her phone.

On her way back to her car, she dumped the phone in a trash can.

It was in this state of mind that she arrived home and found Clate in her back yard, sitting at her picnic table.

He didn't move, said nothing as he took in her wet pantyhose, the wet hem of her skirt.

Piper could taste the salt water on her mouth. "I lost my cell phone in the bay."

"I see."

"I lost my cell phone in the bay, I had to fish it out, and so I got wet."

Silence.

"It's true," she said.

"What was your cell phone doing in the bay?"

"I threw it there."

His eyes darkened. "You received another threatening call."

She fought back tears she had no intention of shedding. By God, she could take care of herself. She could stand up for Hannah. She didn't need Clate insinuating himself into her relationship with her aunt, into her problems with the anonymous caller, the treasure, her life. Anything.

She stared out at the marsh, could feel fog settling in; her wet clothes were cold against her skin. "I can see why Hannah waited eighty years to tell anyone about that night. Even if she didn't remember until recently, her subconscious could have just been trying to protect her. Telling makes it real. The calls—" Suddenly breathless, she had to gulp for air. "If I don't tell anyone, I can pretend they didn't happen."

Clate didn't respond at once. Whether he was absorbing what she'd said or just waiting for her to continue, she didn't know.

"Except I can't," she said quietly. "I have to look life straight in the eye."

Without responding, Clate got to his feet. It occurred to Piper that he hadn't explained why he was in her yard. She hadn't asked. This trespassing thing obviously wasn't going to be tit for tat.

"Let's go inside," he said. "I'll fix you something to drink. We'll figure out where to go from here."

She nodded, not just because she was too confused and upset to argue. She appreciated having him there.

He followed her into her tiny office adjoining her keeping room and waited while she checked her messages. She could feel him surveying her small office from the doorway, taking in her cluttered antique rolltop oak desk, her drop-front bookcase, her old side-by-side oak filing cabinet, her oak swivel chair. She had sewed a cushion for the chair herself, refinished the furniture, and framed the cross-stitched sampler that hung on the wall, stitched in a careful hand by an Abigail Macintosh in 1803, perhaps an ancestor, perhaps not.

The message tape whirred as it rewound. "Most of my work is hands-on. I don't spend hours and hours at a time in here. I like the view of the flower garden."

"It's pretty," he said.

"Thanks. This house hasn't had as many additions and updates as the Frye—as your house. The kitchen fireplace was plastered over, and the place had been ranchified to a degree, but that's it." She glanced at him, aware of how sexy he was slouched against the door frame. She couldn't remember the last man, other than her father and brothers, and Stan Carlucci and Paul Shepherd, she'd had over. Her social life, somehow, had dried up in recent months. Hannah maintained it was all part of her destiny. "Your house in Nashville is new, isn't it? You built it?"

"That's right. Piper—"

"I know, I know. You're not going to be distracted from tales of threatening phone calls and hurled cell phones." She sighed. "You are nothing if not relentless, Mr. Jackson."

He smiled. "Remember it."

The tape started on its six messages. Tension gripped her neck and shoulders, made her breathing shallow. She had to concentrate to keep from shaking. Clate remained in the doorway, apparently calm.

The first three messages were inquiries about her various classes, the fourth from a friend about sailing next week, the fifth from Andrew, the sixth from her father.

Andrew wanted to know when she planned to come clean about "whatever the hell else you've got going on." Her father wanted to know if she had any idea why her brothers ground their teeth whenever her name came up.

"Well." She rolled her shoulders in an effort to uncrick the muscles. "Nothing nasty at least. But whoever's harassing me has been careful not to let his voice be recorded."

Clate drew himself up from the doorjamb. He looked every inch the hard, competent, I'll-take-charge-now male that Piper had long vowed she would avoid. "That's why you got the charming rap excerpt yesterday. What did he say in this last call?"

"Nothing much, just that he was losing patience."

"That's enough."

"I still can't be sure it's a man."

"Understood."

His quiet tone, his easy stance, were not to be misjudged. He was alert, processing every nuance of what she said, how she looked, what his next move ought to be. And he wasn't happy about what he was hearing. No question. But he was controlled, measured in his responses. He wasn't the sort of man who exploded.

Piper bit back a touch of panic at the image—it was almost like watching herself from a camera—of her in her car, driving along in her business outfit, feeling okay about her ability to handle her family, Clate, her work. Until the call. Until she'd heard that unrecognizable, mean, insidious voice on the other end of the line and knew the calls weren't going to stop just because she wanted them to stop.

She shivered in her wet clothes. "I could use a cup of hot tea."

Without a word, Clate returned to her keeping-room kitchen. Piper followed, feeling a bit steadier. It was her favorite room. It had a warm, cheerful, homey feeling whether she was alone or had a crowd in. Clate was a crowd all by himself. He got the copper kettle off her stove while she stood by the huge fireplace. On chilly days, she kept a kettle of water simmering on the fire. She'd hung handmade pot holders on hooks, had set her favorite wingback chair close to the fire, and had a soft-cushioned loveseat for guests and times when she wanted to stretch out with a book, relishing her quiet life. She would imagine herself living out her days here, alone.

"Go on upstairs and change," Clate said in that quiet drawl. "I'll make tea."

"The tea bags are in that little brown crock, and a mug—"

"I'll manage, Piper." He walked over to her, grabbed her by the elbows, turned her back to him, and whispered in her ear from behind. "Go upstairs."

She left him to it and headed through her work-in-progress parlor and up the steep stairs in her front vestibule, straight into her bathroom. Every step was an effort. She enjoyed the pretty femininity of her little bathroom with its white fixtures, rose-flowered wallpaper, fluffy, rose-colored towels. She had arranged a small, antique chest with an array of scented candles she'd made herself, tubs of various creams and potions Hannah had pressed upon her, tiny vials of essential oils, a basket of pretty-smelling soaps.

First she peeled off her stockings and tossed them in the trash. Her skirt was next, flung into the wicker laundry basket. Her blue-striped cotton shirt hung to her hips. It was a lost cause, too. The sleeves were soaked, the rear hem damp. She remembered reaching into the water, frantically combing the bottom with both hands, as if one cell phone would turn Cape Cod Bay into a Superfund toxic waste site. If her brothers had ventured by at that particular moment, that would have been that. Off to the loony bin with her. Or under a hot light for further interrogation.

She discarded her shirt in the basket and washed up with rosewater-and-glycerine soap that had never felt and smelled so luxurious, so sweet and comforting. She took her time drying off with a fresh towel, splashed on rosewater toner, then rubbed in some of Hannah's special hand cream, made of an infusion of lady's-mantle and essential oil of geranium.

In her bedroom, she put on clean underwear and, given the fog, was debating between long pants and shorts when she heard footsteps on her stairs.

She went still. "Clate?"

"I've got your tea."

"Great, thanks." But her reaction just to his voice was dramatic, awareness sparking, flaring, before he'd even reached the top of the stairs.

She slipped on her terry bathrobe, just wrapping it tightly around her without tying it as she met him at the door.

Seeing him under the low, slanted ceiling of her upstairs shattered whatever equilibrium she'd succeeded in regaining. And he hadn't touched her. He hadn't even looked at her.

A muscle in his jaw worked as his gaze swept over her quickly and efficiently. He was trying not to capitalize on the situation, she realized. Emotionally, physically, she was exposed, unable to hide anything from herself much less him.

"Here." His voice was husky, the drawl barely detectable. He held out the steaming mug for her to take from him. "Drink up. Hope it helps."

"It won't as much as one of Hannah's teas. I wonder what she'd recommend for a situation such as this." But her attempt at humor faltered, and she cupped the mug in her palms, soaking in its warmth. "Thank you."

"No problem."

He turned to go.

Piper managed a sip of the tea. Ordinary, orange pekoe tea, with a touch of honey.

But it was no use. She couldn't concentrate on tea, on changing clothes, on anything except the man retreating from her bedroom. He was doing the honorable thing, of course. She'd just had a fright, she'd been fishing cell phones out of the bay. Yet she wanted him. She was hot and quivering just with the thought of him staying with her while she dressed.

"Clate, I—"

He glanced back at her, his eyes a smoky blue in the gray light.

She smiled. "Please stay."

He didn't move from the doorway. Although he wasn't over six feet, his head skimmed the frame, which she had carefully sanded and painted a rosy taupe. This was her space. She'd chosen it, worked on it, decorated it. It fit her dimensions, her tastes, her varying moods. Yet somehow—she couldn't describe how—his presence wasn't jarring.

"Unless," she went on, still smiling, "you want to get back to your tea."

"Not hardly." His laughter didn't quite reach his eyes. He was holding back, playing the Southern gentleman, and the effort it required—the restraint—crackled in the air between them. He moved toward her, and when she still didn't send him back downstairs, didn't change her mind now that he was there, close enough to touch, he took her mug from her hands and set it on her dresser. "Hot tea doesn't do anything for me right now."

He came back to her, slid his arms around her, inside her bathrobe, his palms settling on the small of her back, on her bare skin.

"I'm not cold anymore," she said, the slightest quaver in her voice. She hoped he didn't mistake it for nervousness. Because she wasn't nervous. Shaky with want and anticipation, yes. But not nervous.

He smoothed his palms over her hips, downward to her thighs, where her skin was still cool from her dash into the bay. "You're cool here." His eyes darkened. "Cool and still a little damp."

His palms slipped around to the fronts of her thighs, until finally she gripped his upper arms, desire like hot pin prickles all over her. He didn't stop, but moved up her thighs, inward, excruciatingly slowly, until she was throbbing, aching just with the thought of those hands. She dropped her head against his chest as he slid one hand between her thighs, not moving any faster. One finger drew back her underpants, slipped inside to where she was decidedly hot and damp.

"Don't stop," she moaned half to herself. "Don't ever stop."

She could feel his erection hard between them, knew he had no intention of stopping unless she said so, and that knowledge—that certainty—only added to her sense of urgency.

His mouth found hers, his tongue spearing inside her with the same fierceness she felt. Her breasts swelled inside her bra. And all the while his hand moved slowly, with delicious agony, probing, circling, teasing out every emotion, every sensual urge she had.

Suddenly, he lifted her, carried her to the bed, and laid her down. Her bathrobe fell off in the process. "You're so beautiful," he murmured, unclasping her bra, exposing her breasts to his gaze, his palms, his mouth. His hands moved lower, as he cast off her underpants. When she was right on the edge, he quickly pulled off his own clothes, and it was all she could do not to gasp and stare at his hard body. Small scars she hadn't seen before scored one shoulder and upper thigh, only adding to his air of rough masculinity. Yet he had brought her tea. He would, now, leave if she changed her mind.

But she had no desire to change her mind. No intention.

"I have protection," she said. "In the drawer." At his amused look, she added, unembarrassed, "You know us Yankees. We like to be prepared for anything." She had her evacuation plan for the next Category 5 hurricane, too, which of late she'd thought was more likely than finding a man she'd want to make love with. "I'm not sure about the expiration date, though."

As he reached over to her nightstand, she ran her fingers down his hips, curved inward, and skimmed his huge erection, exulting in the feel of him. Even when Hannah had been casting out into the universe for a man for her niece, Piper hadn't in her wildest fantasies come up with any who thrilled her more than this one.

"Date's good." He eased back to her, grinned. "Not that I'm ever unprepared."

"You mean you—"

"In my wallet. Always." He winked, settled his palm over her stomach. "Just in case an old Yankee witch summons me to the woman of my dreams."

His words, his sexy drawl, the gleam in his eyes were enough to rekindle her earlier sense of urgency. Then he added more fuel by easing his firm, naked body onto her, letting her touch, taste, explore, until finally he drew her hands from him and raised up off her, gazing into her eyes. "I want to love you, Piper." His drawl was husky, his body rigid, a hint of the control that he was exercising.

She nodded, unable to speak herself, feeling breathless, already spent. Yet when he dealt with protection and came to her again, fresh energy surged through her. She guided him to the hot, wet entry, gasped when he thrust into her, gently at first, through the tightness, letting her get used to the feel of him, the size of him. Then he thrust harder, faster. She shut her eyes and concentrated on the slick, hard feel of him inside her as she went still one moment, arched up to meet his thrust the next.

But concentration, experimentation, even real consciousness quickly became impossible. Her world was spinning, sparking, shimmering. Nothing mattered but *now,* this moment.

She thought he called her name. She knew she called his. And it seemed so right, so perfect. *Clate.* It was as if she'd been waiting her entire life to cry out that name.

Slowly, she became aware of the fog settling in over the marsh. The tiny house, the low, slanted ceilings, the isolation of their little spit of land. They might as well have been alone in the universe.

Stretched out beside her, Clate touched her hair. "You're wondering if your aunt's not a witch after all."

"Does it matter?"

He smiled. "Not to me."

"This wasn't—I didn't—" She grimaced, unable to find the right words.

From her hair, his fingers moved down her cheek, touched her mouth lightly. "It's okay, sweetheart. We don't have to talk now. You don't have to think."

"Whatever I feel for you, *I* feel. It's not Hannah's doing. It's my own." She grinned suddenly, skimmed a knuckle across the scar on his jaw. "I won't have her taking the blame for you."

"Piper, whatever happens between us, happens. No one gets the credit or takes the blame."

"You don't know my brothers," she said dryly, only half seriously.

He laughed. "Maybe it's a good thing I live a thousand miles away."

"And have a house with a high fence and big dogs."

"Not that you've ever let your brothers intimidate you."

"Never. But they've totally intimidated most of the men on Cape Cod."

He grinned, kissed her softly, and whispered, "Then I say good for your brothers."

Chapter

12

⁓

While Piper showered and drank a fresh cup of tea Clate had brought her, he ventured out into her herb garden. Fog had descended over the bay and was fast encroaching on the marsh, distorting sounds, heightening the senses. Everything seemed closer, saltier, cooler, damper. He noted purple and yellow blossoms among Piper's herbs, recognized chives, parsley, maybe basil, not much else.

He sipped on his mug of tea. He didn't want it, but he'd poured it anyway. Gave him something to do. Helped stop him from charging upstairs and into the shower with Piper, soaping her up, making love to her again. But her life was already in enough of a turmoil without adding him to the boiling cauldron.

He could still feel her body against his, his body inside her. The soft, smooth skin, the firm muscles, the fragrant hair.

A sip of tea. Helped unclench the jaw, it did.

"Hell," he muttered.

He needed to be straightforward with her. That was a

point of honor with him. He did not delude women in order to keep them in his bed. He never made promises he had no intention of keeping.

But Piper had asked no promises of him, and he'd made none. If he tried to be straightforward with her now, he didn't know what the hell he'd say because he didn't know what the hell he wanted.

As satisfying as the prospect of more good, rousing sex with her was, it left him feeling limited, even diminished. What Piper wanted from him, what she gave to him, was up to her. That wasn't what was eating at him. It was that he didn't know what he wanted from himself.

She joined him in the garden, inhaling deeply. "I can smell the mint. Can you?"

He smiled. The woman had seeped into his soul. That was the problem. An affair never touched him. "Mint and everything else."

She'd changed into jeans and an ivory cotton sweater, the fog having dragged down the temperature. She had her mug of tea. She looked steady, unrepentant about what had happened upstairs, even well pleased with herself. Clate stifled a stab of lust at the memory of how she'd moaned his name, dug her fingers into his upper arms as she'd climaxed.

He jerked himself up straight. "There's something I need to show you in my yard. Got a minute?"

She shrugged, but he could see the spark of suspicion. He remained unpredictable to her, which, he supposed, was just as well. "Sure."

They left their mugs on the picnic table and started down the path along the hedgerow. To avoid prejudicing her, Clate refused to explain what he wanted to show her until they reached Hannah's herb garden and he pointed out the scalped area. "Tuck spotted it first."

"He didn't do it?"

"He says he didn't."

"Well, I didn't. The only use I have for foxglove is as a flower, and monkshood I don't have any use for. Its flower is pretty enough, but it's nasty stuff. I think it's only use is as a cleaning agent. Hannah planted it before she really knew what she was doing. I hope whoever did this used gloves."

Clate eyed her, noted the slight loss of color in her cheeks. Lovemaking had temporarily put thoughts of her aunt's troubles out of her mind. With a sudden jolt, he realized he didn't want their lovemaking to be a mere diversion, not a way out of the moment but into it.

"What about Hannah?" he asked.

She gave a tight shake of the head. "That's not the way she harvests herbs. It's too radical. After she's done, you can hardly tell she's touched anything. And why would she do all this work when she could just get me to do it for her?" A small, uneasy smile. "Besides, one of us would have spotted that raspberry car of hers."

"You're sure?"

Her shoulders slumped. "No, I'm not sure. I'm not sure of anything right now."

Including him, he realized. Maybe especially him.

"I'll go see her." She squinted at him through the glare of the fog and her own confusion. "We mapped out a whole plan of where to look next for the treasure, you know."

"I figured as much."

"She still doesn't want to involve you."

He nodded. "That's her right."

"But it's your land."

"I didn't say I'd cooperate."

That brought a smile, but it quickly faded. "The letters in her shoebox were compelling, Clate, but I wish they'd been more conclusive, one way or the other. There's no proof there's any treasure, here or anywhere else. I think it's time I went back to the library. Maybe I'll stop on my way to see Hannah." She scanned the area of cut poisonous herbs. "I really can't imagine that this was her doing."

"I agree."

"My caller?"

"I don't know, Piper. Maybe your family—"

She cut him off, starting down his sloping lawn. "The minute my father and brothers find out about any of this, I'll lose all room to maneuver."

"They might know something."

"Uh-uh. They'd have told me."

"Maybe they're thinking the same thing about you."

She swung around, and he was surprised to see her grinning. "Are you kidding? My father and brothers would never assume I'd tell them *anything.*"

"I wonder why," he said dryly.

She laughed. "I'll give it some thought, okay? Meanwhile"—she took a breath—"I guess I'll see you around."

It was her signal to him. He understood. She needed to walk back to her house alone, without him.

Watching her go wasn't easy. Someone was out there who could be mean, desperate, or just plain stupid enough to do anything. If threats weren't working, what would come next?

But Piper was no fool. She knew the score, the risks. And she knew what she needed.

She stopped halfway down the path, whirled around, and yelled to him. "I have no regrets, you know."

He grinned. "I know."

Piper started a small fire in her keeping-room fireplace to take the damp chill out of the air and sat on her wingback chair with a bit of knitting. The fog distorted sound, made the bay seem closer, the wind fiercer. She'd locked her doors, although her locks were totally inadequate.

She knew she had only to say the word, and Clate would be over. To deal with an intruder, to spend the night.

"Your destiny isn't my destiny, Piper. It's yours to discover and to live."

Only Hannah. How was conjuring a man up for her niece letting her discover and live her destiny?

But no one could have conjured up Clate Jackson. Not even Hannah Frye.

Finally, Piper laid down her knitting needles and headed up to bed. She peered out her dormer window, but saw only the fog. When she climbed between her sheets and pulled her quilt up to her chin, she stared at her ceiling. What time did Clate go to bed? What would he think when he did?

It was a long time before sleep overtook her, her thoughts filled with images of how explosive and wild and free she'd felt that afternoon.

No one needed to warn her about Clate Jackson.

By morning the fog had burned off, the sun was shining, and after a morning class in making beeswax candles, Piper set out on her bicycle. Bypassing everyone and everything she knew in town, she ensconced herself in a remote corner of the Frye's Cove Public Library. If she ever hoped to sort out her relationship with Clate, she needed to sort out her business with Hannah. Plainly, she was getting on someone's nerves. Maybe it had to do with buried treasure, maybe not. But she meant to find out.

She checked every article, every mention she could find, of the mysterious shipwreck of Caleb and Phoebe Macintosh. She read up on the Russian royal family tree. She dug into princesses and baronesses and other wealthy upper-class women whose escape from revolution in Russia might have coincided with her great-grandfather's time in Europe. There were a few possibilities, none concrete, none she could examine with any precision from an old Cape Cod library on an early summer morning.

As facts and tidbits came to her, she jotted down everything that had happened, everything she knew, on a spiral notepad. She hoped that putting it all together, right there in front of her, would help her make sense of what, on the face of it, made no sense. An old woman who claimed she'd lured a Tennessean to Frye's Cove as the love of her niece's life. Disturbing phone calls. Recovered memory of treasure. Rumors of the Tennessean wanting to develop his newly purchased land. Signs of digging. Hacked poisonous herbs. Piper wrote it all down in chronological order.

She skipped the parts about midnight kisses and afternoon lovemaking. Relevant or not, she needed no reminders about when, where, and how they fit into her time line of events.

Had the caller known she'd been on Clate's property or just guessed? If he'd known, how? Was he spying on her, on Clate? From where?

Piper shut her eyes and let the questions wash over her. Maybe some insight would come just from formulating the right question.

"There you are."

Andrew's voice.

Piper's eyes flew open. Both brothers loomed over her. Her first impulse was to cover up her table of articles, books, notes, scratchings of card-catalog numbers. But that would only alert them that she was working on something she didn't want them to know about.

"We recognized your bike out front," Benjamin said, and Piper could feel her stomach lurch as she recognized his expression for what it was: masked fear. She turned to Andrew and saw that mix of irritation and gravity that she'd always known—probably since the day their mother died—hid his fear.

"Hannah?" She almost couldn't get it out.

"She passed out at the wheel." Benjamin kept his tone crisp, businesslike, as if that would keep his sister from panicking, himself from panicking. "She ran off the road and smashed into a trash can. Just missed a couple of old people out for their afternoon walk. They called an ambulance, the police."

"She's okay," Andrew said. "A few bumps and bruises. Liddy and Pop are at the hospital with her now."

Benjamin nodded. "We thought you'd want to go see her."

They didn't ask about her notepad, her time lines, her books on the Russian revolution, her histories of Cape

Cod, and stacks of old magazines, although she noticed Andrew's flicker of interest. But he restrained himself as she scooped everything up, shoved it in her knapsack, and nodded, her pulse racing, her stomach twisted, that she was ready.

Twenty minutes later, they were at the hospital.

Hannah had been admitted with dizziness and nausea; her few bruises were of little concern. Doctors wanted to run tests to find out what had caused her to pass out.

She, of course, had her own ideas, which she articulated to Piper the moment her brothers, father, and sister-in-law had grudgingly left them alone together. Andrew retreated, muttering that this was what always got the two of them into trouble in the first place.

"I was poisoned," Hannah announced.

Piper immediately glanced around to make sure no one was within earshot, but Hannah looked so green and frail that Piper couldn't even summon up a good warning glare. "It was warm today. Maybe you had too much sun."

"I wasn't even in the sun. No, I was poisoned. I'm not sure what it was, but the doctors will never find it in my blood because they won't know to look for it. It's probably dissipated by now anyway."

"Did you try a new tea?"

Hannah scowled. "I didn't poison myself. Someone else poisoned me."

Piper suppressed a groan of disbelief, frustration, exasperation. She was at her wit's end. Her aunt was driving her insane.

"Hannah, how on earth could someone poison you?"

"Very easily. A few drops of the right poison in my springwater, and here I am, nauseated and dizzy. I don't keep an armed guard at my townhouse, Piper. A clever sort could easily have slipped in and done the deed. Perhaps it was even a guest."

"Hannah."

"You mustn't be shocked, dear. We know someone's trying to stop you from digging up my father's treasure."

"No, we don't know that. We know I've been receiving nasty phone calls warning me off Clate's land, but that's all. Besides, you said nobody knows about the treasure."

"I said I didn't tell anybody about it. That doesn't mean someone didn't already know." She took a shallow breath, her eyes clear and sparkling green, a contrast to the sickly green of her skin. "Possibly the killer."

The killer? It took a moment, but Piper finally realized what her aunt was saying. "Oh, Hannah. The person who lured your parents onto the sandbar would be even older than you are by now! I can't see some old codger slipping you a mickey and leaving lines from rap songs on my message machine."

"Old codger, Piper? Oh, I see. You can believe everyone in town will blame *me* for making those calls to you, *me* for sneaking out behind your back to dig treasure. I'm eighty-seven. Why not someone ninety-seven or a hundred?"

Piper stared at her old aunt. She was so slim that her body barely made a lump in the thin hospital blanket. "Okay. Name me a ninety-seven-year-old candidate."

Hannah snorted, annoyed. "Always such a pragmatist. Maybe he's not alive."

"What do you mean, a ghost is responsible for the call on my cell phone? Oh, come on, Hannah, even you can't believe that."

"I'm keeping an open mind," she said airily. "And now that I've had a chance to think about it, I'm sure the poison was in the springwater your father delivered yesterday."

"Hannah!" Piper quickly lowered her voice before her father and brothers heard her and burst through the door. She leaned forward, her voice shaking she was so upset. "Hannah, are you suggesting my father poisoned you?"

"Heavens, no. He's always been such a sweet boy. I remember when—"

"Hannah."

She sighed. "Oh, all right. Someone must have gotten

to the water before him. It's the only sensible option. I'll have to speak to him."

"No, don't." Piper could just imagine the results of that conversation: a straitjacket for her aunt. "Let me handle this, okay? You just concentrate on feeling better."

She looked as if her last drop of energy had drained out of her. "I have a lovely sage tea I don't suppose the doctors would let me near. They'll be pushing pills and needles at me."

"If you want sage tea, Hannah, I'll bring you sage tea."

"You won't worry about me, will you, dear? I've had a long, long time to think about what I'd do when I got old." She managed a thin, wretched-looking smile. "And here I am."

Piper fought back tears. Yes, here was her aunt, this solid, unwavering presence in her life, finally undeniably old. Who knew how much time she had left?

How much time *they* had left, Piper thought, pushing back any image of her own life without her aunt.

Hannah lifted a hand, and Piper took it, felt how cold and skinny it was. "Now don't you cry," her aunt said. "That won't accomplish anything. We all die, my dear. Some sooner, some later."

"Don't talk like that!"

"Phooey. I'll talk any way I please. It's no mystery to the elderly that they're old, you know. And death—I'm sorry, but it just doesn't scare me. I've seen too many go before me to worry about the great beyond." Another wan smile. "Now. I threw out the springwater. I didn't like the taste. Your father fetched me another bottle. I want you to confiscate it before anyone else can get into my townhouse and replace it, in case it's poisoned, too."

"You want me to have it tested?"

A spark of pleasure in her eyes. "Now you're catching on. And have the empty bottle tested. There might be enough residue of the poison to identify it."

"I'll do it," Piper said quickly. "I'll do anything for you, Hannah. You know that."

"You're a dear girl." Her eyelids were drooping. "I think those damned doctors gave me a chemical sedative. I have that nice valerian decoction at home . . ."

She trailed off, and Piper gave her frail hand a gentle squeeze. "You get some rest. I'll take care of everything."

"And your man, Clate . . . fate . . ."

But she was asleep. Piper withdrew, finding her father, her brothers, Liddy, and—no surprise—Clate in the small waiting room. The damned firing squad. They knew something was up, every damned one of them. Poison. Hell's bells.

"She's asleep." It wasn't all they wanted to hear, but it was a start. She glanced at Clate, felt her heartbeat jump at how good-looking and sexy he was, even in ragged, expensive chinos and polo shirt. She felt stronger, surer, for having him there, and it surprised her that it wasn't a feeling she remotely wanted to fight. "You heard?"

"I stopped by the tavern for a drink, and Paul and Sally Shepherd told me."

"We were working there when we got the news," Benjamin explained.

Liddy stood beside her younger sister-in-law. She was an attractive, athletic woman, unintimidated by the protective urges of her husband and brother-in-law. "Thank God Hannah's going to be all right."

Piper nodded, numb. What did all right mean when you were eighty-seven?

"Piper." Her father's voice held that familiar note of paternal authority. "Clate tells us we need to hear you out on a few things."

Her first reaction was anger. Bastard. Traitor. How could he rat her out? But there was no treachery in Clate's return gaze, and she knew he'd acted out of decent enough motives, that he was being clear eyed and objective where conflicting emotions had her darting off in a thousand different directions at once.

"We can go up to the house," her father added gently.

"I'll stay here with Hannah," Liddy said. "She'll probably sleep through the night and be right as rain in the morning. The doctors are optimistic it was nothing serious."

Andrew grunted. "Damned lucky she didn't mow anyone down or drive herself into the bay and drown."

Before Piper could snap back at him, Benjamin and Liddy moved them toward the door. She'd ride with her brothers. Those were her instructions. "Hear her out" was a euphemism for "you're telling us everything." If Clate didn't know it, Piper did.

He smiled, unrepentant. "Have fun. I'll stay here with Liddy a while."

Oh, sure. Throw her to the lions and run. Yet as she left the hospital with her father and brothers, with Liddy and Clate looking after Hannah, she didn't feel nearly as alone as she had last night, knitting in front of her fire.

The Macintosh men were not happy with her.

Piper told herself this was to be expected. She'd been receiving threatening phone calls, digging for buried treasure, trying to explain inexplicable digging and cutting on Clate's property, and protecting Hannah, all under their noses, without saying a word.

Andrew's reaction was predictably the most extreme. He wanted his sister to move in with Benjamin and Liddy and stay away from her house until things settled down.

"I can't do that," Piper said, with limited patience. "I have a business to run. Besides, I make my own decisions about my life."

"Yeah, and look where they've led you."

If he had any idea of how far her relationship with her new neighbor had gone, he had the courtesy to keep his mouth shut.

She resisted the urge to tell him to go to blazes. "This is what I get for not moving to Wyoming when I turned eighteen."

"Piper," her father said, his tone reasonable, "if this were happening to one of us, you'd be here right now, listening, worrying—"

"Pissing us off," Andrew added with a small grin.

It was true. Sometimes, because she was the youngest and the only female and usually was the one on the hot seat, she forgot that she had interceded on her brothers' behalf countless times in the past. Meddled. Told them what she thought in no uncertain terms.

"If you didn't have the same protective streak we do," Benjamin said, "you wouldn't have taken on Hannah's latest cause."

Her father settled back in his old, overstuffed chair. He lived simply, in a small reproduction Cape Cod house off the water where he had raised his three children, Piper for the most part alone, with, they would argue, the help of her older brothers. A picture of her mother on her parents' wedding day stood on the mantel, as it always had. "Your grandfather never mentioned any Russian princess or treasure, Piper. Don't you think he would have known?"

She shrugged. "Maybe, maybe not. I'm not saying I believe Hannah. I'm just doing as she asks. If there's no treasure, I won't find any. So far we've only checked under the wisteria."

Andrew pounced on her slip of the tongue. "We?"

"Clate's helped out on occasion, although he's as skeptical as you all are. I'm trying to keep an open mind."

Benjamin got to his feet, paced. Andrew had never sat down. "You think this crackpot who's calling you knows about the treasure?"

"I don't know. He just warned me off Clate's land. That's as specific as he's ever gotten."

"And of course you paid no attention," Andrew said sarcastically.

"I wasn't taking him seriously."

Benjamin groaned, exasperated. "Why the hell didn't you say something?"

"I was worried people would think it might be Hannah." She left it at that, letting them sort out what she meant.

They did. When realization dawned, Andrew bit off a curse, and Benjamin shook his head in amazement. "Because of this crazy spell to conjure up a man for you!"

"I know it's illogical and contradictory," Piper said.

Andrew grunted. "That won't matter with Hannah. Everyone knows how she hates to be proved wrong."

They batted around theories over a quick dinner. Then it was decided, after much argument, that Piper would go on about her business more or less as usual, with a few modifications for safety. Benjamin would return to the hospital to check on Hannah and pick up Liddy. If their aunt was released as expected in the morning, Liddy and Piper could pick her up.

"What?" Piper said, recalcitrant to the end. "You don't want Hannah and me alone together?"

Andrew got his keys out. "That about sums it up."

"Well, tough. You see why I don't tell you everything? Nobody around here knows how to mind their own damned business."

"Don't sit there on your moral high horse pretending you've never meddled in our lives and never would."

"As if I ever had any power over you two! I'm so much younger than you and Benjamin—"

He snorted, summing up his opinion of her protest.

Her father held up a hand. They'd been over this same ground hundreds of times since his daughter was two. He would drive her home and check her house, make sure no one was hiding in the cellar, had planted a bomb, or left another few bars of unpleasant lyrics on her message machine. Come morning, Andrew, Benjamin, and Liddy would check in on her at various points during the day. That was the plan, by Robert Macintosh's decree. No one argued.

In the car, her father said, "And I expect this Clate Jackson's looking after you, too."

"I can look after myself, Pop."

"That wasn't my point."

She sighed. "I know it wasn't. I'm sorry. I just hate

feeling this—" She searched for the right word. "This vulnerable."

"Some son of a bitch gets a bee in his bonnet about any of us, we're vulnerable. It's not because you're a woman, young, have two older brothers, and are stubborn and independent as the day is long that you're feeling vulnerable right now and hating it. It's because you've got some creep out there pestering you."

"Then you don't think it's Hannah?"

He shook his head, confident. She noticed the deepening lines at the corners of his eyes, the gray in his hair, but he was still a strong, vital man. "Even Andrew doesn't think this is Hannah's doing, and you know he's thought she was crazy ever since he was thirteen and she tried to feed him candied violets."

"They were good." Piper laughed, remembering. And laughing was a welcome release as her father turned into her driveway. "I'll be fine, Pop. Really."

"I know you will, kid. I think it's a testament to your spirit that you're even willing to spend the night alone." He glanced over at her. "If you are."

"Pop—"

"That wasn't a question, Piper. It doesn't need an answer."

Five years ago—even two years ago—she would have gone to great lengths to assure her father that Clate Jackson wasn't spending the night with her. She supposed it was progress that she could just let it be and let him think whatever it was he was thinking.

She and her father scoured her house and listened to her messages together, and when he left, he kissed her on her cheek. "Good night, Piper."

"Good night, Pop."

"You get spooked, give a yell."

Under the circumstances, she felt an enormous twist of guilt that she hadn't mentioned Hannah's poison theory to him and her brothers. But she just couldn't. Best to test that second jug of water first. Or to let

Hannah tell them herself, which doubtless wouldn't happen any time soon.

As it was, Piper felt her only option after her father left was to climb into her car, drive over to Hannah's, and check for poisoned water.

On her way out to her car, Paul Shepherd arrived with her bicycle. Grim-faced, he dragged it out of his trunk and set it out on her driveway. "Sally and I give Hannah our best and hope she has a speedy recovery. It's a good thing she's as ornery as she is, I suppose. If there's anything Sally or I can do—"

"Thanks, but the doctors think Hannah will be fine."

"That's a relief." He hesitated, averting his eyes. "Piper, I hate bringing this up now, but I think you should know. Stan Carlucci has suggested, privately, that Hannah could have passed out after drinking one of her experimental concoctions."

"You mean that she poisoned herself?"

"Basically, yes."

"Well, I asked her, and she didn't."

"She wouldn't admit she'd made a mistake, would she?"

His tone was mild, reasonable. Piper swallowed her fury. "Please tell Stan Carlucci that I appreciate his concern."

Paul winced at her sarcasm. "Piper, Stan means well. Truly. If Hannah accidentally overdosed on one of her teas, or drank the wrong one, it's no worse than other elderly people forgetting they've taken their medication for the day and doubling up. This sort of thing—well, as hard as it is on family members, it's to be expected."

"I don't go for the old-people-are-all-daffy theory."

His expression turned cool. "That wasn't a generalization."

"I'm sorry. It's been a difficult day."

He softened. "Forget it. Stan's willing to keep quiet for now, provided you or your father or one of your brothers—or her doctor—does a thorough check of her townhouse. He—none of us wants her or anyone else to get hurt. We all wish her nothing but the best, Piper. Hannah and Stan have their political differences, but that's not interfering with his judgment."

Piper nodded, feeling drawn and tired and in no mood to argue about Stan Carlucci. "I know he wouldn't want any harm to come to Hannah."

Looking relieved, Paul started back toward his car. "And Sally's happy to help in any way she can. You know she looks upon Hannah as a grandmother."

"Tell her thanks."

"I will."

"And thank you, too, Paul. You've been walking a fine line in this thing, and I appreciate your neutrality. I know Frye's Cove isn't always easy on newcomers."

He laughed. "No, it isn't, but it certainly helps being married to a Frye, even if no one around here would ever admit it makes a difference. Now, don't go and tell Sally I said that. You know how discreet she is about using her family name." He winked as he pulled open the driver's door of his car. "I'll see you around."

"Sure. And thanks for bringing me my bike."

"Where would Piper Macintosh be without her bicycle?"

She watched him slide back into his car, then gave him a ten-minute head start before charging off to Hannah's housing complex, debating whether to limit her poison hunt to jugs of springwater or open it up to everything in her aunt's townhouse.

Chapter

13

⚭

There were moments when Clate felt as if he were caught up in one of the Miss Marple murder mysteries Irma liked to read, only without a murder. This wasn't one of them.

He walked on the beach right at the point where sand and water met and tried to concentrate on the soothing rhythms of the waves. The tide was in. After returning from the hospital, he'd walked down to the water. A sunset of vibrant oranges and reds fired the entire sky. This beauty and solitude were why he'd come to Cape Cod, not to get embroiled in Macintosh family troubles with a chestnut-haired woman he couldn't get out of his mind.

Tension gnawed at every muscle, every fiber of his body. Nothing about what was going on in Frye's Cove felt neat and tidy, eventually to be resolved in a drawing room gathering. He sensed that events were getting more and more unpredictable, on the verge of spinning out of control altogether.

Or maybe it was just having made love to Piper Macintosh. He was losing perspective, objectivity.

Ultimately, it was possible that everything could be laid at the feet of an eighty-seven-year-old woman whose body and mind were failing, and the difficulties her family, particularly her grandniece, had accepting that hard fact.

The calls were the most disturbing of the odd events of the past days. Buried treasure, rumors, mysterious digging and herb cuttings—connected or unconnected—weren't necessarily sinister. They could even, deliberately or not, be Hannah's doing. But the calls resisted easy explanation. As cynical as he could be about the bonds of family and community, Clate didn't believe that even a slightly dotty, ever-determined Hannah Frye would terrorize her niece.

With a snarl of impatience, he plunged up the narrow strip of beach into the far reaches of his land. No, an old woman's desire to see her niece hooked up with him didn't explain everything going on in pretty little Frye's Cove. He didn't need a body through the ceiling to convince him. He *knew*.

The cool breeze off the water, the quiet of this unpopulated stretch of Cape Cod, finally penetrated, soothed. He came to a small inlet and could see across the calm water to the wildlife preserve adjoining his property. For a moment, he stood still, listening to the water and shorebirds, watching the scrub pine and oak and wild grasses shift in the breeze. He'd never been obsessive. He would look at the facts, consider theories and rumors, and decide what to do.

But he'd also never been one to meddle in other people's families. He preferred to act alone and trust his instincts, to maintain and use to his advantage the objectivity and perspective of an outsider.

In Frye's Cove, he was an outsider. He could move his entire company up here, bring up his dogs and every scrap of furniture he owned, and he would remain an outsider. The Southerner. That rich guy from Tennessee.

He smiled, surprisingly amused at the thought.

He returned to his house along the same route, half expecting to find the Macintosh men on his doorstep. If Piper told them even half of what had been going on out on her dead-end road, they wouldn't be pleased. But his doorstep was empty, and he was alone, dusk upon him.

He stood out on his terrace, swatting at bugs and wondering about buried treasure.

Then he spotted Piper slinking through the break in the hedges. She had a shovel slung over one shoulder and had on overalls and a flannel shirt that made her look like a lumberjack. Her hair was pulled back with a red bandanna. She hesitated for a half second, seeing him, then kept coming.

She stopped on the lower terrace and slid the shovel off her shoulder, jabbing it into the ground. Even from a distance of yards, Clate could see the paleness of her cheeks, the drawn look around her mouth. The determination.

"Hannah says I should try near the honeysuckle," she called to him. "She's not sure it was the wisteria after all."

"She's not," he said, keeping his tone mild.

"What does a seven-year-old know about wisteria?"

"A fair point."

She didn't seem to hear him. "I had a cup of coffee and a huge piece of strawberry shortcake before I came over. I'm hyper enough to dig up the whole yard if I have to."

"You think the treasure's here?"

"I think I have to prove to Hannah it's not."

Clate moved toward her, his muscles still loose from his long walk on the beach. "And yourself?"

She met his gaze. "And myself."

"I have a shovel in the shed. I'll help."

Her shoulders slumped. He could see the relief wash over her. She almost smiled. "We're crazy, you know."

"Ah-huh," he said, and fetched his shovel.

After two hours, they had nothing to show for their efforts but a handful of old nails, rusted tin cans, and something Piper claimed was a Wampanoag arrowhead. They'd dug under the honeysuckle and all around the wisteria, still Hannah's best bet for where she'd seen the shadowy figure digging eighty years ago.

Clate was sweating, feeling strangely exhilarated as he leaned against his shovel, which looked old enough to have been the one Hannah's murdering thief had used. "Worked off your caffeine and sugar yet?"

"About an hour ago, I think." Piper was breathing hard, apparently undeterred by their lack of success. "You know, you could be right. Someone else could have known about the treasure eighty years ago and it's long gone."

"Or there was no treasure."

"Hannah saw what she saw that night. It just has to be explained to her satisfaction." With noticeable effort, she slung her shovel back over her shoulder. Even in the dark, Clate could see the sheen of perspiration on her arms and neck. There was none of the pale, drawn look of earlier. "I need to be up early to pick her up at the hospital. She won't want to stay a minute longer than necessary."

"Where were you earlier?"

His question had come out of nowhere, something he'd been saving up, and she responded with a jolt of surprise. "I was talking to my father and brothers."

"Afterwards. You didn't have your car. One of them must have driven you home."

"My father did. So?"

"So your car was gone when I got back from the hospital."

She gave him a deer-in-the-headlights look, then scowled. "I can't do anything in this town without someone breathing down my neck."

"Don't keep dragging that one out, Piper. It won't work. People have damned good reason to keep an eye on you and you know it." He gave her a long, probing look. "You're hiding something."

"Oh, all right. Geez, if I'm going to face the damned inquisition. I went by Hannah's, okay? I got her fresh clothes for tomorrow. A nice, comfortable calico dress and kerchief."

Clate didn't back off. "And what else?"

She pursed her lips. "Underwear."

"Piper, what did Hannah tell you when you were alone in her hospital room together?"

Her mouth snapped shut.

"You know," he said easily, slinging his shovel onto one shoulder, not feeling the fatigue of two hours of fruitless digging, "if I were one of your brothers, I'd have drowned you years ago."

She sniffed, about-faced, and marched down his sloping lawn. Clate felt a rush at the sight of her backside, her lean, trim legs moving fast.

So what had Hannah told her? Hannah, who, he reminded himself, hadn't told even Piper everything she knew.

"Bet you didn't tell your brothers either," Clate called to her.

She didn't even break stride.

"You're a devious woman, Piper Macintosh." Her gait faltered, but she still didn't turn around. The cool breeze felt good on his overheated body and was probably all that kept him from charging after her. "But I will allow that you lead a complicated life. I don't have to answer to anyone but myself. You've got your aunt, your father, your brothers, half the damned town."

She stopped, looked around at him. "I don't envy you, you know."

"No reason you should."

He saw her hesitating, that sharp Yankee mind debating, plotting, sorting through the complications and exasperations of her life. "I broke a lot of promises I made to Hannah tonight."

"By talking to your father and brothers?"

She nodded. "It felt necessary at the time. Right now,

I'm not so sure. I need—" She glanced up at the sky, the stars just coming out, then back at him. "I need to keep this one promise. For now."

He left his shovel on a pile of dirt and started down the yard toward her. Now a good ache had started in his shoulders and arms. "Does this promise include spending the night alone?"

She smiled as he came up beside her, and a glimmer of real certainty sparked in her eyes. "No, as a matter of fact it doesn't."

Piper made coffee in her cozy kitchen and popped an English muffin into the toaster. She could hear the shower running upstairs. Not since moving into her crumbling little house three years ago had she had a man spend the night. The occasional friend from Boston would drive down for a weekend, but never anyone in whom she had a romantic interest.

A romantic interest. How innocent that sounded. She remembered aching spirals of need as they groped, tore, pounded, made love last night, until they were panting and slick and almost bruised. She'd held nothing back. Neither, she felt, had he.

No, nothing at all, she thought dryly as her muffin popped. Had he guessed her relative inexperience? Had he deliberately unleashed every last inhibition she had? Even now, with the morning light slanting through her windows, she quivered with anticipation at the mere thought of him walking into her kitchen.

"Get a grip," she murmured. "Liddy will be here soon."

Yet she knew she'd never get enough of him. A dangerous thought, that. Even as they'd whispered to each other in the dark, she'd sensed that Clate Jackson was a solitary, skeptical, difficult man, never mind that last night he'd wanted her every bit as much as she'd wanted him. In fact, she'd tried to suggest he sleep on the parlor couch. He'd laughed, sauntered across the room, trailed one finger slowly, torturously across her lower lip, and had asked her if she expected him to stay on the couch.

"Do you always do what's expected of you?" she'd asked.

"Almost never." His eyes had seemed more black than blue. "Except tonight. Tonight's your call."

And she'd made it. "Not the couch, then."

With a shaking hand, she slathered peanut butter and her homemade strawberry-rhubarb jam on the halves of her muffin. She wasn't a bit fatigued. Treasure digging and lovemaking half the night had led to the sleep of the dead. She felt unreasonably refreshed, her muscles loose, just a touch of soreness where soreness was not a problem.

He materialized in her kitchen, smiled a good morning as he took down a mug and poured himself coffee. Then he saw she had none, and he poured her a mug. It was the sort of thoughtful, intimate gesture that fired the imagination. Yet Piper had no illusions. This man wanted entirely different things out of life than she did. Sex to him was easy, casual, done without much consideration of the past or the future, even if proper physical precautions were observed. He enjoyed sex. Absolutely no question there. He'd fallen on her with a hunger and need that were unmistakable, dizzying. But his lovemaking was rooted in the present only and didn't mean anything.

The point was, she'd be a fool to fall in love with a man like Clate Jackson, to demand from him—or herself—what neither could give, or could give up. Enjoy what he had to offer, she warned herself, and leave the rest to fate.

Which would undoubtedly please Hannah no end.

Thought of her aunt sobered Piper. She straightened, thanked Clate for the coffee, and offered him an English muffin. He shook his head. "Coffee first." His eyes had turned to slits as he studied her. "Piper, last night—"

"We don't need to talk about last night." A quick thought jarred. "Do you have regrets?"

He smiled. "Only that it had to begin with two hours of digging. I can think of several ways we could have spent that time."

A shudder of pleasure ran through her, just imagining the possibilities.

He seemed to read her mind. "And *I'm* the rogue."

"You are, for stirring me up that way."

It hadn't exactly left him unstirred, she noted. But he laughed and moved off to the terrace, giving her his back. "I'll take my coffee and clear out before your sister-in-law arrives. Give my best to Hannah. I trust that whatever you two are cooking up now, you won't let it get out of hand."

And that was the first time that morning that Piper remembered the poison. She'd searched Hannah's town-house kitchen the night before—and found nothing incriminating. No extra jug of springwater. No old jug of springwater. Either Hannah had tossed them out and forgotten, her father had collected them for refills, or someone had stolen them.

Piper had checked the entire kitchen while she was at it. No decoctions, tinctures, or teas that were anything out of the ordinary for Hannah's pantry and refrigerator.

Before she talked to anyone else about the missing water jugs, Piper wanted to talk to Hannah. Maybe she'd want to change her poison story or abandon it altogether now that she was feeling better and could admit she'd passed out for possibly no reason at all beyond the infirmities that came with advancing years.

Liddy Macintosh arrived well after Clate had slipped back through the hedges. But Piper's sister-in-law had a nose for romance, or perhaps just a lot of common sense. "I can't believe you'd spend the night out here alone with some sicko calling you. I can't believe Andrew and Benjamin let you."

"They told you everything?"

"Benjamin was up half the night ranting and raving. Of course he told me. I think the more he thought about it, the less he liked it."

"It referring to—"

"These phone calls, first of all. Hannah's behavior secondly. Yours thirdly."

"Mine?"

Liddy laughed. "You know, I take your side a lot. Benjamin and Andrew do treat you as if you're twelve half the time, even if they know better. But I think sometimes that's easier for you. Having two older brothers to call upon when the going gets tough helps to keep the going from getting tough. If you know what I mean."

"I don't."

"I mean, ass," she said affectionately, "that your role in your relationship with your brothers is just as important as theirs. You use them to get yourself off the hook with men."

"Off the hook with what men? They've scared half the men in town away, and the other half they won't let near me."

Liddy hooted in disbelief. "And you name me one man in town that ever seriously interested you. Just one, Piper."

"That's not the point."

"It's exactly the point. Which isn't to say Andrew and Benjamin aren't utter pains in the ass at times." She flipped back long, blond hair with one hand, blue eyes twinkling. "And, of course, you know I wasn't including Clate Jackson among the men from town."

"So?"

"Piper, I swear, I don't know why your brothers haven't tied a rock around your ankle and pitched you into the bay by now. Speaking of pains in the ass! So," she said, "I am not blind, I am not stupid, I am not naïve. I saw the sparks flying between you and Jackson yesterday at the hospital."

"You imagined—"

"I saw. And so did Andrew and Benjamin."

Piper blanched. "They told you?"

"Are you kidding? They're pretending if they don't say anything, what they saw won't be real. That's nonsense, of course. What they saw was real enough. They'd just feel a whole lot better if they remotely trusted Clate Jackson to do right by you."

"Do you trust him?"

They exited Piper's house through the front door. Liddy stopped in the walk and gave her sister-in-law a sly grin. "After seeing him, I figure trust is probably not real high on your list of priorities involving our rich Tennessean. This is something I understand. I won't say your brothers do. The double standard and all that."

Piper couldn't stop a flush of embarrassment at Liddy's obvious conclusion that her sister-in-law and Clate Jackson had been to bed together.

"Oh," Liddy squealed, sliding into her car, "I love being right."

When they arrived at the hospital, Hannah was chomping at the bit to go. She got dressed while Piper spoke to her doctor, which irritated Hannah no end. She could see to her own medical affairs, thank you. But Piper insisted.

The doctor, no youngster himself, said he could find no physical reason why Hannah might have passed out. Without coming right out and saying so, he indicated his belief that she'd simply dozed off at the wheel, and it seemed less frightening and embarrassing to her to claim to have passed out.

Hannah sat up front with Liddy and scowled around to Piper in back. "That old fool told you I faked passing out to save face, didn't he?"

"He was really very polite about it."

"I'm old, not stupid. I know the difference between passing out and falling asleep. And who on earth would I want to save face for? You all have seen me at my best and my worst since you were tots."

This was true. Piper sighed. "It doesn't matter, Hannah. You're out of there."

"Yes." She sat back with satisfaction, hands folded on her lap. "Thank you for bringing me my clothes, Piper. You found everything all right?"

"Not everything," Piper said cryptically.

But not cryptically enough. Her sister-in-law glanced suspiciously into her rearview mirror, and Piper tried to keep a neutral expression. As circumspect as Liddy was, she wasn't above tattling to her husband and brother-in-law that sister Piper and aunt Hannah hadn't quite told them everything.

When they arrived at her townhouse, Hannah announced that Piper should stay for a while. "I'm feeling a little wobbly." This, Piper knew, was pure fiction. Even if true, Hannah would never admit to feeling lousy unless it suited her. "A night in the hospital will do that to anyone." She shuddered. "Modern medicine."

Liddy was in no mood. "It's better than leeches."

Hannah gave her a cool look. "I suppose you have a point. But I believe in promoting good health through preventive care, and resorting to needles, pharmaceuticals, machines, and carving knives only when absolutely necessary, and not just to pay the light bill or provide new boats for the doctors."

"Since when have you become so cynical?"

Hannah gave an airy toss of the head, apparently forgetting she was supposed to look wobbly. "Since this morning when I insisted on seeing my bill before I left. One night in the hospital! One night! A family of four could have lived on that much for a year in nineteen seventeen. And did."

Liddy glanced at her. "I suppose you would know. Look, I have specific orders not to leave you two alone. Piper doesn't have her car, and yours is in the shop."

"But she can call you, can't she? Or her father or one of her brothers?" Hannah smiled sweetly, but was immovable. "There's always that nice man who bought my house. He has a lovely car."

"You're making this hard on me." Liddy appealed to her sister-in-law. "Piper, you know Benjamin and Andrew are going to think you two are up to something."

Which they were. Piper shrugged. "Let them. If

they're so suspicious, they can come over. They'll only find us brewing sage tea."

"It's not just suspicion, it's worry."

"Phooey." Hannah climbed out of the car in a spurt of energy, but she quickly shot a hand to her temple and pretended to ward off a dizzy spell. She smiled at Liddy. "You're a sweet woman, my dear. But if Piper and I are to be attacked by wild dogs, so be it. There's not a thing you could do if you stayed."

Liddy gripped the wheel. "I'm not sticking up for either of you ever again."

Piper laughed. "Liddy, you're a sweetheart. You got more than you bargained for when you married into this crazy family. I'll be careful, and I'll watch Hannah. Promise."

Reluctantly, Liddy finally agreed and left her husband's sister and great-aunt to their own devices. Hannah made a point of taking Piper's arm as they headed up the walk to her front door. "Your hand's cold," Piper said.

"It's that hospital," Hannah sneered, and left it at that.

She had to have a hot, restorative cup of sage tea before she would even permit the mention of poisoned water jugs. Piper was fidgety enough, she had a cup as well. Sage was considered a woman's herb, its healing and preventive qualities on the female reproductive system well known. Where there was a thriving sage garden, there was a strong woman. Or so the belief went. And, used externally, it was a good hair rinse, something Piper kept in mind when she was drinking the stuff.

"There." Hannah rested back against the tall wing-backed chair in her living room. "I feel much better. I should have had you smuggle me in a cup last night."

"I've done enough sneaking around on your behalf."

"So you have. Now. Am I to assume you didn't find the water jugs?"

Piper set down her china cup; she'd only drunk half her tea. "I looked everywhere, Hannah. I didn't find either of them. No fresh jug filled with water, no empty jug. Unless you keep your water somewhere I didn't look, they're gone."

She looked mildly offended. "I keep my water in the refrigerator or store it in the broom closet."

"I looked both places, and on the deck, and in the trash."

"Then someone stole them."

Piper had guessed that was coming. "There's no sign of forced entry, and your doors were all locked. Who else has a key besides me?"

"The director of the complex and your father."

"I can speak to both of them and make sure their copy wasn't stolen. But that'll mean explaining to them why I want to know."

Hannah's brow furrowed, and she was thoughtful a moment, finally emitting a small sigh. "Perhaps you should hold off."

Piper's heart jumped. "Hannah, *were* there any water jugs?"

"Of course there were." She spoke without irritation, almost absently; her green eyes had glazed over. She rubbed her temple. "I need to think. My dreams—" With obvious effort, she jerked her chin up and focused on her niece. "You should go now, Piper. I need to be alone."

Piper remained in her chair. "What is it, Hannah?"

She shook her head. "Leave. Please."

"Hannah."

A small smile. "I'm fine. Truly. Now call someone for a ride and wait outside. I must be alone."

"I'll walk into town," Piper said. She remembered Clate's opinion that her aunt was withholding information. "It's not that far, and I need the exercise. Frankly, there's not a single soul I want to see right now. I'm not in the mood to argue about where I've been, what I'm doing. Geez, I'm going to be watched like a bug on a pin." She shook off the indignity of her situation. "Look, Hannah, if this is some witchy thing you're doing—"

"What difference does it make to you? And walk, if you wish. I expect your Clate will be along before you get too far."

If she were so damned clairvoyant, why couldn't she have sensed her water was poisoned? But Piper let that inconsistency go for now. "Hannah, he's not my anything."

"Oh, but he is. I'm more sure of it now than ever."

Piper's brothers paid Clate a visit after he'd made a few business calls, read his morning faxes from Mabel Porter, and refilled the holes in his back yard that were empty of buried treasure.

From their dusty, paint-stained appearance in his driveway, he guessed the two men had sacrificed their lunch hour to read him the riot act or do whatever it was they'd come to do. Macintosh & Sons, he'd discovered, was a class outfit. The father and two sons were knowledgeable, skilled, hardworking, and principled. Clate could have chosen a similar path at sixteen. He'd liked the physical part of his work, that incomparable sense of accomplishment when, at the end of the day, he had something concrete to show for his labor. But he'd relished the excitement of putting together deals, getting fresh projects off the ground, finishing them, moving on to the next. The money, the thrill, the power, the respect—they all contributed to his satisfaction with what he did.

Yet here he was, alone on Cape Cod, having a white-hot affair with a woman who valued her life and reputation in her little hometown.

It was Benjamin who spoke first. "I'll be straight with you, Clate. People are talking behind your back. I don't like it, and neither does Andrew, but we can't help hearing things. It's a small town. We've been the subject of that kind of talk ourselves." He paused, apparently waiting for Clate to respond. "Okay. I'll put it this way. We'd better not find out you're at the bottom of what's been going on with Piper and Hannah."

Clate gave the man credit for laying it out to him straight. "And why would I be?"

Andrew stirred. "Because something's in it for you."

"Such as?"

Benjamin shrugged expansively. "Profit. You wouldn't be the first outsider to take advantage of the locals around here." As if Cape Codders themselves had never done damage to their own land and futures by going for short-term gain. "You make a few calls, get Piper all worked up about living out here alone. Next thing, she sells you her land."

As upset as she was about the calls, Piper was taking them in enviable stride, Clate thought. If anything, she'd only dig in her heels and stay put if she guessed someone was trying to move her, much less sell her land to a Nashville developer. Her brothers, however, had their own ideas about their younger sister.

"I don't resort to scare tactics when I want something. And most of my projects have been in downtown Nashville, except for my hotel, which was on land that everyone agreed was open to development." But he understood what the brothers were trying to tell him. "I bought this place because I needed a retreat. That's the best I can explain it. A resort on thirty acres." He sighed. "That's not what I do."

"Then if it's not you," Andrew said, "someone in your outfit's talking out of turn."

"I suppose someone from Tennessee could be making inquiries." He considered the prospect a moment, liked it less and less. "Could be an enemy rather than a friend. Someone who wants to know my plans. If I'm distracted up here, perhaps they can move in on me down there."

Benjamin shifted his weight from one leg to the other. "You don't trust anyone, do you?"

"I have no illusions about people."

"Must be a hard way to live," Andrew said.

Clate had the feeling Andrew Macintosh understood just how hard, if for different reasons. "The point is, even if I would employ such tactics, I have nothing to gain by harassing your sister and exploiting your aunt."

"You bought her house."

"It was for sale, and I paid far more than I needed to pay."

"Why?"

Clate met Andrew's intent stare. "I liked the location."

"What about the house itself?" Benjamin asked.

"I don't care about the house." And then he knew: there was more. He frowned. "What is it?"

Benjamin sighed. "Another credible rumor floated to us this morning. Says you're looking into the historic value of the Frye house so you can have it moved or torn down."

He gave a short, bitter laugh. "Why bother? If I do nothing, it'll collapse on its own before too long."

Both brothers' professional interest was piqued. They muttered for a few moments about how they'd warned Hannah for years to fix up the place, about its pristine lines, its potential. But they quickly brought themselves back to their point. Benjamin said, "So is that a denial? You're not interested in having this house moved, either to make way for a resort or a new house?"

"What difference does it make if I want to build a new house?"

A stupid question. He knew it instantly. This was Cape Cod, this was New England, and his was, by any definition, a historic house, even if never placed on the national register. There'd be pickets, letters to the editor, and general hell to pay if he decided to take an ax to the place and put up something new, to better take advantage of the sea breeze, the views, the technological advances of the past century or two. No wonder Hannah had decided to sell.

And he'd paid her every last dime of her asking price. He hadn't negotiated, as much proof as he probably needed that the old woman was a witch after all.

"Never mind," he said. "I haven't even decided if I like Cape Cod, never mind what to do with this house."

The brothers seemed surprised that someone might not actually like Cape Cod, but after a few more questions along the same lines, they departed. Clate wasn't sure how satisfied they were with his explanations, and he wondered who the hell was spreading credible rumors about his intentions.

The thought propelled him to his car and into town. Time he and Mrs. Frye had a talk about what she was holding back.

Hurtling herself down the main road from Hannah's house, without benefit of bicycle or car, was Piper Macintosh. He pulled over, rolled down his window. She started, jumping up a good foot and nearly tripping on the sandy shoulder. "Oh, it's you. Gosh, you startled me. My mind was wandering."

"I'm surprised to see you out on your own."

She smiled wryly. "So am I."

"How's your aunt doing?"

"Fine. I just came from there. She kicked me out, in fact. She wanted to be alone. I think a night in the hospital has sobered her." Piper tilted her head back and studied him, her chestnut hair gleaming in the midday sun. "She predicted you'd come along, you know."

"Did she?" Clate was amused. "A lucky guess, although I suspect she knows I've run out of patience with her. I'm not one to grill old women, especially when they've just been released from the hospital, but I think it's time she told us the rest."

Piper made a small noise to register her disgust. "I don't know how you can stand being suspicious all the time."

"I couldn't if I weren't also right most of the time." He spoke lightly, but held his ground. "She *is* holding back, Piper. She has been from the beginning. Just as you are now."

"That's not fair."

"I'm right and you know it. You want a ride?"

"Not if you're going to go off and harass my aunt."

"No. If she wants to be alone, I'll hold off for now. Where you headed?"

She slid into his passenger seat with the air of someone who was doing something she really wasn't convinced she wanted to do. Nothing like daylight and an aunt fresh out of the hospital to spark clear thinking. He was a danger to her status quo, her life as she knew it, and yet no amount of rational thinking was going to stop her from wanting to make love to him again. He understood, because he was in the same damned boat. Loving Piper Macintosh wasn't an easy proposition. And loving him—well, she already had a taste of what that was like or she wouldn't be so jumpy about sitting in his car.

"I should go home," she said. "I need to spend a few hours in my office. I'm behind on a million things."

"Did you tell Hannah we dug for her treasure?"

"Not yet. I didn't have a chance before she threw me out."

He paused as he turned the car around and started back toward town. "You're sure it's not because you don't want to disappoint her?"

"Disappoint her? Clate, she won't be convinced that treasure's not out there until we've dug up the entire yard right down to the marsh. Then we'll probably have to start on the preserve."

His grip on the wheel tightened. "Piper, there's no treasure."

"There might have been eighty years ago. Someone could have moved it in the interim and Hannah just never knew. I'm going to reread everything in her shoebox, all my notes, finish the timetable I was working on yesterday at the library." She was talking to herself more than to him, planning, trying to establish control over her life. "I keep thinking there's something I've missed."

Clate acknowledged her words with a neutral nod. "If you need any help, let me know. I'll be around. I have to go to Nashville at some point, but I can put it off for a few days."

Out of the corner of his eye, he saw her swallow at the intrusion of his life—his real life. Nashville was another world. His business, his friends, his life there. Hell, she'd never even met his dogs. He'd planned to decide how he was going to use his place on Cape Cod, get the lay of the land, before bringing them up. Now he'd already fallen for a woman.

Which was an inadequate way to explain his relationship with Piper Macintosh. He'd more than fallen for her.

He said, "Your brothers checked up on me, just in case I'm plotting against you, your aunt, and all of Frye's Cove. If you could follow their circuitous reasoning, they had a point. Depends whether they choose to believe me or what they've been hearing about me."

"More rumors?"

He told her. She listened without interruption, and finally he said, "I have to say, I didn't think much about what the Macintosh family might be losing out on when I bought your aunt's place. I thought more about the Fryes. Here's this woman who married late into the family, selling out everything: land, house, furnishings, the silverware, tangible pieces of Frye history. She let her husband's granddaughter have any family papers she wanted, but that's it."

"That's all Sally said she wanted. She wasn't interested in the rest."

"Why not?"

"She didn't feel attached to it. She grew up in a Boston suburb. She visited her grandfather here, but that was about it until she and Paul bought the inn. Sally's always adored Hannah. I think she didn't want to interfere with whatever Hannah chose to do. Besides, the Frye house has its problems, and Sally and Paul might not have wanted to be saddled with them right now, given the money they're sinking into the inn."

"What about furnishings?"

Piper smiled. "Let's just say Sally has very definite likes and dislikes."

Clate slowed as he drove through the village center, where dappled sunlight fell on the town green and flowers glinted in boxes on the porch of the Macintosh Inn. Very pretty. Easy to get caught up in the myth and the fantasy of Cape Cod. He glanced over at Piper. "You don't think Sally was hoping Hannah would change her mind or that she just didn't want to make a scene? You know, alienate townspeople while she and her husband were trying to get an inn up and running."

"Sally's not that labyrinthine in her thinking."

"Well, I'm getting off the track. As I said, I considered that the Fryes might get their noses out of joint. But I didn't consider your family."

She jumped in her seat, spun around at him. *"My* family?"

"Whoa, there. I'm not making any accusations. Your brothers have made it clear they don't like having such a prime piece of Frye's Cove real estate in the hands of an outsider."

"Only an outsider could afford her price," Piper said. "I think Hannah knew that going in."

"Part of her strategy to lure the man of your dreams here?"

"The man of my destiny." She shot him a dry, amused look. "I'm not sure my dreams had anything to do with it. But do go on."

Clate eased his car down toward the water, the winding, narrow, picturesque roads feeling more familiar to him. He noticed a sailboat out in the bay. If he came up here on a regular basis, he could learn to sail. "I just started wondering if your brothers had anything to gain—"

"You suspect my *brothers?"*

"I'm not willing to rule anyone out. That's the only point I'm making. I don't actually suspect anyone. Their visit made me realize that we need to maintain a certain amount of neutrality and objectivity—"

"You do," she said curtly. "I don't."

He bit off a sigh. He'd done a hellishly bad job of explaining himself.

"I suppose you haven't ruled me out, either?" she asked coolly. "I could be making the calls up. To get attention, to get revenge for my aunt selling out, to get you onto the hot seat. I could come up with a dozen wild reasons that make about as much sense as suspecting my brothers."

"That wasn't my point." His teeth were clenched. The woman damn well knew that wasn't his point. "I'm just trying to encourage you to keep your eyes open and to withhold judgment."

"Not of my brothers. I refuse."

"All right, then, not of your brothers. Hell. But of everyone else, okay?"

She remained rigid, arms folded across her chest. "I would hate to be so cynical that I couldn't trust anyone."

"Yes," he said, glancing over at her as he turned into her driveway, "you would."

Chapter

14

All afternoon Clate could feel Piper's presence on the other side of the hedge. He imagined her picking vegetables and herbs, gathering wildflowers, working at her out-of-date computer in her office, snipping fabric in her studio with her ancient pinking shears. Irma Bryar would have liked and understood his Cape Cod neighbor and her simple ways. A good garden, a solid house, good friends. *"They're all I need, Clayton. I'm a happy woman."*

He remembered his yearning to make his mother happy. The flowers, the chores, the times he'd bring her coffee and toast and offer to do anything, anything, if only she would be happy. All thrown into the abyss. Nothing he could do. Nothing she could do. Happiness, contentment, were beyond her.

Not so with Piper. He thought of her delight at seeing the roseate tern, at picking strawberries in her little garden. Her happiness might mean everything to whoever loved her, but she would never make it their responsibility, their burden.

Tuck stopped over, and together he and Clate reseeded the areas where he and Piper had dug for treasure. Tuck asked for no explanation. Not wanting to lie to a man he intended to entrust with his property while he was in Tennessee, Clate offered none. As far as O'Rourke was concerned, the entire lawn needed reseeding and fertilizing. Never mind that it was lusher and greener than most in Frye's Cove, certainly than Piper's; she was into naturalizing.

"You know," Tuck said, leading up to something. He peeled off his Red Sox cap and scratched his sweaty head. "I've been thinking about those herbs we found cut down, then Hannah turning up sick."

"The doctors didn't find anything wrong with her."

"Yeah, exactly."

Clate narrowed his eyes. "What are you saying?"

"I'm not saying anything. I'm just wondering if she—I don't know, if she got in to something, I guess, and made herself sick. I had a sheep once that nearly died eating moldy hay."

"You're saying Hannah could have poisoned herself."

Tuck reddened. "Not on purpose. I mean, my sheep wasn't looking to make himself sick. Hannah . . ." He replaced his hat, rolled his big shoulders. "It's none of my business, but I think maybe it's time she stopped messing around with herbs and stuff. She's going to kill somebody one of these days, if not herself."

Clate nodded, walking out to Tuck's truck with him. "It's none of my business, either, but I'll give it some thought."

Tuck had barely backed out of the driveway when Hannah herself arrived in her little raspberry sedan.

"I thought you were supposed to be on the mend today," Clate said as she climbed out in one of her weird prairie dresses.

"A few cups of sage tea and I'm right as rain." She gave her long skirt a good shake and inhaled deeply. "Oh, I do miss my fresh sea air. May I come in?"

"Of course."

She smiled, deceptively sweet. "You're a Southern gentleman, aren't you?"

He laughed. "Not hardly."

"Meaning you were raised to exercise good manners," she clarified, "not that you're necessarily gentlemanly with money. Although I suspect you are, more than you're willing to admit."

"I was raised to get along on my own."

Pursing her lips, she gave a tight, confident shake of the head. "No. Someone taught you proper manners. You know what to do, what to say, even if your baser instincts are to be less polite." Her green eyes sparkled with insight, understanding. "And you often have been."

Clate pulled open the creaking front door and held it for her. "Certain of yourself, aren't you?"

"Almost always."

"I have a feeling, Mrs. Frye," he laid on the southern drawl, "that you're just a real good guesser."

"An excellent guesser," she said, unoffended, "but I don't need to guess when I already know, do I?"

Clate let that one go. She led the way to the formal front parlor, which, thus far, he hadn't so much as sat in. With her old-fashioned dress and white hair, she looked as if she belonged amidst the antique furnishings. He could imagine her waiting for a sea captain to return from the Far East, bringing home the china plates displayed on the mantel, the intricately carved chest off to one side of the prim, uncomfortable sofa, the ivory statue, the chess set made of whalebone.

She settled on the edge of a Queen Anne chair. He offered her something to drink. She declined. Her eyes leveled on his as he remained standing next to the cold fireplace. "It was my husband."

"What?"

"The man I saw that night."

Clate didn't move. "The night your parents died?"

"Yes. I had no memory of it until I moved out of here." She glanced around the musty room, but her expression didn't change. She was eerily calm for a woman who'd just accused her husband of killing her parents. "And even then, it came to me in a dream. A clear dream. There's no doubt. Jason Frye lured my parents onto a sandbar, robbed them, and left them. He took their treasure and buried it that same night out here, in his own back yard."

"Why?"

"So he wouldn't get caught." She spoke without hesitation or bitterness. "It would have ruined him, his family name. That was important to him. The Fryes don't have the scoundrels in their family tree that the Macintoshes do. I'm sure he was terribly sorry about what he'd done. It was probably a prank, something he did to make himself feel courageous and daring. Jason always wanted to feel courageous and daring. I expect he had no idea my parents would actually die."

"But if your parents recognized him when he robbed them—"

"He could have been wearing a mask."

Clate said nothing, trying to imagine the horror Hannah must have felt when she realized her husband of seven years had caused her parents' death, even if unintentionally.

Provided her memory of that night so long ago was reliable.

"He tried to make it up to me," she went on with conviction. "I can see that now, in hindsight. He helped my brother and me find housing, helped first him and then me find work, was always there if we needed anything. He supported me in all my arguments with the board of selectmen over the direction the town was taking. Eventually he even married me." She shut her eyes briefly. "It all makes sense now."

Clate edged toward the sofa. A breeze lifted the soft, faded white curtain, brought with it the smell of the Frye gardens. How had she lived here for twenty-five years, knowing yet not knowing? Had her subconscious not permitted her to remember? Or was she just nuts? "Mrs. Frye—"

"It all must seem so far-fetched to you." Her tone was patient, her expression still unchanged. "I understand. You're so young."

"Memory can be a tricky thing."

She smiled placidly. "I'm eighty-seven, Clate. I know just how tricky memory can be. But I do remember."

"Eighty years later, in a dream."

"Yes. Eighty years later, in a dream."

He swallowed. He could hear the old grandfather clock in the library ticking, and a boat out on the water, big from the sound of it. The wind rustled in the tall marsh grasses. Hannah Macintosh Frye believed she had watched the man she would marry more than five decades later dig a hole in his back yard the night her parents died. She had lived in this house, amidst its quiet sounds and fragrances, for twenty-five years. And only now, after she'd sold it, did she remember.

She was eyeing him. "I knew it would be difficult with you. This winter, when I decided to put this place on the market and expected you would come, I knew."

"Mrs. Frye, you're welcome to your fantasies, but I—"

"But it's even more difficult than I imagined."

He bit off a sigh. "Do you really believe you summoned me here?"

She smiled. "Does it matter?" She didn't wait for him to answer. She leaned over, touched his hand. "Thank you for making me tell you. I feel better now that someone else knows."

Clate didn't feel very good at all. Before she left, he took her out to her witch's garden. She frowned at the missing herbs, mystified. "You have no use for these plants, Clate. You don't have the knowledge—" She stopped, gasping, her voice hoarse as she stared wide eyed at the chopped area. "Burn them. Burn them all. *Promise me!*"

* * *

Piper came round to the front of her house, only to find Sally Shepherd standing in her driveway. Sally jumped back in surprise. "I'd just given up on you."

"Sorry. I was talking a walk on the beach. I needed to clear my head."

"I understand. It's been hectic for you, I'm sure. At least Hannah seems to be doing well. I stopped in earlier, and she's looking quite fit and spry."

"She's amazing. Would you like to come in?"

Sally glanced around, as if someone might pop out from the roses. She was unusually nervous, clasping and unclasping her hands; she kept her nails blunt-cut and wore only a thin gold wedding band. Today's outfit was straight out of the Talbot's catalogue: a striped top and walking shorts in white and primary red. "If I'm not disturbing you."

"Not at all. I don't have any classes coming in today."

She relaxed somewhat. "I've been wanting to sign up for your scented candles class. I'd never put candles in the rooms at the inn, of course, but I'd like to make some for myself. They're wonderful. I especially love the smell of strawberry in the winter. Strawberry candles and a hot bath." She gave a small, almost embarrassed laugh as she followed Piper through the rose-embroiled fence and up her front walk. "Decadent."

Piper laughed. "So long as you have warm apple cobbler to go with it."

"No. Warm chocolate-pudding cake."

They exclaimed over desserts and fragrances until they reached the kitchen, where Piper offered iced tea to drink. "It's all I have, except for water, of course." She grinned. "No chocolate cake."

"Well, I suppose tea is safe here." She blanched. "I'm sorry. I meant that as a joke, but the timing—"

"It's okay, Sally. I say the same thing about Hannah and her teas. At best, most of them taste lousy. I'm surprised Stan Carlucci managed to drink enough to make him sick." Piper opened her refrigerator, withdrew a glass pitcher of tea. Her walk on the beach had left her thirsty, if not clearheaded about poisons, treasures, and her next-door neighbor. "He and Paul haven't mentioned the tincture episode to anyone?"

Sally accepted the glass of tea. The temperatures had fallen dramatically since morning, the air feeling more like early spring than the onset of summer. She lowered her eyes, spooning in sugar as she sat at Piper's kitchen table. "That's one of the reasons I stopped by. They're thinking about it. Stan—well, you know how he is. He has it in his head that Hannah passed out because of some tea or infusion or whatever she drank."

Hannah had the same thing in her head, with the difference that it had been slipped to her, not that she'd slipped it to herself. Piper shrugged, trying not to seem disturbed at what Sally was saying. "Who would he tell? I already know what he thinks, and my father and Andrew and Benjamin lost patience with her potions ages ago."

"I think he might tell her doctors." She tried her tea, then added another quarter teaspoon of sugar. Her eyes didn't meet Piper's. "And perhaps the police."

"You think he might, or the plan's in the works?"

"I think it might already be in the works."

Piper gritted her teeth. "Sally—"

Sally breathed out, looking older than her thirty-eight years. Piper felt a stab of sympathy. It couldn't be easy coming to her with this news. Sally swallowed hard, visibly, then blurted, "He told Paul he's going to her doctor, then to the police, first thing in the morning."

"And he has the best of intentions, I'm sure," Piper said sarcastically.

"That's what he says."

"Oh, Sally. Hannah didn't leave him that tincture, and she didn't poison herself. Stan's just going to end up looking like an even bigger ass."

Sally didn't answer, but simply stared out the window at the gusting wind and gathering dusk. "When I was growing up, Hannah was always so wonderful to me. We didn't come here that often, but once, I remember, we got caught in a hurricane. I was ten. I wanted to leave, I was so scared, but my grandfather didn't think it would be that bad on this side of the Cape. And I suppose it wasn't." She drank more of her tea. "I remember everything about those two days."

"Jason stayed put, of course."

"Oh, yes. We rode it out. Hannah had me help her set aside water, food, candles, matches. She tried to get me to think of it as a grand adventure, but I only remember feeling terrified. I didn't think so much of Cape Cod after that."

"You tend to remember your first hurricane." Piper sat across from her, welcoming the cold air blowing in through her open windows. Not a hurricane-force wind by any stretch of the imagination. "I've no illusions. The right hurricane comes along, my little strip of coast'll be rearranged."

"They say in five or six thousand years Cape Cod will be entirely underwater. Geologically, that's tomorrow."

Piper nodded. She'd heard the same predictions. They were common knowledge along the precarious, wind-swept, sandy shores of the peninsula that jutted out into the Atlantic. "Our ancestors' cutting down all the trees didn't help."

"I guess they were thinking about getting through the winter, not the next few millennia." Sally set her glass down with an unexpectedly sharp thud. "Or their profit margin."

"Either way, what's done is done."

"After that first hurricane, I never had any fantasies about the Frye house. I never wanted it, even as a child. My friends didn't understand. I'm not sure Paul did, at first. Cape Cod's so romantic to everyone, so beautiful. But all I could think of was crouching down in the dark with Hannah and my grandfather while the wind howled and the rain lashed at the windows and the roof and walls creaked, and there was no one in walking distance who could help us. No one." She turned to Piper. "I like living in town. I don't know how Hannah stood it out here by herself after Grandfather died. Then you came, but I guess I still didn't understand."

Piper drank more of her iced tea, seeing a side of Sally Shepherd she'd never seen before. "I never thought of us being out here alone. Pop and my brothers were within calling distance—"

"Not if the power lines were down."

"Trust me, if the lines were down, they'd come hunting for us. And with the sophistication of hurricane warnings, there's no reason to stick around if a Category Five's charging up the coast."

"Unless you're Jason Frye," Sally said, not with bitterness, not with affection, but a sort of studied neutrality.

"Or a few other diehards. Most of us have been through enough hurricanes that we batten down the hatches as best we can and clear out when the evacuation orders come. So, Sally, if you're not much on the Cape, why did you buy the inn?"

She smiled, looking more relaxed. "Because it was just impossible to resist. Paul and I both fell in love with it. He wasn't happy practicing law, and we both knew immediately that this was our chance. The location in the heart of the village is perfect, we get to be around people, and it's as well protected as any spot on the Cape can be. It's not ostentatious, it's just a pretty, tasteful New England inn."

That would be important to Sally. "No regrets, then?"

"None." There wasn't a flicker of hesitation. She went on, more subdued, "And I want you to know I have no regrets about Hannah having sold the Frye house to Clate Jackson. If I'd wanted it or any of the furnishings I'd have said something. But I didn't, and in any case, I wouldn't have felt it was right to lay claim to anything."

"Why not?"

"That would have been so crass. If Hannah wanted to sell every last teacup, that was entirely her right as my grandfather's widow. Piper—" Sally jumped suddenly to her feet and put her glass in the sink. Whirling back around, her intensity, rare for so self-contained a woman, was palpable. "Piper, do you think she's happy?"

"Who, Hannah?"

"Yes. When I was a little girl I always just wanted that reassurance that she was truly happy. I don't know why. My grandfather wasn't a bad man. Frugal, a bit of a perfectionist, something of a stick-in-the-mud, but he was reliable and pragmatic. I think she could count on him. Anyway." She seemed to catch herself, and smiled, embarrassed by her own intensity. "I suppose at eighty-seven one doesn't worry too much about happiness."

Piper sensed the older woman's embarrassment. "I think we all want to be happy, Sally, no matter our age. It's nice of you to care about Hannah this way. I'm sure she'd be touched."

"Yes, I suppose." She'd retreated into the composed, dignified, rather plain woman who'd married a Boston attorney and bought a country inn in a Cape Cod village named after her family. "I'm sure I've taken up enough of your time, Piper. By the way, thank you for your advice on the inn. Paul and I both are thrilled with the results so far. We've done more work since you were there last. Please stop by, and I'll give you the updated grand tour."

"I'd like that."

Piper saw her out, and they agreed that Sally would encourage Stan Carlucci to wait another day or two, at least to give Hannah a chance to fully recover, before he ratted her out to her doctors and the police. In the meantime, Piper promised herself she'd try to find the damned water jugs. Maybe she should talk to her father about Hannah's poison theory. He'd brought her the springwater and might remember what the jugs looked like, who might have had access to them.

After Sally left, Piper settled herself down by weeding her garden and picking a couple of baby zucchini for dinner. She wondered if Clate had already figured out that the private conversation she'd had with Hannah at the hospital had involved talk of poison. With Stan Carlucci thinking along those lines, it wouldn't be long before the whole town would be speculating.

Of course, Piper thought, she could walk over there and tell Clate herself.

She pitched an armload of weeds into her compost heap. She had no idea why she was so damned mad at him. It was as if she had all this pent-up anxiety that had to go somewhere, and he was just handy. Sure, in his zeal to keep an open mind, he was willing to suspect her brothers of terrorizing her. But that was nothing, really.

"You slept with him," she muttered. "Twice. That's what's bothering you."

And she was falling in love with him. Which was absurd. She knew next to nothing about his life in Tennessee and nothing at all about his life before the age of sixteen. She just thought she was falling in love with him because of the sex.

"That sure explains it," she said sarcastically, taking off inside. The temperature was still falling. The weather was never certain on Cape Cod.

What was worse, she decided as she tossed kindling into her big keeping-room fireplace, was that she didn't trust herself to know what in blue blazes she did feel. Love, anger, lust, anxiety. All of the above. If she fell in love with Clate, her life would change. There was no question of that. He was a rich, driven Tennessean who wasn't even sure he liked Cape Cod.

"Good, Macintosh. You don't know what you're doing in the next twenty minutes, and you're fretting about the next twenty years."

Twenty years. Her mind leaped into the future, tried to imagine it without Clate in her life, couldn't. Or didn't want to.

She struck a match, setting the kindling on fire. In a few minutes, she had a good blaze going. She added a small log, hoping for enough of a fire just to take the chill out of the air.

The telephone rang. She picked up the extension in the kitchen. "Piper Macintosh."

"Bitch. You're finished."

"That's it. I'm hanging up and calling the police."

"You're too late."

She slammed down the receiver. Too late or not, she'd had enough. A strange, vaguely threatening call was one thing. This was direct and to the point. She picked up the phone again, breathed in, and started to dial.

But she stopped, hand in midair.

Someone—something—was in the house with her.

Adrenaline sliced through her, but she didn't move. Had she heard a noise? Had the events of the past days made her hopelessly paranoid?

No. Someone was here.

Trying to pretend she was invisible wasn't going to help her situation. Grabbing an antique cast-iron poker from her fireplace, she started for her back door, the quickest route outside. She had her car keys in her pocket. She'd jump in her car, lock the doors, and either head next door or straight into town.

No, not next door. Clate might not be home. Straight into town made more sense. But she wanted him. Here, now. She wanted him desperately.

If she hadn't thrown her cell phone into the bay, she could have called the police. Her portable phone was out. No way was she doubling back a single step.

A gust of wind tangled her hair and penetrated her cotton shirt, sprouting goosebumps on her arms. She raced through her herb garden, out onto her lawn, and past her vegetable garden.

Where she stopped dead and breathed.

Smoke.

She stared up at her roof. Red-orange flames shot out of her chimney. Thick, black smoke billowed.

The presence she'd felt wasn't someone in the house with her. It was fire. Not a contained fire in her fireplace. A chimney fire. She knew the signs.

The poker fell from her hand. Her stomach lurched. A chimney fire was a nightmare for any house, but particularly an old one. Two-hundred-year-old timbers burned fast. Her father and brothers' services had been called upon after more than one chimney fire.

Her paralysis lasted less than a couple of seconds. Stifling a wave of nausea, she raced back inside. She needed to close down the dampers in each of the fireplaces to shut off the oxygen to the fire before the heat of the intricate brick chimney caught the walls on fire, before sparks hit the roof.

Her smoke alarms were screeching. She snatched the portable phone as she flung herself at the keeping-room fireplace, smelling the smoke inside now, hearing the crackle of the fire up in the chimney. She had a chimney sweep coming at the end of the summer. He came every year. She knew the dangers of a chimney fire.

She hit the automatic dial, got the dispatcher. "Alice, it's Piper Macintosh. I've got a chimney fire. *Ouch!*" In her fury to get the dampers shut, she scraped her knuckles on the brick. "It's okay, I'm just trying to—"

"Piper, get out of the damned house. We'll have someone there in five minutes."

Two more fireplaces to go. Piper cut Alice off and raced into the living room, where the smoke was heavier. She dropped to her knees. It'd be worse upstairs. Smoke rose. She'd never make it. She'd collapse. Her eyes stung with tears and smoke, and she reached up into the chimney and hit the damper, trying not to think. *My house, my house.*

Even on her hands and knees, she was coughing, choking in the smoke. She couldn't make it upstairs. She dropped all the way down onto her belly and half crawled, half slithered out the front door. The fire department would be too late.

Energized by adrenaline, panic, determination, she charged around back. Damned if she'd stand there and watch her house—her dream—go up in flames.

She dragged out her hose, slung it over one shoulder as

she clambered up the sturdiest of her trellises. Rose thorns pricked her arms and face. She could feel the trellis giving way under her. But she grabbed hold of a gutter with one hand, the edge of the roof with the other, and hoisted herself up onto the shingles. The wind, which mercifully had abated, was pushing the smoke in the opposite direction.

Hot tongues of flames roared three feet into the air. The fire was still getting enough oxygen from the one remaining fireplace in her bedroom. Crawling to her feet, Piper dragged the hose up the pitched roof. It caught on the trellis. She tugged gently, impatiently, careful not to tear it or kink it or pull it off its spigot. The spigot was on. She'd left it on after watering her tomatoes, after her walk, but before she'd realized Sally was there. She'd meant to come back and give her entire garden a good drink. The sandy soil was so porous.

"Think," she shouted at herself. "Concentrate!"

She could feel the heat of the fire. The house could already be burning under her. In a minute, she could go through the roof.

Sirens wailed in the distance, coming closer.

"Piper!"

Clate's voice. Not happy. She coughed, nearly blinded by smoke, her eyes stinging and tearing. She got the hose turned on, the water spraying out at the flames as she moved closer.

"Piper!" Her brother's voice now. Andrew. Furious. "Get the hell off the goddamned roof!"

The stream of water from her hose hardly dampened the flames. If she could only get it straight down the chimney.

She moved closer. Were the shingles hot under her feet? She couldn't tell. Maybe it was just the heat from the sun. Tears streamed down her face, mostly from the irritation of the smoke and soot. She was too caught up in her task to cry.

An arm clamped around her middle, and Clate took the hose. She hadn't heard him on the roof, hadn't even felt his presence. "The fire truck's here." His voice was soft, his drawl melodic. "They'll take care of it."

"My house." She gulped for air. "I keep a clean chimney. I always keep a clean chimney."

"It's all right, Piper. It's all right."

He edged her down the steeply pitched roof onto her ladder, which he'd set against the rose trellis. The fire fighters were already setting up their own ladders, chasing into her house with their axes and hoses. She stumbled on the ladder, half blinded, choking, her knees shaking.

When she landed on firm ground, Andrew dragged her away from the fire fighters. He looked ready to tear her head off. "Jesus Christ, Piper, do you have to do everything yourself? You could have been killed up there!"

She spat something black and icky over the fence into her vegetable garden. "I tried to get the dampers shut first. I couldn't get upstairs."

He inhaled sharply. "Too much smoke?"

She nodded, and Clate came up. A film of black soot covered his face, arms, the V at his neck where his black shirt was open. She glanced at her own arms, her shirt, her pants. She was head-to-toe soot. "Dick Van Dyke," she said.

Andrew glared. "What?"

"In *Mary Poppins.*" This from Clate, his tone soft. "He played the chimney sweep. There's a scene where he looks pretty much like your sister does now."

"Christ, the two of you."

Piper had her back to her house. She couldn't see what was happening. Clate and her brother urged her down the yard, toward the marsh. She could hear yelling, talking, urgent sounds of the men and women doing their job, but she couldn't distinguish words. It was as if her mind wouldn't let her understand what they were saying.

"Here." Andrew handed her a folded bandanna from his back pocket. "It's clean."

She wiped her face and eyes, and suddenly her legs

went out from under her, blood pounded in her ears, and her face felt hot and tingly. She swore even as Clate braced her with one arm, even as she knew she couldn't stay on her feet. Mortified, she felt herself being lowered onto the ground, the cool shade steadying her.

"Shove her head down," Andrew said.

"Don't you dare. I'll be fine. I just—" She stifled a surge of nausea. If she threw up, Andrew would be calling in the paramedics, getting her oxygen. "I need to catch my breath."

Clate squatted down beside her, his presence steady, unshakable. "You want anything?"

"A gun to shoot whoever set my house on fire."

"It was a chimney fire," Andrew said. "You're going to burn someone's house down, you don't set a damned chimney fire. You toss a Molotov cocktail through the window or pour on gasoline. Jesus, Piper. You're getting paranoid."

She glared at him. "I keep a clean chimney."

"Yeah, well, not clean enough."

He marched off to the fire fighters. Still squatting in front of her, Clate watched him go, then turned back to her with a small smile. "Worry makes him irritable."

Her teeth were chattering. She stiffened her muscles to control her shaking. "I *hate* this. I hate every minute. You should have left me on the roof. I almost had the fire out."

"If I'd left you on the roof, the fire fighters—most of whom seem to know you—would have cheerfully turned a fire hose on you. Piper, you can't always take on the world by yourself." He bit off a sigh. "You know, for someone so in to family and community, you sure as hell don't like taking their help. You'd rather do the giving than the receiving."

"Excuse me, but I don't need a lecture right now."

"No, you don't. You probably need a shot of sugar. You're white as a damned sheet under all that soot."

"At least I didn't pass out."

A glimmer of humor in his eyes. "God forbid."

She closed her lips around her teeth, as if that would help the chattering. She made herself glance back at her house. It wasn't engulfed in flames, at least. And the flames spilling out of the chimney had died down. But there was smoke, a lot of smoke, and the fire fighters were still inside, and who knew about water damage, smoke damage.

"Hannah's shoebox." A jolt of adrenaline launched her to her feet. "I have to get her letters. I don't have that much I can't replace, most of the family stuff is at my father's house, but Hannah's letters—"

She bolted out of the shade, Clate fast on her heels with a growl of frustration as he called after her. She didn't listen. The fire fighters wouldn't know an old shoebox contained valuable, even priceless, materials. They'd hose it down, let it burn, who knew what.

"Piper, hold up. They won't let you in."

"It's my house, damn it!"

Her father and Benjamin intercepted her before she reached her back door. She was tempted to make a scene. She held back tears of frustration, anger, grief. She muttered about her clean chimney, her little fire in the kitchen not being enough to get a raging chimney fire going, her promises to Hannah, who was counting on her.

But then Hannah was there, too. A fire fighter screamed at someone to get the old lady the hell out of the way, and she ignored him as she walked around the perimeter of the damage zone. "I heard the news from my neighbor," she said. "He's an old goat, but he has a scanner. Come, Piper. Let's sit in the shade."

Ernie, the police chief, had arrived and asked loudly if Piper needed a hypodermic to calm her down. She whipped around, planning to tell him where he could stick his hypodermic, but Andrew slid in between them and, exercising more patience than he ever had with his sister, thanked Ernie for showing up for a little old chimney fire. "Piper try to put it out herself?" Ernie asked.

Hannah's hand was cool on her wrist as she coaxed her niece to the picnic table. Benjamin and her father joined them, but Clate hung back. She glanced up at him, seeing better now that tears and Andrew's bandanna had helped clear some of the soot from her eyes. He cut such a lonely figure, she thought suddenly, unexpectedly. No one knew him well enough to yell at him.

"There, now," Hannah said. "This is much better. I noticed your wax beans are almost ripe enough to pick."

"Your hand," Piper sniffled, touching her aunt's frail, bony hand. "It's all sooty."

"No bother. I have a lovely oatmeal scrub that will take care of it."

Piper turned to her father and Benjamin, back to Hannah. "I'd invite you all in for iced tea, but my house is burning down." She blinked back fresh tears. "I can't believe it."

"It's not going to burn down," her father said. "We'll have to wait and see what kind of damage there is."

Andrew joined them. "She's lucky. Looks as if there's minimal fire damage, some water damage. Closing the dampers on the downstairs fireplaces helped. It was a dumb thing to do, but it helped."

"Andrew's right, Piper." Her father's expression was grave. "You could have passed out from smoke inhalation and ended up getting carted out of here on a board."

"Any one of you would have done the same thing."

Hannah patted her hand. "Not I. If the Frye house had ever caught fire, I'd have let it burn to the ground. I might have even poured some gasoline on it." She smiled at her family's look of shock. "Well, why not?"

"Because it's illegal, for one thing," Andrew said.

"A pristine, historic house like that, Hannah." Benjamin shook his head. "It's a beauty."

She sniffed. "You never lived there."

Andrew dropped down onto the picnic table and said, half amiably, half seriously, "Don't give Jackson here any ammunition, in case he decides to put in that resort."

Clate took the half-hearted jibe in stride. "I'd invite you all over to my pristine, historic house, but I know you Macintoshes like to stay in the thick of things."

"Well, someone should bring Piper a blanket or a shawl," Hannah said. "She's freezing."

Piper stiffened to keep herself from shaking and shivering. "I'll be fine."

Everyone ignored her. "I've got a blanket in the truck," Benjamin said.

She sighed in resignation. "There's a shawl in my studio. It's closer."

"I'll get it," Clate said, and moved off. In Piper's estimation, he looked as calm and in control as he would if he hadn't just pulled a woman off a burning house.

When he was out of earshot, Piper frowned at her two brothers. "I can't believe you two would think he could do something like this."

Andrew looked mystified. "Like what? You're the one who didn't get her chimney properly cleaned."

"I did, too. Someone set that fire, I tell you. I *felt* it."

He groaned. Benjamin held his temper in check, and their father said, "Piper, be careful. You don't want to start flinging unwarranted accusations of arson. A chimney fire's not that easy to set. It could have been an accident."

"It wasn't an accident."

Hannah had shrunk down into the bench, her brows drawn together in concentrated thought, her green eyes as clear and bright and vivid as Piper had ever seen them. It was the same sort of expression she'd had when she first mentioned her father's treasure.

"Piper's right." At first, the men didn't hear her. Then she raised her chin and drew her own handwoven shawl about her thin shoulders and repeated herself in a louder, stronger voice. "Piper's right. It wasn't an accident. Someone set the fire."

Andrew snorted. "Well, hell, let's just go find Ernie and tell him. He'll take your word for it, Hannah. Let's get Stan Carlucci to vouch for you."

"You needn't be nasty," Hannah said airily.

"You want to see nasty, Hannah? Walk over there and tell Ernie you've divined that someone set Piper's chimney on fire." Andrew was red hot himself now. Nothing drove him crazier than the people he loved not heeding his version of common sense. "People are asking enough questions about you as it is."

"Phooey. I stopped caring what people thought of me in 1935 when this town practically ran out of money and decided to blame me." She pursed her lips. "It was arson."

"Pop, you talk to her."

"What? Me? Aunt Hannah hasn't had to account for her actions to anyone in eighty years. She's not going to listen to me."

She smiled. "Your father did spoil me."

"Yes, he did."

"Maybe someone stuck something up in the chimney," Piper said, "and when I built a regular, ordinary fire in the kitchen, it caught fire, set whatever creosote was there on fire, and—"

"And who the hell would stick jellied gas or napalm or God knows what up in your chimney?" Andrew asked derisively. "He'd have had to get up on your roof or get inside and stick it up your chimney, which wouldn't be easy, and in case you haven't noticed, you live out on an isolated road. You come and go as you please. Clate comes and goes as he pleases. Who would risk being seen?"

Piper jumped up in a rush of impatience. "I don't know who. If I did, I'd be trying to run him down with my car right now. I am *trying* to go through proper channels."

"A day late there," Benjamin said mildly.

She supposed he had a point. "Well, at least we all know now it wasn't Hannah, don't we?"

Hannah perked up at this prospect. "Are you implying I can't climb up on a roof?"

They were about to dive into a fresh round of arguing

when Clate returned from the studio with Piper's shawl. He slipped it over her shoulders. Her brothers and father noticed the intimacy of the gesture, but said nothing; Hannah was looking on with satisfaction. If her prediction did come true, Piper knew, she'd take the credit. If it didn't, she'd find some way to take herself off the hook. Clate sat next to her on the bench, and she sank against his shoulder. She didn't care about the future right now, didn't care what her family might think.

The fire fighters finished their work. Piper got a lecture on the dangers of creosote buildup from Ernie, who told her she needed to have her chimney cleaned regularly and avoid burning green wood. In his opinion, she was damned lucky that the house was salvageable. Most of the damage was limited to the second floor and the roof.

"What if the fire was set?" Piper asked, in full hearing range of her father, Andrew, Benjamin, and Clate.

Ernie frowned. "How?"

"I don't know how. I'm not an arsonist."

"Piper, damn it—"

"Hypothetically."

"Hypothetically, if the fire was set, it was set. It was a hell of a hot fire. Chimney's like a damned blast furnace. There might be traces of a starter left, but who knows? Be tough to find." He eyed her, sarcasm creeping in. "You want me to call in the FBI?"

She clutched the shawl under her breasts. "That's not funny."

Ernie straightened, squaring his shoulders as he returned to his professional demeanor. "You've had a rough day, Piper. This thing looks like an accident. Let's leave it at that."

The phone call, she thought. She'd received it right before the fire. Had he known she'd just lit a fire that would catch the starter in the chimney? Had he been out there in the woods across the road somewhere, watching? She could feel her stomach lurching, her whole body trembling. Suddenly it all seemed so complicated to try to explain to Ernie, to anyone. What could he do without a suspect, evidence, even a good reason for the calls? What would he say if she started yammering about buried treasure?

"You're probably right." She had to talk through chattering teeth. "Tell the guys thanks, okay? They saved my house."

After the police and fire departments left, the Macintosh men decided to go in and check out Piper's house, urging her to go over to Clate's to get cleaned up. Their abrupt change in attitude toward him took Piper by surprise. Clate seemed hardly to notice.

"Your clothes'll probably be ruined from smoke damage," her father said.

"I can call Liddy," Benjamin said, "and have her bring over a couple outfits."

Piper readied a smile, but it didn't quite come off. "Thanks."

She and Clate walked down along the path, and the closer they got to the marsh, the clearer and cleaner the air. Except for the odors clinging to her clothes, her hair, her skin, the acrid smells of the fire had dissipated. She concentrated on the ordinary sounds of the birds and the sea. Clate was a solid, silent presence next to her.

But as they went through the break in the privet, she turned to him. "Something's on your mind."

"It'll keep."

The shawl had dropped down her shoulders; the walk, the air, had helped steady her. "It's okay, Clate, I've done all the falling apart I'm going to do today."

He started up the path and she caught up with him. He glanced at her. "All right. What didn't you tell the police chief?"

"Ernie? You noticed?" A stupid question. Clate was a man who noticed everything; it probably had been a means of survival. He was an observer, someone who'd learned, probably early on, to protect himself by watching, seeing beneath the surface. She sighed. "I received another phone call right before the fire. It just seemed too much to go into."

"Did the caller mention the fire?"

She repeated his exact words, then asked, "Do you think my father and brothers saw I was holding back?"

He gave a small smile. "They don't look at you the same way I do."

She smiled back, and for the first time in hours, she felt composed and almost calm, never mind that her house had just about burned down.

Chapter

15

Clate had a pot of hot tea ready when Piper joined him in the kitchen after her shower. She'd put on his flannel robe, and if her house hadn't just caught on fire, he'd have carried her right back upstairs. But her sister-in-law was on her way with clothes, and her father and brothers with their report on how her house had fared, and who the hell knew about Hannah. So Clate tore his gaze from her milky, fresh-scrubbed throat and poured the tea.

"Honey in mine, please," she mumbled.

"I don't have honey."

"Sugar, then."

She slid onto a chair at his wobbly, antique kitchen table and stared out the window. It was a long, slow June day, dusk coming late. Gulls arced in the evening sky. She'd stopped shaking, he noticed, but now she was fighting tears. He was watching for signs she was slipping into shock. It wasn't every day even Piper Macintosh tried to put out a chimney fire.

"You can cry, you know." He placed her tea in front of

her; he'd used one of Hannah's pretty cups and saucers from the dining room. "Might release some tension."

Her jaw set. "I wouldn't give the bastard the satisfaction."

"The bastard wouldn't know."

"I'd know."

A woman of a certain integrity. She'd trespass and swipe valerian root from her neighbor's garden, she'd withhold critical information from her family, but she was honest with her emotions. Brutally so at times.

Clate touched her damp hair, kissed her softly on the cheek. "Drink your tea. I'll make another pot. I'm expecting a Macintosh onslaught at any moment."

Her eyes—green, clear, determined—focused on him, and a smile tried to work its way through to him, but didn't quite get there. "Better make coffee, too. My brothers aren't tea drinkers."

"Why doesn't that surprise me?"

He got coffee out of the refrigerator and set it on the counter, then raked a hand through his hair, his back still to Piper. She deserved to know. The calls, the strange goings-on with treasure and poisons and missing herbs and now possible arson—he couldn't not tell her about his conversation with Hannah.

He filled the carafe to his coffeemaker with water, debating. No. Piper wouldn't prefer to sit quietly and drink her tea when there was information to be had. He was doing her no service by holding back.

He poured the water into the coffeemaker, then turned to her. "Hannah stopped by earlier. Remember when I told you I had the feeling she was holding back on you?"

Piper's eyes narrowed, cautious, suspicious. "Yes."

"She was. You'll understand why in a second. Piper, she saw the shadowy figure that night. Or thinks she did."

"It was in her dream?"

He nodded. "She's convinced this dream is really her memory—her seven-year-old self talking to her eighty-seven-year-old self, I guess."

244

"Then she recognized this figure? She knows—"

"She recognized the man who was out there that night, in her dream, burying a chest in the Frye back yard."

"Good God. Who?"

"Jason Frye."

Piper didn't respond. Clate wasn't sure she was even breathing. She simply stared at him, not a tear in either green eye.

"I'm sorry," he said. "I should have waited to tell you."

"No." She shook her head. "No, you shouldn't have waited. I'm just—I just don't know what to make of this one. I don't know if I believe Hannah more or believe her less now. I mean, she and Jason were married for seven years."

"That could be the whole point."

Piper frowned, rubbed her forehead. "Yes, she could be having this dream now that she's out of her husband's house as a way of coming to terms with some new realization that she married the wrong man. This treasure stuff could all be metaphorical."

"A trick of the mind to get her to acknowledge that she and Jason weren't happy together?"

"Exactly."

He got a filter down from the cabinet, set it in the coffeemaker, and scooped in coffee grounds. "And it's something she couldn't do until she'd moved out of here and I'd moved in."

"Apparently not. Her subconscious wouldn't let her deal with the fact that she and Jason weren't happy together while she was still living in his house."

"So why have you hunt treasure?"

Piper's shoulders sagged, making her look even smaller in his robe. She turned back to the window and his miraculous view. Some of the spark of energy had gone out of her voice. "She doesn't know if her dream's a trick of her imagination or if it's real, an event that actually happened. Maybe she wants me to prove it wasn't Jason that night. I don't know. Why didn't she just tell me?"

"To keep you objective. It's nothing that we can solve now." He flipped on the coffeemaker, half an eye on Piper. He was still worried shock would settle in. "Drink your tea. Your family will be descending at any moment."

Liddy arrived first with a suitcase of clothes and two preadolescent boys who wanted to know all about the fire. Were you really up on the roof, Aunt Piper? Did anything blow up? They pelted her with questions, and she tried to answer them, until their mother ran them outside.

"Jesus, Piper," Liddy Macintosh breathed. "The whole town's hopping over this one. Stan Carlucci flagged me down and told me to tell you he'll help you in any way he can."

"He can stop saying Hannah's trying to poison him."

Liddy managed a weak grin. "I think he was thinking more in terms of a basket of fruit. Here." She dropped the suitcase onto the floor. "I'm bigger through the behind than you, but I think most of this stuff'll fit. I brought a couple of pairs of shorts, jeans, sweatshirts, T-shirts. I called a friend, and she's off to the store to pick you up some new underwear." She glanced at Clate, who busied himself getting down mugs, then shifted her gaze back to her sister-in-law. "No fun wearing baggy undies."

"Thanks, Liddy."

"No problem. I also grabbed an extra toothbrush and some cleansing cream Hannah gave me." She smiled encouragingly. "That should help you feel at home."

Before Piper could reply, the front doorbell rang. Liddy went off to answer it as if the place were hers, which was fine with Clate, who understood he was living in a house that the people of Frye's Cove, in general, looked upon as their own. Hannah must not have spent much of her widowhood alone. When Liddy returned, she had a box of doughnuts. A present from Mrs. Carlucci. Clate had the feeling this was only the beginning.

Liddy put the doughnuts on a plate and dug out a big Thermos that Clate didn't even know he had, poured in the coffee, and made another pot. The friend arrived with the new underwear. The boys floated back in, tried to make off with two doughnuts each, were reprimanded, and satisfied themselves with one each.

Sally and Paul Shepherd turned up with a big pot of clam chowder from the tavern at their inn. They expressed their shock and dismay at Piper's ordeal. "At least you and your father and brothers know how to fix up the place," Paul said. "It's salvageable, isn't it?"

Piper nodded. More color was returning to her face. She liked the activity, Clate thought, and appreciated the attention, the fact that people cared. "I think so. It could have been much worse. They'll be over with their report soon."

Sally sat at the table, turning down Liddy's offer of coffee and a doughnut. "It's true, then, that you ran back inside to shut down the dampers?" She seemed amazed, and she struck Clate as a woman with a certain strength of character, an almost prudish sense of propriety, but without real courage.

"I acted without thinking."

"Oh, Piper! You could have passed out with all the smoke."

"I know. It was dumb."

"But you probably saved your house," Paul said, standing above his wife.

Piper nibbled at a honey-covered doughnut. Rising, Sally laid a hand on her husband's elbow, ladylike, utterly composed. "We should go, Paul." She smiled kindly at Piper. "If you need anything, please don't hesitate to call on us. We certainly have room at the inn if you need a place to stay."

"Thank you." Again, tears threatened. "Everyone's been great."

As the Shepherds left, the Macintosh men arrived. They smelled of smoke and had splotches of soot on their hands, arms, faces, clothes. Andrew looked as if he'd crawled up the fireplace. He retreated to Clate's downstairs bathroom to wash up. The other two washed up at the kitchen sink, much to Liddy's irritation. Benjamin grinned at his wife. "Pour us coffee, woman, and keep quiet."

She kneed him in the thigh, muttered something to him that sounded pretty much like "go to hell," and they both laughed. Benjamin did, however, pour his own coffee. Liddy offered him and her father-in-law doughnuts.

They were eating, all talking at once, when Hannah made her entrance. She'd gone home for a jar of a greenish tea that she insisted Piper drink immediately, without benefit of a cup, heat, or sugar. Piper opened the jar and sniffed. "What is it?"

"A restorative mixture."

"Of what?"

"I don't remember, exactly. I wrote it down somewhere. Oh, for heaven's sake. I drank some myself last night, and I'm still here." She gave a haughty toss of her head. "I didn't poison myself. That, presumably, was the work of whoever set fire to your house."

Andrew emerged from the hallway. "What was that?"

They were off and running. Poisons, arson, threatening phone calls, who hadn't told whom what, who was still holding back pertinent information. This last was reiterated by each Macintosh man, eyes on Piper and Hannah, who ignored them. Listening carefully, Clate gathered that Piper's house was salvageable, but unlivable at the moment. Part of the roof had burned, and the wall around the chimney on the second floor had caught fire, forcing the fire fighters to rip it up. Smoke damage had probably ruined most of what Piper owned, although some stuff downstairs, especially closer to her kitchen and back rooms, might be okay.

Liddy Macintosh dipped chowder into mugs and bowls. She smiled at Clate. "You'll get used to it. The more worried they are, the louder they shout."

He leaned against the counter, watching Piper hold

her own with her father and brothers. They never crossed the line with her, and in their own way, they treated her as an equal. She'd have to bear up under their scrutiny and high standards, just like anyone else. And they under hers.

"She'd be right there yelling with Benjamin," Liddy said, "if Andrew had just nearly gotten himself killed trying to keep his house from burning down."

"Tight-knit family."

She laughed. "Don't I know it."

When they launched into a rehash of everything they'd just gone over, Clate took his mug of coffee outside. The boys were rampaging through his yard with a familiarity that was disconcerting him less and less. Hannah, perhaps, had done a disservice to them all by selling this place.

She materialized next to him; he hadn't even heard the door open. Wisps of white hair floated around her gently wrinkled face. She said, "I assume you've told Piper it was Jason I saw that night, out here."

"I told her."

"And you're both even more uncertain of my memory now." She wandered down from the terrace, through the lush grass toward her enclosed herb garden. Tall flowers—pale pink, dark purple, frothy white, creamy yellow—glinted in the last of the evening sun. She glanced back at Clate, and he noticed there was no kerchief or crocheted snood today, just pins and cloisonné combs. "If Jason was responsible for my parents' deaths, I want to know. I *have* to know. What I saw that night could have been coincidence. Maybe he was burying something that had nothing to do with the shipwreck. Maybe I'm misinterpreting what I remember."

"Is that what you believe?"

"This isn't about what I believe. It's about what really happened here. The truth."

"What about what's happening now? The calls, the rest of it."

"They're related." She spoke with conviction. "I just

don't know how. But Jason's dead. He didn't set Piper's house on fire."

"So you really do believe the fire was set?"

She eyed him. "Don't you?"

He didn't answer at once. He could hear the boys whooping as they raced down through the marsh, the family inside talking more quietly now, occasional laughter punctuating their conversation. His head ached. He hadn't noticed before. It was the tension, he knew. It was caring about these people. About Piper. He wasn't accustomed to these sorts of complications in his life.

"Yes," he said at last. "I do."

The screen door banged open and shut, and Piper burst out onto the terrace in baggy jeans, an oversized sweatshirt, and, presumably, new underwear delivered by Liddy's friend. She was carrying a fresh mug. "Hannah, this tea is swill. Absolute swill. I'm not going to dump it on the grass because it'll probably kill it."

"I never said it had a pleasant taste."

"I'd rather drink out of a mud puddle." She fastened her eyes—a vivid, lively green now—on Clate and thrust the mug up at him. "You want to try?"

He laughed. "Thank you, I'll pass."

"You're looking much better," her aunt said. "I think the tea's working."

"I had two sips."

"Perfect."

Piper let that one go and turned to Clate. "Did you show her the missing herbs?" When he nodded, she waved her mug at her great-aunt. "Come, Hannah, and tell me what misery the missing herbs can cause and cure. I want to be ready, just in case someone poisons *my* water."

Clate left them to it, and he walked down his sloping lawn, trying to get some space around him. He could hear car doors shutting, more people arriving. Who the hell would show up with chowder and doughnuts if his place in Tennessee burned down? Nobody he didn't ask to show up, that was for sure. Another indication of how different Piper's world was from his own.

She eased in beside him, not quite touching him. "My family and friends tend to hover in a crisis. When it gets claustrophobic, I send them home." She sighed out at the view. "I hate being in the position of needing their support."

"You'd rather be the one bringing the chowder."

She smiled, turning to him. "It was good chowder. Did you have any?"

He shook his head. He wanted to slide his arm around her, hold her close, ease the last edges of panic and shock out of her, but he could feel her restraint. Leaning against him at the picnic table, in the thick of the crisis, was one thing. Now the shock had receded, and her family and friends were watching, on alert. In spite of her straightforwardness about almost everything else, she was reserved, even self-conscious, about her romantic life, even when it was uncomplicated and unconfused, which, with him, it wasn't. Clate understood. Enough, for now, that they just walk together.

"You must be climbing the walls," she said. "All these people, everyone making themselves right at home. Getting a little claustrophobic yourself, Clate?"

"Just carving out some space for a few minutes."

"I can leave you alone."

"No." He glanced at her and smiled. "I like having you in my space."

She almost managed a laugh. "You're a devil, Clate Jackson. Well, I told them I was going to look at my house. I declined all offers to join me. I don't need a lecture right now on eighteenth-century chimney construction and plaster replacement. I just want to see the place."

He gave her a long look, saw past the fatigue, the shock. "Bullshit." He drawled it out, lightened it with a wryness in his tone. "You want to check on Hannah's shoebox and your research notes."

She grinned up at him, unrepentant. "Don't you?"
He laughed. "Lead the way, Miss Macintosh."

The shoebox was there, smoky smelling but un-charred. All her notes—her notebook, scraps of paper, printouts, copies—were gone.

Her throat raw from the residual effects of the smoke, Piper stared down at her desk. Her mind had gone numb. Clate was checking the rest of the house, just to make sure she hadn't put them somewhere else and, in all the hoopla of the day, forgotten. But she hadn't forgotten. She'd brought everything into her office and left it on her rolltop desk, and now it was gone.

"Why not take the letters, too?" She was musing out loud, trying to force herself into clear, logical thinking. One step at a time. That was all she needed to manage.

But Clate was there, in the doorway. "Because he wanted to know how much you knew. You said yourself the stuff in the shoebox doesn't prove there's any trea-sure or give any clues where it might be." He was silent a moment; Piper, who hadn't turned around, could sense his concentration. He went on, "I'm wondering if he already knows where it is."

She spun around. "The treasure, you mean? Then it exists."

"Maybe. Or maybe this guy knows it doesn't exist, and there's another reason he doesn't want you on this mission, only we don't see it yet."

The quick movement, the tension, had blood rushing to her head, pounding in her ears. She sank onto her chair. Even here, a thin, gray film of soot covered virtually everything. Water from upstairs had seeped through the ceiling. She couldn't imagine what her bedroom looked like. "I should tell Ernie."

"The police chief?"

She nodded, even her eyeballs throbbing. "I've been robbed. I've been threatened. Someone tried to burn down my house. Someone poisoned my great-aunt. She didn't just fall asleep at the wheel. Two water jugs are missing from her house. I think she's right and she was poisoned. Then there's the unexplained digging in your yard, the poisonous plants that were cut down. I know I don't have any evidence, any clue as to who's responsible, but I—well, if I don't tell Ernie, my father and brothers will once they learn about my missing notes and stuff here."

"What about Hannah? You've kept quiet this long for her sake. Suppose Ernie decides this whole thing's goofy and she's probably responsible for everything, all of it?"

"She can't be."

"But suppose this Ernie decides nothing that's happened is beyond what an eighty-seven-year-old woman who's losing touch with reality could do."

She stared at him. "Is that what you think?"

"No, it's not. I think Hannah's an eccentric, relatively harmless old lady. I think she has moments of great wisdom. I also think she's weird as hell wearing those old dresses, but that's neither here nor there. The point is, your buddy Ernie could have heard enough about her in recent weeks to make him wonder."

"Are you suggesting I not tell him?"

Clate shook his head. "I'm suggesting you prepare yourself for the authorities wanting to take a good, long, hard look at your aunt's mental state."

Ignoring her headache, Piper hurled herself to her feet. Pain shot through her head, and she staggered backward. Clate steadied her. She smiled weakly. His iron grip on her arm felt good, comforting, welcome, not at all confining. "Thanks. I'm okay. I want to have a look upstairs before I call Ernie."

"It's a mess."

"I need to see it."

A mess it was. Water still trickled down her steep stairs. Soot blackened everything, her rosy bathroom a dreary, cheerless place. But her bedroom was worse. It looked like the stuff of the eleven o'clock local news. The water from the fire hoses had turned the soot into black puddles that formed in the low spots of her floor and sopped into her hand-hooked throw rugs. The awful smell was enough to keep her in the doorway. Her cross-stitched sampler lay in the middle of the muck in front of her shattered fireplace. The fire fighters had taken axes and sledgehammers to a good part of it in their efforts to make sure they got all the fire. She could still feel some of its heat.

The bed where she'd made love to Clate only a short time ago was a wreck, the linens, mattress, and box springs a total loss. She could possibly clean and refinish the four-poster frame. Possibly. Right now, nothing was certain.

She took in the rest with a quick scan that didn't penetrate her mind and heart too deeply. So, she had her work cut out. She'd have to invest in a new wardrobe, new furniture, new artwork. New walls. The chimney would have to be repaired.

"My brothers'll insist on authenticity when I repair the chimney," she said numbly.

Clate had remained on the stair landing behind her. "And you wouldn't?"

She turned. "I would. It's part of the fun in having an antique house."

He smiled, understanding. "Sure. If you say so. Ready?"

"I should call my insurance agent." She started past him to the stairs. "Well, after I call Ernie. Think my family will have saved me a bowl of chowder?"

But Clate touched her shoulder, gently, and he said her name in that rasping, sexy drawl, and it was all over. She fell against him, burying her face in his chest as the tears came, at last. He settled both arms around her, and he held her close, saying nothing. She sobbed, aware of his warmth, his strong body, his patience, even as she cried for her house, for herself, for an aunt who meant everything to her and whom she might be losing. Clate didn't give her any platitudes, didn't shush her, just held her.

Finally, she raised her head and brushed back her tears with her wrists and gave a small, phony laugh. "God, crying on your shoulder. Anybody's shoulder. That's not my style, you know."

"I know."

"Thanks."

He smiled. "You're welcome."

"And thanks for not trying to dry my tears for me. I hate it when men do that. None have ever done it with me, of course, but you know—in the movies, in books. It always strikes me as so—I don't know, patronizing. I'd rather dry my own damned tears."

"I think it's supposed to be romantic."

"It's not."

"To you self-sufficient Yankee types, probably not."

She grinned at him, already feeling better. "And kissing a woman's tears—yuck. That's even worse. I mean, you don't see women kissing men's tears, do you?" She eyed him. "And I'm not repressed."

"No, you're embarrassed over crying."

"I am not. Crying's a healthy response to—"

"Of course it is. But crying's for other people, not for Piper Macintosh. No, she's supposed to do everything, handle everything, maintain that stiff upper lip, especially over something as measly as a chimney fire and an aunt whose eccentricities may be getting the better of her. She doesn't break down and cry."

"Oh, I see. And you would?"

"I haven't cried since I was sixteen."

She narrowed her eyes on him, aware that this conversation suddenly wasn't about her. He'd just opened a window to his soul. "What happened when you were sixteen?"

"My mother died. She was thirty-two. I buried her and left home."

And the window banged shut.

"We should go," he said, tugging on her elbow. "You have things to do, and I sense your nephews are itching to get into the last of the chowder."

But Piper didn't move.

He gave a small sigh, impatient more with himself, she sensed, than with her. "Another time, Piper. This one's not right."

"I know. That's not why I'm not moving."

"Then what—"

She took his hand, lifted it to her face, and brushed his curved finger across a stream of tears she'd missed. Before she could do anything else, his mouth found hers, tentatively at first, as if testing just how close to crumbling she was. He must have realized that she wasn't that close, or just thought he had the antidote, because he dropped an arm around her and drew her to him, sliding his tongue into her mouth, along the edge of her teeth. She draped her own arms around his neck and laced her fingers together, just to keep herself from sliding onto the floor. She was weak, but not from shock and nervousness this time.

"I'm sorry, Piper," he whispered into her mouth, "for your house, for everything that's happening. You're sweet and generous under all that Yankee reserve, and I know it hurts you to think that someone you might know is tormenting you."

She looked into his eyes, that searing blue, those dark, dark lashes. They seemed soft all at once, sincere, the eyes of a man who cared more than he ever wanted to admit he cared. She didn't know what to say. "Thank you."

The blue eyes gleamed with sudden amusement. "You're welcome."

"Don't tell my brothers you think I'm sweet and generous."

"I won't tell a soul." The amusement reached the corners of his mouth as he stood back from her, his arms still light on her back. "It'll be our secret."

They walked back to his house, and Piper went in, picked up the phone, and dialed the police station right in front of everyone gathered in the kitchen. Someone had brought cranberry muffins, a couple of six-packs of sodas had appeared, and a slow-cooker of baked beans was simmering on the counter. Tuck O'Rourke was finishing off a doughnut. One of the fire fighters, a friend of Andrew and Benjamin's, had stopped in after he'd gone home and showered. The only women in the place were Hannah, Liddy, and herself. Her female friends tended not to come around when they thought she was in trouble with her father and brothers, and having a chimney fire almost burn her house down was a sure sign of trouble.

All eyes were on her, all voices silent, when she asked to have Ernie please stop by the Frye house when he got the chance, she had a robbery to report. No, she didn't want to talk to anyone else about it. She wanted to talk to Ernie. Frye's Cove's police department was small, and she'd have to explain the whole thing to Ernie eventually, anyway.

She hung up the phone.

Andrew said, "What now, kid?"

She pushed her hair back with both hands. She hadn't fussed with it after showering, and it had gone every which way as it dried. Her sister-in-law's baggy jeans made her feel as if she'd shrunk through the day, her ordeal slowly withering her down to nothing. She wondered if she had a red nose and red eyes from crying.

"Piper," her father said, and she realized her mind had drifted.

Hannah got creakily up from the table and withdrew her jar of miracle tea from the refrigerator. "I'll have her perked up in a jiffy."

But Clate said, "Piper found some things missing in her house. She received a threatening call right before the fire. It's possible someone intended the fire not only to terrorize her, but to cover up for an earlier theft."

The place erupted. What precisely was missing? When did Piper last see it in her office? Could one of the fire fighters have destroyed it because it was on fire? Misplaced it? Mistakenly tossed it? Questions and theories abounded, and Piper was shoved onto a chair, a bowl of chowder planted in front of her, orders given from all around for her to eat. And talk. Of course she'd have to be comatose before they'd let her off the hook.

And she had to go through it all over again, several times, when Ernie arrived with his notepad and a long, long list of skeptical questions. He'd at least kicked everyone out of the front parlor while she talked.

When they finished, and he'd put away his notepad and was just Ernie, friend of the Macintosh family, he settled back against a musty wingbacked chair. "I'm going to have to talk to Hannah."

"I expected as much."

"You should have come to me with this sooner."

"Yes, I should have. If I'd had a crystal ball, I would have." There was no sarcasm in her tone; she meant what she said.

"There's not any more I could have done then than I can do now, but at least word'd be out and this character maybe wouldn't have been so bold as to steal these notes and things right out from under your nose, maybe even set your house on fire."

She nodded, glum. He was making a lot of sense. "I guess this is a case of hindsight being twenty-twenty."

"Or it's a case of a niece trying to protect her elderly aunt." His tone was surprisingly gentle, and he leaned over his paunch. "She means well, Piper. I'm not saying she doesn't. But when we sort this thing out, we still might find her at the bottom of it. She'll have her reasons. Some spell, some potion. Who knows?"

Piper sank back in her chair. She'd spent countless evenings in this room, talking with Hannah, knitting, reading, just watching the fire.

Ernie got heavily to his feet. "If she thinks this Clate

Jackson character's the love of your life, I wouldn't put much past her to get you two together. You know, she's eighty-seven. She might not care if she scares the living shit out of you and burns your house down, provided it works and you end up with this guy."

"That doesn't explain the treasure."

"Sure it does. All part of her little game to get you to the altar."

Piper sighed. If Clate had been in the room, he'd at least have understood why she'd been reluctant to go to Frye's Cove's chief of police. "Ernie, you don't understand at all. She believed—don't ask me why—that the only way the love of my life and I would ever find each other was if she sold her house. So she sold it. It's got nothing to do with wanting to get me married off. It's got to do with wanting to bring two people together."

"If you believe her."

"True. She could have just used this spell thing as a way to get her off the hook with people in town who're ticked at her for selling to an outsider."

"Yeah, well, from what I hear, she's lucked out on this one. Think she knew Jackson wasn't a troll before she claimed she'd conjured him up?"

Gathering together her last shreds of patience, Piper rose. "I have no idea. Thanks for coming by, Ernie."

"There's not much I can do, you understand."

She nodded. "Can you wait and talk to Hannah tomorrow?"

"Sure." His gaze softened, and he cuffed her on the shoulder. "Buck up, kid. You'll get through this."

"Thanks."

She received similar encouragement from her father and brothers as they and Liddy and Hannah finished cleaning Clate's kitchen. They'd told him to sit down and leave them to it because he didn't know where anything went. He watched silently from the table as Piper said her good-nights to her family.

"You'll be all right here?" her father asked.

She nodded. "Yes, fine."

"I'm leaving the tea for you," Hannah said. "A half cup before bed will make all the difference."

"I'll try to choke some down." She felt her eyes fill with tears as she gave her aunt a quick hug and squeeze. "Ernie's coming by tomorrow. He needs to talk to you."

Hannah gave an irreverent grin. "I'll have my broomstick ready."

Piper laughed. "Oh, Hannah."

"You and I need to talk."

"I know. Tomorrow."

Hannah nodded, looking troubled. Piper kissed her on her cheek. "I'll see you in the morning. Promise."

Liddy offered to bring more clothes if needed, Benjamin said he'd help clean up her house, and their boys made off with a stack of cookies someone had dropped off while Piper was in talking with Ernie. Andrew, however, couldn't shed his concern. Instead of expressing it to his sister, he addressed Clate. "You'll see to her, right?"

Clate nodded. "Absolutely."

That wasn't the answer Piper was looking for from him. "I'll see to myself, thank you very much. I'm not helpless. Just because—"

"Jesus, Piper." Andrew glared at her. "If Clate hadn't come by, there'd be a big hole in your roof where your butt went through."

"There would not. I was in perfect control of the situation."

"The hell you were."

Liddy rolled her eyes, and the boys giggled. Benjamin seemed ready to jump in on Andrew's side. Piper could feel herself firing up for another round with her brothers, but her father stepped forward. "You need sleep, Piper, and so do your brothers. We all had a scare today." He clamped an arm over her shoulder, his version of a hug. "None of us could stand to lose you, kid. It's not that we don't believe in you or appreciate your abilities."

She knew. It was just easier to argue and snipe than to

admit that she'd scared herself today. "I'm glad I can count on you all."

"You can," her father said, "anytime."

They left, and the house was suddenly very quiet and dark, and Clate Jackson was still sitting at the kitchen table.

Chapter
16

Welcoming the sudden quiet of his house, Clate stretched out his legs and watched Piper pace. She wrung her hands together, pushed them through her hair, occasionally balled them into fists and punched them at her sides. Whether or not she was willing to admit it, under all that brusqueness and argumentativeness was a sweetness and generosity that most in Frye's Cove seemed to recognize. No wonder Hannah had conjured up a man for her and her brothers tended to be overprotective.

Finally, she threw up her fists and let them flop down to her sides. "I give up. I can't sleep here."

"So that's why you're pacing. And here I thought it might have something to do with your house almost burning down." He smiled, still settled back in his chair. "Piper, there's more than one bedroom in this house. You don't have to sleep with me."

She scowled at him. "That's not what I meant. I want to sleep with you." She caught herself, a touch of color coming into cheeks that had been pale too long. Clate thought this rather interesting, considering they'd already slept together more than once. She said, carefully, "I mean, that's not why I'm reluctant to sleep here. It's because of Jason Frye."

"He's dead, Piper."

"I know that, but this was his house, and if he killed my great-grandparents and then had the gall to marry Hannah—" She shuddered visibly, the rush of color disappearing fast. "It gives me the creeps."

"We don't know if he meant to kill them. Or even if he did."

"It doesn't matter."

"What's it got to do with where you sleep?"

She stared at him. "This was his house, Clate. He lived here his whole life."

"I'd think someone as attached to old houses as you are wouldn't worry about what ghosts and spirits might be lurking under the rafters. What's your alternative?"

"My tent," she said with sudden decisiveness, and marched out the back door.

Clate rolled up off his chair and followed her out. It was dark and chilly, a stiff breeze kicking up. He admired the purposefulness of her walk as she headed across the terrace and down onto his lawn. A woman with a plan. After a day like hers, he'd have sunk into the nearest bed by now, never mind who else had slept under the same roof in the past two centuries. But she was off to pitch a tent.

"Where are you going to pitch this tent?" he asked, coming up beside her. He didn't relish the idea of spending the night in a tent, but he'd do it. Not that she planned to invite him. But he didn't plan to wait for an invitation, either. She wasn't spending the night out here alone.

"Outside my studio. It's far enough from the house it shouldn't smell there, and the ground's nice and even. I don't think it'll rain." She glanced up at the sky as if to check, then marched on toward the break in the hedge. "And there aren't any rabid animals around."

"Always a positive."

She ducked through the hedges, and he went right after her. He supposed she could accuse him of hovering. He didn't care. He planned to hover until whoever had said she was finished this afternoon on the phone was in the custody of Ernie-the-police-chief.

The stars were just coming out, the moon almost full. Piper stumbled several times on the way up to her studio, but never fell. The tent was musty and old, up on a high shelf in her studio closet. They got it down and laid it out on the ground just outside the little shed she'd fixed up, painted, and converted into her studio. He imagined her doing it, working hard, planning, arguing, dreaming.

"I suppose you're not planning to let me sleep out here alone," she said, hands on hips, breathing hard.

He gave her a steady look. "I don't think that's what you want, Piper."

"Would it matter?"

"Not in this case, no."

A small smile. "If I had a dog, it might be different."

He grinned back at her. "It'd have to be a big dog."

She stood back to calculate which spike and pole went where, and Clate could feel the peace settle between them. It was decided. He would stay—which she knew already had been decided—but she wouldn't argue. She'd had a bad scare today, and her first impulse, Clate knew, was to assert her independence. The lingering effect, he expected, of losing a mother at two and having a father and two older brothers raise her.

Familiar with the tent's design, Clate started in to work. "I used to sleep in a tent a lot like this when I first came to Nashville. I'd pitch it way out in Percy Warner Park. I'd get kicked out periodically, go out on the river, get kicked out there. Finally, I saved up enough for a little apartment on West End." He reached for a spike, glinting in the silvery light. He hadn't talked about those early days in Nashville in a long, long time. "Irma Bryar gave that tent to me. I think I still have it somewhere."

Piper was quiet next to him. "Irma Bryar. She's the woman who died."

"That's right. She took me under her wing when I was eleven and on the road to hell." He stopped, glanced up at her. Could she ever imagine, ever understand? "My parents married young. My mother was self-destructive, and my father was a mean drunk. They couldn't take responsibility for themselves much less a kid. Irma Bryar helped me take responsibility for myself. When my mother died in a fall when she was drunk one night, I left home."

Piper's face had gone deathly pale against the night sky. "I'm so sorry."

When he saw her expression, he regretted having said anything. She had enough of her own problems.

"What about your father?" she asked quietly. "Is he still alive?"

His shoulders ached, and the wind suddenly seemed colder. "He's tried to see me a couple of times. Supposedly he's been sober twelve years and has a new wife, two kids. A boy and a girl. Seven and nine years old. God, I hope he can do better by them than he did me. For their sake. I've accepted my own past. It was what it was."

But Piper wasn't interested in his past. "You mean you have a brother and sister you've never seen?" He could hear the shock in her voice, the absolute certainty of what she would do. She shook her head. "I couldn't stand it. I'd have to see them."

He stopped working and looked up at her. She could never really understand what his childhood had been like, and he was glad for it. "I expect you would."

Piper's eyes popped open, her heartbeat surging as she stared into the pitch dark. Something had jarred her out of her sleep. She remained very still, listening, uncertain of what had awakened her. An owl. The wash of the tide. She could smell the mustiness of the tent and feel Clate next to her and the hard ground beneath. Had she simply had a bad dream? She couldn't remember dreaming at all, remembered only Clate making love to her. That was the only way to describe what had happened between them. He understood that she was wrung out, empty, and he'd given himself to her, slowly, tenderly, asking for nothing in return but her shimmering release. She'd been so tired, so utterly relaxed, that she'd fallen off into a dead, restful sleep.

There it was. A different sound, one not of nighttime along a sea marsh. But she couldn't identify it.

She sat up on her elbows, alert to every sound.

Clate reached out gently and touched her upper arm. "It's okay," he whispered.

"What—"

"Shhh."

He'd heard something, too. As she listened carefully, she could distinguish the sounds of movement out in her yard. Footsteps. Heavy breathing. A scrape of what sounded like metal against dirt. They weren't steady sounds. They came intermittently, as if whoever was out there was trying desperately not to make any noise.

Clate eased up into a sitting position and leaned toward her, whispering, "He must have parked down the road and walked in. I heard him on the road."

"Who is it?"

"Someone who doesn't know you and I are up here in a tent."

She tried to control her racing pulse. "I wish I'd brought my baseball bat."

"Not to worry." He spoke in a whisper as he fumbled in the darkness, quietly, and produced something that he held up. Piper couldn't quite make it out. "I supplied myself with some nasty-looking tool out of your studio."

She reached over, found his hand, and felt the smooth, cool metal outline of his intended weapon. "It's an antique whalebone knitting needle."

"Figured it couldn't be new. Well, it'll do for my purposes."

He threw off their blanket and managed to pull on his

jeans without making a great deal of noise. Skills learned in his youth, Piper thought. There was so much she still needed to learn about him, *wanted* to learn.

She heard his fly zip, then came the flash of his grin as he kissed her. "Wait here. I'll be back."

He crawled to the end of the tent, unzipped the screen flap, and was out.

Piper pulled on Liddy's jeans and sweatshirt, grabbed the flashlight—a serviceable weapon in a pinch—and slipped out after him. The order for her to wait was just a reflex on his part, she rationalized; if he thought about it, he'd assume she'd pay no attention.

The stars and nearly full moon cast the landscape in a silvery light that produced long, eerie shadows across gardens, lawn, and marsh. She could see well enough to make out Clate's glare when she caught up with him after a few steps.

But she saw the dark silhouette down toward the hedgerow and pointed.

The moonlight, their shifting shadows, must have given them away. The figure went still for a breath, said nothing, then bolted.

Clate Jackson's was not a subtle temperament. He shouted, "Hey! Hold on!"

He didn't wait for an answer. Using his sprinter's body to advantage, he shot down across her meadow with his antique whalebone knitting needle tight in his fist. Piper didn't dare turn on her flashlight in case it blinded him or startled him and threw him off his stride, tripped him up in any way.

She followed at a half run, her mind reeling. Who were they chasing? A man. Definitely. She hadn't made out his face, couldn't put a name to the thick body she'd seen silhouetted against the night sky. It was someone, obviously, who didn't want to deal with Clate Jackson.

A stitch in her side slowed her down. Too much stress, not enough sleep and proper food. Should she run up to Clate's house and call the police? She didn't know if her own phones were working. What if whoever was out there managed to elude Clate and came after her instead? Suddenly her flashlight seemed less like a suitable weapon. She wished she had the knitting needle. But cowering in her tent would have been worse. At least out here she had room to run, if necessary.

The dark figure slipped through the break in the hedgerow. Clate streaked after him. Piper hesitated for a beat, debating her options. She spotted a shovel cast off on the path, picked it up along with the flashlight, then followed the two men through the hedges.

Two yards ahead, Clate already had the man on the ground and the knitting needle up against his captive's eyeball. "Don't move. Got it?"

Piper jerked to a dead stop, gulped in air as she stared down in shock. "Tuck!"

Tuck O'Rourke remained focused on Clate and his knitting needle. "I didn't do anything." His voice was near panic. "I swear."

Clate rose, his knitting needle at the ready. "Up on your feet, O'Rourke. One wrong move, and I'm cutting loose."

"All right, all right. Jesus." Tuck climbed unsteadily to his feet. His breathing was ragged, and he wiped a big hand across his mouth and beard as he kept a wary eye on Clate. "You're one crazy bastard, you know?"

"My chief asset in business. Now, turn around and walk—slowly—up to the house. We'll call the police, and you can explain to them."

Piper laid Tuck's shovel on her shoulder and followed the two men up the sloping lawn. Some pieces started fitting into place, others didn't. "Why was he digging in my yard? Why not over here?"

Clate answered. "Hell if I know."

Tuck snorted ahead of them. "Because I listened to your lunatic aunt, that's why."

"Hannah?" Piper asked, mystified.

"Yes, Hannah," Tuck growled in disgust. "Hell. I

should have known never to listen to anything that crazy bitch says. She told me on my way out last night that you'd found an old map in the wall of your house after the fire—"

"I didn't find any map."

"No shit. If I'd been thinking straight, I'd have realized she was telling me a lie, setting me up. She said the treasure had been moved into your yard, that it was buried down at the end of the hedges."

Piper held her shock in check. That explained Hannah's troubled look as she'd left last night. Something had made her suspect Tuck—something he'd said, something she'd dreamed up—and she'd made up the map to manipulate him into coming out here tonight.

"Crazy bitch," Tuck repeated under his breath.

"We can't all be crazy," Clate said in that easy southern drawl, but he glanced at Piper and shook his head as if to reconsider his statement. "It would have been nice if she'd warned us."

"She tried, but she didn't have a chance," Piper said. "Too many people around who'd have argued with her and blown the setup, alerted Tuck that she was on to him. There's not much room to maneuver in my family. You either tell all, or you keep your mouth shut. If she tried to call after everyone was gone, well, we were in the tent."

Clate didn't look particularly satisfied. "Just keep moving, O'Rourke."

"You're lucky I'm cooperating. I outweigh you by fifty pounds. I could take you down."

"Maybe," Clate said calmly, "but I have my knitting needle, and Piper, here, she has your shovel. I'm sure she wouldn't need much of a reason to hit you over the head with it. You almost got her killed yesterday."

Tuck's step faltered. "That wasn't me." His voice was strangled, less cocky, but he talked fast, panicked. "I didn't do anything but try to get to the treasure before you did. My daddy told me about it. He'd heard talk from back after the shipwreck, only he didn't believe it. When I started working here, I put two and two together, figured Piper was after the treasure, and—"

"And you decided to get to it first."

"Yeah. But I just snuck over and dug that one time, when you thought it might have been her or animals. Then now."

"In the meantime, you terrorized her to keep her from digging on her own."

He stopped, turned. His big, amiable face was pale under his beard. "No. I didn't. Look, I don't see eye to eye with the Macintosh bunch. Andrew and Benjamin didn't think I was good enough to date their little sister. Well, screw them. Screw her. If I could get my hands on the Macintosh treasure, I'd hock it and bank the money. I'm not saying I wouldn't. But I didn't make those phone calls, and I didn't try to burn down her house."

Clate was unmoved. "Tell it to the police."

Twenty minutes later, he did. Ernie himself turned up at the police station and listened to what happened from Tuck's point of view, Clate's, and Piper's. Tuck, waiving his right to an attorney, maintained he'd done nothing more nefarious than trespass.

Ernie sent him home. "Hell, he could just say he was out digging clams," he told Piper and Clate. "Look, go home. Get some rest. We'll sort this out in the morning."

One the way home, Clate had such a tight grip on the steering wheel of his expensive leased car that his knuckles turned white. Piper settled back in the comfortable seat, wishing away her fatigue and confusion and yet determined to look with clear eyes at what was in front of her. "Ernie's right. Tuck's not our guy."

"Agreed."

"At least he's not *the* guy." She breathed out, suddenly feeling exhausted. "I think he's telling the truth. I wonder if Hannah—what tipped her off. He must have said something and she just took the bull by the horns, told him that phony story about the map, and prodded him into coming out here."

Clate glanced at her. "No question, Piper. You and your aunt are related."

When they got back to his house, they discovered that Hannah had indeed called while they were off pitching their tent. In Hannah's crisp, confident voice on Clate's answering machine was her warning: "I think you'd better expect company in Piper's yard tonight."

Clate stared at the machine. "Has she always been like this?"

"Pretty much. She's just less likely to second-guess herself these days."

"Why didn't she try calling again if she got the machine?"

"I expect she figured we were . . . indisposed."

He grinned then, some of the intensity and anger easing. "So we were. Tired?"

She shook her head. "I couldn't sleep now. Maybe I'll just make coffee and do some work in my studio. I'd bake bread if I had a kitchen. I think I'll—I don't know, maybe I'll make potpourri."

He glanced over at her. It wasn't yet dawn. But he seemed to understand. "Go to your studio, Piper. I'll bring the coffee."

Chapter

17

Piper's day filled up with her insurance adjuster, a quick trip out of town to a real store for basics, and explanations to her father and brothers about what had happened the night before. They were furious Hannah had set a trap for Tuck without mentioning it to anyone. If she'd waited, they might have caught Tuck at more than carrying a shovel across Piper's yard. As it was, the police had released him. Tuck was making noises about pressing charges against Clate for threatening him with a knitting needle, and he wanted his shovel back.

Hannah, however, was unrepentant. She'd told Ernie as much as she intended to tell him, and the rest she told Piper when she finally was able to get over to see her aunt late in the afternoon. Hannah served her lemonade—ordinary, fresh-squeezed lemonade—on her deck. "Frankly," she said, "I was afraid Tuck would end up getting himself hurt if he wasn't stopped."

Piper tried her lemonade; it wasn't very sweet. "Then you don't think he's responsible for the calls?"

"Nor did he poison my springwater, steal the herbs

from my—Clate's garden, put the tincture on Stan Carlucci's doorstep, or set your house on fire. That," she said emphatically as she settled back in her chair on her deck, "was someone else." She inhaled deeply, shutting her eyes as she settled back in her deck chair, fatigue visibly washing over her. "Ernie put me through the wringer, you know."

"I'm sorry, Hannah. If you were just a regular old lady, nobody'd never dream of suspecting you."

Her eyes popped open. "I *am* a regular old lady."

This from a woman in a nineteenth-century yellow calico dress.

"Piper Macintosh, I'll have you know that I am what eighty-seven looks like. I'm no different now than I was at forty-seven. I'm just more focused in my energies, and I know more about the things I take pleasure in doing, and about myself, and I don't bother trying to hide who I am in case someone might not like me. And," she added emphatically, "I'm more aware of how little time I have left." She gave a small smile. "And how much. When you're eighty-seven, eternity stretches before you."

Piper didn't want to think about eternity right now; she was more concerned with the here and now. "Were the police satisfied?"

"That I'm not terrorizing you and setting houses on fire, I think so. They're not convinced I didn't poison myself accidentally, and Ernie—I remember when his mother was born, the nerve of him—had the audacity to suggest that I'm using your troubles to cover my tracks with Stan Carlucci." She sniffed. "Just how devious do they think I am?"

"Pretty devious, Hannah."

Her deep, beautiful, old green eyes sparkled. "I don't know. I think I like being considered devious."

"What made you suspect Tuck of trying to find the treasure?"

"The way his eyes shifted, his general demeanor last night. He wanted his greed and envy of Andrew and Benjamin to pay off financially, but he was afraid he'd end up getting blamed for things he didn't do. My mention of the map offered him the chance to try one last time to get to the treasure before anyone else did."

"Clever. But he didn't actually say anything incriminating?"

"Not that anyone else would have noticed, no," Hannah said, smug.

Piper let her aunt enjoy her victory. "Well, if it wasn't Tuck and it's not you, who in blazes is it? Does Ernie have any ideas?"

"The calls concern him, but in his opinion, everything else can be explained by blaming Tuck or me."

"You?"

"Of course. The daffy witch. The crazy aunt who conjured up a man for her niece. What Tuck didn't do, I did."

"You know I don't believe that," Piper said.

Hannah smiled. "I know. Piper, I had a dream last night." Her vivid green eyes grew distant, but she frowned, visibly shaking off whatever was on her mind. "No, it's not clear to me yet. When I'm meant to understand it, I will. I need to be patient."

She shifted the conversation to Piper's new wardrobe, which she made her go out to the car and fetch to show her. She asked about her plans for fixing her house and gave her advice on what decoctions and infusions she should be adding to her diet while under such stress. "And Clate Jackson," Hannah said as Piper started toward the sliding-glass doors. "He's the one, isn't he?"

Piper imagined his body in hers last night, the night so dark she couldn't even see his face, yet everything about him had seemed so clear, so distinct in her mind. And yet, a part of him remained elusive. "Hannah, I'm just not sure—" She hesitated, searching for the right words, the focus of her thoughts. With a pang of regret, she knew what she needed to say, to hear herself say. "He may be the one, but I'm not sure that Clate and I were meant to find each other. Not in this lifetime." It was the kind of talk her aunt would understand.

Hannah nodded in understanding, if not agreement. "You'll know soon."

"You already know, don't you?"

"Yes."

When Piper arrived back at her house, no one was around. The insurance adjuster, her brothers, her father, concerned friends, and students had all been and gone, and she was alone, if not for long. She'd promised to meet Clate next door and have dinner with him. Andrew and Benjamin would show up later to put plastic over her roof for protection when it rained. So much work had to be done, and meanwhile, her life was in limbo.

Fatigue had worked its way into every muscle of her body, into her brain. The aftereffects of yesterday. The expected low after such an adrenaline surge. Yet it was more. She could feel it somehow.

A father he hadn't seen in eighteen years, a brother and a sister he had never seen.

She didn't understand. She couldn't. If his father was sober now and was trying to make amends, why not at least see him? He hadn't accepted his past. That much was obvious to her. But her parents hadn't been self-destructive, abusive alcoholics. Although she'd lost her mother at two, she'd always been surrounded with love and support. Sometimes she felt confined and claustrophobic, but that was nothing compared to what Clate had endured.

Then there was the business in Tennessee, his high-profile life there, his fancy hotel, his employees, his house on the river with the tall fence and the big dogs. She'd never met his dogs. How could she say she was in love with a man when she'd never met his dogs?

She didn't know him. He was an illusion. She'd gotten caught up in Hannah's fantasy and had fallen in love with the man she'd wanted Clate Jackson to be, not the man he was.

But she *had* fallen in love with him. Suddenly there was no question of that.

A truck came down the road, and Andrew pulled over,

his tires spitting gravel and sand. He rolled down his window. "Pondering your losses, kid?"

She squinted at him. "I guess. It all feels worse today."

"Bound to." His expression was serious; he hadn't switched off his truck engine. "Piper, I don't know if it's my place to tell you this, but I thought about it, and I figured, hell, if it was me, I'd want you to tell me. But I'll give you the option. You want me to talk or you want me to shut up and you go on over and ask Clate yourself?"

"Ask Clate what?"

"About his real plans for his property."

Piper frowned. "You've heard something," she said.

"A letter from a research historian here in town. I found it on my windshield when I finished work." He handed over a neatly folded, heavy sheet of stationery. "Apparently this guy was hired by Clate's company to research the history of the Frye house. The original house was built in the center of town—"

"That's not news."

"It is to Jackson and company. If he knows the Frye house was moved here back in the 1880s, he can use that to justify having it moved again and push forward his plans to develop the land."

"Who left you the letter?"

"I don't know. Could be the research historian, only he didn't want to let it be known he was a snitch. Could also be this guy who's been making the calls, hoping to stir up more trouble. I'm not accusing Jackson of anything, Piper. He could have a loose cannon employee on his hands, or this could be a hoax, part of this scheme to harass you to distraction." He shifted his truck into gear. "Ask him."

"I did ask him, and he said he had no plans to develop his land here."

"He wouldn't lie to you, would he?"

"I don't think so."

"Me, neither."

She tried to smile, but couldn't. "Thanks."

"Jesus, Piper, don't thank me. I already feel like a

crawling piece of—well, never mind. You need anything?"

She shook her head, holding the offending letter, still folded, between her thumb and forefinger, as if it might suddenly ignite in her hand.

"Don't stay out here too long by yourself. Tuck won't dare make a move in this direction, but if he's the wrong guy—"

"I'm on my way over to Clate's now."

"I'll be back in an hour or so with Benjamin to see about your roof."

She nodded dully, and waited for him to turn around and head back down her narrow, isolated road before unfolding the letter.

The name on the letterhead was vaguely familiar, that of a Bostonian who summered in Frye's Cove. The letter was addressed specifically to Clate, at his offices in Nashville. It outlined the basic history of the Frye house. The building itself, she thought, not the people who'd lived there. In 1886, the letter noted, the house had been moved from its location on the Frye's Cove green to its present location.

Ammunition for the review boards. He'd need more. The environmental hurdles alone, especially with so much protected salt marsh on his thirty-acre parcel, would probably stymie any major development plans. She wasn't automatically opposed to any and all development. She did believe, with Cape Cod already facing so many problems as a result of its past mistakes, many of them made by her own ancestors, that any new development should be well conceived, in harmony with the land itself.

But that wasn't the point.

The point was, this letter was addressed to Clate Jackson.

Stuffing it into the pocket of her new cotton-linen cardigan, she marched into her back yard and down along the path, through grasses and beach peas and bayberry, to the edge of the marsh and through the break in the privet. The long, long June day was slowly settling into evening, the sun low in the sky, shorebirds arcing in over the marsh for whatever food they could find. The wind had died down, and there was a stillness, a peace, that seemed to come only at this hour, before dusk.

She spotted a figure out across the lawn, just beyond the grape arbor that had been the first Mrs. Frye's pride and joy. Every fall, Hannah used to let Piper pick all the concord grapes she wanted, and she'd make jelly and conserves to her heart's content. Doubtless, Clate wouldn't want a grape arbor in his resort. Maybe she wouldn't warn him about the poison ivy growing in its midst.

"You're getting ahead of yourself," she warned, half aloud. She didn't have the facts. Clate deserved a chance to explain.

But when she waved to him and he didn't wave back, she could feel a spark of anger. Irritated, she wouldn't have to think about loving him, about her house, about Hannah, about anything except how annoyed she was, how white hot. A resort. She didn't care if that was what he did, a function of who he was. She didn't care if he planned to get around to telling her after her own troubles had eased. If he'd lied to her, he'd lied. Period.

Of course, he could have a good explanation.

"Hey, Clate!" She waved again, and picked up her pace as she crossed the lawn. "I've got something to ask you!"

No response. How could he not have heard her with no wind, no competition from birds, traffic, anything? With the tangles of grape vines, poison ivy, and brush, she couldn't make him out clearly. Maybe he was absorbed in his task and just hadn't heard.

"Clate!"

She hated being ignored.

The closer she got, the less sure she was about what she'd seen. Or thought she'd seen. Now he'd dropped out of her line of vision altogether. She looked back over her shoulder, up to the Frye house on the rise above the bay, its pristine lines familiar to her, comforting. He wasn't on the terrace. No one seemed to be around at all.

She took a step backward, debating. She hadn't actually seen the man's face. She couldn't think of anything—body shape, hair color, clothing—that specifically made her think he was Clate, except that he was there, on his posted property.

Biting the inside corner of her mouth, she decided to retrace her steps back to her house and regroup. Maybe she was just paranoid after yesterday, but the vicious, determined voice of her caller sounded in her mind. *"Bitch."*

Yes, a quick retreat was the prudent option.

"Not so fast."

The voice came from among the pines, and before she could move, Paul Shepherd ducked under a low branch and emerged into the open. "Just stay right there, Piper."

She gaped at him. "Paul? What're you doing out here?"

"I wish you hadn't come." His voice was small, filled with regret. "Now it's too late."

"Too late for what?" She was mystified. What was he talking about? "It's not Stan again, is it? Look, Hannah didn't leave him that tincture of bistort and agrimony—"

"No, she didn't. I did."

Piper went still. "You?"

"I wanted people to think she was crazy, out of control. What did Stan call her? A menace. It suited my purposes."

"Your purposes being—oh, geez. You're the caller. You—"

"Yes, me, Piper. Surprised?"

She nodded. She had to buy time. She had to get away and get help and never mind the jumble of questions assaulting her. Why? How? What did Paul Shepherd care about an eighty-year-old Cape Cod mystery, about buried Russian treasure?

"If you'd done as I asked," he said mildly, "everything would have been fine."

Now. She spun around and bolted across the lawn. Where was Clate with his damned antique knitting needle? Where were her brothers? Adrenaline and terror and crazy thoughts sped her along, but the tension of the last days, the fatigue, had taken their toll on her legs. She couldn't get breaths deep enough, fast enough. She dug hard, concentrated on running, running, running.

Paul shot out after her. He smashed one hand into her back and sent her sprawling face first in a move so vicious her mind reeled. This was Paul Shepherd? This was Sally's husband, a Cape Cod innkeeper?

Piper went down hard, her hands coming up just in time to keep her from landing on her jaw. The wind went out of her, and she gulped for air and tried to scramble to her knees.

Paul stomped her down with one foot on her back. "Don't move until I tell you to move."

"Paul, what the hell's the matter with you? You can't want to do this. It doesn't make any sense. Hannah's treasure doesn't exist. It's a dream she's had. I was humoring her."

He pressed his foot harder into the small of her back. *"Stop!"*

His voice sounded strangled, close to tears. If he pressed down any harder, she wouldn't be able to breathe at all. As it was, she could smell the grass and sand, could feel clover tickling her nose. "Paul, don't say any more." She tried to control her mounting terror. She had to think, be rational, reason with him. "I can't prove anything. Whatever you've done, the police have no evidence. It'd be like Tuck. They let him go."

"It's too late. It's gone too far." He sucked in a breath, eased back on her. "Now. On your feet. Slowly, Piper. No tricks. Trust me, I'm not some big stupid beef like Tuck O'Rourke. You won't get a second chance to cooperate."

As if a first chance would get her anywhere. But when

he removed his foot, she got up onto her hands and knees, stifling a wave of nausea as she spat out dirt and grass, then, slowly, as instructed, climbed to her feet. Her head spun. *Clate. Where are you?*

She focused on Paul Shepherd. His hair was a mess, his eyes wild, his clothing impeccable. He was perspiring heavily, but not breathing hard at all. He was in better physical shape than Tuck. Sending a woman flying hadn't winded him. "Paul, don't let this thing escalate further. So far, you haven't hurt anyone. Clate's up at the house. He's waiting for me. My brothers will be here any minute. You can't succeed."

A terrible smile at the corners of his mouth widened to show his straight, white teeth, and finally erupted into a cold, amused, miserable sound that was half laugh, half sob. "You think the love of your life is going to rescue you? Ah, Cinderella. Think again."

"Paul—"

"He's dead, Piper. *Dead.*"

"No!" A croak, a gasp as the air, the energy, the spark, went out of her. Yet she knew it wasn't true. He was bluffing, or he was wrong. Clate wasn't dead. She knew.

"I killed him." Tears welled in his eyes, and he took a breath, calming himself. "Just the right amount of a few of Hannah's special herbs in his iced tea. I'm sure it tasted awful, but by the time he realized it, it was too late." He sniffled, croaked a sob. "Oh, God, I've never killed anyone before."

"Paul, don't. You can't—he can't—"

He straightened, collecting himself. "I know it's hard for you, Piper. You finally find a man, and I kill him. I'm sorry. Truly. But I have work to finish, and I've just gone too far." He pulled his lips in between his teeth, as if to hold back his emotions. "I never planned for any of this to happen."

"Paul, I'm sure Clate's not dead." Piper spoke carefully, not wanting to spin him deeper into whatever vortex he'd created for himself. "I'm sure of it."

"Come," he said. He straightened, in control of himself, the man, she thought, on the other end of the phone yesterday before her house caught fire. "You can help me dig buried treasure."

Clate moaned. Even with his eyes shut, everything was spinning. His stomach rolled and lurched. Bile crawled up his throat and burned in his mouth. Sweat drenched his clothes, his hair. And the foulest smell on the planet seemed stuck under his nose. He couldn't escape it. Finally, he turned onto his side and heaved his guts out onto the floor. He saw, vaguely, that someone had put down newspaper as if he were a sick dog. He started to swear, groaned, heaved again.

"Jesus, Hannah." Andrew Macintosh's voice boomed through the haze of Clate's consciousness. "What the hell is that stuff?"

"It's something I made up when Jason was having those spells." Hannah's voice was as placid as ever.

"Well, don't tell the police. They'll dig him up and have his body tested, make sure you didn't poison the poor bastard."

"I had him cremated, remember?"

Clate tried to sit up, his stomach slightly less turbulent. Hannah had removed her vial of God-only-knew-what from under his nose. He had his eyes half opened. Where the hell was he? The library, he decided. Someone must have brought him there. Last he remembered, he was passing out on the kitchen floor.

"He'll be fine now," Hannah pronounced.

"Clate." Andrew's voice again. Clate hadn't brought him into his line of vision yet. "Jackson, where's Piper? She was supposed to be here for dinner."

Piper. Clate staggered to his feet. A strong arm—Andrew's—caught him by the elbow and steadied him. His eyes focused. His vision was blurred still. "Piper?"

"She's not here and she's not at her house," Andrew said. "Her car and bike are still here."

Clate took in the words, took in Andrew's terror, even

as he rolled off the couch and staggered out of the library, down the hall to the kitchen. His head throbbed, his legs shook, his stomach undulated. *Piper.* He turned the sink faucet on cold and stuck his head under. He soaked his hair, his face, the back of his neck. He switched off the water, stood up, and just dared himself to throw up.

Hannah was sniffing his iced-tea glass. "Don't wash this. We'll have it tested for poison."

Clate didn't argue. Even Andrew kept quiet.

"Jackson, Piper was pissed at you. I showed her a letter—"

"I haven't seen her. I was starting dinner when I collapsed. She's not—" He took a breath. "Hell."

Andrew straightened, his face pale. "I'm calling the police. Benjamin's at her house working on the roof. I'll get him over. Hannah, you can call Pop and Liddy, Sally and Paul, Carlucci, anybody you can think of. We'll find her."

But Hannah had sunk against the counter, her little bony hand shaking; her frail body looked bloodless. "Not Sally and Paul." Her voice quavered, yet her tone was confident. "That's what my dream meant." Her eyes focused on Clate, her mouth drawn down in a mix of determination and terror. "My God, we have to hurry."

"Clate's not dead," Piper said as she jabbed the spade into the hard ground. "You're bluffing."

"Hannah's missing herbs, Piper. The police will blame her. Either she made a mistake because she's old and crazy or she intentionally poisoned him to get her house back and stop him from putting in a resort. He is, you know. I've heard it on good authority. Men like that, nothing stops them." He spoke with a note of admiration, envy. "Keep digging."

Her arm and shoulder muscles screamed in agony, but she couldn't stop. If she did, Paul would kick her. He had several times already. "Paul, listen to me. You're not that desperate. Clate's not dead. I'd know it if he were. You can make a case that you were trying to disable him, not kill him. You don't have to do this."

"Shut up. Dig, damn it."

She could hear the panic bearing down on him. She continued digging. One spadeful at a time. Through roots and worms and rock. It was exhausting work, and whenever she tried to catch her breath, he kicked or hit her, not hard enough to disable her, just hard enough to scare her into thinking about what came after the hole was dug.

"I need water," she said.

"Tough. Dig."

"There's no treasure."

"It's another eighteen inches down, Piper."

"The treasure's a myth. It's a story Hannah's father told her while he was off in the war. It doesn't exist."

He kicked her, harder this time, on the outside of her right shin. She bit back a cry of pain. She wouldn't give him the satisfaction. This whole thing was about him, his ego, his need to be the big man with the name, the reputation, the money. He was a sniveling, arrogant, miserable coward who'd turned a hunger for the easy way out—for treasure—into a campaign of terror. One mistake had piled onto another, until a neat, tidy operation was entirely out of hand, and he was willing to commit murder to get what he wanted and keep from owning up to what he'd done.

And he knew, she thought. He knew what he was. That was why he kicked her, hit her, enjoyed, on some level, having her in his power.

"The hole's too deep," she said. "I have to get down in it."

"Do it."

Once he took his eyes off her, the moment his attention flagged even for a split second, she'd have at him with the shovel. She was just waiting for her chance. She jumped down into the hole. This spot wasn't on Hannah's list. It wasn't even visible from the bedroom window from which she'd watched her shadowy figure. Jason Frye. Dead for nineteen years, and now his handiwork eighty years ago was causing more trouble.

If Hannah hadn't imagined the whole thing.

The muscles in her shoulders and arms aching, Piper hacked the shovel into the dirt. She was on relatively high ground, and the scrub trees and brush produced organic matter that had enriched the soil, making it heavier, denser, less sandy.

"I want the treasure, Piper. Don't mistake me. This isn't just to cover my tracks." His voice was hoarse, every fiber of him focused on her as she dug. "I want the money it'll bring. If Sally had more spark, I'd have the house, the land, *and* the treasure. But she's the Frye, and she doesn't care what I want. Thinks it's unseemly for someone of her social status to want anything."

"It's not wrong to want," Piper said carefully.

"Oh, it is if you're Sally Shepherd. Wanting implies you don't have everything already, that you need more. It's a reflection on your family, on your status in the community. That's why this damned house is so frigging pristine. Can't fix it up. That's for crass materialists."

"Paul, I consult with people all the time who have names and reputations, but who aren't snobs, who take pride in having their places looking nice. They don't not spend money just so people won't think they're crass. Sally never struck me—"

"Sally's a *cow*." Spittle flew out of his mouth, and when she shot him a glance, she could see the pain underneath the anger, the knowledge that there was no turning back. He'd gone too far.

Piper dumped a shovelful of dirt onto the pile she'd already dug and tried to appeal to what reason he had left. "I don't think she had a say in whether Hannah sold the Frye house or not. If you and she could have afforded to buy it—"

"Not with the Macintosh Inn dragging us down." He sneered, furious at the memory. "A nice, prestigious property that all our uppity friends approve of. We can be the proper New England innkeepers. No five-star hotel near the Grand Ole Opry for me."

So, he wanted to be a Clate Jackson. He was envious. Eaten alive by the realities of his life and his own inadequacies. He wanted to be a player, and instead he was leading a quiet life as a Cape Cod innkeeper. What had he thought when he'd married Sally? That her family name and reputation would launch him into commercial success? Later he'd discovered that she thought such success beneath her. Piper shuddered. What a reason to marry anyone.

She thought of the letter in her pocket. It wasn't the prospect of Clate Jackson doing what Clate Jackson did that had so irritated her. A resort on his particular Cape Cod property would never make it through the review boards. It was lying to her, manipulating her, making her believe in him.

But she did believe in him, she realized. Whatever lay behind the letter, it wasn't lying and manipulation. It was a mistake, it was the work of a subordinate, it was even Paul Shepherd's doing. Damn it, she wasn't being naïve, not this time. She knew Clate. He wouldn't do something like this behind her back.

And he wasn't dead, she told herself again. She was sure of it.

"Dig," Paul ordered.

"How do you know the treasure's here?"

"Sweet Sally told me. It was her way of explaining why she didn't want to make a stink about Hannah selling the Frye house out from under her. Seems old Jason made a deathbed confession to her."

"Then it's true," Piper said. "He lured my great-grandparents onto that sandbar."

"Apparently he succumbed to the pressures of adolescence. He'd read the letters from Hannah's father to her, and he thought he was in some sort of adventure novel. He wanted to prove himself courageous and daring. A war was going on. He had to show he was a man."

"By robbing two innocent people and leaving them to die?"

Paul shrugged, and Piper could see that the horror of that night—what Caleb and Phoebe Macintosh must have suffered—didn't reach his soul. It was all an intellectual exercise that had nothing to do with him. "He never meant for them to die. He thought someone would save them before the elements did their work. He'd disguised himself so they wouldn't recognize him. When his plans went awry, so to speak, he was distraught, racked with guilt. He buried the treasure out here and left it."

"But Hannah saw him from her window. It couldn't have been here."

"My lovely Sally was a step ahead of her. She suspected Hannah might have seen something that night and would eventually remember, or had already. Either way, Sally wasn't willing to take the risk. The Frye name and reputation, of course, had to be preserved at all costs. After her grandfather's sordid confession, she came out here, dug up the treasure—"

"It was under the wisteria?"

"Yes. Sally moved it. She never even looked inside. She insists she was trying to preserve her grandfather's honor and refused to profit from what he'd done." Paul regarded Piper with smug, miserable satisfaction. "I had to persuade her to tell me where she'd buried it. This took time. In the meanwhile, I needed to keep you from stumbling on it first. If I'd known it was way out here, I wouldn't have worried so much."

"So the calls, the attempts to discredit Hannah—"

"Very clever, I thought." He leaned over the hole and touched her hair, and it was all she could do not to pull back in revulsion. "I discovered I enjoyed threatening you. I liked hearing the fear and the anger in your voice. The edge of danger, every moment thinking I'd be caught spying on you out here in the middle of nowhere, sneaking into your house. I'll bet Jason Frye was more intoxicated with what he'd done than he ever wanted to admit, no matter what price he paid. Two lives in his hands. Think of it. Sally says he led a tortured life. I don't believe it."

Piper grimaced. "You're disgusting."

He laughed, but even then, his eyes didn't leave her. And she knew. When she found his damned treasure, he was going to smash her over the head with the shovel and bury her in its place. In his own mind, he'd left himself no other way out.

Clate scanned the horizon from his upper terrace, his eyes throbbing, his throat on fire. The sun had dipped low, the sky was a soft, lavender-blue as dusk settled. If Piper had a letter proving he was a snake in the grass, she'd have marched straight over with it and shoved it under her nose.

Something or someone must have distracted her.

"She's in the woods."

He turned, and Sally Shepherd emerged from the kitchen, ghostlike. If he had tried to touch her, Clate wouldn't have been surprised to see his hand go through her. She had no color in her face. He noticed a swollen, colorless bruise at the corner of her right eye. Yet her mouth was set, a grim dignity about her.

"At least that's where I expect she is." She breathed, maintaining the set of her mouth. "My husband left the house about an hour and a half ago. If Piper saw him—if he—" She swallowed, faltering.

Andrew and Benjamin were searching their sister's property; their father and the police were on their way. Hannah came out onto the terrace. She hugged a shawl around her slim, old woman's body. "I understand now. Before he died, Jason told Sally what he'd done. Sally, please. Take Clate to your husband. Hurry."

"I moved the chest," she said in a clear, steady voice. "I—I had to. But I never looked inside. I couldn't. It was all I could think to do at the time. I didn't want to know if there was treasure inside. My grandfather was so horrified by what had happened to Hannah's parents. He'd lived an exemplary life. It didn't seem to me that whatever was inside that chest made any difference."

Neither Hannah nor Clate spoke.

Sally swallowed, her dignity ragged but in place. "I was wrong."

"You were young," Hannah said, touching the other woman's hand. "Sally, dear, where did you move the chest? Take Clate. Now."

Lifting a hand, Sally pointed across the marsh. "It's out there. Paul made me tell him. He hit me."

Clate straightened, ignoring the residual effects of his poisoned iced tea. If Paul Shepherd was out there, Piper was in danger. "Show me."

Nodding, summoning the last shreds of her dignity, Sally led him off the terrace and down across the lawn, past the grape arbor, and into the woods. Scrub trees gradually gave way to larger pine, cedar, oak. He could see where deer had been chewing on trees. Mosquitoes buzzed in his ears. Fresh assaults of nausea threatened to drop him to his knees. His throat burned. He pushed on, gripped in a terror he'd never known, not even when he'd gone down to the county hospital and identified his mother's body.

Piper. If he was too late, if he lost her—

He couldn't finish the thought.

He and Sally ducked under the low branches of an oak into a small clearing of soft, high grass, golden in the evening sun.

On the far edge of the clearing, in front of a stout, lone hemlock, stood Paul Shepherd. Piper was on her knees next to him, at a strategic angle for the shovel he had in his hands.

Piper smiled weakly at Clate. Dirt and sweat smudged her face, an ugly red swelling at the corner of her eye, in the same place the bastard had hit his wife. Clate could feel himself going rigid, reaching deep into his soul for control, for calm, for the courage to wait for his moment. There were more cuts, more bruises. On her arms, on her hands. He couldn't see her legs. Blood mixed with dirt on her fingers.

His head cleared. Anger pushed back his nausea, his fatigue and pain. He noticed a small, unimpressive looking steel-and-wood chest to Shepherd's right. Hannah's treasure. What she'd dreamed about that night eighty years ago had happened. Her memory of when she was a little girl drawn to her window by the wind, the scents of the night, was real.

"Oh, Paul." Sally's voice was barely audible. She choked back tears and stood back from Clate, away from her husband. "Stop now, *please,* before you do anything else. The police are on their way. You can't possibly—"

"Get away. Both of you." He croaked out the words, his grip tightening visibly on the shovel. Desperation showed in his wild eyes, his trembling lip. "I can crush her head with one swipe. That's all it'll take."

Sally sucked in a small, strangled breath. "*Why,* Paul? What can you possibly hope to gain?"

"*Shut up!*"

Clate eased forward. He was acutely aware of his surroundings—sounds, smells, the slightest stir of the breeze. Yet all his energy was focused on the man in front of him. Everything depended on the choice he made now. Everything. He couldn't look at Piper. If he did, Shepherd would know just what was at stake.

"You're not going to hit anybody," Clate said in a steady, calm voice. "You don't have enough time to get the arc you need to bash her head in. I'd be on you before the shovel came down."

His eyes flashed. "You want to risk it?" He waved the shovel. "Go on, both of you. Get out of here. I just want the treasure. Right now, it's all I've got left. When I have it and I'm free, I'll let her go."

Sally stifled a sob, and Clate eased another half step forward. Shepherd had a good angle on Piper's head. If

Clate was a second off, she would be severely hurt, if not dead. His gaze descended to hers, just for an instant.

A flicker of pure, little-sister, in-your-face nerve.

Hell, Clate thought, and lunged forward just as Piper went for Shepherd, elbowing him hard on his shin. He yowled, and Clate plowed into his shoulders with both hands, sending him sprawling backward into his treasure hole. The shovel smacked Clate's chest, and he caught it before it could hit on the ground. Shepherd had landed badly, his head and shoulders and most of his torso in the hole, his legs half out. He wasn't stupid. He realized what had happened, and he started to sob miserably. Sally hung back, unable to go to him, her misery etched in her plain face as she fought for self-control.

Piper scrambled to her feet. "What took you so long? You should have just hit him and been done with it. The damned arc he needs to bash my head in. What kind of talk is that? Geez, I'm on my knees, half dead already after digging that damned hole, and you two are discussing *my goddamned life!*"

"You were scared," Clate said patiently.

"Damned right I was scared!"

"So was I."

Her mouth snapped shut. She stared at him. Tears welled in her eyes and she brushed at them with her dirty, bloody fingers. He held his shovel with one hand and scooped his free arm around her. She felt so good. She was all hot and sweaty, and when he looked at her bruises and cuts, he had to fight not to hit Shepherd over the head with his shovel.

She blinked back more tears. "Hannah's treasure. It's real."

But before they could deal with treasure, they had to deal with the Macintosh men and most of the police department of Frye's Cove, Massachusetts, who arrived in force, dispatched into the woods by Hannah herself. Paul Shepherd acted as if he were the victim, as if anyone in his position—with such a stupid wife, with such provocation as he'd endured—would have done exactly what he'd done. Then he shut up and refused to speak to anyone but his lawyer.

Sally didn't speak to anyone, just walked silently with Robert Macintosh back to the house that had been in her family for over two hundred years. Whatever demons she was fighting, she'd fight alone. By her own choice. Instead of sharing her grandfather's deathbed confession with the woman he'd married and tried to make amends for what he'd done, she'd kept it to herself.

Hannah was waiting on the terrace, gazing patiently out at the view that had been hers for so many years. With Ernie's permission, her nephew Robert had carried his grandfather's chest up from the woods. He set it in front of the Adirondack chair where his aunt sat.

Hannah turned to Sally Shepherd. "Jason didn't ask you to move it, did he?"

She shook her head. She hadn't cried since that first sob at seeing her husband with Piper, Clate noted. Whether it was shock or that Yankee stiff upper lip, he didn't know. She said, "After what he'd done, he couldn't bring himself to look inside the chest. He just buried it. He wanted me—he wanted me to do the right thing. He said he'd done what he could, but he was never able to bring himself to tell anyone the truth. Except me. He could have died with the truth. He could have spared me." She inhaled, struggling to hang onto her self-control. "But he didn't."

Hannah reached out a hand, but Sally didn't take it.

"He never asked me to forgive him," she went on. "The one he should have asked was you, Hannah. But he knew you'd never forgive him, and so he never asked."

"No." Hannah spoke calmly, confidently. "He knew I *would* forgive him, and so he never asked for my forgiveness. His was a foolish, impulsive, terrible mistake that led to the deaths of two people. He never intended anything bad to come of that night. When it did, he couldn't face what he'd done. He didn't want forgiveness, Sally. He wanted to live with his guilt. Perhaps he deserved to live with it."

"Then why tell me what he'd done?"

"So you could know. So you could look at reality for what it is, and accept the truth about him."

Piper sighed, impatient, fidgety, her energy all but spent. "Hannah, don't you want to know what's inside?"

"I was wondering how long you could stand it," Hannah said, a sudden, unexpected twinkle in her eye. Her niece had that effect on her, Clate realized.

With her family looking on, Hannah leaned over and tried the latches. "They're stuck. Andrew, would you mind?"

Obviously glad to have something physical to do, Andrew worked the latches free, then stood back. "Hannah, if you want to do this alone—"

"Alone?" She stared at him, mystified. "No, I don't want to do this alone. I was alone that night, when the Fryes broke the news of my parents' death, when I saw the man I was later to marry out here, only to forget for eighty years." She shook her head. "Caleb and Phoebe Macintosh were your great-grandparents. They'd want you here, and so do I. Now, lift the lid, will you?"

He complied, and Hannah's expression immediately changed. Her eyes widened, and she gave a small gasp of delight. "Oh, *look!*"

Clate couldn't see inside the small chest. Hannah reached in, as excited as a seven-year-old, and withdrew something wrapped in oilcloth, presumably to protect it at sea. Two tiny, booted feet poked out the bottom. Hannah unwrapped it, and for a moment, she was the little girl she was meant to have been eighty years ago, welcoming her parents home.

A porcelain doll smiled up at her. It was a princess, decked out in Czarist Russian garb.

"She comes with her own little Fabergé egg," Hannah said, rushing her words, ignoring the faded, tattered condition of the doll, "and, oh, look, a little velvet bag of gems. Oh, this is wonderful. Wonderful!"

Benjamin Macintosh took a breath and held it, tears not far off. Andrew paced, unable to watch. Their father cried openly, as did Liddy.

Piper sat on the arm of her aunt's chair and pointed out the doll's authentic buttons, how the porcelain had survived eighty years of being buried, and the clothes, although rotted, could have been in so much worse condition, but not to worry, they could stitch up some new ones.

She touched Hannah's shoulder. "Look, Hannah. There's more."

Her old aunt reached into the chest again, producing a small, waterproof pouch. "You open it, Piper. My hands are shaking."

"Mine are dirty."

"Phooey. Open it."

Taking the pouch on her lap, Piper reached carefully inside. "There's a note."

"I don't have my reading glasses," Hannah said. "Read it."

"Are you sure? I wouldn't want to intrude."

Clate smiled. Of course she did. He could see that same knowledge in every pair of eyes on the terrace. At eighty-seven, Piper Macintosh would probably be every bit as nosy and meddlesome as her great-aunt.

"Oh, read it, for heaven's sake."

Obviously excited, Piper opened up the yellowed envelope and withdrew a folded sheet of notepaper. "Some of the lettering's faded." She caught her breath. "It's from your father. 'Dearest Hannah, I hope you enjoy Anna, the Russian princess I rescued while I was in Europe. You're a darling daughter. Thank you for waiting so long for me. Love, Father.'"

The terrace fell silent. Even Clate, who until a short time ago had never known any of these people, felt the tenderness and loneliness of a father and daughter stretch across the decades.

Hannah sat quietly, not bothering to blink back the tears.

"There's more," Piper said quietly. She dipped into the pouch and produced a small box, with a tiny card on top. "It says, 'My sweet Hannah, I love you, Mama.' You want to open it, Hannah?"

She shook her head. "You."

Piper complied, and inside the box were four tiny glass vials. "Lavender water, rose water, glycerin, and witch hazel. Oh, Hannah! Your mother knew you were a witch even at seven!"

Chapter

18

Three days after Cape Cod's most celebrated mystery was solved and Hannah Macintosh Frye was reunited with her parents' treasure, Clate headed south.

Piper understood. His refuge on Cape Cod had become a frenzy of activity. Reporters, friends, family, police, the curious. Everyone in Frye's Cove now knew about his relationship with Piper Macintosh and naturally made it their business.

"No wonder it took a spell to get a man up here for you," he'd said, part in exasperation, part in amusement, finally appreciating the complexities of her romantic life.

The national media had a field day with Hannah Frye and her nineteenth-century dresses and spells and potions and memory of a crime that had occurred eighty years ago. She was in her element. The reporters stayed longer than was necessary because it was Cape Cod and the weather was beautiful, and because they—this Piper could not figure out—liked the tea Hannah served them.

Paul Shepherd refused to talk to anyone. The Macintosh brothers tried to get Ernie to let them have ten minutes alone with him. Ernie, a man of principle in spite of his prejudices against the Macintosh women, declined. Since Tuck had admitted digging once in Clate's yard, that meant Paul was responsible for everything else. Andrew figured out that Shepherd must have poisoned Hannah's water jugs while they were at the inn, before Robert Macintosh had run them out to her. Then, when father and sons rushed off to see Hannah in the hospital, Paul took advantage of the chaos to borrow one of their keys to her townhouse, slip in, and remove the jugs, to prevent them from being tested for poison. Afterward, he resumed whipping Stan Carlucci into a frenzy over Hannah's designs on his digestive system.

Carlucci had apologized to Hannah for jumping to the wrong conclusions about her. They still disagreed on everything, he still didn't appreciate her help with his problem, but he knew the tincture of bistort and agrimony was Paul's doing, not hers.

Sally Shepherd was cooperating with the investigation of her husband's activities, neither rising to his defense nor condemning him. She was calm and dignified, throughout. Piper couldn't decide if this was a result of Sally's nature, or if she just didn't feel any real emotion where her husband was concerned, as if the last drop of any passion that had ever been there had drained out of their relationship long ago.

When Clate left for Tennessee, he promised to return soon. He indicated that business duties called, but Piper suspected otherwise. Not that he was lying to her, precisely. Just that he wasn't telling her everything. She sensed unfinished business that concerned not just him, but *them*. Which, in her view, made it her business, too.

So, she decided to let her curiosity get the better of her.

She discovered he didn't fly commercial. He had his own plane at the airport in Hyannis. He flew it himself. A pilot. Every time she thought she had the man figured out, she learned something new about him.

When she decided to follow him to Tennessee, she bought her ticket through a travel agent, drove to Boston, and climbed on a Boeing 737 at Logan Airport. She'd had to pay top price because she had only had fourteen hours' notice. Her flight was uneventful, which was just fine with her, and when she landed, she hoisted her borrowed overnight bag on her shoulder and marched out to the taxi stand, suddenly realizing she hadn't the vaguest idea where to go.

She didn't know the name of Clate's company. She didn't know the address of his house. She didn't even know the name of his hotel.

So she climbed into a cab and asked the driver, "You know Clate Jackson's hotel?"

"Yes, ma'am."

She loved the South already. "Take me there."

Nashville occupied a basin of rolling hills of oak and cedar and hickory between the Cumberland plateau and the higher plains of western Tennessee. It was pretty country, and as her cab shot out onto the bustling interstate, Piper could feel its energy. Clate must have responded to that energy when he'd wandered down from the hills at sixteen. Through hard work, drive, and nerve, he'd survived. Now he owned a company that employed hundreds. And it still wasn't enough, not because it was wrong, but because he'd hoped it could do what it couldn't do. In her mind, commerce was never a good substitute for family. More manageable and less intrusive in some ways, but no substitute.

The hotel was on a tree-lined road off the interstate, an impressive building of contemporary design and convenience and old-fashioned service and sensibility. Hard to believe the builder and owner was only in his mid-thirties. Piper overpaid the driver, since he'd known Clate Jackson, and slid out, turning down a doorman's offer to take her bag. Doors opened, and she heard more "ma'am's" than she had since she'd turned old enough to be called ma'am.

She walked up to the front desk and asked for a room. There were no rooms. The hotel was booked. They were sorry, ma'am, but would be happy to direct her to another hotel.

She frowned. So much for Plan A. "Do you know if Clate Jackson's here?"

"Ma'am?"

"The owner," she said blithely. She was small-town Cape Cod. This was big-city South. She wasn't sure how things worked down here, but she was pretty sure front desk clerks would know the name of the owner of the hotel that employed them. "I figure there's no point in trying to find his office if he's not even here. He's why I came to Nashville. I'm his—he's my—" She sighed. "We know each other."

Out of the corner of her eye, she saw one of the clerks motioning for someone, probably security. Plan B wasn't working, either. Her case might have been strengthened if she'd combed her hair and reapplied lipstick after she'd landed. As it was, she was a still-bloodied-and-bruised, chestnut-haired woman in a Red Sox T-shirt with a borrowed overnight bag slung over her shoulder, asking about a man who owned an opulent southern hotel. She'd worn traveling clothes. Her new Tennessee outfits were in her bag.

"We do," she said. "Give him a buzz and ask him. My name's Piper. Piper Macintosh. I'm from Cape Cod."

A big man in a dark suit touched her elbow. "May I help you over here, ma'am?"

Ten minutes later, she persuaded him to call Clate's assistant. A minute after that, he installed her on a polished elevator while eyebrows raised all through the lobby. She was to get off on a high floor, and a woman would be there to greet her.

The woman was named Mabel Porter, all of twenty-four, smartly dressed, professional, and very surprised, except she tried not to show it. She apologized, for what Piper wasn't exactly sure, and explained that Clate was out of town, but that he'd be back later that evening. "He'll be so surprised to see you," she said.

Piper grinned, pleased with herself. "This is true."

Mabel showed her to a suite whose living room alone was bigger than the downstairs of Piper's eighteenth-century house. There were also a bedroom, a bathroom, and a bar area. The decor was Southern in flavor, very expensive, flowery, and tasteful. No layers of paint to scrape off the wainscoting, no creaky wide pineboard floors. Piper thanked Mabel, then asked, on sudden impulse, "Are you the one who inquired about the history of the Frye house?"

Mabel's mouth dropped open and her face paled.

Piper smiled brightly. "Oh, don't worry. I think it took initiative on your part. You were anticipating your boss's needs. He—well, I am sure that if he hadn't caught me stealing valerian root a couple of weeks ago he'd have thought resort sooner or later."

"I don't think so. He—that kind of development isn't his sort of thing. I know that now. I hope you don't—I didn't mean any harm. Mr. Jackson—"

"It's okay, Mabel. If I know Mr. Jackson, he figured it was you when I first showed him the letter from the research historian. He crumpled it up, tossed it in the fireplace, and forgot about it. I think he's probably more forgiving these days than he used to be." She liked this impulse thing. Maybe she'd be as good as Hannah in another fifty or sixty years. "Anyway, I was just curious."

"I see." Mabel regarded her with fresh appreciation. Here was not just some crazy Yankee, but a woman who understood the fundamentals of business, which, when it came down to it, was just having good instincts about people. "You're not what I expected, Ms. Macintosh. If there's anything you need, please don't hesitate to let me know."

After Mabel left, Piper threw open all the drapes and drank in the view while hot water poured into her enormous, spotless tub. She'd added a few drops of Hannah's infusion of meadowsweet to help her relax.

Wherever Clate was, whenever he returned, she wanted to be ready.

She smiled as she sank beneath the water. It didn't occur to her that he might not be happy to see her.

Summer had arrived in the Cumberland hills, hot and humid, thunder rumbling in the distance. Clate could smell the sweet, overpowering scent of Irma's honeysuckle as he stood with one foot on the bottom step of her front porch. Hers was a little yellow clapboard house, simple and pretty. In her final effort to get him to understand right from wrong, she had left her house to Clayton Jackson, Sr., and his new family. At her insistence, they'd moved in when she'd had to go into the nursing home in the weeks before her death. The senior Jackson had been helping her out for years, without pay.

Clate heard the kids out back, had seen them when he'd pulled in. A boy and a girl. Dark haired, tanned, barefoot. They were squealing as they ran through a sprinkler. He couldn't stop staring at them. Beautiful kids. More than he could have ever expected.

A crow cawed overhead, bees hummed in the honeysuckle. He could hear his car engine running behind him. Security. He needed to know he could leave fast, in case coming here was a mistake.

The old screen door opened, and a thin, wiry gray-haired man walked out. Clate recognized the loping gait. He had gotten his own thick build from his mother's side of the family.

Family. No, that wasn't what they'd been. Three people caught in the same horrible windstorm was more like it. A couple of troubled teenagers with a baby they didn't know how to raise properly. They'd done their best. And their worst.

The door shut. His father walked down the steps. He wasn't much over fifty, still young. He rubbed the back of his neck, awkward, even afraid. "Hello, Clate."

"Hello."

"Reckon you heard about the house. I did some work

for Miss Irma from time to time, but other'n that—" He shrugged. "I don't know why she did half the things she did. But I thank the good Lord she was here for you."

Clate managed a smile. "Me, too. Mabel Porter, my assistant in Nashville, told me about the house. But that's not why I'm here. I just—" He stopped, squinting in the heat, trying to put words to the sense of urgency that had gripped him in the past three days, since he'd watched Hannah Frye pull an old doll out of her treasure chest and he'd fallen in love with her niece. Somehow he had the feeling if he didn't come here, if he left now, that whatever he had with Piper would slip through his fingers. He licked his lips, sighed. "I just wanted to come by and say hello."

His father cleared his throat, shoved his knotty hands into his threadbare pockets. "Well, I'm glad you did. You want a drink or something? I've got iced tea inside. Francie, she likes those flavored teas—you know, mango and raspberry and things—but I just like regular old tea. She's a nurse up at the county hospital. She'll be back home soon." He took a breath, awkward, trying so damned hard. Clate could sense his father's nervousness. "You don't have to drink it inside. I can bring it out."

"It's okay. I'm not that thirsty."

Finally, his father's watery eyes focused on him, and he said, "I think about you every day, Clate. Have for years. You're in my prayers and have been ever since I got sober. Before that—" He shook his head. "The devil had hold of me, son. That's all I know. But I gave him the hold on me. I gave it to him, and I know I did. I can't say it any plainer than that."

He wasn't going to beg forgiveness. In all Clate's youthful fantasies of what his father would do when—if—they saw each other again, he had him on his knees, begging. And Clate would refuse. Deny him that easing of his guilt and misery. Only now, his father wasn't asking for forgiveness. He wasn't asking for anything.

"Regular iced tea?" Clate asked.

"Lipton. I bought the tea bags myself."

"The kids?"

"I made a pitcher of Kool-Aid for them."

Clate rocked back on his heels, and he breathed in the sweet honeysuckle. Vengeance. Irma Bryar had warned him against its seductiveness, its power to deceive, warp, destroy. Now, finally, he understood.

He looked back at his father. "I need to turn the car off."

"Go ahead. I'll pour the tea and call Sammy and Miranda."

No fear that he'd get in his car and drive back to Nashville. Whatever he chose to do, his father would accept. "Sammy and Miranda. Nice names."

"Francie picked 'em out. Me, I'm no good at that stuff. They're good kids. Like you were."

When he sat behind the wheel, felt the hum of his car's engine, Clate knew he could drive on down out of the hills and wind his way back to Nashville. He didn't have to have iced tea with his father. He didn't have to meet his brother and sister. He could get out of here, go back to his work, his meetings, his responsibilities—to the status quo of his life. He had a choice.

But if he went back, he'd lose Piper. She hadn't asked him to come here. She didn't even know he'd come. Yet he knew, with a certainty that Hannah herself would have understood, that he would lose her. The status quo was no longer enough.

He climbed back out of the car, and he walked up onto the front porch where Irma Bryar had sat in her rocking chair for so many decades. He could see her now, that worn, wise woman so willing to give of herself. She knew he'd be back. One day, he would have to come home and see his father.

A head popped up over the porch rail, and a gap-toothed smile flashed at him. "Are you my brother?"

"You must be Miranda."

"He's your half-brother, nit." Another head popped up, the grin snaggle toothed on the older child, Sammy. "Aren't you?"

"Yes, I am. My name's Clate."

"Like Daddy's," Miranda said.

"I think your father—" He stopped himself, instantly noting their confusion. "I think our daddy's pouring us drinks."

"Kool-Aid, Kool-Aid," they chanted, giggling, and clattered up onto the porch, and Clate followed them inside.

Clate had asked that unless there was a bomb in the hotel, no one disturb him until he returned to Nashville. When he did, he immediately knew something was up. He could feel it in the air as he walked through the lobby. Then he noticed the odd looks, the quickly suppressed smiles. He started for the elevator, and stopped.

Piper.

She was here.

"Hell fire," he muttered, figuring Hannah was having her effect on him. He was thinking he knew things that he couldn't possibly, on any rational basis, know.

But she was here. He knew it.

It was late, and Mabel had gone home, but she'd left a message and a key on his desk. "A woman who says she's Piper Macintosh arrived at 3:40 p.m. Red-brown hair, slim, Red Sox shirt, nasty bruise on her right eye, *very* smart. Enjoy, Mabel."

Taking long strides out of the office and down the hall, he was at her door. He knocked, and her voice called, "I'll bet our Miss Mabel left you a key."

He used it, and when he pushed open the door, he heard soft music and the pop of a champagne cork. Piper walked over to him in a sleek black dress, a cameo necklace, and sparkly black velvet shoes. "The shoes are a bit big," she said, handing him a glass of champagne. "A woman in my open-hearth cooking class insisted I borrow them once she saw the dress. Anyway, there's not much opportunity to wear sparkly shoes in Frye's Cove. The necklace is Hannah's. She says—well, you can imagine."

"Something about the love of your life being drawn to cameos?"

"Something."

"The dress?"

"It's mine," she said. "It's my Tennessee dress. I bought it just for you. I wanted you to see that I can—" She struggled for the right words. "That I can make a place for myself in your life here."

He smiled, watching her mouth as she sipped her champagne.

"I'm not sure I covered up my bruises too well," she said.

"You don't have to cover up anything." His voice was husky, his heart hammering. He set down his glass, took hers and set it down, too, and held her by the elbows. "And never a bruise, Piper. Never."

"Clate—"

"As for my life here—" He looked around the beautiful room, acknowledged a tug of pride at what he'd accomplished; then he looked back at her. "It's changing. It *has* changed. I've got good people I trust working for me. I don't need to be here on a day-to-day basis. I don't want to be. I'm not saying I'm surrendering all control—"

"Oh, never."

"Then again, I might just sell the whole damned company. I have options now I didn't see before. But I'm in no rush. I'd like to take some time to restore my house on Cape Cod and—" He stopped, noticing that Piper was shaking her head. "What?"

"We're moving the Frye house."

"We?"

"The town. We held a meeting last night after you left. The historical society wants to move it onto a lot they have near the cove and restore it. They've been looking for just such a project." She smiled. "We're all very excited."

"That's all well and good, but *we* don't own the Frye house. I do."

She waved a hand in dismissal. "You and this me and mine stuff. If you're going to make a place for yourself on Cape Cod, you've got to understand a few things—"

"Piper, do you have any idea—"

"I thought we could build our own house. You being a builder and all."

He narrowed his eyes on her. Their own house.

"With proper attention to the past, of course, but I do want plenty of outlets and at least a couple of tall ceilings and big windows. I like light."

"Outlets, tall ceilings, big windows. That's it?"

She shrugged. "I'm not as in to a fireplace in every room as I was a week or two ago. I figure I'll keep my house, use it as a showcase for my students and my business. I'm thinking of doing a book, and maybe a cable TV show. I've had a few inquiries over the years. I think one of them might have been based in Nashville."

"You've been doing a lot of thinking in the past few days."

"Comes from having your house burned down, your head nearly bashed in, and being around you Type As," she allowed. "What about you?"

He moved in closer. "I've been visiting my father and my little brother and sister. They're good kids, Piper."

The lightheartedness went out of her eyes, and he could see that she knew, understood, what he'd done. And why. "And your father?"

"He's a good man. Under it all, once he got sober and stayed sober, he was a good man. He's good to Sammy and Miranda. They adore him."

"I'm glad you went," she said softly. "I don't know if I'd have had the courage."

He smiled. "You gave me the courage, Piper. Loving you did."

Her eyes widened, and she bit down on her lower lip. "Clate—"

"I do love you, you know. I think I have since the moment I caught you in your aunt's crazy garden at four in the morning."

"Not before?"

He laughed. "I hadn't met you before."

She grinned, a glint of mischief in her dark green eyes. "So?"

"So—" He breathed in. "It's going to be like this, isn't it?"

"Yep. Forever." She stretched sexily, the glint still there. Then it vanished, as abruptly as it had appeared, and she said, "I think I've loved you my whole life, Clate. Before we even met. Long before."

Another step closer, so that he could smell whatever herbal concoction she'd been bathing in, so he could breathe in the scent of her. "Tell me, were you planning to spend the night here?"

"I've no objection, unless you have a better suggestion."

"I have a place on the river."

"Tall fence, big dogs."

"And tall ceilings and big windows." He slid his arms around her, kissed her neck. "How long have you been in that dress?"

"An hour."

"Long enough, don't you think?"

"I want to meet your dogs," she murmured as his mouth found hers.

"You will," he said, tasting her, loving her, "but not in this dress."

"You'll take care of it?"

"With pleasure."

**POCKET BOOKS
PROUDLY PRESENTS**

WHITE HOT

CARLA NEGGERS

**Available in Paperback
from
Pocket Books**

**Turn the page
for a preview of *White Hot*. . . .**

After a restless night, Mollie got up early and jogged on the beach three blocks from Leonardo's house. He had refused to buy on the water out of fear of hurricanes. As if living three blocks "inland" would make a difference. She had learned as a tot not to quarrel with the incomparable logic of Leonardo Pascarelli.

The cool, sweet-smelling morning and cathartic run helped ease the effects of last night's overindulgence on chocolate desserts and the passing horror of thinking she'd seen Jeremiah Tabak. Never mind hurricanes, Mollie thought. Jeremiah Tabak was her great nightmare of living in south Florida.

She arrived back at Leonardo's in time to let in his husband-and-wife gardener-and-housekeeper team. The security gate and fence had required a lifestyle change for Mollie, who had managed in Boston with six locks on her door and a primitive intercom system. Leonardo even had his windows and a few choice closets wired.

Louis, who did the grounds, and Georgia, who did the house, parked their truck in the short driveway and greeted Mollie warmly. They were somewhere between fifty and a hundred and obviously liked Leonardo, the son of a butcher in Boston's Italian North End. They kept his place immaculate and beautiful. Mollie had learned to stay out of their way and not try to understand why an empty house needed to be cleaned once a week. More Leonardo logic, she supposed. And it would be like him to lend his house to friends from Paris at a moment's notice.

With Louis and Georgia off to the main house, Mollie started across the driveway to head up to the guest quarters over the garage, which she cleaned herself. A good stretch, a shower, coffee and toast, and she'd be ready for her day.

The Tabak incident must have been the product of consuming too much chocolate. She had not actually seen him. She'd only *thought* she'd seen him. It was like her early weeks in south Florida, when she kept thinking she was seeing poisonous snakes, lizards, and big spiders at every turn. Once, while coming out of Leonardo's pool, she was convinced an alligator had just slithered across her path. It turned out the movement had been the shadow of a passing gull. Before long, she'd adjusted, realizing that she wasn't likely to confront alligators and such in Leonardo Pascarelli's backyard.

It would be that way with last night, too. Unaccustomed to Palm Beach parties, she was a bit nervous, and her mind had conjured up Jeremiah Tabak, turning a simple stranger in a truck into her worst-case scenario of life far from home. Once she adjusted to this new social scene, she would stop thinking she'd seen him.

She shuddered, hoping she wouldn't conjure him up again any time soon. That kind of distraction she did not need in her life. But Jeremiah Tabak, star investigative reporter for the *Miami Tribune,* operated in very different circles than did Mollie Lavender, brand-new south Florida publicist. Last night's dessert concert was just the sort of society function Jeremiah would disdain. He wrote about crime, drugs, gangs, corruption—not dessert concerts and charity balls. The Tabak stories Mollie had read in her months in Florida had been upsetting, gritty, unpleasantly realistic. They had a way of ripping the rose-colored glasses off people's faces, forcing them to look at a world they wanted to pretend didn't exist.

And yet, Mollie had to admit, whether he was covering the scum of the universe or the lowliest, sorriest victim of the lowliest, sorriest crime, Jeremiah Tabak managed to get at the humanity of his subject—which could be frightening or heartbreaking or, perhaps most unsettling of all, both.

Mollie gave the man credit where credit was deserved. His work was top-notch. It was everything else about him she had learned to distrust.

She was halfway across the driveway when a brown pickup truck pulled up in front of Leonardo's gates, which she'd left open.

The same brown pickup from last night.

It showed no indication of turning in. Mollie heard the rattle of its engine, noticed that the passenger window was rolled down. A dark-haired man was behind the wheel, peering across the seat out at her.

Her heart beat wildly, but she didn't move, trying to convince herself this was just like her alligator that turned out to be a seagull. She was perspiring from her jog, her Miami Dolphins shirt and running shorts matted to her, her legs glistening, her feet hot. But she wasn't out of breath.

It couldn't be Tabak. It just couldn't. She had to be seeing things.

"Well, well, well. Mollie Lavender. Ain't you a sight for these poor, sore, old eyes."

His voice. His lazy, easy, obnoxious Florida drawl

with its slight twang. He could lay it on thick when he wanted. It hadn't changed. And she hadn't forgotten it, hadn't forgotten how it could melt her spine.

He climbed out of the truck and grinned at her over the roof. Sexy, confident as ever. "Hi, there, darlin'. It's been a while."

Mollie squinted at him. She tried to look as if she hadn't thought about Jeremiah Tabak in ten years and couldn't quite figure out who this man at the foot of her driveway was. "Excuse me?"

His grin broadened. He knew she knew *exactly* who he was. She supposed his natural cockiness enabled him to do the kind of work he did. But she'd have sold her soul to the devil for a hunk of Boston pothole to hurl through his windshield.

He patted his battered truck roof with one hand. His eyes were hidden behind sunglasses that only made him look sexier, cockier. "Sweet Mollie, you're not going to pretend you don't remember me, are you?"

Remember him? She had nightmares about him. Unsettling dreams. Sweet, terrible memories. She banked back her emotions, continued to squint dumbly. "I'm sorry, I—"

"Ten years ago. Spring break. Daytona Beach. Your parting words: 'I hope you rot in hell, Tabak.' Well, you got your wish, sweetheart." A half-beat's hesitation. "If you read the *Trib,* you know I spend a lot of time in hell."

Beneath the easy grin, she could see he wasn't unaffected by his work.

Naturally, he took advantage of her surprise. "Mind if I come in?"

Before she could answer, Victoria arrived, squeezing her little car around his truck and into the driveway next to Louis and Georgia's truck. She bounced out. "Jeremiah Tabak? I thought I recognized you. What are you doing here? Mollie, do you know him? He's *famous.* He—"

"He was just leaving," Mollie said with no detectable trace of rancor.

Jeremiah walked around the front of his truck, onto the driveway. Heat was beginning to radiate up from the tar. He still had that saunter. He was still trim and well-muscled, a flat six feet tall. He wore his near-black hair shorter. He had the same blade of a nose, the same thin, hard mouth. She didn't need him to take off his sunglasses for her to see his eyes, the mix of grays and greens and golds that had intrigued her for the week they'd had together, and the ten years since.

"Actually," he said, addressing Victoria, who was already smitten, "I wanted to talk to Miss Lavender about taking me on as a client."

Mollie felt herself going purple, her self-control slipping. A client?

A client?

It was as bald-faced a lie as she had ever heard.

Victoria barely contained her delight. "She has an hour free right now. Her first appointment isn't until ten-thirty. Park your truck and come on inside, Mr. Tabak. I'll run up and put on some coffee."

She was off, moving faster than anyone had a right to in the heeled sandals she wore.

Tabak sauntered up to Mollie. He touched his sunglasses with one finger, savoring his victory but not pushing his luck. "Your whirlwind make good coffee?"

"Her name's Victoria. Victoria Miranda. Yes, she makes excellent coffee. Everything she does is excellent, including her tae kwon do."

A twitch of that thin mouth. "That a warning?"

Mollie could feel the sweat dripping down her back. Better the alligator in Leonardo's backyard than Jeremiah Tabak in his driveway. "I'm giving you five minutes, and only because if I didn't, Victoria would hound me until I told her why not. No one knows about you, Tabak. No one."

"Not even your flaky family?"

"No one."

He wasn't chastened. Not Jeremiah. That he'd served as the catalyst for the explosion that had forever changed the life of a twenty-one-year-old college student had no impact on him. His life was unchanged by their affair ten years ago. He had gone on to become one of Miami's most respected, hardest-hitting reporters, just as he'd planned.

"No one at all, eh?" He grinned that slow, lazy, mind-bogglingly sexy grin. "That's good, Mollie. I like being your deepest, darkest secret."

"How did you find me?" Mollie asked as she poured the dark, aromatic coffee Victoria had prepared before retreating, reluctantly, to her computer in the living room. Jeremiah had settled onto a high stool at the breakfast bar in the guest quarters' cozy, honey-colored kitchen. Sun streamed through the windows, and Mollie could see Louis working down in the backyard.

"Easy," Jeremiah said. "You've already made a name for yourself. One of my colleagues over in arts and entertainment knew all about you. You used to work at a big p.r. firm in Boston. About six or eight months ago, you moved to south Florida and set up your own shop. Lucky for you, your godfather is a world-renowned tenor who was willing to lend you his place for a year."

"Not lend. I'm house-sitting for him."

"Ah. Of course."

She shoved a mug of coffee at him. He'd removed his sunglasses, his eyes that deadly swirl of color that had haunted her for a decade. She wondered if he noticed just how on edge he made her. Probably. Jeremiah Tabak noticed everything.

"It's a leg up," he went on, "having Leonardo Pascarelli in your corner."

"I don't deny it."

"My friend in A&E also says you have an eccentric client list. Dogs, has-been ventriloquists, a spooky ex-astronaut."

Mollie frowned. This, she thought, was why her clients

needed her. "One dog. One ventriloquist. And my ex-astronaut isn't spooky at all."

"Doesn't he say he met aliens on the moon?"

"He's been widely misquoted as having said he met aliens on the moon."

"Ah."

More sarcasm. Jeremiah was hard news all the way. He would have nothing but scorn for publicists and the work they did. Remaining stiffly on her feet, Mollie sipped her coffee. She had once slept with this man. Thought herself wildly in love with him. But she'd been just twenty-one, and she'd learned from her mistake.

"If my client list is so odd, why would you be interested in hiring me?"

He shrugged, an air of unconcern. He wore a dusk-colored shirt that fit close, chinos, canvas shoes. Casual, not inexpensive. Deliberate. He was, Mollie remembered with a sudden jolt of heat, a very deliberate man. If her question took him by surprise—if he thought she was still naïve and easily misled—he didn't show it. Given his profession, his natural reserve, he would be accustomed to keeping tight rein on his reactions. Even ten years ago, she'd seldom known what he was thinking.

"My contact also says you're fun, energetic, and optimistic," he said. "People appreciate your fresh approach and high integrity."

Mollie couldn't deny a rush of satisfaction. "That's nice to hear."

"Yeah, in a sleazy profession like yours, a good reputation—"

She glared him into silence.

He grinned, unrepentant. "I'll allow there are sleazy reporters. You can allow there are sleazy publicists."

"There are bad apples in any profession. You indicated my profession itself was—" She sighed, set down her mug. "Oh, never mind. Tell me, Mr. Tabak. Why do you want to hire a publicist at all?"

"Because my life's gotten complicated. I need someone to handle that end of things. You know, the requests for interviews, speeches, advice. I need to have someone I can toss that stuff to. So, when I saw you last night, I thought, perfect."

Mollie dragged her mug across the counter, picked it up, sipped, sipped again, and decided, no. No, he was definitely lying. Or at least skirting the truth. "I didn't have 'publicist' stamped on my forehead last night. For all you knew, I was still a flutist."

"But I found out different, didn't I? I went to arts and entertainment thinking you were playing flute in the area. When I learned you were a publicist, just starting out and not too set in your ways, I figured you were what I needed."

"I see."

She didn't bother to conceal her doubt. Unchagrined, he picked up his mug, eyed her back. His gaze was as unreadable and intense as she remembered, and not for one second did she think he was telling her everything—or even anything. Jeremiah Tabak believed in himself, and he believed in expediency. Period. He used what means were at hand to attain a desired end. Once, she'd been those means. Never again.

"Mollie, if our past history—"

She sniffed, her grip on her mug tightening. "Don't get your hopes up, Tabak. I haven't thought about you in ten years."

Victoria appeared in the doorway. Her dark eyes shifted to Jeremiah even as she spoke. "Excuse me, Mollie, I'm sorry to interrupt—I've got the reporter from *Boca Raton* magazine on the line. Do you want me to have her call back?"

"No, I've been trying to catch her for two weeks. I'll take the call."

With a quick smile at Tabak, Victoria withdrew, and Mollie automatically reached for the kitchen extension; it was where she took all her private calls.

She glanced at Jeremiah. "Would you mind waiting in the den?" She motioned to an open doorway on the other side of the kitchen table. Generally she kept her den off-limits to business, but she didn't want him in with a madly curious Victoria.

He slid off the stool, and Mollie watched him saunter into the den with his mug of coffee. Even if his growing fame as a reporter was making demands on his time, she didn't believe he was seriously considering hiring a publicist, never mind her. He'd just ignore calls he didn't want to return. Jeremiah did what he wanted to do and only what he wanted to do.

With an inward groan, Mollie put him out of her mind and focused on her call. "Hello, this is Mollie Lavender. I'm so glad you called. I've been——"

The den!

Mollie choked. She sank against the counter to keep her knees from giving out under her. Calling upon every ounce of professionalism, upon her limited background as a performing artist, she said, "Excuse me, something's just come up. I'll call you back in ten minutes."

She hung up and, steadying herself, rushed into the den.

She was too late.

Standing in the middle of the room, Jeremiah turned and gave her a dry, amused look. "You haven't thought about me in ten years, hmm?"

Mollie stood very still just inside the doorway. It was a small room, its furnishings simple and comfortable. She'd added a few personal belongings she'd brought down from Boston: two photo albums, a framed picture of her family and Leonardo at Symphony Hall, movie videos, her CD player and CD collection. And her dartboard. She'd nailed it to the wall above a rattan chair in the corner.

Something had possessed her—she now couldn't imagine what—to blow up a black-and-white photo of Jeremiah Tabak on Victoria's Xerox machine and tack it to her dartboard. It was a candid shot from a magazine piece on Miami's star reporters. He'd refused to pose on the grounds that he wasn't into self-aggrandizement and public relations.

"That was just—I was just amusing myself. I was bored one night, and I saw that picture and . . . and . . ." She took a breath, summoning her last shreds of dignity. "I have no animosity toward you."

"That why most of the darts landed between my eyes?"

She forced a laugh. "I'm a good shot."

He settled back on his heels, glanced at the dartboard, then back at her. "I guess I should consider myself lucky you aimed for my forehead."

If he looked any closer, he'd see that she'd taken aim elsewhere on occasion. "Look, don't think just because I threw a few darts at your picture that I've been carrying a torch for you or plotting revenge against you for the past ten years." There, she sounded reasonable. "I'd bet I hadn't thought of you a half-dozen times when I arrived in Florida last summer and discovered you were a well-known reporter. When I saw your picture, it simply caught my fancy, and—and—"

"And it ended up on your dartboard."

"Yes. Yes, that's pretty much it. You shouldn't feel flattered or insulted."

"No? What was on your dartboard before me?"

"What? Oh, nothing. It was just a regular dartboard." She swallowed, her mortification easing. "No one comes in here but me. I'd never leave your picture up with company here."

"Because you don't want anyone to know about us," he said, taking a step toward her.

"There is no 'us,' Jeremiah. There never was any 'us.'"

His brow furrowed, and if he was attempting to figure out what she was thinking, feeling, Mollie gave him no further opportunity. She charged back into the kitchen. Why had she ever let him upstairs? Why hadn't she shooed him on her way? She could have explained to Victoria. She didn't *need* to explain to Victoria. She was Victoria's boss.

Jeremiah rejoined her in the kitchen, but before he could slide back onto his seat at her breakfast bar, Mollie flew around at him. "What do you want from me, Tabak?"

No visible reaction to her display of temper. He picked up his sunglasses. "I just need someone to handle the aggravations of my quote-unquote celebrity status. Mostly you'd just blow people off—"

"I'm not that kind of publicist. I take on clients who want my help. You want a private pitbull." She was breathless with indignation now, falling apart, unable to get any kind of handle on why Jeremiah Tabak had finally looked her up after ten years. "Well, that's not me. I have ethics. I have integrity. I—"

"Okay, Mollie. Forget it." There was no emotion in his tone, none in his face. The earlier cockiness was gone. Whatever he was thinking, he kept it to himself. "It was a bad idea."

Mollie caught her breath. There. She'd won. He was backing off. She was stronger than she'd been ten years ago. Tougher. Wiser. But she wasn't cynical, she wasn't mean-spirited or vengeful; she didn't live in the past.

Jeremiah started for the door. "Good seeing you again, Mollie."

"You, too, Jeremiah."

He stopped, glancing back at her, the gold coming out in his eyes. "You still play the flute?"

She shook her head. "I haven't even picked it up in five years. To play at a level I consider even tolerable, I'd have to put in a minimum of an hour or two a day. I don't have that kind of time. Or the commitment."

"What made you quit?"

"I realized that playing flute wasn't what I wanted to do with my life. I wasn't meant to be a world-class musician. It wasn't who I am."

"Was your family surprised?"

"*I* was surprised."

He gave a curt nod, that straight-line mouth giving away nothing. "Took guts to quit. Maybe I'll see you around sometime."

"Maybe."

The door shut. He was gone.

Mollie let out a long, slow, cleansing breath and collapsed onto a barstool. He was wrong. It hadn't taken guts to quit the flute. She'd never felt so uncertain in her life as when she'd returned to Boston and dropped out of the conservatory. She'd only known that was what she had to do, and her week with Jeremiah Tabak, for all its drama, had forced her to recognize that unalterable fact.

Before Victoria realized Jeremiah had gone and came in to pump her boss for information, Mollie returned to the den and peeled his picture off her dartboard. Twenty-one years old, on her first trip over spring break. She'd spent previous spring breaks in Boston, playing flute in tiny, dingy, windowless, soundproof practice rooms. That week, she'd indulged in Florida sun and sand . . . and she'd had her first and only flirtation with a "dark and dangerous" man. Jeremiah Tabak had been a young reporter with the *Miami Tribune,* digging into drug use among college students on spring break. He'd used Mollie to help him find those answers. He hadn't realized she didn't smoke, didn't drink, didn't use drugs—barely even knew anyone who did. Her life was music. Hours and hours of solo and ensemble practice a day. Classes in music theory and composition, music history, in addition to regular academic classes. Excursions to concerts in Boston and New York.

And, of course, her family. Her father was a violinist, her mother a violist, her sister a cellist. It had been something of a rebellion even for Mollie to take up a wind instrument, never mind to quit music altogether.

She remembered trying to explain that to Jeremiah in the predawn darkness after a night of lovemaking. He'd been mystified—not unsympathetic, simply blank on the rivalries, prejudices, expectations, and ambitions of classical musicians. Her family, she'd told him, weren't snobs. They had eclectic taste in music and played all kinds, although they were best at the classics. Growing up, Mollie had lived here, there, and everywhere, her parents never settling into a career with one symphony orchestra, one string ensemble, one university or conservatory. Boston had always been their base, but they taught and played wherever it suited them. They fancied themselves itinerant musicians. Traditional notions of home and hearth simply had no meaning for them.

"They're flakes," Jeremiah had pronounced.

They were. Loving, tolerant, impractical, devoted to their work and their daughters—but not tuned into the world in any conventional way. Not the way Mollie was.

She smiled, thinking of them.

Her smile faded quickly as she thought of Jeremiah Tabak standing in the middle of her den, ever confident, sexy as hell. She'd convinced herself she was well removed from his seedy world, that she didn't have to worry about running into the *Miami Tribune*'s star investigative reporter. His visit had unsettled her more than she wanted to admit.

And it could mean only one thing: he was on a story.

Not sure what to read next?

Visit Pocket Books online at
www.simonsays.com

Reading suggestions for
you and your reading group
New release news
Author appearances
Online chats with your favorite writers
Special offers
Order books online
And much, much more!